BIRMINGHAM LIBRARY SERVICES

DISCARD

KU-662-116

Goodbye, Ruby Tuesday

By the same author

Waiting in the Wings

Kiss & Tell

Such a Perfect Sister

Some Kind of Hero

Goodbye, Ruby Tuesday

DONNA HAY

ORION

First published in Great Britain in 2004
by Orion,
an imprint of the Orion Publishing Group Ltd.

Copyright © 2004 Donna Hay

The moral right of Donna Hay to be identified as the
author of this work has been asserted in accordance
with the Copyright, Designs and Patents Act of 1988.

All rights reserved. No part of this publication may be
reproduced, stored in a retrieval system, or transmitted
in any form or by any means, electronic, mechanical,
photocopying, recording, or otherwise, without the prior
permission of both the copyright owner and the above
publisher of this book.

A CIP catalogue record for this book
is available from the British Library.

ISBN 0 75285 997 8 (hardback)
0 75286 022 4 (trade paperback)

Typeset at The Spartan Press Ltd,
Lymington, Hants

Printed in Great Britain by Clays Ltd, St Ives plc

All the characters in this book are fictitious,
and any resemblance to actual persons, living
or dead, is purely coincidental.

The Orion Publishing Group Ltd
Orion House
5 Upper St Martin's Lane
London WC2H 9EA

BIRMINGHAM CITY COUNCIL (CBC)	
H J	16/08/2004
F	£17.99

www.orionbooks.co.uk

To the players and fans
of Wakefield Trinity Wildcats

Acknowledgements

Although I spent most of my time alone at my computer, there are many people who helped shape this book. First I'd like to thank the Clark family – Maureen, Brian, Rebecca and Alex – for coming up with real-life suggestions for the fictional Norman-ford, and for taking us on a minibus tour of the wilds of West Yorkshire. Sorry if I haven't mentioned Wakefield Trinity enough – I did my best! I hope the dedication makes up for it. Also, to Jan Devos for explaining the intricacies of management consultancy – don't be too shocked by what I came up with, will you? – and my nursing expert Pauline Case for supplying a plausible deathbed scene. Thanks also to my agent Sarah Molloy and to everyone at Orion, especially Jane, Juliet, Sara and Gaby.

Last but not least I would like to thank my husband Ken and daughter Harriet for their (almost) endless patience and support, even when I locked myself away for eighteen hours a day, and for still being there when I finally emerged. I love you both.

Prologue

Sadie Moon stubbed out her cigarette in the rose bushes and climbed back in through the window of the Willow Lodge Diocesan Home for Unmarried Mothers, pulling her dressing gown around her.

Her room-mate Janey looked up, her baby clamped to her breast. 'You're taking a risk. Mrs Walcross would kill you.'

'I'd like to see her try.' Evelyn Walcross didn't scare Sadie. She called herself the home's Moral Welfare Officer, but she was a sadistic bitch who made sure the girls in her care suffered for their 'sins'. They slept in chilly rooms and worked like slaves, cleaning the home and scrubbing shirt collars in the laundry until their hands were raw. The whole place reeked of damp and carbolic soap.

All the other girls were terrified of Mrs Walcross, but Sadie was a rebel. She wore her skirts short, bleached her hair and sneaked outside to smoke Woodbines while all the other girls were in the chapel praying for their souls.

Mrs Walcross had had it in for Sadie ever since she'd caught her smuggling in a bottle of Cherry B under her maternity smock. She'd done her best to make Sadie mend her ways. She'd had her on her hands and knees cleaning floors. She'd given her extra kitchen duties. She'd taken away every last privilege she had, done everything but beaten the sin out of her with her bare hands. But Sadie just laughed at her, undaunted and defiant.

Janey stroked her baby's face, murmuring to him. She'd given birth three weeks before Sadie, the day before her eighteenth birthday. Her little boy had chunky limbs and a shock of black hair. Just like his father, Janey said. Her boyfriend played rugby for Wakefield Trinity. He'd wanted to marry her but her parents wouldn't allow it because he was Catholic and they didn't want their daughter to marry a Papist.

Today was Janey's last day at Willow Lodge. Mrs Walcross had come to her last night and told her to be ready to leave by teatime.

'I am doing the right thing, aren't I?' she said.

Sadie shrugged. 'What choice did you have?'

Mrs Walcross had spelled it out when she gave her the adoption papers to sign. If she didn't, her baby would be taken away from her and put in a children's home. There was no way she would be allowed to keep it. If she tried, she would end up on the streets and the authorities would never allow her to have more children.

'It's up to you,' she'd said. 'Do you want your baby to be brought up in an orphans' home, or in a proper family?'

'It's going to be so hard to say goodbye,' Janey said.

'I know.' Sadie stared at the pokerwork plaque on the wall. 'THEN LUST WHEN IT HAS CONCEIVED GIVES BIRTH TO SIN – James 1:15.' It was the first thing she saw every morning.

She looked into her baby's cot. She slept soundly, her long dark lashes curling on her soft round cheeks, her tiny starfish hands flung up on the pillow beside her. Seeing her made Sadie's stomach flip.

No one told her it would be like this. No one warned her she would be ambushed by love.

It shouldn't have happened, not after the nightmare of everything that had gone before. Finding out she was five months pregnant – how could she not have realised sooner? – then having to break the news to her mum. And of course *she* told Sadie's brother Tom who, being the man of the house, decided Sadie should come to Willow Lodge. Did he know what this place was like? she wondered. Not that it would have mattered to him. He would have sent her to hell if it might stop the neighbours gossiping.

At the time she hadn't cared what became of her. She was past caring about anything by then. She didn't want a baby, especially not this one.

Anyway, she had other plans. She was going to be a singer, move to London and become as rich and famous as Shirley Bassey. She had it all worked out in her head. She even had a stage name – Sadie Starr. She could almost see it, up there in lights at The Talk of the Town.

But then, a week ago, this thing she'd been carrying around inside her had become real. A little person who grunted in her sleep and screamed with rage and curled her tiny fingers tightly around Sadie's and stared up at her with dark, unfocused intensity, as if she was the only person in the whole world who mattered.

It wasn't her fault, she reasoned. She couldn't help how she'd come into the world, or who her father was. She was Sadie's and Sadie was hers. She'd even given her a name, although she'd never said it out loud. Only in her head.

She knew she'd have to give her up eventually, but she tried not to think about it. She couldn't take care of a baby, and her family wouldn't allow it. Tom wouldn't, anyway. It was the only thing that stopped her packing her bags and leaving the misery of Willow Lodge, the fact that she would have to leave her baby behind, too.

Mrs Walcross came into their room just before lunch. Janey's suitcase was on the bed. She'd dressed her little boy, Stephen, in the blue leggings and matinee coat she'd spent so long knitting that Sadie had got sick of the laborious click of her needles and threatened to throw them out of the window. Now she was feeding him again, sitting in the hard armchair between their beds.

Sadie was on her third attempt at changing her baby's nappy. She still hadn't got the hang of folding all that bulky towelling, or where to stick the pins. But the baby didn't seem to mind. She kicked her little naked legs, surprising herself when they moved. She looked so funny Sadie couldn't help giggling.

But she stopped when Mrs Walcross walked in with a grim-looking social worker. She went straight across to Janey and said, 'Time to say goodbye.'

Janey looked up, startled. 'But you said teatime! Can't I just finish feeding him?'

'His mother and father are waiting for him.' Mrs Walcross nodded to the social worker, who lunged at Janey and roughly took Stephen from her. Janey screamed and Sadie yelled, 'Leave her alone, you bitch!' but the social worker was already gone, her soft shoes squeaking down the corridor.

Sadie's scream startled her baby. Her tiny face crumpled and she wailed. Janey cried too, rocking in her chair and howling like a wounded animal.

'Shh, shh, it's all right, Ruby.' She swept her into her arms and held her close.

Mrs Walcross turned. 'What did you call her?'

'Ruby. It's her name.'

Mrs Walcross gave her a look of pure spite. 'We'll see what her new parents say about that.'

Sadie sat on the edge of the bed as the door closed, holding her baby close, trembling with shock and rage.

Over my dead body, she said to herself.

Irene Moon sipped her sherry with a grimace and tried to listen as Glenys Kitchener droned on.

'You're so lucky to be able to get away with such a small do, Mrs Moon.' She was only twenty but looked and acted much older, in a prissy pastel-blue two-piece and white gloves, a hat shaped like a fruit bowl perched on her curls. Her legs were buckling under the weight of the baby propped on her hip. He was trussed up in a sailor suit, his fat red face framed by a frilly bonnet. 'When little William was christened we had to go all the way to Leeds to find a place big enough. Such a fuss! But I suppose you have to expect these things when you're in public life, don't you?'

Irene fought to keep the smile off her face. Public life indeed! Glenys might have come up in the world since she married Bernard Kitchener, just because he was a local councillor and ten years older than her, but it wasn't that long since she'd been playing hopscotch down their street. Now to listen to her anyone would think she'd been brought up in a palace instead of a poky flat over a fish shop in Coalpit Lane.

She looked around at the small gathering in her front room. Her son Tom was parading around with baby Catherine in his arms, showing her off to everyone. At twenty-one, he looked too young to be married, let alone a father. It didn't seem too many years since she'd brought him home from hospital herself.

Jackie stood at his side, smiling nervously. Irene knew what her daughter-in-law was thinking. She was hoping Tom wouldn't wake the bairn. There were already purple shadows under Jackie's eyes from all the sleepless nights she'd had.

Poor Jackie, Irene thought. Motherhood hadn't come easily to her. Many was the time she'd heard her crying through their thin bedroom wall.

Glenys lowered her voice. 'I do think you're terribly brave, having a party at all in the circumstances.'

'And what circumstances would those be, Glenys?'

'You know. With your Sadie being . . . away.' Glenys glanced around then leaned forward confidingly. 'Is there any news of her?'

Her concern didn't fool Irene for a moment. All she wanted was the latest gossip. Just like the rest of them.

That was why she hadn't wanted a big christening do. She couldn't face those friends and neighbours she'd known for years, all pointing the finger at her family.

'You will tell her we're thinking about her, won't you?' Glenys' voice dripped sympathy. 'I do feel sorry for her. Although I did warn her what would happen if she ran around with the likes of *him*.' Her mouth pursed. 'You did the right thing, Mrs Moon, sending her away.'

'Did I?' She was beginning to wonder. The only reason she'd done it was to silence nasty gossips like Glenys Kitchener. Now she felt disgusted with herself.

'Definitely. You couldn't have it in the house, could you? Think of the shame. And besides, could you honestly imagine Sadie caring for a baby? She can hardly look after herself, let alone a—'

They were all suddenly aware the room had gone very quiet. Irene turned round.

There, standing in the doorway, was Sadie, her suitcase at her feet and a baby in her arms. She looked pale, exhausted, but utterly defiant.

'Hello, Mum,' she said. 'We've come home.'

Tom reacted before Irene could summon her thoughts. Ignoring the guests, he grabbed Sadie's elbow and steered her out of the room into the kitchen. Jackie hurried after them.

Everyone tactfully started to leave. Glenys was the last to go.

'Are you sure there isn't anything I can do?' she said, craning her neck to catch a glimpse of what was going on in the kitchen.

'We can manage.' Irene hustled her towards the door and closed it firmly in her face. She leaned against it and shut her eyes. Give me strength, she prayed. Then she headed for the kitchen.

'I'm telling you, you're not having it in this house.'

'It's my baby.'

Sadie sat at the kitchen table, still clutching the bundle in her arms. Her hair was damp with rain and she was shivering inside her pink mohair coat. Tom loomed over her, while Jackie looked helplessly from one to the other. Somewhere upstairs, baby Catherine yelled at being left out of the action.

'It's a little bastard. And you're not keeping it under this roof. Tell her, Ma!' But before his mother could speak, he went on. 'And I hope you're pleased with yourself, ruining my daughter's christening?'

'I didn't plan it, did I?'

'Trust you to make a spectacle of yourself. Never mind anyone else, Sadie Moon always has to be the centre of attention.'

'I had nowhere else to go. What did you want me to do, sit in the bus shelter in the rain until you'd finished showing off to the neighbours?'

'I wanted you to do as you were told for once and leave that behind.' He pointed at the baby in her arms.

'I changed my mind.'

'You can't do that! We agreed—'

'She's my baby and I'm keeping her.' Sadie's face was thin and wretched, but her eyes blazed with determination.

'But—'

'That's enough, Tom.' Irene spoke up. 'We're not going to get anywhere by shouting, are we? Jackie, love, go upstairs and see to Catherine before she screams the place down.' Jackie ran off, relieved to have something useful to do. Irene reached for the kettle and filled it under the tap. 'Have you eaten?' she asked Sadie.

'Not since this morning. But I'm not hungry.'

'You've got to have something. I'll get you some sandwiches from the buffet in a minute.'

'What is this?' Tom demanded. 'Has everyone in this house gone mad? She turns up out of the blue with that . . . that thing, and you treat her like she's the flaming vicar dropped in for Sunday tea!'

'Like I said, there's nowt to be gained by shouting.' Irene turned to Sadie. 'So what did the social workers say when you told them you'd changed your mind?'

Sadie fiddled with the baby's shawl. 'I didn't tell them. I just walked out.'

Tom snorted with rage. 'You did what?'

'I walked out. You don't know what it was like there. They were so cruel—'

'What did you expect? Bloody Butlins?'

Irene looked at the bundle in her daughter's arms. It was only a week old, just a few weeks younger than Catherine. She longed to see if the baby had her cousin's soft, fair colouring.

Ever since Catherine was born, Irene had been haunted by thoughts of her other grandchild, the one she'd never know. That vile woman at Willow Lodge had tried to make out it was none of her business when she telephoned every day to find out if the baby had arrived, but she'd got it out of her in the end.

And now she was here. 'You're in no state to be out of bed, let alone traipsing halfway across the country,' she said.

'I had to leave. They would have taken her away from me.'

7

'That was the point!' Tom said. 'You don't get it, do you? Do you really think they're going to let you keep her after this?'

'They can't stop me. I didn't sign any papers. Besides, I'm her mother.'

Tom laughed unkindly. 'Some mother you are! If you really cared about that kid you'd do what's best for it and give it the chance of a decent home.'

'She's got a home here.'

'I told you, you're not bringing it into this house. Haven't you done enough to drag this family's name through the mud? Ma can't hold her head up any more as it is, without you making it worse for her!'

Sadie stared at him for a moment. Then, gathering her baby to her, she stood up. 'All right. If that's the way you want it—'

'Wait. You're not going anywhere.'

'Ma!'

'Tom, your sister's just given birth. Can't you see she's not in a fit state?' She looked at Sadie. 'Why don't you go upstairs and rest? You look dead on your feet. I'll bring you up some food in a minute.'

Sadie shot a wary look at Tom, then left. They listened to her footsteps climbing the stairs, then Tom turned on Irene. 'Why did you say she could stay?'

'She's my daughter. And that baby's our flesh and blood, whether you like it or not.'

Tom's hands clenched and unclenched at his sides. 'If she stays, we're going.'

'Don't be daft, Tom.'

'I mean it, Ma. It's her or us.'

Irene looked pleadingly at him. 'I can't put her out on the street, Tom.'

'Fine. We'll move out, then.'

'Where will you go?'

'We'll find a flat somewhere. Don't worry about us. Worry about *your daughter*.' Tom slammed out of the room. A moment later the bedroom door banged overhead and she heard him shouting something to Jackie, and her quiet voice trying to reason with him. Not that it would do any good.

Irene sighed. She couldn't seem to please one of her children without upsetting the other.

She felt torn. Tom had been so good since his father died three years ago. But she couldn't turn her back on Sadie, no matter how much trouble she brought with her.

Sadie shivered in bed, the covers pulled up to her chin. It was strange to see her there, surrounded by all her teenage paraphernalia – posters on the walls, Dansette record player propped up on the chest of drawers. It reminded Irene that she was only sixteen, barely more than a child herself.

The baby was tucked in beside her, sleeping peacefully. How she'd slept through all that shouting Irene had no idea. She seemed very contented, unlike her screeching cousin next door. Her daughter must be doing something right, she decided.

'Sorry, Mum,' Sadie whispered. 'I didn't mean to cause trouble.'

'You never do, do you? It just seems to follow you around.' Irene put the tray of sandwiches and tea on the bedside table.

Sadie looked down at the baby, tucked in the crook of her arm. 'Do you think I've done a stupid thing?'

'It doesn't matter what I think. It's done now, and we've got to make the best of it, haven't we?' She held out her arms. 'Can I?'

Sadie warily handed her over, as if afraid Irene might take her away. Irene looked closely at her granddaughter for the first time. She was heartbreakingly beautiful, as dark as Catherine was fair. Just like her father. Sadie had stubbornly refused to tell anyone his name, but like everyone else Irene had a good idea who it was. Especially as the lad in question had left town just after finding out Sadie was pregnant.

She was better off without him, anyway. Irene pushed the shawl back off the baby's face with the tip of her finger. She would never admit it to Sadie or Tom, but she was secretly relieved her grandchild was home where she belonged. 'So does this one have a name yet?'

'Ruby Tuesday.'

'What kind of a name is that?'

'It's a song by the Rolling Stones. I like it.'

'I might have known you'd come up with summat daft!' She looked down at the baby again, smiling in spite of herself.

Daft name or not, she couldn't have given her up either.

Chapter 1

Present Day

'How much? And does that include free light sabres? How about the personal appearance by Darth Vader? I see, and that's how much extra? Yes, I agree, it does seem a lot of money. For that amount I'd expect you to teleport the real thing direct from the Death Star . . .'

Ten minutes later Roo Hennessy put the phone down, feeling pleased with herself. In the past two hours, she'd fired off more than a dozen overdue emails, taken a conference call from Tokyo, waded through the complexities of a pharmaceutical merger in Frankfurt, and organised a *Star Wars* themed party for her son's sixth birthday.

And her PA Carole still hadn't managed to struggle in on the tube from Kensal Rise.

Carole finally appeared just before ten, an appeasing cup of coffee in her hand. 'Have you got a minute?' she asked.

'I am rather busy—'

'I won't keep you.' Carole was a nice woman, but she was forever in the middle of some domestic crisis or other. As she plonked herself down in the seat opposite, Roo steeled herself for another saga about her husband's ongoing back problems, or her son's unpaid parking tickets. 'I just wondered if I could take a bit longer for lunch today.'

'You've just come in!'

'I know. I'm sorry. I'll make up the time later, I promise.'

Roo rolled her eyes. 'So what is it this time? Car failed its MOT again? Your youngest due at the orthodontist?'

'Actually, it's my birthday. A few of the girls are taking me out to celebrate. But if it isn't convenient, I'll just tell them—'

'No. That's fine. You take as long as you want.' Roo felt ashamed. After three years of working together, she should have known when her PA's birthday was. Most of the time she forgot her own, let alone everyone else's.

'Thanks.' Carole reached the door and stopped. 'You can come if you want. It's only the wine bar, but you're very welcome.'

'I'd love to, but I'm up to my eyes in it.' Roo held up a wad of cost benefit analyses. 'Some other time, maybe.'

'Sure.' Carole smiled back, but they both knew she didn't mean it. Roo Hennessy didn't take lunch breaks, or socialise with the rest of the staff. She stayed welded to her desk from dawn to dusk.

She opened her laptop and called up her notes on the Homeworks project. She'd been working with the DIY chain for four months, visiting stores, meeting the staff and management and generally seeing how everything fitted together. Now she was due to meet the directors the following day to present her report on how the whole operation could be run better and more efficiently. And cheaper, of course. That was the bottom line for most of the companies that employed her. They weren't interested in a pleasanter, more motivated workplace. Most of them wanted to know where they could safely cut corners, how they could get more work out of their staff for less money.

And Roo usually delivered. She was good at her job, which was why she was now one of Warner and Hicks' senior management consultants. She loved smoothing out glitches in the system, spotting where the numbers didn't balance, where the workforce weren't using their time and skills efficiently enough. It didn't always make her popular with the staff, who were laid off or forced to work harder to cover the lost jobs. But they weren't the ones who hired her, and her decisions almost always found favour with the management. She found it immensely satisfying to make the figures add up, to bring order to confusion.

Two hours later, the acid-burning sensation in her stomach told her it was lunchtime. She rifled in her desk drawer for her antacid tablets and crunched a couple. How the hell did she manage to get indigestion when she lived on black coffee and illicit cigarettes?

She shook the packet. Empty again. It was no good, she'd have to go down to the chemist for more. She had two meetings and a presentation to prepare later and she couldn't get through the afternoon without them.

On her way she nipped to the loo. She was just about to come out of the cubicle when the door swung open and a group of women clattered in, laughing.

'I can't believe you did that!' She recognised the voice of Marion, one of the admin staff. 'What did you have to invite her for?'

'I couldn't really *not* invite her, could I?' Carole said helplessly. 'Besides, I knew she wouldn't come. She never leaves her desk.'

Roo stiffened, her hand still on the cistern handle. She peered through the crack in the door. They were all at the mirror, putting on their make-up ready to go out.

'Talk about obsessive!' Marion said, applying lipgloss. 'You know what Roo's short for? Ruthless.'

'She's not that bad,' Carole said. 'Actually, I feel a bit sorry for her.'

'Sorry? For the Ice Queen?'

'I reckon she's lonely. There can't be much going on in her life if all she wants to do is work. Can I borrow your lippy?'

'She's like a flaming robot,' Marion said. 'I don't know how you stand working for her, Caz.'

Carole muttered something Roo couldn't hear, and they went off laughing. She flushed the toilet quickly and came out to wash her hands. She was so mortified she couldn't meet her own eyes in the mirror.

Carole felt sorry for her! How could that be? Roo had a fabulous home and a company Audi TT. She took expensive holidays and spent more on moisturisers than Carole did on feeding her family. She had a lifestyle, for heaven's sake! Why should anyone feel sorry for her?

As for being ruthless – well, that was plain ridiculous. She was ambitious and she worked hard. You had to, if you wanted to compete with the big boys at Warner and Hicks. It was a very male-dominated environment, and Roo had to fit in. She knew she would never have made it to senior consultant if she'd taken time off every time Ollie was sick, or littered her desk with family photos. She couldn't help it if she was caught in the middle, too female to be part of the old boys' network, but too tough to be one of the girls.

And yes, sometimes she did feel as if work was taking over her life. But Carole had no right to feel sorry for her. Just because she didn't advertise the fact didn't mean she didn't have a life outside work. A very good life, actually.

She went down to the chemist in the precinct and bought her Rennies and a bottle of Chanel No. 5 for Carole. Then she hurried back to her office.

Her office. Her own space, beautifully decorated with pale wood furniture, Eames chairs and a plate glass wall that looked down the glittering ribbon of the Thames as far as the Palace of Westminster. How could anyone not envy her all this? There were people at Warner and Hicks who would give their grannies for this view. Now *they* were ruthless! All Roo had ever done was work hard and try to be the best at what she did.

But as much as she told herself she deserved it, there were still times when she felt like a fraud. What was she doing here, sitting at a big desk, telling corporations how to run their businesses? Didn't they know she was just a kid from the backstreets of a rundown Yorkshire town? She might be able to fool everyone else with her posh accent and designer clothes, but she didn't fool herself. Sometimes she could almost imagine Gerry Matthews, the principal consultant, storming in and telling her to clear her desk because she'd been found out.

The door opened and Gerry Matthews stormed in. Roo almost screamed.

'Got a good one for you.' He was in his early forties, Armani-suited and never wasted time on greetings. 'Failing business. The bank has asked us to take a look at it, see if we can do something with it before they end up in even more trouble.' He slapped the file down on her desk. 'Three-month job. I've told them you'll be there on Monday.'

Today was Thursday. That gave her just three days to get up to speed, if she worked flat out all weekend. Roo nodded thoughtfully to hide her surge of panic.

'And the bank wants us to try and turn it around?'

'Or close it down. Worst case scenario, they can take their assets and get their money back that way. It's up to you which way they go. Make a go of it, or help take it apart.'

'I'd better get started straight away.' She glanced at the name on the file and froze. 'Wait a minute. Fairbanks Fine Furniture? Not in Normanford?' She flicked over the page, her heart speeding up a fraction. There was no reason why it should be the same place. No reason at all.

But it was.

'Have you heard of it?'

'You could say that.' Roo stared down at the address printed in front of her. 'I was born in Normanford.'

'Great. So you'll have local knowledge?'

Oh yes, Roo thought. I know it all right. Only too well. 'Can't you send someone else?'

'Why don't you want to go?'

'Personal reasons.'

Gerry considered it for a moment. 'Obviously you don't have to go if you don't feel you can,' he said. Then, just as Roo was letting out a sigh of relief he went on, 'There are other places. Funnily enough, I was talking to Iceman Frozen Foods the other day. They're still looking for someone.'

There it was. The unspoken threat. Take this job, or spend the next six months in eternal darkness on a fish processing plant in Norway, away from her family and well out of the Warner and Hicks loop. By the time she returned, the only thing anyone would remember about her was a lingering smell of cod.

'I'll go to Normanford,' she said.

'Are you sure? I don't want to force you into anything. And I hear Bergen is very nice this time of year. Bit cold, but—'

'I said I'll go.'

'Great.' Gerry beamed. 'Don't look so fed up. It's only for three months. And it'll be a good chance to catch up with your family and old friends again.'

Roo looked down at the file in her hands. That's what I'm afraid of, she thought.

She decided she deserved to get home before Ollie's bedtime for once. She left Carole trying to compose a letter while under the influence of several large Frascatis and headed back to Wandsworth.

Ollie was in the kitchen eating his tea while his nanny Shauna packed his lunchbox for the following morning.

'May the Force be with you,' he intoned solemnly through a mouthful of food as Roo swept past, collecting the evening paper and the post that was crammed behind the toaster.

'Um, thanks.' Roo swooped down to kiss her son's cheek. She glanced at his plate and stopped short. 'What are you eating?'

'Chicken nuggets and chips.' Shauna looked defensive. 'He won't eat the stuff you left for him.'

Or you're too bone idle to cook it, Roo thought. Honestly, what was the point of stocking the fridge with healthy foods when her nanny poisoned him with junk?

She and Shauna eyeballed each other across the kitchen. She kept meaning to talk to her about her attitude, but she was terrified she'd leave. And useless or not, finding a new nanny at short notice was a working mother's dread. Roo even had a recurring nightmare that she was about to jet off to give a presentation in New York when Shauna arrived at the airport with Ollie in his pyjamas and handed in her notice.

She gave up and searched through the fridge for something to cook for supper.

'You've got to hear my spelling words,' Ollie broke the silence. 'We're supposed to practise every day. Only you never do.'

'Doesn't Shauna do it?'

'Of course I do,' Shauna snapped. 'He just likes you to do it sometimes. It's important for him to know you're interested.'

'Everyone else's mummies listen to them,' Ollie piled on the guilt.

'Yes, well, other mummies don't have busy jobs like mine, do they?'

'Being a mummy is a job,' Ollie pointed out, as Shauna smirked.

Yes, but being a mummy doesn't pay wages, does it? Roo wanted to shout. It doesn't pay for toys, or school trips, or birthday parties. Or, come to think of it, for nannies who seemed to think their only role was to stuff rubbish into their charges and swan around in the family Shogun.

But instead she smiled at Ollie. 'I'd love to hear your spellings.'

'Great!' The speed with which he rushed to fetch his book made her feel awful. Maybe she hadn't been spending enough time with him lately. She tried to get home in time to give him his bath and a story every night. When she wasn't in Frankfurt, or New York, or burning the midnight oil on some other project. She did her best, but it was hard to give a five-year-old quality time when your eyelids were drooping and you knew you still had to pull together some figures for a boardroom presentation.

She peeled potatoes and defrosted chicken breasts as he struggled through his spellings. But then a headline on the front page of the *Standard* caught her eye. One of her former clients had just reported record profits in the first six months after implementing the new working system she'd suggested. Her eye wandered down the column. Maybe she'd get a mention.

'Mummy! You're not listening.'

She looked up sharply. 'I am.'

'No, you're not! You're reading the newspaper!'

'What's all the shouting about?' David wandered in.

'I was reading to Mummy and she wasn't listening.'

'I *was* listening. I can do more than one thing at once. It's called multi-tasking.'

'There you are,' David ruffled Ollie's fair hair and went to the fridge for a bottle of wine. 'Mummy's multi-tasking. She's a very busy lady, Ollie. We can't expect her full attention all the time, can we?'

Roo glared at him. He was being unfair, but she let it pass. She seemed to be letting a lot of David's comments pass these days. They'd be arguing all the time otherwise. She went on peeling and chopping while David poured himself a glass of wine and Shauna read the Sits Vac column in the paper. Roo was convinced she only did it to make her feel insecure.

'You haven't forgotten Ollie needs to take his money for the school trip tomorrow?' she asked, dashing away a tear brought on by the onions. 'And you have to let his teacher know he has a dental appointment on Tuesday . . . Shauna, are you listening?'

'What? Oh, yeah.' Shauna looked up vaguely.

'Maybe she's multi-tasking.' David caught Shauna's eye and they both grinned.

'Very funny. And don't forget he needs to do his violin practice tonight. He's got a lesson after the school trip.'

'Bloody violin,' Ollie mumbled, kicking the table leg.

'Ollie!'

'I hate it!' Ollie's lower lip jutted. He looked just like David when he was in a bad mood. 'What do I have to learn the stupid violin for, anyway?'

'Because—' Roo opened her mouth and found she couldn't think of a single reason. Except that all the other kids in his class went to clarinet, junior astrophysics or pre-school Japanese classes, and she didn't want to be a bad mother. 'You might enjoy it one day.'

'I won't. And I'm no good at it.'

'That's because you never practise.'

'That's because I hate it!'

'He's got a point,' David said. 'He's never going to be Yehudi Menuhin, so why put him through it?'

'Because I've just paid for six months of lessons, that's why.'

'I don't know why you bothered. The way you push him, he'll be suffering from executive burnout within three.'

'I'm not pushing him. I just don't want him to be left behind.'

'Oh God, heaven forbid!' David rolled his eyes. 'I don't know why you don't start setting him achievement targets, then you can sit down and have a monthly performance review. At least that way he might see you occasionally.'

18

Shauna hurried Ollie upstairs to do the dreaded violin practice, leaving them glaring at each other.

'Why do you have to be so hostile?' Roo demanded.

'Why do you have to be such a control freak?'

'That's not true.'

He refilled his glass. Roo regarded the bottle anxiously. He'd been drinking a lot more since he lost his job. But she didn't dare mention it. She didn't want him to fly off the handle again. Not now.

'Gerry Matthews has given me another project,' she said.

'So you'll be putting another bunch of poor sods out of work? I bet you'll enjoy that.'

She ignored the jibe. 'It's in Normanford.' Just saying it made her feel sick.

'Does that mean you're going away again?'

'Only for three months. And I'll be home every weekend.'

'Great. Just great. We never see you these days.'

What's the point when all we do is argue? Roo felt like asking. 'Look, I didn't want to take this job. I had to. It was either that or six months on a fish farm in Norway.'

'You could have said no.'

'Don't you think I tried? I haven't got much choice, have I? One of us has to earn a living.'

She could have bitten off her tongue as soon as she said it. She'd tried not to make a big deal out of them living off her income. But it was like treading on eggshells and sometimes she forgot to be careful.

'Great. Thanks for throwing that back in my face. I'm well aware who controls the purse strings around here.'

'David, I didn't mean that—'

'I know what you meant. Don't you think I'm trying to get another job? Don't you think I feel bad enough, being chucked on the scrapheap before I'm forty?'

'Being made redundant wasn't a reflection on your abilities. It was just—'

'Spare me the pep talk. You're not talking to your clients now.'

No, Roo thought. If I was, I'd tell them to stop feeling so bloody sorry for themselves and sort their lives out.

But she could never say that to David. He was a totally different man these days – moody, argumentative and resentful of her career since he lost his own job as an IT manager. She realised it was a difficult time for him and she'd tried to be supportive and understanding. She'd even tried to offer practical suggestions. She'd fixed up several meetings for David with useful contacts, and tracked down information on small business grants he could apply for if he decided to start up on his own. But he rejected all her efforts and now she was getting tired of tiptoeing around his fragile self-esteem.

They ate supper in silence. Afterwards David went off to watch television, leaving her to catch up with paperwork at the kitchen table. Roo wanted to talk to him about going back to Norman-ford, and how much she was dreading it. She wanted him to be sympathetic, to take her in his arms and tell her she didn't have to go, that he'd take care of her. But all he'd done was give her a hard time, as if she wanted to leave her home and family and go to a place that held nothing but bad memories for her.

She closed her laptop and stretched her cramped shoulders. The light had faded, filling the kitchen with shadows. Was it really ten o'clock already?

She felt a brief surge of satisfaction as she looked around the kitchen. It was a sleek, beautiful room, with handmade maple units, big stainless steel appliances and black granite worktops that shone like glass. She'd seen it in *House and Garden* and copied the whole look, right down to the pale wood floor and Alessi coffee pot. At the time she'd imagined holding informal supper parties with lots of friends around the long table. But in reality she was far too busy to think about cooking, she talked to her friends by email, and the only time she sat down at the table was to work.

Later that night she followed David up to bed. In the darkness she could see his hunched shape under the bedclothes, his back to her. Roo changed into her silky Janet Reger nightdress, taking time to hang her clothes up. It was a habit with her; she couldn't sleep if everything wasn't tidied away. David's clothes were abandoned over a chair. She fought the urge to tidy them, knowing it would infuriate him.

'David?' she whispered, climbing into bed beside him. She reached for him, feeling the warmth of his skin. But he was already asleep. Or pretending to be.

Roo stared up at the ceiling in frustration. She couldn't remember the last time they'd made love. It must have been more than four months ago. About the same time David was made redundant.

Maybe going away would be a good thing, she thought. Didn't they say absence made the heart grow fonder?

Chapter 2

It was raining on Sunday evening when Roo Hennessy returned to Normanford.

She hadn't been home for nearly two years, and then it was only a quick duty visit. Normanford had once been a thriving mining town in West Yorkshire, but the pit closures of the 1980s had torn its heart out. It depressed her to see how down-at-heel it still looked. The precinct was full of charity shops, cut-price electrical retailers and cheap boutiques. Some shop fronts were boarded up and covered with tattered fly posters. The library was now a job centre, and the lovely old Majestic cinema had been turned into a bingo hall, its art deco walls covered with neon signs advertising the Nightly Jackpot.

She suddenly felt deeply miserable. The only thing that stopped her turning her car round and heading straight back to London was the thought of the Norwegian fish factory. Even that was beginning to look more attractive.

It had only been a few hours but she already missed Ollie and David. She'd fought back the tears when she kissed her son goodbye, although he was more preoccupied with watching his favourite TV show than his mother leaving.

'It's a good sign he's not clingy,' Shauna said. 'It shows he's well-adjusted.' She'd been unusually nice all weekend. Whether it was genuine or just relief that Roo was going she wasn't sure.

'Either that or he's so used to her not being here it makes no difference,' David muttered. Unlike Shauna, he was making no effort to be nice.

But at least he'd taken her out for dinner on Saturday night. And they'd made love, although it was hardly earth-shattering. Roo was too exhausted with packing, reorganising her workload and worrying about the Fairbanks paperwork she still hadn't finished reading. In the end she'd faked it, then when David was asleep she'd got up to compose yet another feverish list of things everyone else had to remember while she was gone.

'I hope you've put "breathing" down,' David said. 'You know we won't remember to do it unless you're there to remind us.'

'I'm not that bad.'

'You're worse. I must say I find it a bit insulting that you think we can't organise our own lives without you doing it for us.'

There speaks a man who doesn't know where we keep the iron, Roo thought. But deep down she was worried. Not that they wouldn't cope without her, but that they would cope too well. The waters of family life might close over her head, and she wouldn't leave a ripple.

Usually the company would have put her up in a hotel. But since Normanford only had a couple of B & Bs, they'd rented her a house instead.

'We could have found you a hotel in Leeds, but we thought this would save you all that commuting,' Tina, Gerry's PA, explained. But Roo would have gladly swapped twenty minutes on the motorway for the bliss of room service. Especially when she found out where she was staying.

She didn't need the faxed directions from the letting agents to find the house the company had rented for her. By some sick irony, it was in exactly the same street she and her mother had lived in before she went to university.

Apart from the UPVC double glazing and a crop of satellite dishes, the redbrick terrace hadn't changed much. She'd forgotten how narrow the houses were, their front doors spilling straight onto the pavement. Roo suddenly longed for her bright, spacious bedroom with its antique *bateau lit*, walk-in wardrobes and luxurious ensuite. She didn't quite know what would be waiting for her behind the door of number sixteen Sykes Street but she had a feeling it wouldn't be his and hers limestone vanity units.

She only hoped the residents had changed in the past twenty years. Sykes Street had always had a reputation in Normanford. It was where the problem families ended up. Barely a night went by without a fight breaking out or a police car screeching into the street.

'It's better than the telly!' her mother would laugh, peering out of the net curtains while Roo curled up on the sagging old sofa, mortified to be there. The only good thing about living on Sykes Street was that no one noticed them. Among all the law-breakers, the late-payers and the loudmouths, for once they appeared almost normal.

She couldn't park outside the house because the space was taken up by a beaten-up Mini Traveller. Roo pulled up at the far end of the street. There, beyond a row of rusty iron railings, a steep grassy embankment ran down to the river.

On the other side of the railings, a gang of youths were entertaining themselves lobbing rubbish into the water. The long grass was a dumping ground for broken bicycles, old shopping trolleys and beer cans.

Roo was indignant until she remembered how she used to sit in that very same spot with her cousin Cat and Billy Kitchener. Sometimes she'd stay there until long after dark, not wanting to go home and watch her mother acting daft with her latest boy-friend.

She reached number sixteen and was searching in her handbag for her keys when the neighbour's door flew open and a blonde woman rushed out, pulling on her coat.

'Bastard!' she called behind her.

'Rachel, wait—' A man followed her, fair-haired, in his twen-ties, dressed in nothing but a pair of faded jeans.

'So who was she?' Her voice was shrill enough for the whole street to hear. Some things never changed, Roo thought.

'No one you'd know. Look, it wasn't serious—'

'And that makes it all right, does it? You shag some stranger and that's meant to make me feel better? Just answer me one question. Why did you do it? Why?'

'I don't know. I'm an idiot, I suppose.'

'You said it!' She stormed off down the road. Seconds later she was back, jabbing her finger in his face. 'You know what your problem is? You're afraid to commit. As soon as a woman starts getting too close, you have to press the self-destruct button. I think you should take a long, hard look at your behaviour, because I really think you have some esteem issues to sort out.'

'And I think you've been reading too many self-help books.'

'Screw you!'

As she flounced away, the man turned to Roo and said, 'Hi, you must be my new neighbour. I'm Matt.'

'Roo Hennessy.' Roo shook his hand, nonplussed. It was as if the last five minutes hadn't happened. Or maybe this happened to him all the time. He looked the type, with that bad-boy grin of his. 'Is that your car?'

'It certainly is,' he said with pride. 'I bought it last week off a bloke in a pub. Beautiful, isn't it?'

'It's also in my space.'

'Technically, it isn't. You see, contrary to popular belief you don't actually have any statutory rights to park outside your own house—' He caught Roo's withering look. 'But since you asked so nicely I'll move it, shall I?'

It took him ages. First he had to go inside and find some shoes and a shirt. Then he couldn't get the damn thing started. Roo sat in her car, tapping her hands impatiently on the wheel. She was aware that the youths had given up their litter-lobbing and were watching with interest. Oh well, at least she was doing her bit for the environment.

Finally he appeared at her window. 'Sorry, I can't seem to get it started. I think it needs some fine tuning.'

Roo tutted, got out and slammed the door. She stomped round to the back and flung open the boot to get her luggage out. Matt watched her.

'Nice motor, by the way. You don't get many of those around here.'

'Audis?'

'Cars with hub caps.'

'Alloys, actually.' She shut the boot and went to pick up her bags, but Matt got there first.

'Allow me.' They were heavy but he managed them easily. She opened the front door and he followed her in, looking around. 'Not bad. Better than the dump I live in, anyway.'

Roo had to admit it wasn't as horrible as she'd feared. The two living rooms had been knocked through, with a galley kitchen beyond. Upstairs, she already knew, there would be two bedrooms and a bathroom. The rooms were small, but the place had been newly refurbished, so at least it was all magnolia walls and plain carpets. And it was clean, too. The smell of new paint and pine disinfectant hung in the air.

Matt followed her into the kitchen. 'This is nice.' He ran his hand over the shiny worktop. 'Every place I've ever rented has smelled of boiled cabbage. Why do you think that is?'

'I have no idea. And much as I'd like to discuss it further, I'm afraid I have a lot to do, so—'

'Right. I'll be off.' He didn't move. 'Do you start your new job tomorrow?'

'What makes you think I have a new job?'

'No one comes to a place like this out of choice.'

'I suppose not.' She couldn't help smiling.

'And judging from the number of bags you've brought with you, you're not here on holiday. Unless you're a seriously high-maintenance woman.'

'Very good, Sherlock. Now if you'll excuse me, I've got lots to do.'

'I'll leave you to it.' He'd almost reached the front door when he turned back. 'I don't suppose you'd like to join me for a curry? I've just remembered I ordered a takeaway half an hour ago. For two. But my friend left unexpectedly.' He looked sheepish. 'And partial though I am to an onion bhaji, I don't think I can eat it all.'

'No, thank you.'

'Are you sure? It's lamb bhuna.'

'Like I said, I'm rather busy.'

'I thought I'd ask. I suppose I'll just have to give the rest to Harvey.'

'Harvey?'

'My dog. Although he prefers Chinese.' He smiled. 'It was nice meeting you, Roo. Don't forget I'm only next door if you want a cup of sugar or anything.'

As soon as she was alone she called home. David took a long time to answer. The first thing he said was, 'You're late.'

'The traffic was a nightmare. Can I speak to Ollie?'

'He's gone to bed. He waited up as long as he could, but he couldn't keep his eyes open,' he added reproachfully.

Roo glanced at the clock. 'But it isn't nine o'clock yet!'

'I can't help it if the poor kid's exhausted, can I? Today's been very stressful for him. He misses you.'

'I miss him, too.' Roo felt tears prick the backs of her eyes. 'Both of you,' she said. 'Oh, David, it's horrible up here. I wish I'd never taken the bloody job.'

She wanted him to tell her to come straight home. She wanted him to say it didn't matter if she got fired because he'd landed a fantastic job and could take care of them for ever. And anyway, what did it matter as long as they were all together?

But he didn't. 'You'll get used to it,' he said bracingly. 'And you'll be home at the weekend, won't you?'

'I suppose so.' There were a whole five days to get through before then. Not to mention a mammoth trek back down the motorway.

They chatted for a while. Then David said he had to go because there was a Tom Cruise movie on Sky he wanted to watch.

'Oh. Okay.' Roo fought to keep the disappointment out of her voice. 'I'll call you tomorrow, shall I? To speak to Ollie?'

'You do that. Bye, Roo.'

'Bye, David. I love—' But he'd already hung up. Roo kept the phone to her ear, reluctant to put it down. It was strange, she spent half her life jetting everywhere from Stuttgart to San Francisco, yet she'd never felt so far from home.

The fridge had been cleaned out but fortunately she'd

remembered to pick up some basics from the last service-station shop. She made herself a cup of coffee and took it upstairs to unpack.

The main bedroom was hardly bigger than her walk-in wardrobe at home, but it seemed like heaven. Exhausted after her journey, she dumped her cases on the bed and flipped open the first one. She was too tired to unpack everything, so she pulled out one of her suits and hung it up to let the creases drop out before the following morning.

She ran a bath, adding a generous slosh of L'Occitane lavender. It was barely half full before the water ran cold. Roo sighed. Once again she yearned for the joys of home, and the deep tub she could practically swim in. Or even a hotel bathroom with constant hot water and fluffy towels.

And room service. She couldn't remember the last time she'd eaten. Her stomach growled and she thought about Matt and his curry next door. She dismissed the idea. She had work to do and besides, it wouldn't do to get too cosy with her neighbour. She had a feeling Matt could get the wrong idea if she didn't keep him at arm's length.

She had a quick, lukewarm bath instead of the deep, hot one she'd been hoping for, then changed into her nightclothes. It was barely ten o'clock, but she still hadn't worked out the heating and the radiators were stone cold. And she'd forgotten how chilly it could be in Yorkshire, even in June.

She got into bed, pulled the duvet up to her chin, and settled down to finish the Fairbanks accounts for the last financial year. Skimming through the figures she could see why the bank was so concerned. Fairbanks' sales were poor, and their overheads were far too high. The way they were going, they'd be bust within months.

She made a few preliminary notes, then settled down to sleep. Lamplight seeped through the thin curtains, suffusing the room with faint yellow light. She could hear the teenagers outside laughing and scuffling with each other.

A chill prickled her skin that had nothing to do with the dead radiators. If she closed her eyes she could almost hear her mother singing along to her records as she dolled herself up for another night out, tottering around on her high heels, her hair in rollers.

Sadie Moon. Also known as 'Normanford's answer to Cilla Black', or 'that blonde husband-stealing slut', depending on who you talked to.

She glanced at her mobile phone on the bedside table, wondering if she should call her. She'd been steeling herself to do it all weekend.

It was too late now, she decided. She'd ring her in the morning. Or once she'd settled in properly. Or sometime.

Fuck. Fuck. Fuck.

Roo stared at her car in despair. She couldn't believe it. Fate couldn't do this to her, not on her first day.

But fate had already done a pretty good job of screwing her over. She'd forgotten to set her alarm and for the first time in years she hadn't woken before dawn. She was late, which meant she barely had time to take a cold shower – still no sign of that wretched boiler working – and no time to wash her hair. Racing to get ready, she'd put her fingers through her tights – her best Wolford ones, of course, it couldn't be a cheap pair from Sainsbury's. And she still hadn't had her first cup of coffee.

So much for being at her desk by eight. At this rate she'd be lucky if she made it in by lunchtime.

She felt her panic rising and took deep breaths to control it. Calm down, she told herself. It doesn't matter. You don't have to be perfect.

'Hi there.' Matt greeted her from his doorstep. 'Lovely day.'

'Not from where I'm standing.'

He came up the road to where she stood gazing at the space where her alloy wheels used to be. At all four corners there was a neat pile of bricks. 'Oh dear. Someone's been busy.'

'You do realise this wouldn't have happened if I'd been allowed to park outside my house?'

'I hope you're not blaming me? I already told you, legally—'

'Spare me the lecture.' She pulled out her mobile phone.

'Who are you calling?'

'The police.'

'Why?'

'Why do you think?'

'But you don't know who did it.'

'Surely that's their job? Anyway, I'm sure it was those kids who were hanging around last night.'

'You're not going to tell the police that?'

'Why not?'

'I just don't think it's a good idea to go around accusing people.' He snatched the phone out of her hand.

'Give me that back!'

'Not until you promise not to do anything stupid. I'm warning you, you won't make yourself very popular.'

'So?'

'So you've got to live round here. And it won't just be bricks under the wheels next, it'll be bricks through the window. Seriously, these people's idea of a housewarming is a petrol bomb through the letterbox.'

'I don't care.'

'I do. Suppose they get the wrong house? Anyway, I wouldn't feel happy about it, you being a woman on your own.'

'I'm not on my own.' She flashed her wedding ring at him. 'Anyway, I can take care of myself.'

'I'm sure you can. But I might feel obliged to rush to your rescue. And I'm not very good in a fight.'

'For heaven's sake, they were only kids.'

'Yes, but they have parents. Big ones, with tattoos and criminal records. And that's just their mothers!' He grinned. Roo refused to smile back. She was far too wound up. 'Look, I'll ask around. Give me until tonight and I'll see what I can find out, okay?'

She snatched her phone back and stuffed it into her bag. 'I don't have time to argue about this. I'm late enough as it is.'

'I'd offer you a lift, but I don't think my car's working.'

Roo looked at the Mini again. She could just imagine turning up for her first day in that. 'Thanks, but I'll take a taxi.'

'I'll get you a number. Better still, I'll give them a ring for you. Where shall I say you're going?'

'Fairbanks. And tell them to hurry, please!'

He went back inside the house. Roo kicked at a tuft of grass growing through a crack in the pavement, furious with herself. It wasn't like her to be caught off-guard. She was famous for thinking ahead, always having a contingency plan.

'It should be here in a minute,' Matt said five minutes later.

'Did you tell them it was urgent?'

'Of course.'

They stood together on the pavement, the silence between them stretching into awkwardness. 'Don't let me keep you, if you've got to be somewhere,' Roo said.

'I'm in no hurry.'

Lucky you, she thought, glancing at her watch. A vein began to throb in her temple.

'So you work at Fairbanks, do you? What do you do?'

Roo looked up the road, willing the taxi to appear. 'I advise them.'

'On what?'

'How to run their business.' She pulled her phone out of her bag again, to call the office and let them know she was going to be late.

'I bet you're really good at telling other people what to do.'

'I am, as a matter of fact.' She listened to the ringing tone for a few seconds before giving up. 'There's no one there.'

'It's only eight thirty.'

'I'm usually at my desk before eight.'

'Why doesn't that surprise me?' He considered her for a moment. 'If you don't mind me saying, you could do with chilling out a little.'

'Chill out? CHILL OUT? It's my first day, I'm late, I'm unprepared, and some mindless thug has wrecked my car. How do you expect me to chill out?'

'Calm down. You're just having an off day.'

'I don't *do* off days.' She hit the redial button on her phone. 'I'll try the office again—'

'Hang on, it looks like your taxi's here.'

'Thank God.' Roo watched the Vauxhall Vectra turning with

agonising slowness into the narrow street. At least something was going right.

She got into the taxi, slid into the back seat and slammed the door. 'Fairbanks,' she said shortly. 'And please hurry, I'm late.'

'What's your rush, our Ruby?'

She looked up sharply, meeting the driver's eyes in the mirror. Oh, God. It couldn't be.

But it was.

Chapter 3

'Uncle Tom?' She should have known that in a small town like Normanford she was bound to run into one of her family sooner or later. She just didn't expect it to be so soon.

'I knew it would be you, as soon as they said the fare was to Fairbanks.' He'd put on weight. His faced filled the rearview mirror. 'Looking forward to your first day, are you? Mind you, you'll have your work cut out sorting that place out. It's gone right downhill lately.'

'So I gather.'

'Still, it'll be all right now you're here. It says so in the paper.'

'Sorry?'

'You're famous, didn't you know?' He reached across to the passenger seat, picked up the folded newspaper and passed it to her. The *Normanford News*. That was a joke. She and Cat used to wonder how they brought it out every day when sod-all ever happened.

She scanned the front page. Vandals had torched the community centre. Again. The local rugby team, the Normanford Gorillas, had lost to Wakefield. Again. And there an ad offering cut-price treatments at the local tanning salon, 'Tanz In 'Ere'.

'Page three,' said Uncle Tom. She flipped the page, and there she was.

'Troubleshooter To Save Fairbanks,' the headline said. As if that wasn't bad enough, they'd used that terrible photo from the Warner and Hicks website, the one of her in the severe suit with all her hair scraped back. She'd gone for a no-nonsense, professional image; she actually looked like a scary guard from *Bad Girls*.

The story told how the fate of the factory lay with top management consultant and 'local girl' Roo Hennessy. There was a quote from chairman George Fairbanks saying they expected great things from their new adviser. Oh hell, she thought.

But it was the final paragraph that turned her blood to ice. 'Roo is the daughter of local cabaret singer Sadie Starr. Says Sadie, "I always knew she would do well for herself. I'm looking forward to having her back home."'

Roo put the paper down, feeling sick. Trust her mother to get her name in the paper! It was a wonder she hadn't insisted on a photo of herself. One of those tacky 'artistic' shots she used to keep in her handbag to hand out to talent scouts, all moussed-up hair and thigh-high skirts.

'That's Sadie for you.' Uncle Tom read her thoughts. 'Never could resist sticking her nose in.'

Roo looked back at the article. Sadie Starr indeed! Who the hell did she think she was? She was fifty years old, for heaven's sake! Didn't she ever give up?

'Your Nanna's chuffed to bits,' Uncle Tom went on. 'She's already told all the neighbours. She's very proud of our Ruby.'

'Roo,' she corrected, without thinking.

'Eh?'

'I prefer to be called Roo these days.'

'Oh aye?' He paused, taking it in. 'Well, I can't say I blame you. I always said it was a bloody silly name. Another one of your mother's ideas.' He shook his head as he negotiated a roundabout.

Roo took a deep breath. 'How is she?'

'Just the same, goes from one disaster to another. You'll have heard the latest?' Roo shook her head. 'Got herself shacked up with some bloke a year or two back. She let him take out all these credit cards in their joint names, then he ran off leaving her with all the debts. I warned her what would happen, but did she listen? Oh no. She really knows how to pick 'em, your mother.' He craned his neck to check a junction. 'She's back living with

Nanna now, would you believe? Fifty years old and she still can't keep a roof over her head.'

Roo stared out of the window. They were passing Normanford High Street, a depressing cluster of takeaways, cut-price jewellers and body-piercing parlours.

It's not your problem, she told herself. But she couldn't help feeling disappointed. Why didn't her mother ever learn? No matter how many setbacks she had, or how many times her heart ended up broken, she always went back for more.

For the first few years of her life, while they lived with Nanna Moon in her terraced house on Hope Street, Roo had thought her mother could do no wrong. She looked like a film star, with her blonde hair, pink lipstick and platform shoes. It was Nanna who put the food on the table and made sure Roo always had clean socks for school, while Sadie flitted in and out of the house, leaving nothing behind but a trail of scattered clothes and *Charlie* perfume.

Then, when Roo was nine years old, everything changed. Auntie Jackie died, and Uncle Tom and her cousin Cat moved in with Nanna. It was a tight squeeze, but Roo didn't mind sharing her bedroom with Cat. They were like sisters anyway. The problem was that Sadie and Uncle Tom hated each other, which led to all kinds of rows.

In the end, Sadie and Roo moved out to a cramped flat over an ironmongers' shop. They had to share a bedroom, there were mice skittering behind the skirting boards and the roof leaked into the light fittings when it rained, blowing the lot. The only good thing about it was they weren't there for long. Sadie had a bust-up with the landlord and he kicked them out.

It was the first of many addresses. Sometimes Roo would come home from school to find Sadie throwing her clothes into a suitcase. 'Get a move on,' she'd say, 'they'll be here in a minute.' 'They' could be anyone – bailiffs from the catalogue companies Sadie ordered from but never got around to paying, the gas board come to cut them off, or the landlord looking for his back rent. It didn't matter, the end result was the same; another moonlight flit, and another grotty place. Eventually Roo stopped unpacking, just in case.

If they had nowhere to go, or they couldn't get away fast enough, they'd hide. They'd crouch behind the sofa and try not to make a sound as the landlord pressed his face against the frosted glass. Or they'd lie. Roo was good at making excuses to the debt collectors who came to the door. Or to her grandmother, who wanted to know why Roo was always starving when she came to visit.

'Isn't she feeding you?' she'd say, as Roo ploughed her way through a huge plate of shepherd's pie.

'I'm just growing, that's all.'

'Growing where? I've seen more meat on a butcher's pencil!'

Roo didn't like to admit they mostly lived on beans on toast, or just toast if the money was really tight. At first it was out of loyalty. Then it was embarrassment.

Sadie wasn't like other mothers. Roo realised that the day she sent her to school with a bottle of Newcastle Brown as her contribution to the Harvest Festival. Real mothers were like her friends' mums. They wore pinnies and baked cakes and had husbands. They didn't drink gin, wear hotpants or send their children down to the corner shop to beg cigarettes on credit.

And they certainly didn't leave their kids to go off and sing in dodgy working men's clubs every night.

It was the only job Roo had ever known her mother stick at. They never paid her, except for the tips she collected, but Sadie did it because she was convinced she was going to be a star.

'You wait,' she'd say, as she stuck on her false eyelashes ready for her night out. 'One of these days some big-shot agent is going to walk into that place and sign me up on the spot. We'll be rich, baby. We'll have a mansion in London, and a Rolls Royce. Everyone will be crawling around us then, you'll see.'

But somehow it never happened. In the meantime, Roo would spend most evenings alone. She would have liked to stay with Nanna, but Sadie wouldn't allow it.

'She'll only tell me not to go out, and I don't want her

knowing all my business,' she said. 'You're a big girl, Ruby. You can look after yourself.'

So she did, although she found it scary being at home by herself, especially if they were living in a rough part of town. She'd go to sleep on the sofa with the light on and the telly blaring so she couldn't hear the noises in the street outside.

Then, as she got older, she found she didn't care so much. Sometimes it was a relief not to have Sadie around, with her singing and her music that always had the neighbours bashing on the walls. Then the place was quiet, and Roo could do her homework or read in peace, without Sadie telling her she'd get short-sighted – 'And you know what they say, don't you? Men don't make passes at girls who wear glasses.'

As if Roo cared. She'd seen enough of men to last her a lifetime. Sadie had a never-ending stream of admirers coming through the flat. Sometimes they'd be friendly, but mostly they'd ignore her. Roo would ignore them too, much to her mother's fury.

'Be nice to him,' she'd say, 'he could be your stepdad one day!'

Some hope, Roo thought. She could see what they were after, even if Sadie didn't. And once they'd got it, they'd be off. Never mind that they'd promised to leave their wives, or marry her, or make her a star. And even though it had happened a hundred times, Sadie still got depressed. Then she'd take to her bed and Roo would have to look after her, and hide the gin bottle to stop her drinking herself into a stupor.

That was when she was down. When she was up, it was even worse. There was no shutting her up. She'd sing, she'd shimmy around the house, and she'd buy them both little treats to cheer them up, with money she didn't have.

'What do you need another lipstick for? You've already got loads,' Roo would ask as she watched her mother slapping make-up on.

'I need to look good for my job, don't I? What if that big agent comes in tonight? I don't want him to see me looking a wreck.' Then she'd turn around and smile. 'It wouldn't do you any harm to put a bit of face on. You're a pretty girl, but you're not doing yourself any favours. Anyway, get your coat on, I'm taking you and Cat to the pictures. They're showing *Top Gun* at the Majestic.'

'We haven't got money for the pictures.'

'Don't you worry about that.' So they'd all go, and Cat and Sadie would swoon over Tom Cruise while Roo fretted about what would happen when the rent man called the following week.

'You know your trouble?' Sadie would say. 'You take life too flaming seriously.'

'One of us has to,' Roo snapped back.

But their fiercest arguments were about Roo's father. Normally she couldn't shut Sadie up, but this was the one subject she wouldn't talk about.

'The less you know about him, the better,' she insisted. 'He's not worth bothering about.'

'At least tell me his name!'

'What's the point? It wouldn't mean anything to you anyway. Besides, I don't want to rake over old ground.'

Which was all very well for her to say. But it felt as if part of Roo was missing. Sometimes she'd fantasise that her father would turn out to be rich and successful, and he'd appear out of the blue to claim her. But she knew the truth was that he was probably another of Sadie's no-hoper boyfriends.

As she got older, things got worse. At school, she kept herself to herself. Her only real friend was Cat. She preferred her own company and, besides, making friends meant sooner or later she would have to take them home, and life was tough enough without anyone else finding out about her rundown house or her embarrassing mother. Every time Sadie turned up to a parents' evening in pink full-length fun fur or ra-ra skirt, something inside her would die.

At home, Roo's room became her sanctuary. She stayed in there, listening to the radio and dreaming about what life would be like if it turned out there had been a mix-up at the hospital and she wasn't the daughter of a thirty-something-year-old Bonnie Tyler wannabe after all, but a nice, middle-aged postman and his wife. She even put a lock on the door, much to Sadie's dismay.

'I hope you're not up to no good in there?' she'd yell, hammering on the door. As if Roo was the one with a half bottle of gin, a packet of Players and the Rolling Stones blaring out on the stereo.

In fact, she was plotting her escape. She'd just found out about university; a careers officer came to talk to them about courses and grants, and suddenly she realised that it was possible to go away and study for three years, and the government would pay for it. It seemed like the answer to her prayers. She threw herself into her schoolwork, determined to make the grade. She sent off for prospectuses and sat in her room studying each one, a road map by her side. She didn't care what kind of course she took. She would have studied anything from English to Engineering, as long as the university was as far away from Normanford as she could possibly get.

In the end she chose Bristol, right at the end of the M5. Practically off the end of England. But as she sent off her application form, she secretly wished there had been a University of Land's End.

Her uncle Tom was right: Fairbanks had gone downhill. The main factory building was badly in need of new paint. It was surrounded by an ugly mish-mash of outbuildings that had been tacked on when business was booming. Beyond them she could hear men shouting to each other across the timber yard.

Inside, the reception was even less promising. Roo's glance took in the drab paintwork, dilapidated seating and dried-up plants before coming to rest on the girl chewing gum behind the desk. She didn't look up as she flicked through *Chat* magazine.

'Yeah?'

'Roo Hennessy.'

'Oh!' She dropped the magazine. 'Right. I'll . . . um . . . let them know you're here.'

'Thanks, but I'd prefer to find my own way.' She looked the girl up and down. 'What's your name?'

'Stacey.'

'Let me tell you something, Stacey. First impressions count for a lot in business, and I'm not sure you're giving the impression Fairbanks needs. Would you want to place a big order with a company that looked as if it couldn't be bothered?' Stacey shook her head, her jaw moving slowly like a masticating cow. 'Exactly. So I'd like to see this place cleaned up. Get rid of those plants. And that vending machine. You can't hope to sell high-class furniture from somewhere that looks like a minicab office. And I want you to lose the gum and try to look half awake when people arrive. Do you understand?'

'Hmmph.'

'I'm sorry? I didn't quite catch that.'

'Yes, *Ms* Hennessy.' Stacey glared from beneath the greasy veil of her fringe.

'Thank you.' As she walked away she heard Stacey pick up the phone and say, 'She's on her way up. Seems like a right bitch.'

Necks craned over computers and a tide of whispers followed her as she strode through the main office.

'Is that her, do you think?'

'Must be. She's younger than I thought.'

'She'll take one look at this place and run straight back to London.'

'Ms Hennessy?' Roo turned round and did a double-take. There, standing in the doorway at the far end of the office, was her cousin Cat.

She blinked. No, it couldn't be. But the strawberry blonde hair, freckled nose and mischievous green eyes were exactly the same.

'I'm Becky,' she said. 'Your new assistant.'

Roo frowned. 'Your name wouldn't be Kitchener, by any chance?'

Becky grinned. 'I wondered if you'd recognise me!'

Recognise her? It was like looking at a ghost. Roo did some quick maths in her head. Cat's eldest would be seventeen now. Rebecca Jacqueline. Of course.

'Shall I show you to your office?' Becky said.

Roo's 'office' was a tiny annexe off the main room. With the

40

desk, the chair and a filing cabinet, there wasn't room left for both of them.

She looked around in dismay. 'I've seen stationery cupboards bigger than this.'

'That's what it was. But at least you've got a view.'

That was a matter of opinion. Roo rubbed at the small square of grimy glass and peered out. In the distance she could see the flash of cars streaming down the M62 and the misty outline of the power station. Below her, the sluggish khaki river snaked its way between overgrown banks. It was hardly the majestic sweep of the Thames.

She turned back to Becky. 'Somehow I don't think there'll be room for two of us in here.'

'Oh no, I sit outside. I've been transferred over from accounts to help you.'

'So you drew the short straw?'

'I asked to be moved. I want to learn, you see.' Then, before Roo had time to be impressed she added, 'Besides, it beats processing invoices all day.'

Even the way her nose wrinkled when she smiled was like her mother. It was unnerving. Her mother knew better than to try to talk to her about Cat and her family. Roo wished she had, then she might have been prepared for this.

'I suppose we'd better make a start.' She squeezed herself behind her desk and sat down.

'Can I get you anything?'

'Some coffee would be nice.'

'You haven't tasted Fairbanks coffee!' Becky grimaced. She went off to get it while Roo logged on to her laptop to check her emails. There were the usual screamingly urgent work messages clawing for attention. And others from friends that had been there so long they lay like silt at the bottom of her mailbox, inviting her to events that had long since passed, plaintively begging her to get in touch 'when she had a moment'. As if that ever happened!

She could hear the murmur of voices outside, gossiping. She wasn't used to working so closely with her clients, and it made her uncomfortable. From what she could see of Fairbanks, it was likely she was going to have to make some job cuts, and it would be a lot easier if she wasn't working right next door to the people she was making redundant.

Becky returned with her coffee and lingered beside her desk. Finally she said, 'You know, I always wondered what you were like.'

'I'm surprised your mother didn't tell you.'

'She said you always thought you were too good for Normanford. She said all you ever wanted to do was get out of here.' She lifted her gaze to the window. 'I don't blame you.'

'And what else did she say?'

'Not much. Only that you stopped speaking years ago. She wouldn't say why, though.'

I bet she wouldn't, Roo thought. She looked Becky over. Her clothes were more suitable for a nightclub than an office – white sleeveless top and low-slung black trousers that sunk to her hipbones, showing off a flat expanse of tanned skin and a twinkling emerald in her navel.

For a moment, Roo was tempted to tell her: how she and her mother had been best friends until Cat set her sights on the boy Roo loved and deliberately got pregnant so he'd have to marry her.

'It was a teenage thing,' she said.

She willed herself not to say any more, but as Becky turned to go she blurted out, 'How is your dad?'

'Don't you know? He's—'

'Ms Hennessy?' A tall, silver-haired man stood in the doorway. 'How do you do? I'm Frederick Fairbanks.' He shook her hand. 'I'm sorry my father isn't here to greet you. He's unwell at the moment.'

'I'm sorry to hear that. I was hoping to meet him today.'

'That won't be necessary. As Finance Director, I have my father's authority in the day-to-day running of the company.'

You haven't made a very good job of it, Roo stopped herself saying just in time. 'Then you'll know how grave the situation is?'

'I think that's putting it mildly, Ms Hennessy. I prefer catastrophic. Our trading figures for the last quarter were very poor indeed. Our worst ever, in fact.'

Roo was surprised. He was taking the news very well, considering his family firm was on the skids.

He seemed to guess what she was thinking. 'I'm a realist, Ms Hennessy. I prefer to face our problems head-on rather than shying away from them like some other members of my family.' He perched on a corner of the desk. 'So how bad is it? Bad enough to finish us?'

'I'll know that when I've had a chance to look at the whole picture.'

'But the bank wants to foreclose? They don't think we have a chance?'

'They must think you have some chance or they wouldn't have asked me to come here.'

He studied her face for a long time. Then he smiled. 'Very diplomatic, Ms Hennessy.' He stood up. 'Let me know if there's any way I can help you, won't you?'

'I will, thank you.' As he turned to leave, she said, 'Do you know when I might be able to meet your father?'

Frederick's grey eyes twinkled. 'Oh, you'll meet him soon enough. I just hope you're ready for him when you do!'

Chapter 4

Cat Kitchener looked at the magazine clipping in her hand and back at the client sitting in front of her. 'Are you sure this is really what you want?'

'Oh yes.' Mrs March smiled back at her reflection in the mirror. 'I fancy something different.'

It was different, all right. The model in the photo had a spiky urchin cut tipped with acid blonde. It looked great with her killer cheekbones and sharp designer suit. Cat wasn't quite sure how good it would look on a middle-aged woman with crows' feet and a sensible cardie.

Her heart always sank when customers brought in photos. They were so often disappointed with the result. The worst was a few days ago, when a pensioner had presented her with a picture of Britney Spears.

She knew what Maxine, the salon owner, would say. 'Take the money and give 'em what they want.' But looking at this woman's hopeful face, she knew she couldn't do that to her.

She ran her comb through the greying curls. 'I don't know if it will work with your hair,' she said tactfully. 'But I could try something similar. Something that would really suit you.'

'I'll leave it to you, dear.' Mrs March settled back in her seat. 'You're the expert.'

She sent her over to the basins for a shampoo with Natalie the trainee, and glanced at her watch. Half past two. She'd sent Sadie out for a sandwich over an hour ago. She hoped she hadn't been distracted by the shops again. She'd already been back late twice

44

this week, and Maxine definitely had it in for her. Maxine was right by the door, leaning on the reception desk chatting to Julie Teasdale, the other stylist.

'Great, isn't it?' Avril, the senior stylist, hissed as she whizzed past with a trolley full of rollers. 'We're working our backsides off while those two are gassing! I'm telling you, if it wasn't my last day I'd walk out right now!'

Cat nodded in agreement. No one liked working for Maxine. She usually managed to drive stylists away with her tantrums. Or they took better-paid jobs in other salons, like Avril; Maxine was as mean as she was moody.

She set to work on Mrs March's hair, giving it a conditioning rinse in a warm coppery shade that suited her colouring more than the harsh blonde she'd requested. Then she snipped away at her curls, shaping them into a face-framing style that wasn't too far from the urchin cut she'd wanted, but flattered her face more.

'I haven't seen you in here before,' she chatted as she worked. 'Where do you usually go?'

'Oh, I haven't got the money for hairdressers. I get my sister to do it for me,' Mrs March smiled back. 'But just this once I thought I'd treat myself.'

'Special occasion, is it?'

'You could say that. I start chemotherapy next week.'

She said it so matter-of-factly, Cat almost dropped her scissors. She listened as Mrs March explained that she'd been diagnosed with breast cancer and had had to undergo a mastectomy. But because the cancer had already spread she had to follow it up with a course of chemo and radiotherapy.

'They've already told me I'll probably lose my hair,' she said. 'So I thought I'd make the most of it while I still had it. You know, make myself feel more like a woman?'

Cat nodded, too choked to speak. She was so glad she hadn't taken the lazy route and copied that model's hairstyle. Mrs March deserved better.

As it was, she was delighted with the finished result. 'I look twenty years younger!' she exclaimed. 'How much do I owe you, dear?'

45

Cat glanced around to make sure Maxine wasn't looking and lowered her voice. 'It's on me. On one condition. That you let me do it for you again when the treatment's over and it's grown back.'

Mrs March smiled wistfully. 'Let's hope so,' she said.

Cat was sweeping up the hair from the floor when Julie sneaked up behind her. 'Letting customers off without paying?' she taunted. 'I might have to tell Maxine.'

'And I might have to tell her about you helping yourself to shampoo from the stock room!'

They glared at each other. Julie was tall and scrawny with a nose stud, a lip ring and hair bleached to the texture of candyfloss. A string of tattooed Chinese characters snaked down her left arm. She said they were the symbols for peace and harmony. Cat secretly reckoned she'd copied them off a menu from the Happy Dragon Takeaway and they actually said, 'Set Meal for Four'.

'What are you two gossiping about?' Maxine came over to them, her high heels clicking on the tiled floor. She was in her thirties with tiger-striped hair and far too much make-up. She always dressed in black because she thought it made her look sophisticated. Today it was a trouser suit with nothing underneath the jacket apart from a lot of gold chains and suntanned cleavage.

Julie looked sideways at Cat. 'Nothing,' she muttered. 'I'll be outside having a ciggie if anyone needs me.'

'What's up with her?' Maxine asked, as she stalked off. 'I hope you haven't upset her.'

'Me? Upset her?'

'She's going through a bad time at the moment. Her Dwayne's been arrested again.'

'Now why doesn't that surprise me?' Julie's teenage son spent more time in youth custody than he did in his own home.

'Where's Sadie?' Cat's heart sank as Maxine asked the question she'd been dreading. 'She's been gone longer than an hour. And don't say she hasn't, because I timed her,' she added.

'I . . . um . . . think she had a doctor's appointment.'

'I don't remember seeing it in the diary. Let's look, shall we?' She went over to the desk and flicked through the appointments

46

book with her glossy burgundy talons. 'No, it's definitely not here.'

'She probably forgot to write it down. You know what she's like.'

'Unreliable, you mean.' Maxine slammed the book shut. 'Right, that's it. She's had her last chance.'

'You can't get rid of her!'

'Why not? She's got to learn she can't turn up when she feels like it.'

'But the clients love her.'

'The old biddies love her. And that's not the image I want for this salon any more. I'm trying to take this place upmarket, not cater for the blue rinse brigade!'

Cat almost laughed out loud. Who did she think she was, Nicky Clarke? There was no way Maxine's was ever going upmarket. Not while it was in Normanford precinct, sandwiched between the KFC and the Painted Ladies All-Nite Tattoo Parlour. But the job meant a lot to Sadie.

'If she goes, I go too,' Cat said.

Maxine's eyes narrowed under the weight of her mascara, not sure if Cat was bluffing or not. Finally, she said, 'Fine. I can replace you, no problem.'

'Are you sure about that? Avril leaves today, and you haven't replaced her yet. You wouldn't want to be two stylists down, would you?'

Before Maxine could reply, the bell over the door jangled and Sadie rushed in, her arms full of carrier bags. She stopped dead when she saw Maxine.

'Where the hell have you been?' Maxine hissed.

'I . . . um . . .' Sadie stared at Cat, who furiously mimed behind Maxine's back. 'I was at the . . . er . . . doctor's? That's it! I was at the doctor's,' she finished triumphantly.

'Hmm. Why don't I believe you?' Maxine drummed her nails on the desk. 'This is your last warning, Sadie. If you come back late from lunch one more time, you're out. Is that clear?' She snatched up her fake Gucci bag and stomped out of the salon, slamming the door behind her.

47

Sadie pulled a face. 'Someone's in a bad mood!'

'She means it.' Cat followed her into the staffroom. 'I can't keep covering for you, Sadie. She's got it in for you.'

'Don't I know it! But I couldn't help being late. I had to pick up some groceries for Nanna.'

Cat eyed the carrier bags she was stuffing into her locker. 'Just groceries?'

'Maybe not.' Sadie looked coy. 'I passed Dolcis on the way back, and I couldn't resist these—' she pulled out a pair of crimson stilettoes. Typical Sadie, Cat thought, always dressing to be noticed. Today it was purple pedal-pushers and a bright yellow T-shirt with 'Man Magnet' splashed across the front. 'They'll go with that red dress I bought from the market last week.'

'Sadie! I thought you were still paying off your credit cards?'

'But they were such a bargain! Anyway, I felt like treating myself. I needed cheering up.'

No need to ask why. Sadie had been down since she found out Ruby was coming home and hadn't called her. She pretended she didn't care, but Cat knew different.

And Cat felt hurt on Sadie's behalf. Okay, so her aunt wasn't perfect, but at least she was there. She hadn't left when her daughter needed her, unlike Cat's mother.

'And I got your sandwich.' Sadie handed her the brown paper bag. 'Low-fat tuna mayo and salad, is that right?'

'Unfortunately yes.' Cat unwrapped it without enthusiasm. She craved a great big cheese and pickle barm cake, loaded with extra salad cream. Or a sausage roll. Or a portion of chips from The Friendly Plaice, all hot and greasy with lashings of salt and vinegar. But it was her weekly weigh-in at the slimming club the following day and she had to be strong.

She was picking out the lettuce when Julie came in. 'Shouldn't you two be out there doing some work?' she snapped.

'It's my lunch break, in case you hadn't noticed. And my next client isn't due until three.'

'What about you?' Julie turned on Sadie. 'Why don't you make yourself busy? Go and straighten some towels or something!'

48

'She's got a bloody nerve!' Sadie said, as Julie barged out again. 'Anyone would think she was already senior stylist.'

'Maybe she is. She was getting very cosy with Maxine earlier on. Maybe she's been promoted.'

'Rubbish, that job's as good as yours.'

'I don't know.' Cat tried not to think about it, but ever since Avril had announced she was leaving, she'd been secretly hoping Maxine might consider her for the job. 'I haven't got the experience.'

'Two years working here is enough experience for anyone! Besides, you're really good. Too good for this place, anyway. I'm telling you, if Maxine doesn't make you senior stylist you should tell her where to stick her job.'

'I couldn't do that.' How would she ever get another one? She'd never worked anywhere but Maxine's. After years of drifting from one part-time job to another, she'd decided to retrain when her youngest son Liam was two. Maxine had taken her on as a lowly junior and trained her. Everyone always said she was good at her job but she didn't have the confidence to put herself to the test by looking elsewhere.

Besides, she liked working at Maxine's. Most of the clients were her friends. She enjoyed the laughs and the gossip, and she liked putting a smile on people's faces. They'd come in stressed and leave looking and feeling good.

'I still think you could do a lot better for yourself,' Sadie said.

They were distracted by the sound of shouting in reception. Cat recognised the woman's voice and groaned. 'Oh God, it had to be her, didn't it?' She put down her sandwich. 'I'd better go and see what the old boot wants!'

Glenys Kitchener stood at the reception desk, her handbag swung over her arm, ready to do battle.

'I don't think you understand,' she said to Natalie, the quivering trainee behind the desk. 'I need a wash and blow-dry, and I need it NOW.'

'But we're fully booked. If you could come back in half an hour—'

'No, I couldn't come back in half an hour.'

49

Typical Glenys, Cat thought. She just waltzed in and expected everyone to bow down to her, just because her late husband used to be an MP.

She fixed a smile on her face and went to meet her mother-in-law, Sadie following. 'Glenys, what a pleasant surprise.'

'Catherine.' Glenys' face twitched, but she couldn't bring herself to smile. 'I was just explaining to this – person here – ' she glared at Natalie, 'that I need a wash and blow-dry. And *she* says you're fully booked.'

'She's right. As you can see, we're very busy. With people who've bothered to make appointments.'

'Surely you could fit me in? I'm sure Maxine would insist. She's a personal friend,' she added, for Natalie's benefit.

'Maxine is at lunch. And my client's just arrived,' Cat said, as Pauline Armitage struggled through the door with a pushchair.

Glenys cast a quick, dismissive glance over her shoulder. 'But I have to be at a fundraising committee meeting at four.'

Cat was about to open her mouth when Sadie said, 'I could do it, if you like?'

'Aren't you busy with Mrs Weaver?'

'She hasn't arrived yet. Besides, she won't mind waiting. Poor old dear, she only comes in for a gossip. The longer she's here, the better she likes it.' She smiled at Glenys. 'Just a blow-dry, was it?'

Cat fumed as Glenys whisked off to be gowned up, barely acknowledging Sadie's kindness. She didn't even bother to say thank you, acting as if she was doing Sadie a favour, allowing her to touch her precious curls.

Cat and her mother-in-law had never got on. Glenys made no secret of the fact that she thought Billy had married beneath him. Hers was the only long face on their wedding photo. Even his father had managed a smile, even if he did look as if someone had stuffed a coat hanger in his mouth.

She turned her attention back to her own client. 'What can I do for you today, Pauline? The usual, is it?'

As she washed Pauline's hair she tried to listen to Sadie and Glenys' conversation at the next basin. As she suspected, Glenys was sticking the knife in.

'You mean you haven't heard from your Ruby? How strange.'

'I expect she's busy.'

'Yes, but not to pick up the phone and call her own mother! It isn't right, is it?' Glenys said loudly, for the benefit of all the other customers in the salon. 'But you two were never really close, were you?' She glanced sideways and caught Cat listening. 'Still, you must be very proud,' she went on. 'She's done so well for herself, hasn't she? Mind you, she always was an intelligent girl. I remember thinking she had a wonderful future ahead of her.'

Liar, Cat thought, pouring conditioner into her hand. Glenys had always said she'd come to a bad end, just like her mother.

'Imagine, having a job like that at her age. I expect she earns a fortune. Ouch! Please be careful. I have a very sensitive scalp.'

If she did, it was the only sensitive thing about her! Cat knew very well that while Glenys pretended to be admiring, every word she uttered was meant to be a barb straight into her daughter-in-law's heart.

'Do you remember how friendly she was with my William?' she said. 'Never apart, were they? But I suppose they had a lot in common. Both intelligent, bright people with ambition.' She sighed wistfully. 'You know, there was a time when I thought the two of them might—ow!' She sprang out of the chair, spluttering.

'Oops,' Sadie said. 'Sorry, the spray slipped.' Cat could see she was trying not to laugh. 'Hang on, what's this? I think one of your false eyelashes is stuck in the plughole—'

'I'll take over, shall I?' Cat stepped in quickly and wrestled the shower nozzle out of her aunt's grasp before she could do anything more dangerous with it.

Of course Maxine chose that moment to come back to the salon. 'What on earth's going on?' she demanded.

'She tried to drown me!' Glenys pointed at Sadie. 'I'm drenched! I can't go to my committee meeting like this!'

'Natalie! Fetch some towels for Mrs Kitchener.' Maxine snapped her fingers, summoning the junior. 'Come on, Glenys, let's get you into the back room and dry you off. Then I'll do your hair personally. I'll talk to *you* later.' She glared at Sadie as she hustled the dripping Glenys into the back room.

Cat watched them go. 'You've really done it now.'

'It serves her right, the old witch.' Sadie glanced at Cat. 'Take no notice of her. She doesn't know what she's talking about.'

'I know. She's just being poisonous as usual.' But she had a bad feeling that where her husband and cousin were concerned, Glenys knew only too well.

Cat could still remember the moment she fell in love with Billy Kitchener. His mum and hers were friends, so they often came round to visit. He must have been about nine years old. He looked so out of place with his plastered-down hair and pristine trainers that had never been near a football field. He used to stand on the pavement and watch her and Ruby rattling down the cobbled street in a go-kart they'd made, his dark eyes full of longing. But he'd never joined in.

'Mother says I mustn't get my clothes dirty,' he'd said in that clear, posh voice Cat found so fascinating.

In the end she'd risen to the challenge and pushed him in a mud patch. He'd gone home, filthy and fighting back tears. Cat was terrified of what her mum would do to her, but Billy insisted it was an accident, even when his mother smacked him for being careless. That day he'd stopped being a Mummy's boy and become her hero.

Of course, she never admitted how she felt, not even to Ruby. She was afraid she might laugh and call her stupid. Cat had always preferred to hide her feelings behind a mask of indifference. She pretended she didn't care when she failed most of her O-levels while Roo sailed through every subject with top marks. She pretended she wasn't embarrassed when the lads in the precinct chatted her up and made cheeky comments about her burgeoning bra size. She even pretended to find it funny when her father said she'd never amount to anything.

But deep down she did care. Especially about Billy Kitchener.

Not that it did her any good. Roo was the one he wanted. You only had to see them together to know that. They even looked like they belonged together, both tall and dark and clever-looking. Cat always felt like the odd one out when she was with them.

They understood about politics, read books and watched arty films with subtitles. They laughed at private jokes and talked about things Cat didn't have a clue about. She would have liked to ask questions but she was scared of looking thick. So, as usual, she pretended she couldn't be bothered.

All the time, she told herself that one day Ruby would go to college and she would have Billy to herself. So when Ruby broke the news that she and Billy had decided to go to university together, her whole world collapsed. She felt as lost and abandoned as she had the day she'd come home from school and found her mother dead in bed with an empty bottle of pills. Everyone she loved left her in the end.

But she didn't plan what came next, whatever Ruby said about it. It just happened. Ruby was away at some university interview, and Cat and Billy went out for a drink together. She dressed up specially, knowing it could be their last night alone for a long time, and she could tell straight away Billy fancied her. It felt good; she might not have her cousin's brains, but she could still get his attention. When the evening ended, they went back to his place, as his parents were away at some political do in Westminster.

They both knew what was going to happen, and even though she didn't plan it, she wanted it. She couldn't bear the idea of him going away and her never knowing what it was like to make love to him.

It was the first time for both of them. Billy assumed that because she'd had so many boyfriends she must have been sleeping around for ages, and Cat was too embarrassed to tell him she'd been waiting for him. So when he whispered afterwards, 'Was it all right?' she just smiled and cuddled closer to him.

She'd fallen asleep in his arms, feeling warm, special and wanted. His first time had been with her, not Ruby. Whatever else her cousin took away from her, she couldn't take that.

But then the morning came, and Billy was full of remorse. No matter how much Cat tried to tell him she'd wanted it as much as he did, he blamed himself. She soon realised that it wasn't her he felt guilty about, it was Ruby. He'd betrayed the girl he loved.

When Ruby returned she and Billy were together again, making plans, talking about the future, shutting Cat out. She wanted to make them notice her, to shake them out of their private little world where she had no place.

That was when she came up with the plan. It happened the day her period was due. At first she didn't think about it when it didn't come. But when it didn't arrive after a week, her mind started to work overtime.

What if she was pregnant? Then everyone would have to know what had happened with her and Billy. They couldn't ignore her.

Of course, she knew she wasn't. She'd always been irregular, so it didn't bother her too much. She planned to leave it a few days, then tell them the panic was over. Except it didn't work out like that. Billy insisted he wanted to marry her, in spite of his mother, who said she should have an abortion.

'It'll have to be private; we can't risk any scandal. I can't allow my son to throw his life away marrying you,' she told Cat.

Cat barely heard her. She had a sudden picture of herself married to Billy, living happily ever after in a wonderful home, surrounded by children and love. More than anything in the world she wished she really was pregnant so it could all come true.

She knew it was only a fantasy. She didn't really mean to marry Billy, or to ruin his life. She just wanted to hold on to the wonderful dream a tiny bit longer.

But somehow as time went on she found it harder to let it go. Especially when Ruby confronted her. She told her Billy didn't love her, that he was only marrying her because he had to. She said if Cat really cared she'd get rid of this baby and set him free. She made her feel as if she would never be worthy of him. Between Ruby and Glenys Kitchener, Cat began to believe it.

The only one who didn't make her feel bad was Billy. He was always so sweet and caring, but Cat knew he was only going through with it because he felt sorry for her. The time had come to end the fantasy.

That was when she realised her period still hadn't come. She'd been so preoccupied she hadn't noticed she'd missed a whole month. Panicking, she did a test. It was positive.

The news shattered her. She'd pretended to be pregnant, but the reality was completely different. She felt as if by fantasising about it she'd somehow brought this baby into being all by herself.

She spent the next week hiding away, crying herself to sleep. Her father was unsympathetic. The only one she could talk to was her Aunt Sadie. But even she couldn't see why Cat was so upset when Billy was doing the decent thing.

In desperation, she tried to set Billy free. She told him she didn't want to marry him. She even offered to have an abortion.

'What's brought this on?' he asked. 'Has my mother been talking to you again?'

'I just think we're both too young.'

He thought about it for a long time. 'And is that what you want?'

She couldn't meet his eye. 'I don't want you to be tied down.'

'That wasn't what I asked.'

'I know you don't want this baby.'

'Who says I don't want it?'

'How can you? Your mum's right, it would ruin your future.'

'Maybe you're my future. You and our child.' Cat's heart leapt. He didn't know how much she wanted to believe that.

So they'd got married. His parents bought them a little starter home on the outskirts of town and pretended to be delighted about their wedding to keep up a front. Cat was thrilled to have a place of her own, and set about decorating and buying furniture and getting it ready for the baby.

'I never had you down as a homemaker,' Billy had said, as he watched her doing battle with Aunt Sadie's sewing machine, trying to run up some curtains.

'I've never had a home to make before, have I?' It was true. She hadn't had a proper home since her mum died.

Ruby didn't come to the wedding. And in spite of what Billy had said, Cat could see he was wistful as her cousin got ready to go to university.

He went to see Ruby the night before she left. Cat lay in bed, unable to sleep because the baby was overdue, worrying about what was going on between them. She was haunted by images of him and Ruby making love for the first and last time. She began to think she'd never see him again.

He walked in after midnight, looking shattered. 'Couldn't you sleep?' he asked, rubbing her back. His eyes were red-rimmed.

'I wasn't sure you'd come home.'

'I told you, my future's with you now. You and the baby.' But he didn't smile, and Cat knew why. His future might be with her, but his heart had gone with Ruby.

Chapter 5

It was a dark, wet afternoon and the only sounds in Roo's office were the steady drumming of the rain and the buzz of the faulty striplighting as she studied the balance sheets in front of her.

Then, suddenly, a shout from the main office jolted her back to reality.

'Where is she, then? Where's the woman who reckons she can run my factory better than I can?'

A moment later the door flew open and an old man stood there, leaning heavily on a stick. He was frail and stooped with age, but his gaze was fixed sharply on Roo. George Fairbanks, she guessed. 'So you're Sadie Moon's girl, are you?'

'Mr Fairbanks?' She plastered a smile on her face. 'I didn't think we'd be meeting today. Your son said you were ill.'

'Not too ill to fight for my factory.' He shuffled into the room and lowered himself into the seat opposite hers, wincing with effort. 'So how are you settling in? Office all right for you, is it? I chose it for you myself.'

I bet you did, Roo thought. 'It's fine, thank you.'

'Aye, well, I daresay you won't be staying long.' Behind him, Roo noticed everyone in the main office had stopped typing. She hurried to close the door.

'Just as long as it takes to draw up my report and make my recommendations,' she said.

'And we all know what they'll be!' He leaned forward, his face thrust closer to hers so she could see the yellowing whites of his eyes under baggy lids. 'You can say what you like, but no one's putting us out of business.'

'Well, obviously we all hope it won't come to that—'

'I wasn't born yesterday! I know why the bank sent you sniffing round here. They're like vultures, the lot of them, circling round just because they think we're in trouble.'

'No, Mr Fairbanks, you *are* in trouble. And unless you make some serious changes to the way you do business, you're going out of business.'

He jerked his head away to stare up at the peeling paintwork on the walls. 'We've weathered worse than this.'

'Not this time, I'm afraid.'

There was a long silence. Then he said, 'Do you know how old I was when I started working here? Eleven. I served my apprenticeship on that factory floor, learnt my craft from my father.' His voice wobbled. 'I've been working here for the best part of seventy years, Miss Hennessy. I've forgotten more than you'll ever know about making furniture. So why should I listen to some jumped-up accountant who wouldn't know a dovetail joint from a daffodil, telling me how to run my business?'

They eyed each other across the desk. His age-spotted hands trembled on top of his walking stick.

'Because you don't have much choice. The bank has sent me here to do a job. It would be better for this factory if we could work together. But if you're not going to be able to do that . . . well, I'll just have to do it on my own. Either way, you're not going to stop me carrying out any changes I feel are necessary.'

'We'll see about that.' He suddenly changed tack, smiling at her. 'Have you had a look around the factory yet?'

'I haven't had a chance. There's all this paperwork to get through.'

'Paperwork be blowed! How can you make any decisions about this place if you've never seen it?'

'Well, obviously I will be looking around—'

'How about now?' He struggled to his feet.

The long, low factory building was filled with the whine of electric saws and sanders and the smell of fresh timber and varnish.

58

The men in their brown overalls stopped working and turned to watch them as they went from machine to machine, George explaining how each one worked. Roo had to admit he knew his stuff; there wasn't a part of the furniture-making process he didn't understand. He could tell at a glance which wood was being worked, and he only had to listen to the sound of a machine to know if it was working properly or not.

But what struck her most was the way the thirty or so workers greeted him. Not only did he know them all by name, but he also knew their wives' and kids' names, where they lived and how many brothers and sisters they had. They, in turn, treated him with affectionate respect, like their favourite grandad. Roo had been wondering why the turnover of staff at the factory had been so low and now she knew why; they were like one big family.

When they'd finished their tour, George asked them all to stop working and gather around. Roo was still wondering what he was up to when he turned to her and said, 'Now, Miss Hennessy. Maybe you'd like to look these people in the eye and explain exactly why you're putting them out of a job?'

She glanced around at the arc of expectant faces, her face burning with embarrassment. How could he do this to her? 'I . . . um . . . well, no decisions have been made at the moment . . .' she stammered.

'That's not what you said to me.' George Fairbanks' eyes gleamed with the light of battle.

'Yes, well . . . it's very complicated. I have to produce a report, and . . . um . . . make recommendations according to my find-ings—' she waffled on, aware of everyone looking blankly back at her. Oh hell, this was a nightmare. She didn't do this kind of thing. She compiled lists, made suggestions. They were all just names on a piece of paper, not real people.

She was rescued by a thin-faced man who suddenly appeared and said to George, 'Mr Fairbanks, I think one of the lathes needs looking at.'

'I'll be there in a minute.' George turned to Roo. 'I reckon that's one up to me, don't you?' he said, and shuffled off. Everyone else went back to work, leaving her standing alone in the middle of the factory.

Out in the yard, she met Frederick Fairbanks. 'I was just coming to find you,' he said. 'I hear you've met my father?'

'Oh, I've met him all right.'

'I told you he was a character, didn't I?' Frederick grinned. 'I hope he didn't give you too hard a time?'

'I'll survive.' She brushed a speck of sawdust off her jacket.

'You'll have to excuse him, he's very protective of his business. A bit too protective sometimes. He thinks the world is still the same as when his father made furniture.' He looked around the yard, where some men were unloading a lorry full of timber in the rain. 'But everything's changed since my grandfather opened this place. It's all cheap imports now. That's what people want. They don't want furniture that will last a lifetime. They want something cheap and cheerful they can throw out when they get bored.'

'And what does your father say about that?'

'I wouldn't dare tell him. It would be tantamount to heresy in our family to mention the dreaded F-word. Flatpack,' he explained, as Roo looked blank. 'He already thinks I've failed the Fairbanks name just because I didn't pass my O-level woodwork.' He smiled ruefully. 'He thinks the whole family was born with sawdust under our fingernails.'

'You can't run a business by harking back to the past. You have to look to the future.'

'My thoughts exactly.' Frederick beamed. 'I think we're going to get on very well, Ms Hennessy.'

That night Roo was too tired to cook, so she called in to the pizza place in the precinct for a takeaway. Pizza Paradise looked anything but. Unless paradise was decked out in Lego colours and as bright as a floodlit football ground, with a whiff of stale grease and garlic in the air. A group of depressed-looking teenagers clustered around a single cup of Coke, while over by the window a family squabbled over garlic bread.

'Hello there. Fancy seeing you.' It took Roo a moment to recognise her neighbour Matt behind the till. He wore a yellow

T-shirt, his bright red baseball cap at a rakish angle on his messy fair hair. 'What's a nice girl like you doing in a dump like this?'

'Would you believe, ordering a pizza?' She looked around. 'Do you have a menu?'

'Up there.' He pointed above his head at the row of illuminated pictures that separated him from the clattering kitchen beyond. 'A lot of our customers have trouble with the written word, if you know what I mean,' he explained.

Roo studied the photos. None of them looked appealing. 'What do you recommend?'

'Personally, I'd recommend you go to the Star of Bengal. They do a very nice chicken Madras. Although you don't really strike me as a junk-food sort of woman.'

He didn't strike her as a pizza boy, either. Even in that lurid T-shirt he still managed to look like a Calvin Klein model.

Before she could order, she was interrupted by the father of the family shouldering his way past her.

'Excuse me,' he said, 'but is this fag ash on my Four Seasons?'

Matt made a show of studying and sniffing the congealed pizza before saying finally, 'No sir, I think you'll find that's oregano.'

'Are you sure? It looks like fag ash to me.'

'It's very easy to confuse the two, sir. Chef does it all the time.' The man went off, grumbling. Matt turned to Roo. 'If you must eat at this hellhole, your best bet is the Margarita. Anything with more than two toppings and the chef starts to lose it.'

'Fine. Whatever.'

'Regular or large?'

'Regular.'

'Garlic bread? I wouldn't recommend it,' he said, tapping the keys before she had a chance to reply. 'How about salad?'

'Well—'

'Definitely not.' He rang up the total and took her money. 'By the way, I've got some good news for you. I managed to get your wheels back.'

'You found out who stole them?'

He tapped his nose mysteriously. 'I have to protect my

contacts. But let's just say I talked to a bloke in the pub and he retrieved them.'

'Great.'

'So you owe me fifty quid.'

'What? You're not serious?'

'That's the going rate.'

'It's outrageous! You can tell your friend down the pub the deal's off. I'm not buying back my own property.'

His turquoise eyes lost their warmth. 'But I've already paid for them. What do I do with four useless wheels?'

'You could try putting them on your equally useless car and driving it out of my parking space!'

'I take it you don't want them, then?'

'No, I don't. I'd rather claim on the insurance and buy new ones.'

'Suit yourself. So I'll take the old ones off your car again, shall I? I'm sure you wouldn't mind catching cabs to and from work every day while you wait for your insurance claim to be pro-cessed—'

'All right, I get your point. I'll write you a cheque when I get home.'

'Could you make it cash? I'm not getting on with my bank manager at the moment.'

Roo opened her purse and handed over a handful of notes. 'But this is the last time I get involved in anything like this.'

The chef handed Matt a flat box and he pushed it across the counter to her. 'There you go. Enjoy your meal. And have a nice day,' he called after her.

Roo glared at him. 'Are you being funny?'

A Question of Sport was blaring from the sitting room when Sadie sneaked in just after seven. She closed the door softly behind her, wincing at the rustle of her carrier bags. She paused, listening. Either her mother had dozed off or she was so engrossed in Sue Barker she couldn't hear her.

She hurried past the half-open door into the kitchen, dumped her grocery shopping on the table and had just reached the foot of the stairs when a voice rang out above her.

'And what time do you call this?'

'Mum!' Sadie clutched her chest. 'What have you been told about using those stairs? You could fall.'

'How else am I supposed to get up and down? Fly?'

'You're supposed to use that nice stairlift Social Services put in for you.'

'Stairlift! I don't need a stairlift.' Irene appeared at the top of the stairs. 'I can manage to put one foot in front of the other, thank you very much. It's my house and I'll use the stairs if I want to. Anyway, you haven't answered me. Where have you been?'

'One of the girls at work was leaving. I told you this morning I'd be late. Here, let me help—' She started up the stairs but Irene batted her off.

'Stop fussing, I can manage. The state you're in, it should be me helping *you* up the stairs,' she grumbled.

'I've only had one drink.'

'Oh aye? Must have been a big one. I can smell your breath from here.'

Sadie retreated as her mother began her slow, awkward, sideways shuffle, her gnarled hands gripping the banister rail. Her knuckles were swollen and angry-looking, a sure sign her arthritis was bad today.

Not that Irene Moon would ever admit it. She might be frail but she was fiercely independent. Even though her last hip operation had left her struggling to take care of herself, she still refused all Social Services' well-meaning help.

'You're not getting your claws into me!' she said the day she sent the occupational therapist packing. 'I know what you lot are like. One day it's handrails and ramps, the next you're bunging me in a wheelchair and carting me off to some flaming care home!'

She reached the bottom, her chest heaving with the effort. Sadie tried to conceal her carrier bag behind her but her mother caught sight of it.

'What's that you're hiding? Been spending again?'

'Just a pair of shoes.'

'Another pair? Why do you need so many? You've only got one pair of feet.'

'They were a bargain.'

'They're not a bargain if you can't afford them. But I suppose they went on that credit card of yours?' She shook her head. 'When are you going to learn you can't keep running up these big bills when you can't pay them off?'

'If it's any of your business, I paid cash. My cash.'

'Burning a hole in your pocket, was it? Maybe you should think about putting some away for a change.'

'It's my money and I'll do what I like with it. I'm not a teenager, Mum! I'm an independent woman and I can please myself.' She edged past her mother and stomped up the stairs.

As she went, Irene called after her, 'If you're so independent, what are you doing still living here?'

Bloody good question! Sadie slammed the door and threw the bag down on the bed. Turned fifty, and here she was still in the same bedroom she'd had when she was fifteen. No wonder her mother never treated her like an adult.

If only she knew the truth. Irene thought Sadie had moved back to Hope Street because her flat was repossessed for rent arrears. She never told her the real reason, that she didn't feel her mother could cope alone. She knew Irene would never have let her move back otherwise. And her mother did need help, even though she'd never admit it.

Of course, it had meant the usual lecture from her brother Tom about not facing up to her responsibilities. As if she didn't know enough about them! Sometimes she wished she hadn't been so quick to give up her own place, then she might have had somewhere to escape. She loved her mother dearly, but living under the same roof could get a bit much at times. Especially when Irene forgot who was supposed to be taking care of whom and insisted on treating her like a kid.

But she wasn't a kid any more, whatever the rest of her family seemed to think. She'd made some mistakes in her life. A lot of mistakes. But she'd learned from them. And yes, she could be daft and impulsive sometimes, but she was still a grown-up, mature woman.

If only everyone would give her a chance to prove it.

She went back downstairs to find Tom had arrived. He and Irene were in the kitchen, admiring a gleaming microwave on the table.

'Look what our Tom's brought,' Irene said. 'Isn't it lovely?'

'I thought you could do with one,' Tom said. 'It'll save you a lot of time.'

'Ooh, yes, I bet it will. Look, Sadie, isn't it good?'

Sadie shook her head pityingly. 'You have no idea what it is, do you?'

'Of course I do.' Irene looked cross.

'You wait, she'll be trying to get the snooker on it,' Sadie said to Tom.

'It's for heating things up quickly, Ma,' Tom explained. 'You could cook your tea in it in five minutes, no problem.'

'I only had bread and jam for my tea tonight,' Irene said glumly. 'She went out drinking.'

Tom glared at Sadie. 'What's this?'

'I left her a casserole. She only had to put it in the oven. Isn't that right, Mum?'

'You'll have to speak up, I'm a bit deaf. Would anyone like a cup of tea?'

'I'll make it.' Sadie reached for the kettle. 'And I've bought some of that jam sponge you like.'

'Oh, I can't eat that. The pips get stuck under my plate.'

'You liked it last week.'

'No, I said I liked Battenberg last week. You don't listen, do you?'

'Give me strength,' Sadie muttered.

'What?'

'I said, I'll buy some Battenberg tomorrow. Okay?'

'You could heat your casserole up in your new microwave now,' said Tom, determined not to be overshadowed.

'Hmm, yes. Is that the time?' Irene looked at the clock. 'Snooker's starting on BBC2 in a minute.'

65

As she went off, Sadie said, 'She'll never use it, you know.'

'She seemed happy with it.'

'Of course she's happy, because you bought it for her. But you wait, in a week's time it'll still have the plastic on it and a vase of flowers on top.'

'Anyway, what's all this about you leaving her to fend for herself?' he changed the subject.

'I'm allowed to go out, aren't I?'

'You shouldn't have left her. She can't manage on her own.'

'If you were that worried, why didn't you come round and look after her?'

That stumped him. 'You're living here. I'm not.'

'You're still her son.'

'And you owe her.' He jabbed his finger at her. 'You're forgetting how many times she's taken you in and given you a roof over your head when you were in trouble. It's about time you starting repaying her for that.'

He walked off, leaving Sadie standing, her mouth open. God, she hated her brother! As long as she could remember he'd made her feel worthless.

He was perfect, of course. Everyone had to feel sorry for him because his wife had killed herself, leaving him to bring up their daughter on his own. So tragic, they all said. Yet no one spared any sympathy for her, struggling single-handed to get by with a child.

She listened to them talking in the sitting room as she arranged the cups on the tray – the best china, of course, nothing less would do for Tom. It was hard not to feel resentful. Despite all her efforts, it was still Tom her mother preferred. Good old Tom, who turned up once a week if they were lucky, usually to tell Sadie how to run her life. He never lifted a finger to help with their mum and yet she still thought the sun shone out of his big backside, while Sadie bore the brunt of all her frustration.

When she came into the sitting room Tom was reading to Irene from the obituaries while she watched snooker with the sound turned down.

'Guess who's died?' she said excitedly. 'Do you remember

66

Lesley Jarvis? Tall woman, walked with a limp. Her husband used to be a friend of your father's. You do remember her. Her sister had that squint. Lived up on Wakefield Road until they got bombed out in the war.'

'And she's dead?'

'No, her brother's next-door neighbour is.' Irene shook her head. 'It'll be me next.'

'You? You'll go on for ever, just to spite me.'

Irene cackled but Tom looked shocked. He made a big show of rustling the paper, then said, 'By the way, I saw our Ruby today.'

Sadie's hand wobbled as she poured the tea. 'Oh aye?'

'I gave her a lift this morning.'

'She hasn't been round yet,' Irene said. Sadie and Tom looked at each other.

'I expect she's busy,' Sadie murmured.

'Too busy to see her own mother?' Tom said. 'Says a lot doesn't it?'

'Oh yes? And when was the last time your daughter invited you round for your Sunday dinner?'

That got him. Tom might like to lay the law down, but his relationship with Cat wasn't good either. Not surprising, since he treated her with the same contempt as he did Sadie. No one was good enough for him. Sometimes she wondered if that was why Jackie had sunk into depression.

'All the same, she should have called. She is family, after all, ' Irene said. 'Where is she living?'

'Sykes Street.'

'You're kidding!' Sadie laughed. Wouldn't her snobbish daughter love that!

'You should call round and see her,' Irene said.

Sadie stopped laughing. 'She knows where we live, if she wants to come.'

'Anyone would think you didn't want to see her.'

'I don't. And don't look at me like that. She hasn't bothered with me all these years, so why should I chase after her?' She stirred her tea. 'We've never been that close, even when she was a kid. I don't see why that should change now.'

'What about your grandson? Don't you want to see him?'

'That's up to his mother, isn't it?'

They sipped their tea and listened to their mother grumbling. 'It isn't right,' she said. 'In my day families stuck together through thick and thin. And look at you lot, falling out all the time.' She looked sorrowful. 'I could be in my box before I see our Ruby again. Mind you, I don't suppose you lot will be at the funeral. None of you will be speaking, I daresay.' She looked at them both over the rim of her teacup and sighed. 'I'm seventy-eight. I doubt if I'll be around for much longer,' she said in a small, trembling voice. 'You wouldn't think it would be too much to ask, to have my family around me in my last years—'

'Oh, for heaven's sake!' Sadie put down her cup. 'You can stop the emotional blackmail, it's not going to work.'

'It's a bad state of affairs when a mother won't even pick up the phone and ring her own daughter!' Irene retorted.

After Tom had gone, Sadie rinsed the cups in hot soapy water, still fuming. Why should she go begging? If Ruby didn't want her around – fine. They'd managed without each other all these years; why should that change just because she was living on her door-step?

It would have been nice to see her grandson again though. She'd seen him only a handful of times since he was a baby. She wondered if he'd even remember her.

She ran the cold tap and rinsed the cups under a blast of icy water. What had she done that was so wrong, anyway? She'd always done her best for her daughter. And although she was the first to admit she wasn't too good at being a mum, at least she'd tried. At least she hadn't given her up to strangers.

And Ruby hadn't been the easiest of daughters, either. Sadie had looked forward to her little girl growing up, but with every passing year she grew further away from her. She wasn't interested in shopping or make-up or having a laugh. All she wanted to do was lock herself in her room and bury her nose in a book. Sadie was proud of her clever daughter, but she was scared of her, too. And the way Ruby used to look at her, so full of disdain . . .

Sometimes Sadie felt as if she was the child and Ruby was the grown-up.

She shook drops of water off the cups and set them down on the draining board. There was no way she was going to beg to be part of Ruby's life, whatever her mother might want.

Irene Moon turned the TV volume up full blast. She'd been looking forward to the snooker semi-final, but now she couldn't concentrate on Stephen Hendry heading for a 147 break.

She knew Sadie was more hurt than she let on about Ruby. She might pretend she didn't care, but she was proud and stubborn and she'd sooner go on hurting than make the first move.

Tom hadn't helped, rubbing it in like that. He never missed the chance for a dig at his sister, even after all these years.

She flexed her fingers gingerly, wincing at the pain. Sadie was a good girl; she deserved better than that. Irene knew she didn't always show her how much she appreciated her. The constant nagging of her arthritis made her short-tempered, and not being independent frustrated her. And sometimes she took that out on poor Sadie.

Wild applause filled the room as Stephen potted the final black. Irene came to a decision. As usual, her family weren't going to sort out their problems, so she would have to do it for them. Bang a few heads together, if necessary, just like she used to do when they were kids.

And she would start with Ruby.

Chapter 6

'Doesn't look like anyone's coming, does it?' Becky said.

Roo looked around at the empty circle of chairs and felt slightly foolish. She'd had such high hopes when she arranged her first staff brainstorming session for that morning. But here she was, in the staffroom, her whiteboard and marker pens at the ready, all set to take down the wonderful flow of ideas, and no one had turned up.

'Perhaps they didn't get the message,' Becky suggested. She was stationed by the tea and coffee pot, ready to meet and greet. 'I could go and round them up, if you like?'

'There's no need.' She already had a feeling no one would come. This was George Fairbanks' way of sending her a message that no one was interested in doing things her way.

'You might as well go back to the office,' she told Becky. 'There's no point in both of us hanging around. I'll tidy up here.'

She packed up the board and put the marker pens back in her briefcase, fuming silently. She'd done her best. She'd given them a chance to say how they felt things should be done. Now it was time to do things her way. No doubt George Fairbanks thought this was all a big joke. She hoped he was still laughing when she had half his workforce made redundant.

'Am I in the right place for the brainstorming?' a voice behind her asked.

Roo swung round. 'No, I was just—' She froze. The man in the doorway was smartly dressed in a suit but looked no different from when she'd last seen him eighteen years ago.

'Long time no see,' said Billy Kitchener.

She dropped the chair she was carrying. 'Billy?'

'Thank God for that. I wasn't sure if you'd remember me.' He grinned. 'Aren't you going to give me a hug? Or are you too grand for that kind of thing these days?'

Stunned, she went into his arms, feeling them wrap around her, holding her close. This couldn't be happening. 'What are you doing here?'

'Didn't Becky tell you? I'm Fairbanks' Sales Director.' He held her at arms' length. 'It's good to see you. You look great.'

'So do you.' She still couldn't believe it. Was this really Billy, the boy who'd broken her heart all those years ago? He was a man now, his dark hair flecked with grey. But those laughing brown eyes and warm smile were just the same.

'Sorry I wasn't here yesterday when you arrived. I had to go down south and sweet-talk a couple of customers. They're dropping like flies at the moment.' He shook his head, marvelling. 'Look at you. Ruby Moon. What happened to the scruffy girl who used to skim stones in the river?'

'She's gone. And it's just Roo now. I stopped being Ruby when I left here.'

He'd let go of her but still held her hand, his fingers wrapped around hers. 'I couldn't believe it when they said they were sending you. I thought you said you'd never come back to Normanford?'

'It was either here or a fish farm in Norway.'

'Put like that, I can see how this place might start to seem attractive.' He smiled, his eyes twinkling. 'So you're our saviour. Imagine that.'

'I'm not sure I can.' She glanced around the empty room. 'I haven't made a very good start.'

'They just need time to get used to you. We're a bit set in our ways at Fairbanks.'

'So how did you end up here?'

'It's a long story. Look, why don't I take you to lunch? We can catch up on old times.'

71

'I'm not sure I can.' She looked at her watch. 'I have some notes to write up—'

'In your lunch hour?'

'I don't usually take lunch hours. I'm too busy.'

'Roo, this is me you're talking to. You know, the old friend you haven't seen for eighteen years?'

She smiled reluctantly. 'Put like that, I don't suppose I can say no, can I?'

'That's more like it!' he grinned. 'I've got a few things to sort out back at the office. I'll see you at the gate in about an hour?'

Back in the office she looked at the pile of paperwork and the Post-it messages stuck around her computer monitor and tried to tell herself it wouldn't hurt to ignore them just this once. It wasn't every day she met up with an old friend.

And this wasn't any old friend. This was Billy Kitchener.

'The Ponderosa. Are you serious?'

'I told you you'd love it.'

'It's . . . unbelievable.' Roo stared around her. The restaurant was done out like an old western saloon, its high beamed ceilings hung with cowboy paraphernalia – saddles, bridles and, in the far corner, what looked like a hangman's noose. The dark panelled walls were covered with sepia photos of skinny men with horses. A big wooden sign over the bar had the words 'Welcome to Wild West Yorkshire' picked out in bullet holes. 'Please tell me you don't bring customers here?'

'Are you kidding? This is Normanford's answer to The Ivy. All the movers and shakers come here. And it's gone a lot more upmarket since they got rid of the spitoons.'

'Oh, please!' Roo turned to the barmaid, a middle-aged woman in a rhinestone stetson, and ordered a mineral water. 'At least we stand a chance of getting a table,' she said, looking around the empty restaurant.

'It livens up in the evening, when they have a cabaret. In fact—' he stopped.

'What?'

'Your mum sings here sometimes. Sorry, maybe I shouldn't have mentioned it.'

'No, it's fine. Honestly. Shall we get a table?'

They found a place under a precarious-looking pack saddle. Roo studied the big laminated menu, with its coloured photos of food-filled plates. It made her think of Pizza Paradise. Couldn't anyone in Normanford read a menu? 'I think I'll stick to salad.'

'And I'll have the Rodeo Rib-Eye.' They didn't look at each other as they handed the menus back to the waiter, a mournful man with 'Clint' on his name badge and an oversized cowboy hat with a bullet hole in it. As soon as he'd gone, they both burst out laughing.

'Have you ever seen an unlikelier-looking Clint?' Billy said.

'I wonder if that bullet hole is real?'

'Could be. Some of the customers can get quite rowdy.'

She kept sneaking glances at him, drinking in the face she hadn't seen for nearly twenty years. Billy had always been good-looking, but he was even more attractive in his mid thirties, lean and square-jawed with a hawklike nose. Roo, married to a blond, had forgotten how intensely sexy dark men could be.

They made feeble jokes about Clint, the stupid western decor and the impossibility of finding any vegetable in Normanford that wasn't oven chips. All small talk, as if they were strangers.

And all the time she was more aware of what they weren't saying, how they were skirting around anything remotely sensitive. Like his marriage.

Their food arrived and Roo grabbed the chance to change the subject.

'I was sorry to hear about your father.' It came as a shock to see the obituary in *The Times* a few years back, saying he'd died from a heart attack at the age of sixty. Not that she could remember much about Bernard Kitchener. He was always away pursuing his political career. 'How is your mum these days?'

'Oh, you know my mother. She never stops. She's got her bridge club, and various charity committees she's on. It keeps her busy, thank God. Otherwise she'd never stop bothering me!' He speared a piece of steak. 'I think she would have liked me to follow in Dad's footsteps and become an MP. She misses the power.'

'So why didn't you?'

'I don't think I'm cut out for politics.'

'All the same, she must be proud of you now. High-powered marketing man and all that!'

He looked rueful. 'Not exactly high-powered. Not enough for her, anyway. She'd much rather I was running some multinational corporation somewhere.'

'And what about you?'

'I'm happy the way I am.'

Are you? she wanted to say. Are you really?

They talked about their jobs, her life in London, her family. They swapped photos of their children – besides Becky, Billy had an eight-year-old daughter and a four-year-old son – and Roo raved about Ollie and David.

'You must miss them, being up here? I don't think Cat would like it if I had to work away for three months.' Roo didn't reply. 'It is all right to talk about her, isn't it?'

'It doesn't bother me. But I'm surprised you're still married,' she added.

'Contrary to your direst predictions. And my mother's.'

They finished their meal and Clint turned up with the dessert menus. Roo waved him away. 'Just the bill, please. I've got a lot of calls to catch up on this afternoon.'

'Don't you ever stop thinking about work?'

'Not often.' She knew she'd got it bad the day she found herself timing how long it took her to eat a sandwich at her desk.

'You know what they say about all work and no play, don't you?'

'It makes Jack very successful and well paid?'

He smiled. 'You always were single-minded. You knew what you wanted and went for it.'

It didn't help me get you though, did it, she thought. As if he could read her mind, he suddenly said, 'I missed you, when you left.'

She reached for her drink, not sure how to reply. 'Did you?'

'What do you think? You were my best friend. To suddenly cut all ties like that and not see each other . . .' He stared at his glass. 'You wouldn't believe how many times I nearly picked up the phone to call you.'

'Why didn't you?'

'I didn't think you'd want to hear from me.'

Roo smiled to herself, thinking of those first lonely weeks at university when she'd longed to talk to him, too. 'I told you, I wasn't angry at you. I was angry *for* you. I didn't want to see you throw your life away.'

'I know. And you're right, it could have been a huge mistake. Getting married and becoming a father before I was twenty – it felt like a nightmare at the time.' He looked across at her. 'But it wasn't. It all worked out. My only regret was losing you as a friend.'

'You didn't lose me.'

'So how come I haven't seen you for eighteen years?'

'We drifted apart. It happens.'

'Not real friends. Not like us.' He paused. 'Cat missed you too.'

'I doubt it.' Cat got all she wanted when she married Billy. She wouldn't need Roo around, spoiling her party.

'It wasn't all her fault, you know. I got her pregnant. I had to take some responsibility. I couldn't just leave her.' His eyes pleaded for her understanding, just as they had that night when he'd told her his future was with Cat.

Clint arrived with their bill, distracting them. They had a brief argument over who was going to pay it, and by the time they'd decided their conversation was forgotten.

They walked back to the factory together and stood for a moment, looking in through the high wire fence.

'Weird, isn't it?' Billy said. 'Remember what we always said about never ending up here? Now look at us!'

'We said a lot of things when we were young and stupid. Most of them didn't happen either.'

'Yours did. You always said you were going to get away and you did it.' He sounded wistful.

They parted at the doors to the office building. 'We should get together again,' Billy said.

'Good idea. I'd like to discuss some changes in the marketing strategy—'

'I was thinking more of dinner tonight. Why don't you come round for a meal? I'm sure Cat would love to see you.'

'I don't think that's a good idea.'

'Why not? Her cooking's improved a lot since you last saw her, I promise.'

'Maybe some other time.'

'Or maybe never? I'm never going to get you two to make friends, am I?'

'Probably not,' she agreed.

As she walked away, he called after her, 'Nearly twenty years is a long time to stay angry at someone, Ruby.'

She didn't turn around. As far as her cousin was concerned, it wasn't nearly long enough.

Ruby and Catherine Moon. The Terrible Twins, everyone called them, even though they were nothing alike. Roo was dark and lanky, Cat was small and enviably curvy, with wicked green eyes and a tumble of red-blonde hair. But they were inseparable, whether it was sitting side by side in class, racing up and down Hope Street on Cat's bike – Roo steering, Cat perched precariously on the handlebars – or sharing secrets after dark in their bedroom. When they got older, they got Saturday jobs together in Woolworths, where they spent most of their time stealing from the Pick'n'Mix counter and eyeing up the boys.

But it was always Cat who got asked out. She was the pretty, flirty one; Roo was quieter, bookish. The only time she went on a date was when Cat fixed her up with her latest boyfriend's equally awkward friend. The rest of the time she spent doing Cat's homework for her and lying to Uncle Tom about why his daughter was still at the school drama club at ten o'clock in the evening.

The only boy who ever noticed her was Billy Kitchener. The three of them were best friends, but Roo had more in common with him than her noisy cousin. They liked the same films, books and music. And like her, he wanted to escape. Especially from his ambitious snob of a mother who always thought she knew what was best for her son. She kept trying to steer him in the direction of her bridge club friends' daughters, girls called Victoria and Olivia who rode horses and belonged to the Young Conservatives.

That was why they came up with their plan to go to university together. They would share a flat, far away from Normanford and their families. It was perfect.

But Cat didn't agree. She threw a fit when Roo told her. She accused her of 'stealing' Billy, of wanting him to herself. Roo couldn't understand why she was so upset – and then it dawned on her.

Cat was in love with him herself.

It was a strange, powerful feeling to know that for once she had the upper hand. All those times Cat had fluttered her eyelashes and flashed her C-cup cleavage and Roo had gone unnoticed. But this time someone wanted her, not her cousin.

Or so she thought. Until a month later, when Cat broke the news that she was having Billy's baby. One look at her smug face and Roo knew straight away she'd planned it all. She'd deliberately set a trap for Billy – and he'd fallen right into it.

She didn't go to the wedding. It was bad enough watching her mother with a mouth full of pins as she worked on the bride's dress. It was big, puffy and filled their tiny sitting room like a gigantic white mushroom cloud. It made Roo feel sick to look at it. It also made her more determined than ever to leave Normanford behind.

Billy came to see her the night before she left for university. For a moment she thought he was going to say he'd changed his mind and was running away with her. But instead, full of regret, he'd told her he couldn't let Cat down. And nothing Roo said could make him change his mind.

'Do you love her?' she'd asked.

'I don't know what I feel at the moment. It's all happened so fast.' He looked so wretched, it made her hate her cousin all over again. There she was, looking forward to her wedding day, getting all dressed up in that joke of a white frock, not caring that her husband-to-be was the unhappiest man in the world.

She'd wished him luck and they'd held each other for the last time. 'You know where I am if you ever change your mind,' she'd said.

That was the last time she'd seen him.

It was after six when she left the office to go home, only to find two of her tyres were flat.

She frowned. Surely they were all right this morning? And how could two of them have gone down at the same time? She wondered if they were really her tyres at all, or some dodgy cheap versions Matt had conned her into buying.

She was on her mobile, trying to track down a garage, when Billy strolled towards her. 'Having a half day? I thought you workaholics stayed at your desks until midnight.'

'Very funny. Actually, I'm taking some work home with me. If I ever get home.' She pointed to the tyres. 'I'm calling the garage now.'

'I've got a better idea. Why don't you come home with me?'

'I can't!'

'Why not? It's about time you met the rest of the family. Cat will be fine about it.' He took her briefcase from her and headed towards his BMW.

Roo couldn't share his optimism. If Cat was anything like she used to be, she'd be anything but fine about it.

Chapter 7

Cat stood in front of the food cupboard, fighting the urge to finish off Liam's Smarties. She'd only lost half a kilo at the slimming club weigh-in. Pam, the woman who ran it, blamed a slowdown in her metabolic rate. Cat blamed her inability to say no to a packet of Pringles.

She edged her finger into the waistband of her jeans. All day she'd imagined they felt looser but now she could hardly breathe in them. Perhaps it was too late? Perhaps after thirty-three years and three children her body had finally given up the ghost. Maybe it was time to accept that she'd worn her last bikini and stop trying to fool herself that every clothing manufacturer in the world had started cutting their size fourteen clothes smaller.

She knew Billy would prefer her to give up dieting. He'd made it clear he was sick of watching her pushing a grilled tomato around her plate while he tucked into steak and chips. But did he really want a fat wife? Voluptuous was one thing, but no one wanted a blob.

And now she had even more reason for needing to be slim. The thought of Billy seeing her cousin looking svelte and chic every day and then coming home to her was enough to keep her on the straight and narrow. Maybe she should stick a photo of Ruby on the fridge door, just in case she was tempted to snack?

A half-naked young man strolled into the kitchen. Becky's boyfriend Dominic was a semi-permanent fixture in their home, especially at mealtimes. He was over six feet of solid muscle, thanks to hours spent in the gym and hefting concrete slabs around his dad's builder's yard. Cat forced herself to remember he was only twenty and therefore young enough to be her son. Just.

'Hi, Mrs K.' He opened one of the cupboards and peered inside. 'Where do you keep your clean plates?'

'We don't have any, since no one bothered to switch the dishwasher on this morning.' Was she the only one who could see the dirty dishes stacked on the draining board? It seemed like it. Just as she was the only one who noticed when the bin needed emptying, or they'd run out of milk.

'By the way, you've run out of milk,' Dominic said.

'And I don't suppose it occurred to anyone else to buy any?' Cat reached into her bag. 'Just as well I remembered, isn't it?'

'Cheers.' Dominic took it from her.

'And if you drink it out of the carton I swear I'll kill you.'

'Sorry.' Abashed, he went to fetch a glass.

Cat looked around. 'Where is everybody?'

'Becky's upstairs doing her hair – again. And the kids are playing in there.' He nodded towards the sitting room.

Cat strained to listen. She couldn't hear them killing each other, which meant she could start cooking dinner in peace.

'What are we having?' Dominic peered over her shoulder as she stared into the fridge.

'Something quick.' She was too tired after her hectic day to create a culinary masterpiece. She reached in the freezer for a family-sized pack of fish fingers. Good old Captain Birdseye to the rescue. It wasn't quite haute cuisine, but it was just about all she could manage.

She was arranging them on the grill pan while Dominic stood at the sink peeling potatoes, when Megan came into the kitchen with Liam in tow. She was dressed in her new stretchy jodhpurs, her black riding hat low over her eyes.

'Megan, what have I told you about wearing those clothes?' She'd been badgering to learn to ride ever since she'd seen *Black Beauty* on the television one Sunday afternoon. Cat had finally given in and booked her a few lessons, hoping she might get tired of it as quickly as she had the ballet dancing and the gymnastics. But three months on she was as obsessed as ever, and Cat had been forced to spend even more money kitting her out. It was only a matter of time before she started pleading for a pony. 'I've said a hundred times—' She stopped dead, noticing her son for the first time. 'What the—? Megan, what have you done to your brother?'

Dominic turned around and laughed out loud. 'Bloody hell!'

Cat covered her mouth, trying not to laugh herself. Liam blinked up at her in confusion, his round green eyes clumsily outlined with bright blue eyeshadow that swept up almost to his ears. His mouth was a gash of vivid pink, and the same pink was blobbed in doll-like circles on his cheeks. A sprout of fair hair was caught up in a silver scrunchy on top of his head.

'He looks like my little sister,' Megan explained.

'He looks like a plonker,' Dominic muttered.

Cat was still trying to think of something to say when an awful thought occurred to her. 'Megan, where did you get that—'

'You little sod! You've been in my make-up again, haven't you?'

The screech from overhead made them all jump. Megan shot out of the room while Liam burst into tears.

Becky rushed into the kitchen, looking furious. 'Where is she? I'll kill her!'

'Calm down. You're upsetting your brother.' Cat put her arms around Liam. 'It's okay, sweetheart, she's not angry at you. It's your sister she wants to kill.'

'Little cow!' Becky flung herself down at the kitchen table. 'Why do I have to share a room with her? It's humiliating. I'm nearly eighteen; I shouldn't have to sleep in a room with Barbie posters on the wall.'

'I don't know, I'd quite like it,' Dominic said thoughtfully. Becky ignored him.

'How come we have to share and he gets a room of his own?' She pointed at Liam.

'You know Liam has to sleep with the light on, and it keeps Megan awake.'

'And I wouldn't share a room with him. He's a *baby*,' Megan said, sticking her head around the door.

'And you're a brat.' Becky snatched up a potato and threatened to hurl it at her. Then she looked at Liam, forlornly twisting his hair around its scrunchy. 'That kid is *so* going to grow up gay,' she sighed.

'Leave him alone. He's in touch with his feminine side,' said Cat.

'So what's for dinner?' Becky asked.

'Fish fingers. And don't look at me like that, I don't see you slaving over a hot stove when you come home from work.'

Becky rolled her eyes. 'I should have gone out for lunch with Dad and Roo.'

Cat grabbed the hot grill pan with her bare hand and nearly dropped it. 'What?'

'He took her out to lunch.' She tossed the potato up in the air and caught it. 'Everyone's been giving her a really hard time. Do you know, she arranged this meeting today, and—'

But Cat wasn't listening. Her mind was too full of the idea of Billy and Ruby having a cosy meal *a deux*. It was just as she'd feared; the first chance he had to be alone with her, he took it.

'It's a cow,' said Liam. At first Cat thought he'd read her thoughts, but then she realised he'd drawn a lumpy-looking animal on the fridge door. In Becky's lipstick.

Suddenly they all seemed to be making a noise – Becky screeching, Liam wailing and Cat trying to make herself heard over the din.

'Will you all just SHUT UP!' she yelled. 'Another word out of any of you and I'm putting you all into care!'

To her amazement, the room fell silent. Cat stood for a moment, marvelling at her unexpected power. Until she realised no one was listening to her.

She turned around slowly. There, in the doorway, was Billy. With Roo.

'Guess who's coming to dinner?' he said.

For a split second she saw the whole ghastly scene through Roo's eyes. The breakfast dishes stacked up on the draining board, her wailing four-year-old son looking like an extra from *The Rocky Horror Show*, her teenage daughter throwing a tantrum. And her in the middle of it all, no make-up, shabby jeans and screaming like a fishwife. She didn't know who she wanted to kill first; Billy, for bringing Roo home, or herself for looking such a wreck.

'Hello,' said Roo. 'Long time no see.'

Not long enough, Cat thought. Oh God, why couldn't she have turned up when the house was spotless, the kids were on their best behaviour and she was half a stone lighter?

'These are our kids,' Billy said. 'Not Dominic, obviously. He's Becky's boyfriend.' Dominic looked sheepish. 'This is Liam, our youngest. And this is Megan.' She'd slunk into the room and wrapped herself around her father's waist, looking shyly up at Roo with her butter-wouldn't-melt expression.

Cat couldn't take her eyes off her either. Those lowlights must have cost a fortune. And God knows what she'd paid for that suit. More than Cat earned in a year, probably. It looked good on her, fitting her slim curves in all the right places. But she didn't look a bit like the Ruby she used to know.

She was suddenly aware they were all watching her expectantly. 'Sorry? What?'

'I said it's okay if Roo stays for dinner, isn't it?'

'Just say if it's not convenient,' Roo said.

'Well—'

'Of course it's convenient,' Billy laughed. 'Anyway, I've been telling her what a domestic goddess you are.' He sniffed the air. 'So what are we having?'

Cat's blush spread up her neck until it reached her ears. 'Fish fingers,' she muttered.

Roo broke the embarrassed silence. 'I haven't had those in years.'

Cat took charge of the situation. 'Becky, why don't you take our guest into the sitting room? Megan, take your brother upstairs and wash that stuff off his face. Billy, could I have a word?' she said, as he made to follow Becky and Roo out of the room. Dominic must have recognised the tone in her voice because he fled.

She slammed the door behind them and turned to face him.

'What the hell are you playing at? You could have warned me you were bringing her here!'

'I thought you'd be pleased!'

'Do I look pleased?'

He frowned. 'What's your problem?'

For someone who was supposed to be intelligent, Billy could be very dense sometimes. 'The problem is this place is a mess and we've nothing decent to eat.'

'Roo doesn't mind.'

'No, but I do.' When she finally met her cousin again she'd wanted it to be on her terms. She wanted to be cool and glamorous and in control, not looking terrible and serving up fish fingers.

Burnt fish fingers! She rushed to rescue them from the grill pan before they went up in flames. 'Oh God, now what am I going to do?'

Billy looked over her shoulder at the blackened remains. 'You could always say they're Cajun?'

The meal was tense. At least the children were quiet for once, stunned into silence by their glamorous guest. The only ones who spoke were Billy and Roo, who chatted about work. Becky joined in, leaving Cat to push her food around her plate, too wound up to eat.

'You're not still on that diet?' Billy said.

'Mum's always on a diet,' Becky chimed in. 'Except they never work because she always cheats. She thinks leftovers don't count.'

'Or anything from someone else's plate,' Megan laughed.

'Or if it's straight from the fridge!'

'Will you stop talking about me as if I wasn't here?' Cat glanced at Roo. She was smirking, the bitch.

'Chill out, Mum. It was only a joke,' Becky said, which made her feel even worse. Now they all thought she was neurotic, as well as lacking in willpower.

By contrast, everyone thought Roo was the coolest person on the planet. Even Becky was impressed that she'd actually been to some of the smart bars and restaurants she'd read about in *Heat* magazine. And when she found out she lived down the road from a famous *EastEnders* actor, she was in ecstasy.

'So do you live in a really big house?' she wanted to know.

'It's big enough for the three of us. And the nanny.'

'Your nanny lives in your house?'

'She's got her own flat upstairs.'

'Her own flat! Did you hear that, Mum? And there's me, sharing a room with my kid sister.' Becky sighed. 'I'd love to live in London.'

'Not everyone in London has a big house, you know,' Cat said.

'How would you know? Mum thinks a trip to Leeds is a big day out,' Becky told Roo. 'Remember that time we went to Alton Towers and she took her passport?'

'I did not!' Cat began to clear the plates away. Billy made a move to help her but she waved him back into his seat. He was the last person she needed around her.

As she stacked the dishwasher she could hear them laughing. No prizes for guessing who they were laughing at! She could take a joke, but she couldn't stand the idea of Roo sneering at her.

It was time she fought back, she decided. As she headed back into the dining room with pudding – apple pie, homemade this time – she said, 'So your family aren't with you?'

'No, they had to stay in London.'

'It must be hard for your little boy, not having you around.'

'He's used to it. I often have to travel in my work.'

'Sounds great,' Becky said.

'You miss a lot of his growing up, then?'

'I think quality is more important than quantity when it comes to children. I'd rather spend an hour having fun with my son than two days shouting at him.'

'Surely that's part of normal family life?'

'It is in this house,' Becky grumbled.

'That depends on what you call normal, doesn't it?'

Cat tried again. 'I don't think it's right for kids not to have their mothers around. They need them.'

'Perhaps. But I'm sure Ollie would rather have a happy, fulfilled mother than a clinging, frustrated one with no life of her own.'

'And you've asked him, have you?' The children looked from

one to the other, eyes sliding from left to right as if they were watching a tennis match. 'I don't see the point in having children if you're going to pay someone else to bring them up.'

'More wine, anyone?' Billy interrupted, reaching for the bottle.

Thankfully Roo left soon after dinner. Billy insisted on driving her home, even though she was perfectly capable of taking a taxi. Cat watched them go. She could just imagine what they were saying about her.

She would have liked to put the whole disastrous evening out of her mind, but Becky was full of talk about her new boss. Cat was forced to listen as her daughter recounted every detail of her cousin's fabulous lifestyle.

'You should see her car. And those clothes. She must have a personal shopper to choose them. She's brilliant.'

'She can't be that brilliant if she can't even choose her own clothes,' Cat muttered, clattering pots and pans.

'I mean she's too busy doing high-powered things to waste time shopping.' There was a faraway look in Becky's eyes. 'I'd love to be like that one day.' Then, just in case Cat wasn't feeling low enough, she added, 'You know, no one would ever believe you two are related.'

'Look, I'm really sorry about Cat,' Billy said for the hundredth time as he dropped her off. 'I never thought she'd be so hostile.'

'I did warn you.'

'I can't understand it. She's never usually like that. Our house is always full of people because she makes everyone feel welcome.'

'Everyone but me,' Roo said dryly. She felt sorry for Billy. She couldn't imagine what it must be like for him, living in that madhouse.

Billy looked embarrassed. 'I'll talk to her.'

'Don't bother on my account. I told you, Cat and I are never going to be bosom buddies. We've got nothing in common any more.'

Except you, she thought. She knew exactly why Cat had been so hostile. She was nervous about Roo being back on the scene, in case she and Billy picked up where they left off.

Well, let her sweat. She deserved to feel insecure after the low trick she'd pulled, stealing him in the first place.

The house was blissfully silent, apart from the sound of Matt's dog barking next door. Didn't it ever sleep?

She dumped her briefcase on the floor and called home.

Shauna answered. 'You're a bit late,' she said. 'Didn't you get my message?'

Panic washed over her. 'What message?'

'The message I left this morning, to say Ollie had to have a tooth out at the dentist's. He was very upset about it. He wanted you,' she added accusingly.

Roo gripped the phone. 'Oh my God, how is he?'

'He's fine *now*. He waited all afternoon for you to call. I even called again at lunchtime because I know you never go out,' Shauna added, piling on the guilt. 'And I tried your mobile but it was switched off.'

Roo thought of all the unread Post-its stuck to her computer screen. Her son was in pain, waiting by the phone for his mummy to call and offer a few words of comfort, and all the time she'd been flirting with an old flame. 'Shauna, I'm so sorry. What's he doing now?'

'He's on the sofa watching *Return of the Jedi*. I've given him some more Calpol. He just needed someone to make a fuss of him.' And you weren't there to do it, her silence said.

'Let me speak to him.'

Ollie came on the line, his voice blurred by tiredness. He listened, yawning, as Roo told him over and over again what a brave boy he was, and how much his mummy loved him.

'Can you come home and tuck me in?' he said.

'Not tonight, darling, I'm too far away. But I'll be home on Friday.'

'That's a long time.'

'Only three days. Three more sleeps.' But that was a long time in a little boy's life, wasn't it? Too long.

'Where's David?' she asked, when Shauna came back on the line.

'He's gone to Oddbins.' There was something strange about

87

the way she said it. Has she noticed he's been drinking heavily? Roo wondered. 'I'll get him to call you when he gets back, shall I?'

Roo put the phone down, feeling wretched. Then she remembered what Cat had said and felt even worse. What kind of mother was she, paying someone to comfort her son while she did some stupid job at the other end of the country?

But what was the alternative? To stay at home? She could never do that. She needed to be able to provide for herself and Ollie, to give him all the security she'd never had when she was growing up.

She made herself some coffee, took a lukewarm bath, then left a brisk message on the letting agents' phone about her faulty boiler.

The dog was still barking when she came downstairs, wrapped in her dressing gown. It was too much. Throwing open the back door, she called out, 'For God's sake, will you shut that thing up?'

The barking grew more frenzied, followed by a clatter of falling dustbins. Roo tightened her dressing gown around her and stepped out into the darkness.

The houses in Sykes Street didn't have gardens. They had tiny yards that backed on to a narrow cobbled alley, or ginnel, as the locals called it. As Roo stepped out, shivering in the drizzling rain, a dark shape flung itself against the fence separating their two houses. Roo leapt away from the flurry of gaping jaws. It would be just like her neighbour to own a crazed monster dog.

But then the barking stopped and she saw it wasn't a monster dog but an over-enthusiastic black Labrador, his paws on the fence, tongue lolling in a friendly way.

Roo tentatively reached out a hand. 'Hello, er . . .' What was its name again? Henry? Herbie? Harvey! That was it. 'Hello, Harvey. Has that cruel man locked you out in the cold?'

There were no lights on in Matt's house. He was probably working, but that was no excuse for leaving his dog out in the freezing rain.

She scratched Harvey's velvety ears and thought for a moment. She couldn't just leave the poor animal shivering outside. She found the number for Pizza Paradise in the phone book.

No, said the weary voice on the other end of the line, Matt Collins wasn't working tonight. No, he couldn't possibly give her his mobile number. And he was sick of women calling up for him and never ordering pizzas.

Roo put the phone down. Outside in the yard, Harvey had started whining plaintively at being abandoned again.

Well, it wasn't her problem. It was Matt's dog, nothing to do with her. If he wanted to leave the poor thing to 'catch pneumonia, that was up to him.

'What the hell am I doing?' she wondered five minutes later as she crept out into the ginnel and lifted the latch to Matt's back gate. For all she knew, Harvey might be madly territorial and sink his teeth into her leg as soon as she stepped into his yard.

But he greeted her like an old friend, nearly knocking her flying. So much for being a menacing guard dog, she thought ruefully. 'Come on, boy.' She curled her fingers under his thick leather collar and hauled him back into her own house, trying to remember if there was anything in her lease about not having pets.

As soon as she let him go she knew it had been a mistake. Harvey rampaged around like a hyperactive toddler, his tail swishing from side to side. As she followed him around, desperately trying to distract him, Roo began to understand why Matt locked him outside.

'Watch out for that vase. No, not on the chair!' She made a grab for him. 'Would you like something to eat? Let's see what we can find, shall we?'

That got his attention. He trotted after her into the kitchen and they both investigated the fridge. 'Don't look at me like that,' she said, as his reproachful brown eyes moved from the bare shelves back to her. 'I didn't expect guests, did I?'

Just at that moment the phone rang. It was David, calling to report that Ollie was fine and making the most of being an invalid. Relieved, Roo put the phone down and returned to the kitchen, only to find Harvey had got tired of waiting and helped himself to a low fat yoghurt, some teabags and the mobile phone out of her handbag.

'Right, that's it.' She wrestled the phone from his jaws. 'This has gone too far.'

She was seething with moral outrage as she rang the RSPCA. Matt couldn't be allowed to get away with treating dumb animals like that. And it wasn't her responsibility to look after them for him.

But as soon as she put the phone down she began to regret it. Perhaps she'd been a bit hasty? Especially now Harvey had settled down – admittedly taking up most of the sofa – and gone to sleep. Roo watched him, his head resting on his paws, breathing out deep sighs of contentment. She felt as if she'd betrayed him.

She felt even worse when the RSPCA inspector arrived, look-ing disturbingly like a police officer in his dark blue uniform. 'Did you report an abandoned dog?'

'Yes, but I've changed my mind.'

'You mean the owner's turned up?'

'Not exactly.'

'So the dog's still abandoned?'

'I wouldn't say abandoned. More sort of . . . home alone.' He lifted an eyebrow. 'Look, I'm sure it was just an accident. Perhaps he got locked out accidentally—'

'The dog was locked outside? In the rain?'

'Well, yes—'

'I see.'

'But like I said, it's all right now. The dog's happy here until his owner comes home. I'm sorry to have wasted your time—'

He shook his head. 'We can't leave the dog here. We have to investigate this matter. We take neglect cases very seriously.'

He shouldered past her and went into the sitting room. Harvey looked up, his tail thumping on the cushion at the sight of another new friend. 'Is this the dog?'

What do you think it is? Roo felt like saying. 'Yes, but as you can see he's fine, so—'

'That's as may be, but we'll still have to take action.'

'What kind of action?'

'We'll have to take him away—' For questioning, she thought he was going to say. She imagined Harvey locked in a room with a lightbulb shining in his trusting eyes while the inspector cross-examined him about his whereabouts on the night of Tuesday 30 June. 'To the rehoming centre,' he said.

'You're not going to give him away?'

'Not until all the circumstances have been thoroughly examined. But if we think there's a case for neglect, we might have to prosecute.'

Roo followed him to the front door. 'But what will I tell his owner?'

The inspector looked ominous. 'Tell him we'll be in touch.'

It broke her heart to see the way Harvey hopped into the van as if they were going for a jolly outing. She dreaded Matt coming home. It was nearly midnight when a car pulled up and she heard his voice in the street. There was a woman with him, but not the blonde from two nights ago.

They let themselves into the house, laughing. Then Matt called out, 'Harvey? Come on mate, I've brought you a burger.' His calls became more urgent as he moved through the house and flung open the back door. 'Harvey?' He called into the night, and then, 'Oh Christ!'

'What is it?' the woman said, coming out behind him.

'The back gate's open. He must have got out!'

For a second Roo thought about saying nothing and letting him think Harvey had escaped. But he was bound to find out the truth once the RSPCA contacted him.

'The daft sod's got no road sense,' Matt's voice was shaking. 'He'll probably walk straight under the first bus . . . oh, Jesus! How the hell did he get out?'

'Mr Collins?' Roo went outside, drawing her dressing gown tightly around her. 'Can I have a word?'

'Have you seen Harvey?' Matt looked distraught. 'I think he's escaped.'

'No, he's safe. He's . . . um . . . at the RSPCA.'

'But I don't understand. How did he get—' Realisation dawned. 'Please tell me you didn't.'

'It wasn't my fault. He was barking, and—'

'And so you decided to have him taken away?' Matt was

furious. 'You had no right to do that! What the hell did you think you were playing at?'

'I wasn't the one who locked him out in the rain,' Roo shouted back, forgetting her remorse. 'You're not fit to keep a dog if you treat it like that. It's cruel.'

'You have no idea what you've done! Harvey isn't even my dog. I'm looking after him for . . . a friend.'

'Then maybe you'd better tell your friend to take him home, since you're not capable of taking care of him.'

'I can't. She's dead.'

The woman appeared before Roo could reply. 'I've called the RSPCA. They want you to go in tomorrow morning.'

'Why can't I go tonight?'

'They won't release him until the office opens at nine.'

'Great. So poor Harvey's got to stay locked up in a cell all night. He'll be terrified.' He glared at Roo. 'I hope you're pleased with yourself.'

'Look, I'm sorry—'

'I don't want to hear it.' He held up his hand, silencing her. 'I've had it with you. I tried to be friendly but you're so up yourself you've made it clear you don't want to know. So from now on, just stay out of my way, okay?'

Chapter 8

It was Friday afternoon and the salon was in chaos, with everyone wanting their hair done for the weekend. Cat ran between Marjorie Prentice's wash and set, a full set of foil highlights and old Mrs Wilmslow's perm. Meanwhile, on the other side of the salon, Julie was snipping at her solitary client's hair strand by strand, saying, 'Of course, just because they found my Dwayne with a box of matches and a can of paraffin doesn't actually mean he set fire to the school. Circumstantial evidence, our brief called it. Cat, could you mix my lady's colour for me?'

Cat skidded to a halt. 'Can't Natalie do it? If I don't get Mrs Wilmslow out from under that dryer soon, those rollers will be welded to her head.' She gave the old lady a wave. Mrs Wilmslow smiled back over her *People's Friend*, blissfully oblivious.

'We're all busy, Cat.'

'I don't see you breaking your neck.'

Julie folded her arms. 'Are you going to mix that colour or not?'

'Do it yourself. Who do you think you are, giving me orders, anyway? You're not the senior stylist, you know.'

'That's what you think.'

Cat swung round. 'What?'

'Didn't Maxine tell you?' Julie looked innocent. 'Must have slipped her mind.'

'When did this happen?'

'She told me this morning, before she went out to the cash and carry.' Julie smirked. 'Now are you going to mix that colour?'

Cat went into the back room, too stunned to argue. It couldn't be true, could it? Surely Maxine couldn't have given her that job? Cat knew they were friends, but Maxine must realise that Julie wasn't up to it?

She was still in a daze when she went to put Marjorie Prentice's rollers in. 'Are you all right?' Marjorie said. 'You're not your usual bouncy self.'

'Sorry. I've just had some bad news.'

'You're not the only one. I've just heard they're cutting my Alan's hours at Fairbanks.'

'No! When did this happen?'

'He got a letter this morning. Said they were putting all the staff on short-time working until the financial situation improved. But how are we supposed to manage on half pay?' She stared glumly at her reflection. She was in her fifties, her blonde hair peppered with strands of grey.

'That's terrible.' Cat felt guilty. She might not like the idea of Julie being promoted over her, but at least she still had a job.

'I'll say this for your cousin. She doesn't waste much time, does she? She's barely been at that place a week, and she's already getting everyone's backs up.'

'That's Ruby for you,' Cat said. She was glad it was Sadie's day off and she couldn't hear what was being said about her daughter.

'But I suppose it's not all down to her,' Marjorie went on. 'Everyone knows Fairbanks is on the skids. It's only a matter of time before they close it down.'

'It's not that bad, surely?'

'Alan says she's already sold off a load of their timber stock. What does that say to you? This time next year there probably won't be a factory.'

Cat was thoughtful. Surely Billy would have told her if things were that bad? 'They can't do that. What about the people who work there?'

'They'll end up on the dole, I suppose, just like they did when the pit closed.'

'Yes, and look what happened then. The town nearly died. You should do something about it if you're that worried.'

94

'What could we do?'

'I don't know. Organise a petition. Talk to your MP or something.'

Maxine came back into the salon as she was putting the finishing touches to Marjorie's set. Cat watched Julie dart over and say something to her, then Maxine sent Cat a quick, panicky glance and disappeared into the back room.

So it was true. Julie was the new senior stylist.

She was so overcome with misery and disappointment that she hardly listened to Marjorie until she said, 'So you'll help, then?'

'With what?'

'This Save Fairbanks campaign. It was your idea.' Cat frowned. Since when had she come up with an idea like that?

'Oh no, I couldn't. The only thing I've ever organised is the Infants School Summer Fair, and that was a disaster. Anyway, maybe it won't come to that. Maybe it will all turn out for the best.'

Marjorie looked grim. 'Maybe pigs will fly,' she said.

After brooding about it all afternoon, Cat finally steeled herself to confront Maxine when her last client left.

Maxine had been locked away in her office doing paperwork. She looked panic-stricken when Cat stuck her head around the door and said, 'Can I have a word?'

'Cat, I've . . . um . . . been meaning to talk to you but I've been so busy with this lot.' She held up an invoice. 'I suppose you've heard about Julie?'

'She told me.'

'I just wanted you to know it's no reflection on your abilities,' Maxine said in a rush. 'You're a highly competent hairdresser and I did consider you for the job, but in the end I had to go with the more experienced candidate.'

'So it's nothing to do with her being your friend?'

'No!' Maxine blushed down to the gold chains nestling in her cleavage. 'Julie has been a hairdresser for years. And she's well-qualified.'

'On paper, maybe. But she's hopeless in the salon. And none of the clients like her.'

95

'That's not true. She just needs time to settle in.' Maxine smiled placatingly. 'Look, I know you're disappointed—'

'You're right, I am disappointed. I've worked really hard these past two years. I don't think you're being very fair.'

Maxine's smile hardened. 'Oh, I think I've been more than fair. Who took you on in the first place? Who trained you, gave you the chance to go to college? Not many people would do that, you know.'

'I know, and I'm grateful. But—'

'You might think you're the queen bee here, but I reckon you'd be surprised if you tried to get a job in another salon. Although you're welcome to try, if you don't like it here.'

'I'm not saying that. I just—' Cat faltered. What was she trying to say, exactly?

Maxine softened. 'Look, you've got the potential to be a very good hairdresser. In a couple of years, if Julie ever left – who knows? But you've still got a lot to learn.'

It was only when she'd left the office that she thought of all the things she should have said. Maxine might have taken her on, but she'd paid her own way through college. It hadn't cost Maxine a penny, and she'd got a qualified stylist at the end of it.

She'd gone in, guns blazing, but Maxine had dented her confidence and put her in her place. Perhaps she was right, she wouldn't stand a chance getting a job anywhere else. Her aunt Sadie might reckon she was too good for Maxine's, but what did she know?

She was still fretting about it when Billy got home. He'd been meeting the account managers so it was after eight when he arrived.

'Hi darling.' He kissed her on the cheek as she stood at the cooker, stirring Bolognese sauce. 'Kids in bed?'

Cat nodded. 'And Becky's gone out with Dominic. How was your day?'

'A nightmare.' He pulled off his tie. 'How about you?'

'The same.' She put the lid back on the sauce. 'Maxine's given the job to Julie.'

'Oh?'

'She said it was because I wasn't experienced enough, but I reckon that's just an excuse . . . are you listening?'

'Hmm?' Billy looked up from the *Normanford News*. 'Sorry, what were you saying?'

'I didn't get the senior stylist's job.'

He was instantly sympathetic. 'Oh, no. Poor you. Come and tell me all about it.' He sat down and pulled her on to his knee.

'Julie only got it because she's Maxine's best mate. I didn't stand a chance.'

'That's terrible.' He eased her cardigan back off her shoulder and kissed her bare skin.

'I'd make a much better senior stylist than her.'

'Definitely.' His lips trailed feathery kisses up her neck.

'I wouldn't mind, but she's so lazy . . . what are you doing?' She squirmed away as he tickled her earlobe with his tongue. 'I'm trying to have a serious discussion with you.'

'Sorry. But you look so sexy when you're angry.'

'You're not helping.' She tried and failed to be furious.

'I thought I was taking your mind off your troubles.'

She wriggled as his tongue traced a warm, sensuous line along her collarbone. 'Maybe you are. A bit.'

She turned her head a fraction and his lips met hers in a greedy kiss. She could already feel the familiar heat flooding through her as he turned her body to press against his, their mouths still locked together, his stubble grazing her skin.

'Let's go to bed,' he murmured.

They made love slowly, exploring each other. After so long together she was amazed he still had the power to turn her on with a look or a touch. But she fancied him just as much as when they were young. He was still incredibly sexy, with his lean, hard-muscled body, the shadowing of dark hair on his broad chest that tapered over his flat stomach. Sometimes she would lie awake, watching his sleeping face, and marvel that he was really hers.

A long time later she stared up at the ceiling. 'I spoke to Marjorie Prentice today. She reckons they're going to close Fairbanks down.'

'Oh yes?' Billy said. 'And what would Marjorie Prentice know about it?'

'Her husband works there. So are they going to close it down?'

'Not that I'm aware of.'

'But there might be redundancies?'

'I doubt it. Why the sudden interest in Fairbanks, anyway?'

'I just wondered.' She pulled the duvet up to her chin. 'Julie Teasdale's going to be unbearable now.'

'Who?'

'Julie. The one who got the senior stylist's job.' Honestly, didn't he ever listen? 'I can hardly face seeing her again.'

'So don't.'

Cat twisted round to look at him. 'What?'

'You don't have to go to work.' He was still on his stomach, his face buried in the pillow. 'It's not as if we need the money or anything. Your wages wouldn't keep Megan in riding boots!'

'Are you saying my job isn't important?'

'No, I'm just saying you've got the choice. Although let's face it, the world wouldn't end if you weren't there to snip off someone's split ends.'

'I see.' Cat's voice was chilly. 'Not like Roo, you mean?'

She heard him sigh. 'I never mentioned her.'

'No, but that's what you meant. Just because I don't wear suits and go to meetings and earn a fortune, my job isn't important.'

'All I said was if you hate it so much you should give it up. I was trying to be supportive!'

'By telling me my job doesn't matter?' She threw off the bedclothes and sat up. 'Let me tell you something, Billy. What I do might not seem very important, but at least I make people happy!'

'I bet that woman with the ginger hair wasn't too happy.'

'Piss off!' She threw a pillow at him. Why didn't he ever take her seriously? Even now he was grinning at her as if everything she said and did was one big joke.

I bet he'd take Roo seriously, she thought. I bet if it was Roo having trouble at work, he wouldn't dare suggest she should just pack it all in and stay at home like a good little housewife.

But Roo wouldn't have those kind of problems. Roo wasn't that kind of woman. She'd soon sort out Julie. In fact, she'd probably be running the place by now.

Not for the first time, Cat wished she could be more like her cousin.

Roo sat in a traffic jam on the M25, heading south, glad that every crawling minute took her closer to home.

She couldn't wait to get back, and not just to see Ollie and David. Normanford was a lonely place and it was about to get even worse once the news about the job cuts got out.

She wasn't used to being the one to implement changes; usually she produced a report and left the company to handle the rest. But the bank had given her the authority to make any changes she felt necessary, rather than wait for George Fairbanks to approve them. Which of course he never would.

It had been a difficult decision to introduce shorter working hours, but she had no choice. She'd gone through the cashflow forecast carefully, making savings where she could. She'd put a stop on company credit cards, cut back on sales bonuses and negotiated new terms with creditors. She'd even managed to sell off the useless timber stock, although George hadn't been happy about it. But in the end she knew she would still have to cut the wages bill somehow. And since production was already down due to falling orders, it made sense to rationalise working hours. At least that way everyone could keep their jobs. And she could increase their hours once the orders picked up.

If they picked up.

Her spirits lifted as she turned off the motorway and entered the tangled snarl-up of roundabouts and one-way systems into London. She could forget her problems and enjoy being with her family for the weekend.

The house was silent as she let herself in. She thought everyone was out until she heard laughter coming from the basement kitchen.

Shauna, Ollie and David were gathered around a shaky tower of Jenga bricks. David was trying to extricate a tricky one from the bottom, to the accompaniment of whoops of derision. There was a half-empty bottle of Merlot on the table. They looked so happy that for a moment it felt as if they were the family and she was the outsider.

She dredged up a smile. 'Sounds like someone's having fun!'

'Mummy!' Ollie jumped from his chair and ran to hug her, wrapping his arms around her waist. Behind him, David let the brick fall and the tower collapsed with a clatter. 'Guess what? We've been to McDonald's!'

'Have you indeed?' So much for the romantic supper she'd been planning since she left Normanford. 'That's nice.' She looked up at David. 'You should have waited for me. I would have come with you.'

He laughed. 'You? In McDonald's?'

'What's so funny about that?'

'Nothing.' But Roo saw the amused look that passed between him and Shauna.

'I had a Big Mac. And fries. And a shake,' Ollie danced around, twisting her around with him.

'I can tell.' He was so wired up on E-numbers he could have powered the National Grid.

'Have you brought me anything?' he demanded.

'Ollie!' Shauna pretended to look shocked.

Roo smiled. 'As a matter of fact, I have. It's in the hall.'

Ollie ran off, dragging Shauna with him. David said, 'Do I get a guilt present too?'

Roo's happiness evaporated. He was trying to start a fight and he hadn't even kissed her yet. 'I didn't think you needed one.' She sat down and poured herself a glass of wine.

'How was Normanford?'

'Awful. I don't want to talk about it.' What she wanted was for him to put his arms around her. But he didn't. 'How about you?'

'Same as usual.'

'No luck on the job front?'

His face darkened. 'No. But thanks for reminding me.'

Ollie rushed in, brandishing his new Millennium Falcon. He threw his arms around Roo's neck and kissed her. 'Thanks, Mum!'

'I'm glad you like it, darling.'

'Must have cost a fortune,' David muttered. 'Mummy must be feeling very guilty indeed.'

Roo scowled at him and hugged Ollie tighter. At least she knew how to put a smile on her son's face, if not her husband's.

'I'm going now,' Shauna announced from the doorway. 'You do remember I've got the weekend off?'

'Going somewhere special?' Roo asked.

'Just staying with a friend.'

Roo looked at her. 'Have you had your hair cut? It looks great.'

'Thanks.' Shauna put her hand up to stroke her shorn locks. She'd also bought some new clothes, Roo noticed. It made a change to see her in something other than jeans.

'So would this friend be male by any chance?' she said archly.

'No!' Shauna's face filled with colour. 'She's just a girl from college, that's all. Excuse me, I want to catch the eight o'clock train.'

'What did you have to say that for?' David said, as she scuttled off. 'You could see the poor kid was mortified.'

'I was only being friendly.'

'Roo, you haven't been friendly to her since she started here. Anyway, it's none of your business whether she's got a boyfriend or not.' He refilled his wine glass.

'It is if she decides to get engaged or move in with him. Then she might decide she wants to leave.' Roo shuddered. The last thing she needed at the moment was to have to start looking for a new nanny.

David glared at her. 'I didn't realise nannies had to take a vow of celibacy these days.'

She was hoping for a weekend relaxing but Shauna had set up a play date for Ollie on Saturday afternoon, which scuppered her plans for a family day out.

'What the hell is a play date, anyway?' David grumbled. 'We never had them in my day. We just knocked on each other's doors if we wanted to play.'

'This is London, not Stow on the Wold. We can't just stick a five-year-old out on the common with a football, can we?' In fact she was as fed up as he was that Shauna had done this to her. And she was even more fed up when she found out the play date was with Miriam Granger's son.

Miriam was an earth-mother fascist, the kind who condemned any woman who didn't bake her own organic bread or give birth in a yurt. She tumbled out of her rainbow-painted camper van with a small army of raggedy children and a baby clamped to her formidable bosom.

'Bloody hell,' David muttered under his breath. 'It's a fucking peace convoy.'

'Helloo!' she greeted them gaily, swishing her shawl around her shoulders. 'Sorry I've had to bring all the sprogs. Jeffrey's gone to an ashram. He needed some inner peace.'

I'm not surprised, Roo thought, as a toddler wandered past in a grubby T-shirt and sagging nappy, his hands covered in chocolate, heading for her Designers Guild curtains.

Miriam released her children into their home and settled herself in the kitchen with a mug of camomile tea. She'd brought it herself, 'because hardly anyone has the organic stuff'. She'd also dragged along a sack full of the kids' toys, which were all boringly educational.

'I think Ollie wanted to show off his new Millennium Falcon,' Roo said, eyeing a jigsaw of third world countries. 'You know – Star Wars?'

'I really don't encourage the children to play with anything that glorifies conflict,' Miriam smiled through clenched teeth. 'We should be encouraging understanding and peace between other races, embracing and celebrating our differences, not trying to wipe each other out.' She rustled through her bag. 'Why don't we find something really fun to play with? How about these lovely ethnic dolls?'

Ollie looked as if he would rather stick needles in his eyes than be caught playing with dolls. But after a long-suffering look at Roo, he set himself down with the stoicism of a British Army officer being sent to work on the Burma Railway.

102

'There! Isn't that fun? I believe in creative, non-sexist, non-threatening toys that stimulate a child while promoting mutual tolerance.'

Roo glanced at Ollie and Miriam's son Ravi, who were yanking the heads off the multi-racial dolls and throwing them at each other.

The baby began to grizzle, and Miriam lopped out a breast to feed her. David averted his gaze to the window.

'I do adore breastfeeding, don't you?' she sighed, as the baby suckled noisily. 'Do you know, I breastfed Gustav until he was five. Didn't I darling?' She beamed at the boy sitting next to her. He was about seven years old, with startlingly pale skin and penetrating, hostile eyes as white as a wolf's.

'Fuck off,' he said.

'You'll have to excuse him,' Miriam said gaily. 'He has some anger issues at the moment. We won't let him join Cubs. He can't understand it's a paramilitary organisation.'

Roo looked at the boy, who was sticking a fork into his hand. She couldn't help feeling the Cubs had had a lucky escape.

'Roo gave up breastfeeding after two weeks,' David suddenly said. 'She had to go back to work.'

'Two weeks?' Miriam looked as horrified as if Roo had gone straight from giving her baby breast milk to gin and tonics.

'He preferred the bottle.' And so did she, after a fortnight of frustration, endless crying and cracked nipples.

Miriam shook her head in pity. 'Poor you. Did you never want any more children? I think being an only child is such a lonely life.'

'I agree,' David said. Roo looked at him in surprise.

'But you're an only child yourself.'

'Exactly. So I know what I'm talking about, don't I?'

They finally went home when Miriam noticed the children had found the Millennium Falcon behind an armchair and were using it to drop bombs on the multi-racial dolls.

'Can I have a baby brother?' Ollie asked, when they'd gone.

'Sorry, old son. No can do,' David replied. 'Mummy's far too busy.'

Roo watched him washing mugs in the sink. 'I didn't realise it bothered you.'

'You've never asked.'

True. She'd just assumed he felt the same as her, that one was enough. 'I'm asking you now. Would you like another baby?'

'Would you?'

Roo considered it. It was a long time since she'd been through the nappies and midnight feeds stage and she wasn't sure she had the energy to repeat it. And it would mean kissing goodbye to any ambitions she might have. With one child she could just about hang on to the career ladder at Warner and Hicks. With two she would have the 'mother' label firmly around her neck.

Although that might not be such a bad thing if it meant saving her marriage.

The thought shocked her. Did her marriage really need saving?

Of course not, she told herself firmly. Her marriage was fine. And even if it wasn't, it was the worst reason in the world to have a baby.

'If you have to think about it that long, you obviously don't,' David said coldly. 'Anyway, I doubt if it will happen. From what I remember, you usually have to be in the same part of the country for at least five minutes for conception to take place.'

They made love that night, but Roo's heart wasn't in it. She ended up faking an orgasm and then couldn't sleep.

At least Sunday was better. They took Ollie to the park and Roo managed to forget about work and Normanford while they ate ice-creams and took turns pushing him on the swings. They almost felt like a family. But that afternoon, as they cuddled up on the sofa watching *The Phantom Menace*, she stared at the clock, watching the minutes tick by and dreading the time she had to leave.

'Don't let us keep you, if you're desperate to get back to work,' David said, misinterpreting her anxious look.

At the door, Roo hugged Ollie tightly, breathing in the wash-ing-powder smell of his *Stars Wars* top. As they parted, he pressed a plastic figure into her hand.

'Anakin Skywalker,' he said. 'Before he went over to the Dark Side.'

A lump rose in her throat. 'Thank you. I'll take good care of it.'

'No,' said Ollie. 'He'll take care of you. May The Force be with you, Mummy.'

It'll take more than The Force to get me through this week, she thought as she drove away, tears blurring her eyes.

Matt's car was still outside her house when she got back. Roo wearily parked at the far end of the street and was taking her luggage out of the boot when she saw him coming up from the river with Harvey.

Harvey greeted her enthusiastically. At least he didn't bear a grudge. But Matt scowled. 'Careful, Harvey. Don't go too close or she'll have you locked up again.'

Roo ignored him. 'Hello, Harvey. I see you've survived your ordeal.'

'No thanks to you. He's very traumatised. I think he may need therapy.'

Roo thought about apologising, then changed her mind. 'I see that heap of junk is still parked outside my house.'

'My car is still parked on the street, if that's what you mean.'

'Can't you just move it outside your house so I don't have to look at it?'

'If it's bothering you that much, why don't you get the RSPCA to take it away?'

'I wish I could get them to take *you* away,' Roo muttered, slamming her front door.

Chapter 9

As she drove through the factory gates on Monday morning a Fairbanks van cut across her, blocking the entrance to the car park. Roo almost drove into the side of it.

She got out of her car and walked across to the driver. 'Excuse me, would you mind moving? You're in my way.'

He cranked up his radio volume, drowning her out. Roo tried again. 'Hello?' He drummed his hands on the steering wheel in time to the music.

Roo reached in the open window and switched off the radio. 'Will you please move this van?'

'Oi! I was listening to that!'

'No, you weren't. You were being pathetic and childish.'

He shot her a look of such venom she felt her legs buckle. 'You want to be more careful what you say to people.' He nodded towards her car. 'See you got your flat tyres fixed?'

'What do you know about that?'

'I couldn't say. But put it this way, you haven't got many friends round here.'

'Is there a problem?' She turned around. Billy had abandoned his BMW behind her car and was coming towards them.

'Nothing I can't handle.' Roo glared at the driver, who thrust the van into gear and sped off, just as Billy caught up with them.

'What was that all about?'

'Just a misunderstanding.' She headed back to her car, Billy following.

'Actually, I meant to come and see you today,' he said. 'I

wondered if you'd like to come and meet one of our retailers sometime.'

'That would be very useful.'

'And there's a furniture show on in Harrogate next month. Maybe you'd like to come along to that, too?'

'I'd love to, if I'm free.' She suddenly felt a whole lot better. 'Thanks,' she said.

'What for?'

'Realising I've got a job to do and being so nice about it.'

Billy shrugged. 'None of this is your fault. You're doing your best.'

'Thanks anyway.' She grimaced. 'I'm about to have a meeting with the bank manager and Frederick Fairbanks. I hope they're as understanding as you are.'

At first Mike Garrett was full of praise about the excellent start Roo had made to keep the company afloat. Then she said, 'I want to reinvest any savings back into the factory. Some of the machinery badly needs updating if we're going to compete long-term.'

Mike and Frederick exchanged wary looks. 'I wouldn't get too carried away,' Mike said. 'You haven't saved that much money. There's still a long way to go before we can talk about reinvesting.'

'I know, but we've shown we're capable of managing our finances. We're no longer an unsound risk. And we need that new machinery.'

'What's the point in buying new machinery if we don't have any orders coming in?' Frederick asked. Roo stared at him. Whose side was he on?

'We'll get the orders,' she said.

'Show me the orders and you'll get the money,' Mike said.

'That's just it. We can't meet the extra capacity unless we have the equipment to deal with them. It's a chicken and egg situation.'

There was silence in the office while the two men considered this. Roo waited for Frederick to back her up, but he didn't. He steepled his fingers together and looked troubled.

'I'm sorry,' Mike said finally. 'If we're going to forward you any more capital we're going to have to see more commitment from you to saving money.'

'But we've already cut our overheads to the bone!'

'You could always lose a few more jobs.'

Another silence. Roo thought about the van driver who'd blocked her way that morning. He'd been aggressive, but only because he'd been desperate. 'I don't know if I can.'

'That's the situation. Take it or leave it.' Mike gathered up his papers. 'Let me know when you've decided on your next move.'

'You could have backed me up,' Roo said to Frederick, when Mike had gone.

'It doesn't do to upset the bank manager, Ms Hennessy. Besides, he's right. Why should the bank advance us more money if we can't prove we can pay it back?'

'But we will be able to pay it back. When the orders come in—'

'It would be far better to gain their confidence by making some more savings first.' He tilted his head on one side. 'What's wrong, Ms Hennessy? I was told you were one of Warner and Hicks' best hatchet women. Don't tell me you're losing your taste for wielding the axe?'

She looked at him with distaste. 'I don't find any pleasure in putting people out of work.'

'Of course you don't. But if it's for the good of the company, you'll just have to bite the bullet, won't you?'

She went back to her office, fuming. She swept straight past Becky, who called after her, 'Roo? I've got—'

'Not now, Becky!' She slammed her door. Bloody man! If Frederick Fairbanks was so keen to put everyone out of work, let *him* do it. She was sick of everyone hating her just because she was trying to sort out his family's mistakes.

Becky crept in behind her. 'There's someone to see you.'

'Tell them to come back.'

'But Roo—'

'Becky, please. I don't want to see anyone, okay?'

'Well, that's very nice I must say.'

Roo heard the voice from the outer office and froze. 'Oh my God. Is that—?'

Becky nodded. 'She was waiting in Grandad's taxi when I got here.'

Roo hurried to the outer office. Sitting at Becky's desk, her handbag perched on her knees, was Nanna Moon. She was dressed for an outing, her old brown coat fastened up to the neck, woollen hat flattened on her head, even though it was July.

'Nanna! What are you doing here?'

'I haven't come to apply for a job, have I?' She was a frail old lady now, but she still had that 'don't mess with me' look in her shrewd eyes.

'Why don't you come through to my office?'

'No thanks, I'm all right here. Anyway, this isn't a social call. I want a word with you, young lady.'

Roo glanced around the office. Everyone was doing their best to look as if they weren't listening. 'Are you sure you wouldn't rather go into my office?'

'I told you, I'm all right where I am. Now then,' she fixed Roo with her beady gaze. 'Why haven't you been round to see me?'

Roo cringed. Suddenly she felt twelve years old again. 'Um . . . well, I've been really busy—'

'Too busy to see your own family?' Nanna shook her head. 'It's not right, Ruby, you putting work before your own flesh and blood. I know what this is all about. It's all to do with your mother, isn't it?' Roo darted an embarrassed glance at the women in the typing pool, who'd given up all pretence of working and were listening avidly.

'But—'

'Don't interrupt me when I'm talking, Ruby.'

'No, Nanna. Sorry,' Roo said humbly.

'It's time to mend this rift with your family. They're important. I should know, at my age.' She fumbled in her handbag for a handkerchief. 'I'm seventy-eight years old,' she sniffed. 'I don't have much time left on this earth. I should be spending my last few years surrounded by my loving family, not sorting out their fights.'

'Nanna, please—'

'I want you to come round for your tea on Wednesday,' she said, her tears mysteriously disappearing.

'I'll have to check my diary—'

'Wednesday,' Nanna said firmly. 'I'll get a nice piece of beef in. I know you like it.'

'Actually, I don't eat red meat any more.'

'Then we'll have lamb.'

'Nanna—'

'Anyway, I'll have to go. Our Tom's waiting to take me to the Over 60s club.' She eased herself out of her chair, wincing with effort. 'Although why I go to listen to all those old fools grumbling about their aches and pains I don't know. God's waiting room, I call it.' She pointed at Roo. 'Wednesday,' she said. 'We'll be expecting you.'

As Becky helped her great-grandmother to the lift, Roo thought how Nanna would have made a great captain of industry. She had all the right qualities: determination, decisiveness, and a ruthless disregard for anyone else's point of view.

She went back into her office, wondering how she'd been bullied into going. Emotional blackmail, she decided. Not to mention the embarrassment factor. She was certain Nanna had deliberately chosen to stay where she had an audience, so she could shame Roo into capitulation.

But whatever Nanna said, she had no intention of becoming part of the Moon family again. She didn't belong there any more, if she ever had.

Sadie was also livid when she found out what her mother had done. 'Why did you have to go and see her? Now she'll think I put you up to it.'

'So what? As long as it gets you two talking again, that's all that matters.'

'Mum, she hates me. What's the point in forcing us together?'

But Irene wouldn't listen. 'Nonsense, you're her mother. This has gone on long enough. I'm going to sort it out before they carry me out in my box. I want us to be a family again.'

Family! That was a joke. 'She probably won't turn up anyway.'

'She will if she knows what's good for her. And so will you,' Irene warned. 'If you even think about doing one of your disappearing acts you can forget about living under my roof.'

Sadie pulled a face. 'Don't blame me if it gets awkward.'

'Why should it be awkward? Anyway, I've invited your brother, Cat, Billy and the kids round as well. So we'll have a nice houseful.'

'Oh, God!' Sometimes she wondered if her mother really didn't see the tension under her nose, or if she just chose to ignore it.

She resented being landed with the job of cooking for them all. Cat and Billy weren't so bad; she liked them, and she adored the kids. But Tom would just find fault with everything she did, as usual. And as for Ruby – why should she go to all that trouble for someone who didn't even want to be in the same room as her?

She'd probably be just like Tom, looking down her nose at her. She always was a little snob, even when she was growing up. And she'd be even worse now, after all those years living in London.

Sadie sighed. She'd given up trying to please her daughter a long time ago.

But that didn't stop her buying herself a new outfit for the occasion. She bypassed her usual shops and headed for Marks and Spencer, where she chose a black calf-length skirt and a soft, grey, high-necked sweater, which she teamed with some tiny pearl earrings and her flattest shoes.

Tom laughed when he saw her. 'Bloody hell, I didn't know it was fancy dress! Bit late to start dressing as a nun, isn't it?'

'Leave her alone,' Irene said. 'She wants to look nice for her daughter.'

'I didn't get it for her,' Sadie said defensively. 'I just fancied a change.'

'Just as well,' Tom said. 'It'll take more than a daft outfit to impress our Ruby.'

★

She was in the middle of cooking when Cat, Billy and the children arrived. None of them looked happy to be there, but they all knew better than to ignore a summons from Nanna.

Cat wandered into the kitchen as she was fussing over the potatoes. 'How's it going?' She'd swapped her usual jeans and T-shirt for smart black trousers and a low-cut red top that clung to her generous curves. Sadie wondered if it was for Ruby's benefit.

'Fine. You look nice.'

'So do you.' They gazed at each other and both burst out laughing. 'Look at us, done up like a pair of dog's dinners. Anyone would think she was visiting royalty.'

'Your nanna thinks she is. You should have heard her fussing.' But secretly Sadie was just as anxious to get everything right. She didn't expect her daughter's approval, but she didn't want Ruby to think she was a hopeless case, either.

'I thought you might need this.' Cat handed her a gin and tonic. 'Don't worry, I managed to smuggle it past Dad and Nanna.'

Sadie hesitated, then took it. She'd promised herself she'd keep her wits about her, but she was desperate for some Dutch courage.

'Anything I can help with?' Cat asked.

'You could finish those carrots.' Sadie poked at the potatoes in the roasting tin. They sizzled and spat back at her. 'These are almost done. They'll be ruined if she doesn't come soon.'

'You do realise she probably won't come?' Cat dropped a carrot into the pan.

Sadie was shocked. 'She wouldn't let Nanna down.'

'I'm not so sure. She's an arrogant cow these days.'

Sadie put the tin back in the oven and adjusted the heat. 'I don't care whether she comes or not,' she said, reaching for her drink. 'I'm not bothered about seeing her. It's Nanna I'm worried about. She'll be so disappointed.'

The doorbell rang. Sadie jumped.

Cat smiled nervously. 'What do you know? Looks like the prodigal daughter decided to show up after all!'

She'd changed so much, Sadie hardly recognised her. Tall and elegant in a black trouser suit, her dark hair glossy, she looked as if she'd just stepped off the pages of *Vogue*.

She had a bunch of flowers in her hand. Big showy gerberas in bright scarlet, Sadie's favourite colour. Her heart gave a little skip.

'Sorry I'm late. I had to go home and change. I brought you these.' She handed the flowers over to Nanna.

'They're lovely, aren't they Mum? I'll put them in water, shall I?' Sadie's smile was fixed as she took them, glancing sideways at her daughter. Close to, she was even more dauntingly grown-up. Even her perfume was sophisticated.

In the kitchen, Sadie found a vase under the sink and filled it with water. She told herself it didn't matter that Ruby hadn't even looked at her, apart from a quick nod of greeting when she'd first walked in. It was no more or less than she'd expected. Ruby might look like an adult, but inside she was still a sulky teenager.

She stuffed the flowers in the vase and got on with dinner. Cat came in as she was trying to beat the lumps out of the gravy. 'Where do you keep the corkscrew?' She opened a drawer and searched inside. 'Her ladyship's brought some wine. You should hear them going on about it. Anyone would think it was vintage Cristal instead of corner shop plonk!' She rattled among the cutlery. 'Are you all right? You seem a bit quiet.'

'The gravy's gone wrong.' Sadie suddenly felt near to tears.

'We'll strain it. No one will ever know.' Cat nudged her aside and took the pan from her trembling hands. 'It's okay,' she said. 'She's only your daughter, not the flaming Queen!'

'She doesn't feel like my daughter.'

They sat crammed together around Nanna's best mahogany table, elbows touching. Sadie would have preferred to be at the far end with Cat and the kids, but her mother had insisted she sit beside her daughter. As if it wasn't awkward enough.

Ruby kept up a forced smile and pretended everything was wonderful. But Sadie noticed the way she kept glancing around Nanna's little front parlour, as if she couldn't quite believe she was there. Sadie couldn't believe it either. It didn't seem that long ago since Ruby was in her high chair and she was shovelling spoonfuls of mashed-up rusk into her.

The silence stretched between them. She couldn't think of a thing to say to her daughter. There were so many questions she wanted to ask, but somehow she couldn't bring herself to get a word out. It didn't help that her mother kept watching her across the table, nodding encouragingly in Ruby's direction.

She topped up her glass and made a brave stab at conversation.

'So . . . um . . . how's the family?'

'Fine.' Her voice was so posh, no trace of Normanford in it at all.

'How old is your little boy now? Five?'

'He'll be six in September.'

She nodded. She already knew that. It was the first date she put in her new diary every year. 'I'd love to see him. Will he be coming up soon?'

'No plans for him to at the moment,' said Ruby, twiddling her fork.

She was playing with her food, Sadie noticed. Was it that bad? Everyone else seemed to be enjoying it, but Ruby was probably used to fancy restaurants.

It was so humiliating, she just wanted to run away. She gulped her wine without thinking, to blot out the awfulness of it all.

'That was very nice.' Nanna pushed her plate away. 'Don't you think your mum's cooking's got better since you've been away, Ruby?'

'Definitely.' Was that why she'd left nearly all of it?

'The meat was a bit dry,' Tom commented, spearing it with his fork.

'Trust you to find something bad to say,' Cat muttered.

Sadie stood up, pushing her chair back. 'I'll fetch the pudding, shall I?'

She went into the kitchen and topped up her glass with more wine. Her head was beginning to feel fuzzy, but at least it took the edge off her embarrassment.

'Do you need any help?' She swung round, glass in hand. Ruby stood in the doorway. 'Nanna sent me.' She eyed the glass. 'I think it was her less than subtle way of getting us alone together.'

'I expect you're right.' Sadie also knew if she sent Ruby away

114

Nanna would find some excuse to send her straight back again. 'You'd better fetch the bowls and spoons. They're in that cupboard behind you.'

She took the trifle out of the fridge and set it down on the worktop, struggling for something to say. 'It must feel strange, being back in Normanford again,' she managed finally.

'You could say that.'

'Fancy you working at Fairbanks! Bet you never expected to end up there.'

'Life's full of surprises.' Ruby put the bowls on the worktop. 'Look, we don't have to do this.'

'Do what?'

'Try to be nice to each other. Nanna's not watching. Let's face it, neither of us wants to be here, do we?'

'Don't we?' Sadie said warily.

'I'm here because Nanna wanted me to come. That's the only reason. She's got some stupid idea about us being one big happy family. But we both know that's never going to happen, so let's just get through it as best we can, shall we?'

'Fine by me,' Sadie shrugged. 'Like you said, I don't want to be here any more than you do.'

Roo picked up the bowls and carried them into the sitting room. Sadie followed with the trifle. Her ears sang from the pressure of keeping her temper under control.

What a high-handed bitch, making out she was doing them all a favour by being there! Sadie didn't want her there. She didn't want to play Happy Families any more than Ruby did.

She could taste the bitter anger in her throat. She had enough of her mother and brother watching her every move, and didn't need her own daughter despising her too.

She set down the trifle down in the middle of the table. 'Excuse me,' she said.

Up in her room, she pulled off the wretched skirt and jumper and flung them into the corner in disgust. Tom was right, it would take more than looking like a librarian to win her daughter's approval.

Not that she needed it. She'd managed this long without it, and she wasn't about to break her heart over it now. She lived her life her way, and if Ruby didn't like it, tough.

She put on her favourite dress: sleeveless, low-cut and a defiant shade of flaming red. And just in case anyone didn't get the message, she added some lipstick to match.

Sadie Moon. Scarlet woman. It was what everyone thought anyway, so why disappoint them?

'Bloody hell!' Tom said, when she sashayed in, this time in her highest heels. 'Where do you think you're going, dressed like that?'

'Out. Don't wait up, will you?'

She left them staring open-mouthed. She knew they'd be bitching about her as soon as the door was closed, but she didn't care. It was nothing new.

'You see what she's like?' Uncle Tom said. 'Nothing changes, does it?'

'I don't blame her, the way you were all treating her. Especially you,' Cat turned on Roo.

'Me? What have I done?'

'Now don't go blaming our Ruby,' her father said.

'Why not? Sadie went to all this trouble for you, and you can't even be nice to her. You just sat there like you had a poker up your backside!'

The children giggled. Roo felt her face burn. 'I didn't ask to come here.'

'That's obvious. You reckon you're too good for us, don't you?'

'I think it's time we left.' Billy stood up. 'Come on Cat, before you say something you regret.'

'I haven't even started.'

Roo headed home shortly afterwards, determined never to go back to Hope Street again. This evening had lived up to her worst expectations. She had been stupid to think anything might have changed. Nothing changed in Normanford. Not the gloomy weather, the depressing shops – or the people. Especially not her mother.

At first she thought she might have got it wrong. Sadie seemed more mature and subdued. But then she started hitting the bottle and the old Sadie returned. It was obvious she was there under sufferance. She wouldn't have said a word to Roo if Nanna hadn't kept prodding her. She was just waiting for the moment she could escape and enjoy herself.

There was a message from Ollie on the answer machine when she got home, reminding her about his cricket match on Saturday and asking when she'd be home.

The day after tomorrow, thank God. She couldn't wait!

'You didn't have to speak to her like that,' Billy said, as he and Cat drove home.

'She deserved it.'

'It was difficult enough for her without you sticking your nose in.'

'Difficult for her? What about poor Sadie?'

'That's between them. It's none of your business.'

'Sadie's my aunt.'

'And she's Roo's mother.'

'She doesn't deserve her.' Cat stared bleakly ahead. Ruby didn't know how lucky she was. She should have tried growing up without a mother at all.

'All the same, just let them get on with it, okay?' Billy warned.

Cat shot him a dark look. 'Trust you to stick up for her,' she muttered.

The Ponderosa was quiet, apart from a group of well-dressed men at the far end of the bar.

'You look like a woman who needs a G&T,' Jan the landlady greeted her as she polished glasses.

'Better make it a large one.' Sadie hitched herself on to the bar stool.

'How did the big family reunion go?'

'Don't ask.' Sadie looked around. 'Quiet tonight, isn't it?' she said, changing the subject.

'It always is when there isn't any entertainment.' Jan reached for a glass from the shelf above the bar. 'Lucky that lot over there are spending, or I'd be tempted to shut up shop.'

Sadie glanced towards the group of men. A couple of them were watching her with interest. She flicked her gaze away. 'I haven't seen them before.'

'I think they're just passing through.' Jan put the drink down on the bar in front of her.

'I'll get that.' One of the men appeared at Sadie's shoulder before she had a chance to reach for her purse. She looked him up and down. In his forties, a bit too tanned for her liking, but good-looking and well-dressed. Then she spotted the ring.

'I can buy my own drinks, thanks.' She passed a five-pound note across the bar.

'Independent lady. I like that.'

'Married man. I don't.'

He slunk away from her withering gaze. 'That wasn't very friendly,' Jan remarked. 'He only wanted to buy you a drink.'

'I know exactly what he wanted.' Sadie glanced sideways at him. 'I bet he's a sales rep. In Leeds on a conference, but looking for some entertainment.' She shook her head. 'I don't go for married men. Not any more.'

'The trouble is, once you get to our age they're nearly all married,' Jan sighed.

'Or divorced and bitter,' Sadie agreed.

'Or no one else will have them!' Jan took some of the empties lined up on the bar and dropped them in a sink of soapy water. 'So how are we supposed to meet a really nice man?'

'Speak for yourself. I stopped looking a long time ago.' Sadie downed her drink and pushed her glass across the bar. 'I've had enough of blokes to last me a lifetime.'

'You don't mean that. Are you telling me that if someone gorgeous and available walked in here now you wouldn't be tempted?'

She shook her head. 'No matter how gorgeous and available they are, they always let you down in the end.'

'Get you, the voice of experience! Well, I haven't given up

yet.' Jan pulled a copy of the *Normanford News* out of her bag. 'What do you think of that?'

'Oh Jan, don't tell me you've been putting lonely hearts ads in the paper again? Don't you remember what happened last time? What was his name – Nigel?'

Jan looked defensive. 'He wasn't that bad.'

'He was four foot two, and his mother still sewed name tags in his jumpers!'

'Anyway, I'm not talking about the lonely hearts. I meant that one.' She pointed at the foot of the page. 'Line dancing. I'm thinking of introducing it here once a week. What do you reckon?'

'Good idea. But what's it got to do with your love life?'

'Nothing – except the teacher sounds quite nice. I've arranged to go along to his class at the community centre on Sunday night to see what it's all about. I wondered if you'd come with me for moral support.'

Sadie couldn't imagine her tough pub landlady friend needing any support. But even though Jan was more than capable of throwing drunken punters out of the bar, Sadie knew that since her divorce she'd lost confidence when it came to men.

'Go on then,' she sighed. 'I don't do much on Sundays anyway, apart from watch *Corrie* and listen to Mum moan about her arthritis. But I'm warning you, if anyone makes me wear a daft hat and a pair of cowboy boots I'm leaving, okay?'

Chapter 10

Two weeks later on a Sunday afternoon, Billy took Liam to kick a football around the park. Becky was shopping in Leeds with Dominic and Megan was absorbed with her Barbies while Cat tackled a pile of ironing in front of the *EastEnders* omnibus.

It should have been a peaceful afternoon, but then . . .

'Coo-ee! It's only me.' Cat and Megan exchanged a look of horror as Glenys walked in. Why had Billy given her a key? Cat was sure she only dropped in unexpectedly to expose her as the domestic slut she'd always suspected her to be.

'My dear, I'm so exhausted.' She plonked herself down on the sofa, narrowly missing the pile of clothes Cat had set out for ironing. 'What a day I've had. Judging the WI bake-off this morning, then lunch with the bishop. Where's William?'

'He's taken Liam to the park.'

'On his day off? Doesn't he ever get a rest? You work my boy far too hard, Catherine.'

Cat rolled her eyes and picked up another of her husband's shirts to iron. Never mind that she came home from work every night, cooked supper, looked after the kids and did most of the housework in her spare time. If Billy so much as lifted a tin-opener he was dubbed a saint by his mother.

'I'll have a cup of tea, if you're making one,' Glenys went on, pushing the ironing pile further away from her. 'Earl Grey if you have it. Very weak. No sugar.'

It wouldn't have hurt her to put the kettle on, Cat thought as she stomped into the kitchen. Anyone else might have offered. But Glenys wasn't like any other mother-in-law.

Which was a shame, because Cat would have liked someone she could get close to, especially after losing her own mother. But Glenys always treated their house like a refugee hostel she was visiting as one of her civic duties.

'Given up the diet, I see?' Glenys commented, when Cat came back in with tea and chocolate digestives. 'Very sensible. When you reach a certain age the weight becomes so hard to shift, doesn't it? Luckily it's not something I've ever had to worry about. Do you know, I'm exactly the same weight I was on my wedding day?'

So am I, Cat thought. Only I was four months pregnant then. She put the biscuit back on the plate, her appetite forgotten.

She went back to her ironing and tried to watch *EastEnders,* but Glenys kept interrupting. Cat gritted her teeth and tried to be polite. Deep down she felt sorry for her. Glenys was obviously lonely, which was why she kept herself busy. But perhaps if she wasn't so poisonous all the time she might have more friends.

'Look, Grandma. This doll's getting married.' Megan held up Liam's Action Man, looking rugged with a daisy in the button-hole of his camouflage gear.

'How lovely!' Glenys joined in enthusiastically. 'So who's the bride? The one in the blue dress?'

'No, silly, that's the bridesmaid. This is the bride.' She held up another Action Man, this time dressed in one of Barbie's tight PVC miniskirts with a matching bra stretched over his pectorals. 'It's a gay wedding,' she explained.

Cat stifled a laugh as she heard Billy's key in the door.

'We're home – oh, hello, Mum.' His smile dropped as he walked into the room and saw Glenys there.

'Sit down, darling. You must be exhausted.' Glenys dumped Cat's ironing on another armchair to make space for her baby boy. 'Let me get you a cup of tea.'

'It's fine, I can get my own—' But Glenys wouldn't hear of it. As she rushed into the kitchen, Billy whispered to Cat, 'How long has she been here?'

'Too long,' Cat hissed back.

'So how's work?' Glenys asked, when she'd put a cup of tea into her son's hands and plumped up his cushions for him.

'Fine, thanks.'

'And how's Ruby?'

'She's okay. I think.' Billy shot Cat a wary look. They had an unspoken agreement not to mention her name. It was the only way they could stop themselves arguing. 'I don't see that much of her, to be honest.'

'It must be so difficult for her, sorting that place out. I'm glad she's taken a tough line. I was saying to Frederick at the golf club yesterday, those redundancies are just what Fairbanks needs—'

Cat looked up sharply. 'What redundancies?'

'Oh dear, was it supposed to be a secret?' Glenys put her fingers to her mouth. 'Silly me.'

Cat turned to Billy. 'What redundancies?'

'They've had to lay off some of the van drivers. It was cheaper to subcontract for the amount of work they were doing.'

'But I thought there weren't going to be any redundancies.'

'There was a change of plan. Look, can we discuss this later?' Billy glanced at his mother.

Glenys stayed for dinner and criticised everything as usual. Afterwards Billy insisted on taking her home. Cat knew he was trying to avoid her.

He came home as she was getting the children out of the bath. He met her on the landing and handed her a glass of wine. 'I'll put them to bed, shall I?'

He tucked them in and read them a story while Cat picked up the trail of damp towels and dirty clothes and put them in the laundry basket. She sensed he was hoping she'd forgotten about Fairbanks. But she tackled him the moment they were downstairs.

'Why didn't you tell me about those redundancies?' she asked.

'I didn't think you'd care. You don't usually take such a keen interest in industrial relations.'

'This is different. People I know are losing their jobs. How could you let that happen?'

'It's not up to me. I'm only the Sales Director, remember?'

'So it's all down to Ruby. I should have known. She doesn't care about this town.'

'She's doing her best. You don't know what that factory is like. If someone doesn't do something we'll all be out of a job. Including me.'

He looked so tired, Cat forgot to be annoyed. 'You should have told me.'

'Believe me, Fairbanks is the last thing I want to talk about.' He put his glass down and pulled her into his arms. 'That's why I'm so glad to get home and forget about it all. Once I shut that door and you and the kids are here, it's like escaping.'

He kissed her softly, but Cat pulled away. 'Those poor van drivers can't escape.'

'I know. And I'm really sorry about it. But what can I do?'

Nothing, she thought. There was only one person to blame for those redundancies, and that was her heartless cousin.

She reached up and pushed Billy's dark hair back off his face and kissed his furrowed brow. 'You should share these things with me,' she said. 'I'm your wife. I want to help.'

'Just being with you is all the help I need.' He was reaching for her when his mobile trilled. He answered it, his expression darkening.

'What? Oh my God, when did it happen? Right, I'll talk to her.'

'What's going on? Billy?' Cat asked, as he reached for his jacket.

'I have to see Roo,' he said. And then he was gone. So much for sharing his troubles, Cat thought.

Roo arrived back from her weekend in London just before ten. She was so tired she hardly noticed the man approaching as she parked her car in Sykes Street.

'Billy? What are you doing here?'

'We need to talk.' He took her elbow and steered her down the path to the river.

'Can't we talk in the house?' She was desperate for a cup of decent coffee instead of that awful service-station stuff.

'It's better if we don't.'

Roo began to feel scared. He looked so serious, she wondered what the hell was going on.

They picked their way down the path, overgrown with weeds and stinging nettles. After a few hundred yards Billy stopped and cleared a space for them to sit down on the bank.

'Billy, what is it? What's going on?'

He turned to her, his face grim in the darkness. 'Someone's died,' he said.

Her mouth felt like it was lined with sand. 'Not Nanna—'

He shook his head. 'A man called Eric Pearson. He was a van driver at Fairbanks.'

'But I don't see—' she stopped. 'How did he die?'

'Suicide. They found him in his car this morning.'

'Oh my God.' She sank her head in her hands.

'Apparently the family had big debts. They'd taken out a loan to pay for his daughter's wedding in Australia. Then he lost his job.' He picked up a beer can and threw it in the river. 'He felt he'd let his family down. They were going to lose their house, everything they'd worked for. He couldn't face it.'

'But couldn't he get another job?'

Billy looked at her with something like pity. 'At fifty-eight? He didn't stand a chance.'

Roo stared out across the river. In the distance the chemical works was spewing God knows what into the sluggish khaki water.

'So why are you telling me all this?' she asked, already half-knowing the answer.

'His family has issued a statement. They're saying Fairbanks drove him to it.'

'By Fairbanks I take it they mean me?' She paused, taking it in. 'Maybe they're right,' she said.

'Oh come on, you don't really believe that? How could it be your fault?'

'If I hadn't made those redundancies he'd still be here.'

'You had no choice.'

'Of course I had a choice! I didn't have to put those people out of work, I could have told the bank to stuff their money. But I didn't.' A tear rolled down her cheek and she dashed it away. 'I was so obsessed with making the figures add up I forgot they weren't just numbers on a balance sheet. They were real people with lives and families, and bills to pay!'

'It's your job.'

'Some fucking job that drives people to kill themselves!'

She broke down in tears. Billy put his arms around her, pulling her to him. 'Shh, don't cry. None of this is your fault. It'll be all right, I promise.'

But they both knew it wasn't going to be all right, not from now on.

Sadie limped home along the river path, her shoes in her hand. Bloody cowboy boots! She'd told Jan there was no way she was going to wear them but she'd insisted and now her feet were covered in blisters. And the bits that weren't blistered were bruised where she'd taken a wrong turning during the Grundy Gallop and ended up being trampled underfoot by a twenty-stone lorry driver called Tex.

Never again, she decided. Although at least Jan had got to meet her dream man, the good-looking teacher called Ray. They'd hit it off and Jan had invited him back to the Ponderosa – 'To see if the floor's suitable for dancing,' she said. They'd politely invited Sadie to join them but she could tell three was definitely a crowd. And anyway, she wanted to get home to check up on Nanna and soak her aching feet.

She was only a few yards away from the couple before she spotted them. They were sitting on the bank, almost hidden by bushes. The man had his arms around the woman, and her dark head was resting on his broad shoulder.

Billy and Ruby.

Sadie felt sick. It couldn't be, not after all these years. She'd thought Ruby's infatuation with Billy was over long ago. But it looked like they'd picked up where they left off.

She hurried home, her mind racing. This wasn't right. Ruby couldn't come back and ruin everything for everyone. She had to put a stop to it before it got out of control and someone got hurt.

★

Everyone was talking about Eric Pearson around the school gates the following morning. Cat couldn't get away from it.

'Poor man,' Marjorie Prentice was saying as she dropped her grandson off. 'Forty years he'd been at that place and he gets thrown on the scrapheap. And we all know who's responsible, don't we?'

Cat said nothing. She handed Liam his lunchbox, planted a kiss on top of his head and sent him through the gates.

Billy hadn't come home until the early hours last night. Cat lay in bed waiting for him. She sat up and switched on the light when he came in. 'Where have you been?'

'I told you. I went to see Roo.' He looked shattered. The lamplight showed up the deeply drawn lines on his face.

'Until this time? You must have had a lot to talk about.'

He sat on the end of the bed and pulled off his shoes. 'Please, Cat. Not now. It's been a long night and I'm tired.'

He fell into bed and switched off the light. For once he didn't reach for her. She could smell Ruby's perfume, faint but unmistakable.

'So what were you talking about?'

'I can't tell you.'

'But I want to help—'

'Look, it was work, okay? Nothing to do with you.'

He turned over, lying with his back to her in the dark. Cat lay stiff and unyielding, staring up at the ceiling. So it was starting. They were shutting her out of their little private world, just like they used to.

'So that's good news, isn't it?'

'Sorry? What?' Cat looked up, brought back to the present to find Marjorie smiling at her.

'The newspaper's really interested in backing our campaign, especially after all this business with poor Eric Pearson. The reporter's coming to talk to us the day after tomorrow.'

'Great.'

'It was a good idea of yours, to get the ball rolling. We've already collected loads of signatures on our Save Fairbanks petition.'

'The list we put in the salon is filling up too. I'll let you have it soon.'

'Why don't you bring it on Wednesday? Then you can talk to the reporter.'

'Me? What would I say to a reporter?'

'You should be there. This campaign was your idea, after all.'

'Was it?' She still wasn't sure how that came about. 'It's nothing to do with me.'

'You said yourself, the Fairbanks closure affects everyone. If all those people are out of work it's bound to have a big impact on the rest of the town.'

'True,' Cat agreed, then shook her head. 'I can't get involved. Billy wouldn't like it.'

'And do you always do what your lord and master says?' Marjorie teased.

I do when my cousin is waiting to snap him up, Cat thought. 'I have my reasons,' she said. 'But I'll bring the petition from the salon round on Wednesday, okay? As long as I don't have to talk to any reporters.'

It had been a bad morning, starting with the story in the *Norman-ford News*. Even though it didn't say she actually drove Eric Pearson to his death, it mentioned the 'tough new regime' as causing stress among the workers. And just in case people didn't put two and two together, there was a photo of her, right next to one of Eric Pearson and his family. No prizes for guessing whose side everyone was on.

There were quotes from other Fairbanks workers who'd been put on the streets. It seemed everyone had a tragic story to tell, from the single mum struggling to bring up her two children on the breadline, to the man who'd had to cancel his disabled daughter's trip to Disneyland. Every name was another barb in the heart no one thought she possessed.

The only one who had a kind word to say to her was Billy. He came in to see her just before lunch.

'I brought you this.' He put a sandwich on the desk. 'I had a feeling you'd be lying low.'

'Do you blame me?' She looked out of the window. She was already dreading the walk back to her car that night. She wouldn't be surprised if there was a brick through the windscreen this time.

'Are they giving you a hard time?'

'It's no more than I deserve, I suppose. After all, a man's dead because of me.'

Billy sighed. 'You're not still blaming yourself?'

'I don't see anyone else in the frame, do you?' She sat down at her desk. 'Have you seen the paper? All those poor people in trouble.'

'They'd be in a hell of a lot more trouble if this factory had to close down completely.'

'You're right.' She managed a smile. 'Thanks for trying to make me feel better.' She nodded towards the bag on her desk. 'What's in the sandwich?'

'Cucumber and salmon paste.'

She looked up. 'You're kidding? That was my favourite when I was a kid!'

'Why do you think I brought it? I thought you might need some comfort food.'

She unwrapped it and took a bite. Immediately she was transported back to her youth, with her and Cat scratching together their supper while her mother was doing a turn at the working men's club. 'This is bliss. How did you remember I liked it?'

'You'd be surprised what I remember about you.'

Their eyes met. Roo suddenly found it hard to swallow her next bite of sandwich. 'Let's talk about work,' she changed the subject briskly. 'Have you fixed up for me to see that retailer?'

'Next Monday. It's all arranged.'

They talked about Billy's ideas for changing the company's marketing strategy, refining the range and repositioning the brand. By the time he left, Roo was feeling more like her old self.

All the same, as she crossed the car park that night, she tensed when she heard a car approaching behind her. She'd almost broken into a run before it pulled alongside and the rear passenger window slid down.

'Bit jumpy, aren't you?' George Fairbanks said. 'Anyone would think you had a guilty conscience.'

'Why should I?' she said, pulling herself together.

'I daresay everyone's been giving you a hard time, have they? I'm not surprised. Eric Pearson was well-liked here. I gave him his first job when he was eighteen years old.' He looked at her shrewdly. 'No one would blame you if you walked away,' he said.

'And leave this place in an even worse mess? I wouldn't be doing my job.'

'You've got some nerve, Ms Hennessy, I'll give you that. Hello, who's this? Looks like someone's waiting for you.'

Roo looked up. There at the gate was Sadie, dressed in a pink trenchcoat, shiny black heels and sunglasses like a 1950s starlet. Great. Just what she needed.

'She's still an attractive woman, your mum,' George commented.

'Excuse me.' Roo hurried over to Sadie. 'What do you want?'

'Are you having an affair with Billy Kitchener?'

Roo was so stunned she laughed. 'Silly me. Do you know, for a moment there I actually thought you might have come because you were worried about me.'

'Why should I be worried about you? Oh, you mean all that stuff in the papers?' Sadie shrugged dismissively. 'It's just gossip, you get used to it. So are you and Billy having an affair?'

'No.'

'Then why were you two by the river last night? And don't bother to deny it, I saw you.'

Roo was incredulous. 'You saw us talking and immediately assumed I must be sleeping with him?'

'I know you used to be fond of him. I just need to know if there's anything going on, that's all.'

'And what if there is?'

'Then you'd better end it before someone gets hurt.'

'I presume you mean Cat?'

'And you. And Billy, and your husband and the kids. You

129

could upset a lot of people, Ruby. I want you to put a stop to it now.'

'You're a fine one to talk! I don't seem to remember you ever saying no to a married man.'

'That's why I know what I'm talking about. I'm warning you, Ruby. Don't get involved. You'll only end up losing him again.'

That wounded her. 'How do you know he's not planning to leave Cat?'

'Because they never do.'

'Is that what happened with my father? Did he go back to his wife?'

Sadie's face became a mask. 'I'm here to talk about you, not me.'

'Why? Why do you always do this? Why won't you tell me who he is?'

'Because it's got nothing to do with you.'

'How can you say that? It's got everything to do with me! He's my father, for Christ's sake!'

'And you're better off without him.'

'Surely that's up to me to decide? What have you got to hide? Is he still alive? Does he live around here? Are you worried I'm going to track him down for a big family reunion?'

Sadie sighed. 'We've been through all this. It was a long time ago. There's no point going over old ground.'

'If it was that long ago there's no harm in me knowing, is there?'

'There's no good can come of it either.'

'But I want to know!'

'I don't have to listen to this.' She started to walk off. 'Just stay away from Billy, all right?'

'Why can't you at least tell me his name?' Roo shouted after her. But Sadie was already gone, her heels clicking down the street.

Her hands clenched in frustration. Why couldn't her mother see how important this was to her? There was a big hole in her life, a gap she couldn't fill. Only her mother could help, and she wouldn't. And she wondered why Roo resented her so badly!

130

And as for Billy, he was her one friend in this hostile place and she wasn't going to give him up. If Cat was stupid enough to feel insecure about it, that was her problem.

Sadie was still angry when she went to do her usual stint at the Ponderosa. In her tiny dressing room she hung her dress up behind the door, plonked herself down and threw her make-up bag on the dressing table. She scowled at her reflection in the mirror. The last thing she felt like doing tonight was singing.

Why couldn't she and Ruby be together for more than five minutes without it turning into a fight? Nearly every conversation they'd had over the past twenty years had ended like this, with one of them storming off.

Why did she insist on dragging up the past? Sadie obviously didn't want to talk about it. And Ruby was better off not knowing. It could only bring pain, and Sadie wanted to spare her that. Couldn't Ruby see she was only trying to protect her? She had a good reason for not wanting her to know who her father was. God knows, Sadie had spent the last thirty-six years trying to forget.

'You all right?' Jan stuck her head around the door as Sadie was applying her foundation. She was dressed in her usual white shirt and diamanté lariat topped off with a purple stetson. 'You hardly said a word when you walked in. And you had a face like thunder.'

Sadie grimaced at her reflection. 'Sorry. Does it show?'

'Only to me, 'cos I know you so well. So what is it this time? Man or money trouble?'

'Neither. It's Ruby. My daughter.'

'Oh.' Jan rolled her eyes knowingly. 'Don't talk to me about them. Mine have never stopped giving me a hard time for divorcing their father.'

'Mine hasn't forgiven me for not telling her who her father is.'

'So why don't you?'

'Because she's better off not knowing.'

Jan frowned. 'Was he that bad?'

'You could say that. So how did it go with the Normanford Cowboy?' she changed the subject.

'You mean Ray?' Jan smiled warmly, remembering. 'We got on very well.'

'How well?'

'He's taking me out to dinner tomorrow night.' Jan tried and failed to hide her excitement. 'Oh, Sadie, he's perfect. I never thought I'd meet anyone else after Kevin and I split up. But Ray's special, I can tell.'

'Lucky you.' If anyone deserved to find happiness, it was Jan. She'd struggled to bring up her daughters since Kevin left her for another woman. He'd treated her so badly. She hoped for Jan's sake that Ray would be different.

'And I've got some good news for you,' Jan went on. 'It turns out Ray knows this agent. He represents most of the big singers on the club circuit. He's promised to get him to come in and see you one night.'

Sadie gazed at her reflection. Imagine that. A big-shot agent was finally coming to hear her sing. If he liked her, she could end up singing in all the big northern clubs.

It might not be The Talk of the Town, but it was a start.

Chapter 11

Cat had never seen the woman in the salon before. She was in her early fifties, well-dressed, well-spoken and obviously well-off, judging by the Merc parked outside.

Which was why Julie nabbed her as soon as she walked in. She could smell a big tip a mile off.

'I wonder what she's doing here?' Cat mused to Sadie, as they washed hair side by side at the basins.

'Just moved to the area, apparently. They've bought Bridge House.'

'Really?' Bridge House overlooked the only scenic part of the river on the edge of town. It sat behind tall, ivy-covered walls in acres of its own grounds. 'I wonder if Glenys knows?' Her mother-in-law had always coveted it and felt it should be rightfully hers. It had rankled that someone in Normanford owned a bigger house than her own. But Bridge House had only recently come on the market after belonging to the same family for years.

'She'll probably be straight round there, introducing herself!' They both laughed. Glenys was the most shameless social climber. But looking at the woman somehow Cat knew they would never be friends. Elizabeth Montague looked like she had genuine class, unlike her mother-in-law.

'It's funny, I swear I know her from somewhere,' Sadie said. 'Her name doesn't ring a bell, though. I must have just seen her in the street.'

'Probably.' Cat frowned, watching Julie. 'I don't like what she's doing to those highlights. She's putting the colour far too close to the roots.'

'So?'

'So if she's not careful it'll expand and leak right out of the foil. It could end up a right mess. Maybe I should tell her.'

'Do you think she'd take any notice of you?'

'I doubt it. But if she's going to ruin that woman's hair I should at least warn her.' She put down her shampoo bottle. 'I won't be a minute,' she told her client.

'She won't thank you for it,' Sadie called after her.

She was right. Julie scowled when Cat called her over. 'Excuse me?' She blinked at her. 'Are you trying to tell me how to do my job?'

'No, but I just thought—'

'Look, who's the senior stylist around here, you or me?'

'You are, but—'

'Exactly. So butt out and let me get on with it, okay? Maxine's not here, so you don't have to suck up to her.'

Cat retreated back to the basins. 'Told you,' Sadie said. 'It'll serve her right if she makes a mess of it.'

'True.' But she felt sorry for Elizabeth Montague. From the look of her sleek ash-blonde head, she was used to the best.

She finished her client's hair and, as it was lunchtime, went off to deliver the salon list of signatures to Marjorie Prentice and the rest of the Fairbanks Action Group, as they'd called themselves. They were meeting the reporter after lunch.

They were having their photo taken at the gates of Fairbanks factory when she arrived. The group were lined up around the high wire fence, clutching their petition and squinting in the sunshine as a photographer tried to arrange them for the shot.

'Can't you at least smile?' he pleaded, lowering his camera. 'Do you have to look so bloody grim?'

'We've nowt to smile about, have we? That's the point,' Marjorie glared back.

'Yes, but you want some sympathy, don't you? You won't get it if you look like a bunch of scowling old—Hello!' He looked round as Cat ran towards them. 'This is more like it. Hi, darling, are you one of this lot?'

'No.' Cat rushed past him to hand over the list to Marjorie. 'Sorry I'm late, I had a client to sort out before I could get away.'

'Better late than never,' Marjorie replied, taking it from her. 'By the way, our MP's got back to us. He wants us to go down to Westminster and hand in our petition. Do you want to come?'

'I'd love to, but—'

'But you're worried your hubby won't like it?'

'I wish I could give more help, but it's just . . . what's he doing?' She faced the photographer, who was lining her up in his lens.

'Trying to photograph your backside, I think.'

'No!' Cat wedged herself against the wire fence. 'I told you, I'm not part of this. I don't want my picture taken.'

She was still wondering how he'd managed to talk her into it as she posed with the others, clutching a corner of the petition. It was a pity Sadie wasn't here. She'd be in her element in front of the camera, giving it all she'd got.

She got back to find the salon in uproar. Julie was shouting at Natalie, who was on the verge of tears. And in the middle of it all, Elizabeth Montague sat quietly, her nylon robe wrapped around her shoulders, the picture of dignity despite the ugly streak of white blonde down the middle of her head.

'You silly cow! You put too much peroxide in that colour!' Julie screeched at Natalie, who bit her lip. Tears brimmed in her eyes.

'She didn't get it wrong. You did.' Cat jumped to Natalie's defence, putting her arm around her. 'I warned you.'

'It's her head that's wrong, not my highlighting!'

'It doesn't matter whose fault it is,' Elizabeth Montague said. 'The question is, what are you going to do about it? I can't go out looking like this, can I?'

Julie looked blank. It was obvious she didn't have a clue. 'You could . . . um . . .'

'You could take it back to its original colour and start again,' Cat suggested.

'And how would you do that?' Elizabeth Montague asked. As Cat explained, she could see Julie turning redder and more furious behind her.

'I don't think that would work,' Julie declared flatly.

'I do. And since you don't seem to be able to come up with a more useful idea I suggest we try it, don't you?' Elizabeth's voice was full of calm authority. 'But not you,' she added, as Julie stepped forward. 'I want this young lady to do it. At least she seems to know what she's talking about.'

Cat was acutely conscious of the hate looks Julie kept sending her across the salon, but she forgot her nerves as she and Elizabeth Montague chatted like old friends. She explained how her family had moved back to her native West Yorkshire after years spent in London where her husband was a barrister. She also talked excitedly about her daughter Charlotte's forthcoming wedding. They were meeting at the bridal shop in Leeds for a wedding dress fitting later that afternoon.

When she'd finished, Elizabeth insisted on paying, even though Cat tried to refuse.

'But you've done such a good job!'

'It was nearly a disaster.' She was just relieved she'd managed to put it right.

'No, I insist. And this is for you.' She pressed something into Cat's hand. 'You saved my life.'

Maxine arrived just as she was leaving. The door had barely closed before she pounced on Cat. 'Was that who I think it was?'

'I don't know. Who do you think it was?'

'You know! Her! That actress. The one in the Bond film with Sean Connery. On the black satin bed wearing nothing but a strategically placed python?'

'Lizzie Yorke! Of course!' Sadie cried. 'I thought I knew her from somewhere. She was a real stunner in the seventies. Fancy you doing a famous film star's hair!'

But Cat wasn't listening. She stared down at the twenty-pound note in her hand. She'd never had such a big tip in her life. She was lucky if most of the old dears in the salon gave her fifty pence for her trouble.

Her good mood lasted until Julie caught her in the staffroom. 'I suppose you think you're clever, don't you?' she growled. 'That tip should have been mine!'

'It might have been, if you hadn't made such a pig's ear of her hair.'

'I suppose you couldn't wait to tell Maxine all about it? I saw you, huddled together over there.'

'Maxine doesn't need me to tell her how useless you are.'

She left Julie staring and went back to the salon, where Sadie was still recounting the story of Lizzie Yorke to the old ladies. 'I can't get over you doing her hair! I'm definitely going to ask for her autograph next time she comes in.'

'I wouldn't hold your breath,' Cat said. 'I've got a feeling after today's disaster we won't be seeing her again.'

'What do you mean, you're not going?'

Roo held the phone away from her ear. Just because Nanna Moon was deaf she assumed everyone else was too. 'It's a funeral, you've got to pay your respects.'

'I don't think Mr Pearson's family would appreciate it under the circumstances.'

'If you don't it will look as if you've got something to hide.'

'But I didn't even know him.'

'No, but I did. His mother and I were old friends.' Roo wasn't surprised. Nanna knew everyone in Normanford. 'So shall I tell Tom to pick you up?'

'No, Nanna. I told you, I'm not going.'

There was an ominous pause. People rarely said no to Nanna. Not twice, anyway.

'I'm disappointed in you, our Ruby.' Her voice was heavy with reproach. 'The Moons don't hide away.'

Roo put the phone down as Becky came in with the morning's post. 'Do you think I should go to Eric Pearson's funeral?'

'No! You'd get lynched.'

'That's what I was thinking.' She picked up the post and a glossy magazine fell out. 'What's this?'

'That's mine.' Becky snatched it back but Roo caught the title. It was an upmarket interiors magazine.

'I didn't know you were interested in interior design.'

'I like to look at the pictures.' Becky blushed. 'I've been reading about a new hotel in Leeds. The interiors have been designed by Salvatore Bellini. It's class.'

'Who?'

'Salvatore Bellini. Don't tell me you haven't heard of him?' Becky frowned at Roo's ignorance. 'He's a hot new designer. Specialises in upmarket home furnishings – they cost an absolute fortune.'

Roo glanced at the photos. The hotel was impressive in a cool, minimalist way. Lots of dark wood, white walls and moody lighting. 'It all looks a bit modern to me.'

'It's lovely.' Becky closed the magazine, her face wistful. 'I wish I could see it.'

'Why don't you go and take a look?'

'What, me? In a place like that?' Becky shook her head. 'It's too posh.'

'Nonsense, you should go.' Then an idea struck her. 'Why don't you go today? Call it a research trip.'

'What about all the work on my desk?'

'Forget work for the day.' Roo could hardly believe she was saying it. Were those words really coming out of her own mouth? Her, the woman who had once crawled in to work with a temperature of 104 degrees, just to finish writing a report?

But today was such a depressing day, what with Eric's funeral, it had put her off the idea of working. She wasn't sure if she could spend another hour in that gloomy little cubbyhole. 'I'll come with you,' she said.

It was a strange, heady feeling, playing truant from work. Roo, who usually regarded a lunchtime sandwich at her desk as the ultimate in slacking, found herself tucking into caesar salad and a cold glass of Chablis in the hotel bar, as if she'd always been a Lady Who Lunched.

'I could get used to this,' Becky grinned, picking sundried tomato out of her panini sandwich.

'Me too.' Roo had to admit the photos in the glossy magazine didn't do the hotel justice. It was a temple to modernism, with tinkling water features, vast, Zen-like white spaces and leather sofas you could lose yourself in. 'I was wrong about this place. It's fabulous.'

'Told you!' Becky looked triumphant. 'When I get a place of my own I'm going to paint it all white like this. And I'm going to save up for really beautiful furniture, even if we have to sit on boxes in the meantime.'

'We?'

'My boyfriend Dominic and me. We'll probably get a place together when he finishes his building apprenticeship. We're already saving for the deposit.' She didn't look very enthusiastic about the idea.

'Sounds like you've got your future all worked out.'

'What else is there to do, in a place like this?'

'You don't have to stay here. I didn't.'

'I'm not like you. I haven't got the qualifications.' She finished her sandwich and pushed her plate away. 'I passed a few GCSEs but I wasn't all that interested at school. Although now I some-times wish I'd stuck it a bit longer.'

'You make it sound like it's too late. You're only seventeen – that's hardly over the hill! You could go back to college and take your A-levels, even go to university if you wanted to—'

'I couldn't do that.'

'Why not? You're very bright.'

'Do you think so?'

'I know you are. You can do anything you want if you're determined enough.'

Becky looked around the hotel bar, taking it all in. Roo could see her imagining herself there, living that life. Then she said, 'Dominic wouldn't like it.'

'What's it got to do with him?'

'We're saving for a flat. I couldn't let him down.'

'Surely if he loved you he'd want you to be happy?'

'Yes, but I don't think he'd want me to be happy miles away at university, living it up with a load of pissed students!'

'Then maybe he's not the right man for you.'

Becky was silent for a moment. 'I'll think about it,' she promised, but Roo knew she wouldn't. She was just like her mother at that age, refusing to see there might be more to life than Normanford.

After lunch, Roo planned to go straight back to the office. But Becky persuaded her to take a detour via the city centre for a meander around Harvey Nicks. It felt strange, wandering around a department store in the middle of the afternoon, browsing, instead of rushing in and grabbing the first things she could find because it was her lunch hour and she had a million other things to do.

Becky couldn't understand it. 'It's weird, isn't it?' she said. 'There's me with all the time in the world and no money. And you're loaded and you don't have any time to spend it.'

They both tried on clothes, something else Roo never had time to do. Becky persuaded her to try on a floaty Stella McCartney dress in a flowery print that she would never have considered before. It was nothing like the practical suits she wore. It was in a rusty, autumnal print that suited her dark colouring, making her look softer and more feminine.

'You should have that,' Becky said.

'I'd never wear it. But it is pretty.' Roo smiled reluctantly at her reflection. She hadn't seen herself looking like that for a long time. 'Maybe I will buy it,' she said, then added, 'but only if I can buy you something too.'

'Me? Oh no, I couldn't!'

'Why not? Call it a staff bonus. What would you like? Some Earl jeans? They've got some nice Miss Sixty stuff over there—'

'I quite fancy a suit,' Becky admitted, shamefaced. 'One like yours. One that would make people take me seriously.'

Roo felt absurdly pleased and flattered. 'Let's see what we can do, shall we?'

'What do you think?' Becky twirled in front of her mother in her new fitted black Nicole Farhi suit. 'I won't even tell you how much it cost, but it was a fortune.'

'It's . . . very nice.' Cat frowned. It looked good, but it didn't look like Becky.

Her face fell. 'You don't like it.'

'I do, it's lovely. It's just a surprise, that's all.'

'I know!' Becky looked pleased. 'It's my new image. The new, improved, ass-kicking Rebecca.'

Rebecca. Cat couldn't remember the last time she'd called herself that. 'There was nothing wrong with the old one,' she said quietly.

Becky didn't hear her. She was too busy preening in front of the mirror, twisting and turning this way and that to catch all the different angles. 'I think I should get my hair cut. Something shorter and choppier.'

Cat tried to be encouraging. At least she could take a small part in her daughter's new image. 'Sounds good. Why don't you pop into the salon on Saturday afternoon, and I'll see what I can do?'

'Oh no,' Becky said, without thinking. 'I thought I'd try Toni and Guy in Leeds. Roo says they're really good. Not that you're not good,' she added, seeing her mother's face change. 'I just fancied something new.'

'Of course. Why not? Everyone needs a change.' Cat turned away and busied herself chopping vegetables for supper. She couldn't help it; she felt jealous. Jealous that Ruby had whisked her off on a shopping trip to Leeds and bought her something Cat couldn't have afforded in a million years. And jealous that Becky adored her glam cousin so much she wanted to turn herself into a carbon copy of her.

Ten minutes later, when Becky had changed back into her jeans and was helping her peel potatoes, she casually announced that she was thinking of giving up her job.

Cat was appalled. 'What will you do?'

'I don't know. Go back to college and take my A-levels, maybe.' Becky concentrated on gouging the eye out of a potato. 'Or Roo's offered me a work placement at her firm in London.'

'London!' Cat dropped the potato in the pan with a splash.

'Don't look so horrified, Mum. It's not Baghdad!'

But Cat wasn't listening. So that was Roo's game. Not content with leading her husband astray, now she was trying to take her daughter, too. 'What do you want to go there for? You've got a decent job here.'

'Hardly! The only prospect I've got is getting my own photocopier one day. I want to be the one making the decisions, not following orders all the time.'

'And you reckon you can do that, do you?'

'Roo thinks I've got what it takes.'

Cat felt a twinge of fear. Once Becky had longed to grow up just like her mum. They had the same haircut, the same outlook on life. They'd enjoyed girly shopping trips and curling up together on the sofa to weep through a movie with a box of chocs. Now she could feel Becky slipping away from her. She was going to lose someone else, just like she lost her mother, like she lost Ruby, like she almost lost Billy. She panicked.

'What does Dominic say about all this?'

'I haven't told him yet.'

'Don't you think you should talk it over with him first? He is your boyfriend.'

'So? He doesn't own me.'

'I'm not saying that. I just think he's got a right to know what your plans are. I mean, last week you two were planning to buy a place together, now you're thinking of going off to London. You need to let the poor boy know where he stands.'

'So I'll tell him.' Becky was even beginning to sound like Ruby, high-handed and arrogant.

'Are you sure you've thought about this?' she said. 'It's a big step.'

'So? I need to do something with my life. I can't stay here and stagnate like—'

'Like me,' Cat said.

A flush crept up Becky's neck. 'I didn't say that.' She didn't have to. It was written all over her face. 'We're not all like you, Mum. You're happy with your life, and that's great. But some of us want to achieve more. You understand that, don't you?'

'Of course.' Who'd want to end up like her? Faced with the

choice of being a dull mum hurtling towards forty, and a strong, independent career woman like Roo, she probably wouldn't choose her either.

Chapter 12

Roo woke up to the sound of her phone ringing. She groped for it blearily.

'Have you seen the paper?' George Fairbanks' gruff voice shocked her awake.

'What? Do you know what time it is?' She squinted at the alarm clock. Just before seven.

'Never mind that. Have you seen it?'

'Of course I haven't seen it. I've only just woken up.'

'Then I suggest you look at it before you come in to work. It's a bad business. Very bad indeed.' He slammed the phone down.

Roo thought about it as she showered and dressed for work. What could the newspaper have to say that was so dramatic George had to call her at the crack of dawn?

She soon found out. The front page leapt out at her from the newsagent's stand.

There was a photo of Eric Pearson's funeral, his flower-laden coffin being carried into the church, followed by his tearful widow and the Fairbanks family bringing up the rear. 'Fairbanks' farewell to faithful Eric', the headline read. Underneath, as a footnote to the story, there was another photo. A blurred, paparazzi-style snap of her coming out of Harvey Nichols, carrier bag in hand, grinning her head off, and next to it the words, 'While tough new boss shops till she drops'.

Roo clamped her hand over her mouth, feeling sick. She looked so cruel, so disrespectful. More than disrespectful. Actually happy the poor man was dead.

She paid for the newspaper quickly, avoiding the stony gaze of the woman behind the counter. As she hurried outside, she had the overwhelming urge to throw all her belongings into her suitcase and drive back to London, leaving this whole sorry mess behind. She didn't need this place and it certainly didn't need her.

She pulled herself together with an effort. That was the coward's way out and whatever else she was, she wasn't a coward. She wasn't going to be scared off by a few words.

Cat stared at page five of the *Normanford News*, horrified. How had she let herself get talked into appearing in that photo? If she'd known, she might have dressed up. She put down the piece of toast she'd been munching. She was sure she wasn't the only one being put off their breakfast by looking at it.

Becky was equally unimpressed. 'Oh my God, how could you? You could at least have brushed your hair!'

'I didn't know I was going to be photographed, did I? Anyway, no one will notice it.'

'Want to bet?' Becky shook her head. 'You'd better not let Dad see this. He'll go ballistic.'

'He'll see the funny side. It's only a photo, for heaven's sake!' But as Billy came downstairs she guiltily stuffed it into the bread bin. Which was where he found it five minutes later.

'Cat, are you having one of your funny turns again?'

'No.'

'So why's the paper in— Bloody hell!'

Cat cringed. 'I know. I'm sorry. It's awful, isn't it?'

'Awful? It's disastrous!'

She glanced at Becky, who gave her an 'I told you so' look and went off to get ready for work.

'I can't believe it,' Billy said. 'Who the hell would be that malicious? It's not as if it was her fault!'

'Sorry? What are we talking about?'

'This!' Billy held up the newspaper and she saw the photo of Ruby on the front page. She'd been so desperate to see how dire her own picture was that she hadn't noticed it before. 'Can you believe it? As if she hasn't been through enough.' He slapped the newspaper down on the table. 'I'm going to ring her.'

'Why? You'll be seeing her at work in half an hour!'

'She needs my support, Cat. She needs to know she has at least one friend in this place.'

But why does it have to be you? Cat thought. She sat down at the table and glanced at the front-page story. Okay, it was harsh, but what did she expect? No one had made her go shopping.

He hadn't even noticed her photo. He'd been so caught up with Ruby and her troubles, she'd disappeared off his radar. As usual.

She got on with the children's breakfast and was refereeing an argument over whose turn it was to claim the free gift in the Rice Krispies when Dominic arrived to give Becky a lift to work.

He nodded at the *Normanford News*, lying on the table. 'All right, Mrs K? You've seen your picture, then?'

Cat groaned. 'Don't remind me.'

'You look great.'

'Yeah – a great advert for WeightWatchers!'

'Don't put yourself down. You look fantastic for someone your age.' He saw Cat's face and added, 'Or any age, really.'

Billy came in, still brooding. Before Cat could stop him, Dominic said brightly, 'What do you reckon to your wife being in the paper, Mr K?'

'What?' Billy looked up, distracted. Dominic pushed it towards him.

'There, on page five. Doesn't she look sensational?'

Cat watched Billy's face as he snatched up the newspaper and scanned it, his brows drawing together in a frown.

He put it down without a word as Becky came in. As she and Dominic left for work she heard Dominic say, 'Do you think your mum would mind if I stuck her photo up in our site office?'

'No, but I would!' Becky snapped back.

The children finished their breakfast and Cat sent them upstairs to brush their teeth. 'I'm sorry,' she said to Billy.

'Bit late for that, isn't it?'

'It was only a bit of fun.'

'Fun? You call that fun? What the hell did you think you were playing at?'

'I just—'

'Do you know what this could do to me? And to Roo? Don't you think she's got enough to deal with without her own family turning on her?' His eyes blazed. 'Why did you get involved? It's not your fight, it doesn't even concern you.'

'It affects the whole community—'

'What do you know about it? You're a hairdresser, not a politician.'

She flinched at his cruelty. 'I'm still allowed an opinion.'

He glanced at his watch. 'We'll talk about this later,' he promised ominously.

'Mustn't keep Roo waiting, must we?' Cat shouted after him as the front door closed. It was the first time he hadn't kissed her before he left the house.

She began to clear away the breakfast dishes while the kids argued over their lunchboxes in the hall.

So now she knew. Her own husband thought she was stupid. It was obvious from the contemptuous way he looked at her.

And then there was Becky. Her own daughter, who'd once thought she was the most wonderful woman in the world, now didn't want to be anything like her.

The children were throwing their shoes at each other as she went into the sitting room and picked up the phone.

'I was going to call you,' Marjorie Prentice said. 'You've seen the paper?'

'I've seen it,' Cat said grimly. 'And I've changed my mind. I want to come to Westminster with you.'

There was dog shit on the pavement outside Roo's house when she came home. No prizes for guessing how it got there. Furious, she hammered on Matt's door.

'Oh, God,' he groaned, when he saw her. 'What is it now?'

She pointed at her doorstep. 'Did you do that?'

'No, I didn't. Maybe Harvey did. I'll ask him, shall I?' He ducked back inside the house. 'Harv? Did you crap on that nice lady next door's doorstep?' He stuck his head out again. 'He says he didn't. Come to think of it, he's too traumatised to go anywhere near your place after what you did to him.'

'Oh, for heaven's sake!' Roo rolled her eyes. 'Look, just get it cleaned up, will you? Having one pile of shit on my doorstep is bad enough.' She nodded at the car.

She'd barely closed the door before Matt's drum and bass music pulsed through the wall. How childish, Roo thought, cranking up Vivaldi. They were deafening each other so much she barely heard the phone ring.

'Are you having a party?' David yelled.

'No, but the man next door is, apparently.' Roo turned down her stereo and bashed on the wall. The music went up a notch. She went back to the phone. 'Hang on, I'm going to have to take this outside.' She took the phone into the back garden and crouched among the dustbins. 'That's better.'

'What have you done to him?'

'I had his dog taken away.'

David chuckled. 'Still winning friends wherever you go?'

You don't know the half of it, Roo thought. George Fairbanks had given her a stinging rebuke that made her feel like a schoolgirl. 'Anyway, what can I do for you? Is Ollie all right? He's not ill or anything?'

'He's fine. Can't I call you without it being a life or death crisis?'

'Yes.' But you very rarely do, she thought. Almost every evening she was the one who called home.

Matt brought the rubbish out. He took a long time doing it, she noticed. Eavesdropping, no doubt.

'I thought I'd bring Ollie up to see you this weekend, to save you the journey back down south. What do you think?'

'Fine.' Then, aware that Matt was still lurking on the other side of the fence she added, 'You're coming up? That's wonderful, darling.'

'I just said so, didn't I?'

'I can't wait to see you and Ollie. I love you so much.'

'Have you been drinking?'

'Oh, you naughty man!' Roo threw back her head and laughed. Matt's back door banged shut.

'I'll call you back when you've sobered up,' David said, bemused, and hung up.

Roo made sure she was home early on Friday night. She rushed around cleaning the house, then showered and changed into white linen trousers and T-shirt. It was a fine, warm evening. Perfect for sharing a bottle of wine in the garden. Or maybe not, she thought, as she stood at the kitchen window and surveyed the tiny back yard, the weeds growing through cracks in the concrete slabs. She wasn't quite sure what David would make of her new home.

As it turned out, David found it all highly amusing. 'You mean you actually live here?' he said, as he hauled their bags into the narrow hall. Quite a lot of bags, it seemed to Roo. 'There's no room to swing a cat with a growth defect.'

'I like it.' Ollie ran around, enjoying the novelty of it all. 'The toilet's got a chain hanging from the ceiling.'

'Very working class,' David remarked. 'Don't tell me, it's up the end of the garden, with cut-up pages from the *Racing Post*?'

'The *Guardian*, actually.' Roo glanced at the clock. Five minutes, and they were already getting on each other's nerves. Was this a record? she wondered.

They had supper together in the tiny kitchen, which was surprisingly cosy. Afterwards Ollie played out in the yard under the setting sun while she and David washed up.

'By the way, I've got a job,' he announced as he dried a pot.

'David, that's wonderful! What? Where?'

'IT support manager at a precision engineering firm. The pay isn't that great, but it's interesting.'

And it was a job. The first step on their road back to normality. Roo couldn't have felt happier if he'd told her he'd been asked to run the NASA space programme.

'Congratulations,' she beamed. 'Why didn't you tell me sooner?'

'I only found out this morning.' He paused. 'There's just one problem. They want me to go on a week's induction at their head office in Bristol. Starting Monday.'

'So? I'm sure Shauna will cope if we offer her a huge bonus.'

'Ah. Well, you see, that's just it.' David looked awkward. 'Shauna's ill. She's had to go and stay with her parents.'

'So who's going to look after Ollie?' She saw his face and it dawned on her.

'Oh no. You can't be serious!'

'He's your son,' David pointed out.

'But I'm working!' She thought desperately. 'Can't you find another nanny? There must be temp agencies—'

'Are you suggesting we leave our son alone in the house with a complete stranger for a week?'

Put like that, it didn't seem like a good idea. 'I wish you'd given me more notice—'

'Look, it's okay. I'll just have to tell them I can't make this course. They won't be too impressed, but if you're too busy to look after your own son—'

'I didn't say that, did I?' Roo gazed out at Ollie, jumping from one paving slab to the other. 'Looks like I don't have much choice, does it?'

The novelty of Staying With Mummy lasted precisely as long as it took Ollie to discover the TV didn't have Nickelodeon or any of the Sky channels on it. That was when reality set in for both of them. Ollie realised he'd left all his best toys, including his extensive video collection and his fully poseable *Star Wars* action figures, back in London. And Roo discovered that her five-year-old son could be as hard to please as a Middle Eastern peace negotiator wrangling over the Gaza Strip.

The last time Roo had felt this helpless was when he was a couple of days old and she had just brought him home from hospital. The first time he'd cried, she'd looked around for the buzzer to summon a nurse, then realised with a shock that it was all down to her.

'I want my daddy!' Ollie wailed.

'You know Daddy's gone back to London.'

'I wanted to go with him!'

'No, you didn't. We talked about it, remember? You wanted to stay with Mummy.' She looked at the clock. Two hours gone and they'd already exhausted her limited repertoire of games. It was ironic, really. All these years she'd craved more time with her son and now she had no idea what to do with it. 'Shall I read you a story?' she asked.

'Don't want a story. I want to watch *Fear Factor.*'

'I don't know what that is, but it doesn't sound suitable.'

'Daddy lets me watch it.'

'Well, we don't have it in this house. Now why don't you play in the garden?'

'It's raining.'

'Draw a nice picture, then.'

'Drawing's for girls.'

Roo stifled a sigh. She'd always thought she'd be good at motherhood if only she had more time. Now she realised she was terrible. 'So what do you want to do?'

His eyes gleamed. 'Go out for a burger!'

Roo opened her mouth to refuse. Then the thought of all those mind-numbing hours of arguing rose up before her. 'Get your coat,' she said.

She'd always disapproved of mothers who let their kids get away with murder. If only they stood firm and enforced their rules, their children would soon get the message. But now she could understand why they caved in. To save their own sanity.

For the first time, she felt sorry for Shauna. While Roo was at her desk, smugly congratulating herself on how well she was bringing up her son, Shauna was engaged in an endless struggle to get Ollie to eat muesli and practise his violin.

Ollie changed his mind halfway down the precinct and decided he wanted to go to Pizza Paradise instead. It was full of bored families, all trying to escape the drizzly Sunday afternoon. And Matt was working there. Roo tried not to meet his eye as she lined up at the counter.

They made their way to an empty table by the window. On one side was a family of mum, dad and two kids. They looked like a family from a soap powder ad, all smiling and whiter than white. Her kind of people. On the other was an exhausted-looking woman in a tracksuit, surrounded by squabbling children of various hues. As Roo and Ollie sat down she starting doling out indiscriminate slaps to their heads.

Roo and the soap powder ad woman exchanged disapproving looks.

'I wanted Coke!' Ollie protested when she unloaded the tray and put his drink in front of him.

'Milk is better for you.'

'I don't care! I want Coke!'

'You'll get nothing if you carry on like that.'

'I don't want nothing.'

'Anything. You don't want anything.'

'I just said so, didn't I?'

The soap powder couple at the next table frowned, while their children munched their pizzas angelically. *Bad mother*, their expressions said. 'Eat your pizza and don't be silly,' she hissed.

'I told you, I don't want it!'

'Look, it was your idea to come here.' She pushed it towards him. He shoved it back at her. It caught his drink and sent it glugging all over the table, soaking Roo's lap. 'Now look what you've done!' She grabbed a handful of napkins and started mopping. As she did, she caught the tracksuit woman's sympathetic look.

Roo was shocked. I'm not like you, she wanted to shout. But to the outside world she was just another single mum who couldn't control her kid.

Matt appeared, with a cloth. 'Having problems?'

'Nothing I can't handle.'

'I wasn't talking to you, I was talking to this young man.' He turned to Ollie. 'Is this person bothering you? Because if she is, I can have her thrown out.'

Roo looked outraged. Ollie laughed with delight. 'Yes! Do it!' he cried.

'Tell you what, I've got a better idea. Why don't I compensate you for your ruined evening? Just a second.' Matt disappeared and returned a moment later with a small plastic toy, a figure of some hideous monster Roo didn't recognise.

Whatever it was, it brought a smile to Ollie's face. 'A Robo-droid!'

'A what?' said Roo, who'd only just got to grips with *Star Wars*.

'The latest thing. You're clearly not a fan of Saturday morning TV.'

'Not as much as you, obviously.' She glared at the toy in Ollie's hands. 'You do realise you've just undermined me completely?'

'Sorry?'

'Here I am, trying to show him right from wrong and now you've just rewarded him for being naughty.'

'Actually I was trying to stop him screaming the place down and scaring all our customers away, and since you didn't seem to be doing a very good job of it—'

'I had the situation under control!'

'It looks like it.' He smiled at Ollie. 'Enjoy your meal,' he said, and walked off.

Chapter 13

The woman at the council offices laughed when on Monday morning Roo asked for a list of registered childminders who'd be able to take Ollie immediately.

'You are joking, aren't you? It's the summer holidays.'

Roo watched Ollie stubbornly refusing to eat his muesli in the absence of his favourite Coco Pops. 'So what do you suggest? It's only for a few days, and I've tried everything else.' She was appalled to find there were no nanny agencies in the local Yellow Pages.

'Don't you have any friends or family you could ask?'

'No,' Roo said. 'Look, I'm desperate. I'll pay anything.'

'I suppose I could give you a few numbers. But don't expect miracles, will you?'

Roo gave a hollow laugh as she noted the numbers down. She'd given up expecting those a long time ago.

At least she wasn't expected into the office that day. But she was supposed to be visiting a retailer with Billy that afternoon. She had to find someone to look after Ollie before then.

She called the childminders, working her way down the list. The first five were fully booked for the whole summer. Three others said they might have vacancies. Roo bundled Ollie out of his pyjamas and into the car, roaring off as if she'd been told the last suit in the Dolce and Gabbana sale had just been reduced to a fiver.

The first answered the door with a howling baby in her arms. She was skinny and dressed from head to toe in denim, like a

Status Quo roadie. Before Roo could open her mouth she said, 'It's twenty quid a day, five days a week, and I charge extra for time after six.' Ash fell from the end of her cigarette on to the baby's rompers and she brushed it away carelessly. 'I expect to be paid for holiday time, and I need three weeks' notice of any change to the arrangements, otherwise I get paid in full. Okay?'

She didn't even look at Ollie. Behind her, a ring of toddlers watched daytime TV, where a female chat show host was telling a man in a football shirt that DNA test results showed he was not the father of someone's baby.

'We'll let you know,' Roo said.

'Don't wait too long,' the woman called after her. 'I'm very sought after.'

The next, Angie, was more promising. Her house was bright and sunny, and the children were busy making flapjacks in the kitchen. It seemed so comforting, Roo felt like asking if she could come there every day too.

Unfortunately, Angie could only take Ollie two days that week. 'It's all I can do at such short notice.'

Roo did some maths in her head. 'I really need someone full-time.'

'Then I can't help you. Sorry.'

Roo was sorry too. Especially when she had to drag Ollie away from the flapjack-making. He was subdued in the car as they drove to the final address.

'Don't worry, darling, we'll find somewhere for you to go.' She reached across and patted his knee reassuringly.

The last woman was called Liz. She seemed very nice, capable and obliging. What a piece of luck, she said. One of her mums had just gone on maternity leave, so she had a vacancy. Ollie could start straight away. It wouldn't be any problem at all.

'Actually, it would help me out too,' she said. 'My husband's been made redundant, so we need the extra money.'

A feeling of dread crept up Roo's spine. 'Where does he work?'

'Fairbanks. Do you know it?'

She and Ollie left. Shortly afterwards, as she'd expected, there was a call on her mobile phone. Something had come up, Liz said, and she couldn't take Ollie after all.

Roo said she understood, and she did. She understood perfectly. She was Public Enemy Number One. No one wanted to look after her child while she made their husband redundant.

She parked the car and sat behind the wheel holding her head in her hands. It was a nightmare. She could feel stress building up like a pressure cooker inside her. This was rapidly turning into a problem she couldn't deal with.

'Don't cry, Mummy,' Ollie said. 'I'm sorry.'

'What?'

'I know you don't want me here. I could go back to Daddy. I could go on the train by myself.'

She suddenly saw the world through his troubled eyes. How she was so desperate to palm him off on someone else that she'd bullied him into the car when he'd barely had his breakfast and driven him around to strangers' houses, begging them to take him.

'Oh Ollie, of course I want you to stay.' She hugged him fiercely. 'Come on, let's go home. And we'll pick up some Coco Pops on the way. How does that sound?'

Billy was sympathetic when she called to let him know she couldn't make their appointment that afternoon.

'Why don't we take Ollie with us?' he asked.

'I don't think that would be a good idea. What if he breaks something?'

'It's a furniture shop. How the hell is he going to break a sofa?'

Roo glanced at her son, kicking a ball around the room. 'You'd be surprised.'

So it was settled. After lunch, Billy picked them up and they headed out to Smythsons Furniture Superstore in a retail park off the M62. It was surrounded by fast-food places, and other huge stores selling furniture and carpets and electrical goods.

'Now don't touch anything,' Roo warned as they entered. 'And for heaven's sake don't wander off.'

They met the manager, Neil, who showed them around the store. It took them a while to find the Fairbanks range. It was hidden in the middle of some end-of-range stock they were selling off cheap.

'It's not very well displayed,' Roo commented. 'How can you expect it to sell well if people can't see it?'

Neil looked pained. 'To be honest, even if they could see it they probably wouldn't want it. Don't get me wrong, Fairbanks stuff is good quality and it's very popular with the, um, older end of the market. But they're not the ones with the spending power, and the younger buyers want something more modern.'

'Do you think they'd pay more if they could get modern design with Fairbanks quality?'

'Maybe. Why? What did you have in mind?'

'Nothing yet. But I'll let you know.'

'Depressing, isn't it?' Billy said when Neil had gone.

'Very,' Roo agreed. 'But it's convinced me we're aiming at the wrong market. Competing with this lot on price isn't working. We need to come up with something big, something sensational that will make the buyers sit up and take notice—' she looked around. 'Where's Ollie?'

'He's probably just wandered off. Kids do it all the time.'

An assistant approached them. 'Excuse me, have you lost a little boy?'

'Where is he? Have you seen him?'

'He's over there. In beds.'

A small crowd had gathered, watching in amusement the small boy curled up asleep on top of a futuristic bunk bed. He looked so innocent, his dark lashes curling on his cheeks, that Roo couldn't help smiling as her panic melted away.

'Looks like someone's ready to go home,' Billy said.

She watched Billy striding ahead of her, Ollie in his arms, admiring his broad shoulders in his navy suit. They could so easily have been a family. They looked like they belonged together, both tall, dark and well-dressed. A sophisticated couple, choosing furniture for their new home . . .

She stopped herself. It was a stupid, dangerous fantasy. Just because she and David weren't getting on, that was no reason to start thinking about what might have been with someone else.

They chatted in the car going home, as Ollie slept in the back. They talked about work, and Roo told him about an idea she'd had for branching into contract furniture for hotel chains and offices. 'I'm sure there must be a market there.' Billy agreed, and promised to look into it.

Then the conversation moved on to their children. 'You know, I never imagined you having a big family,' she said.

'Me neither.'

'There's a big gap between Becky and Megan. About ten years, isn't it?'

'There wasn't supposed to be.' His face grew sombre. 'Cat had a stillbirth three years after Becky. A boy, Michael.'

'Oh, I'm sorry. That must have been awful.'

'It was.' Emotion flickered across his face. 'But we pulled through. And then Megan came along, and Liam.' He paused. 'Sometimes you wonder if things happen for a reason. We were very young when we lost Michael. We still had so much growing up to do.'

'Have you ever had any regrets about marrying so young?'

'Regrets are a dangerous thing, Roo. Sometimes it's best just to get on with the hand fate's dealt you.'

They changed the subject and discussed her problems with childcare. 'I could have a word with Cat about it,' Billy said. 'Perhaps she could have a word with our childminder, see if she can take you on—'

'No thanks. I can sort it out.' The last thing she wanted was Cat thinking she couldn't cope.

'How about your mum? Can't she help?'

Roo laughed so loudly it woke Ollie up. 'You've got to be joking!'

'Why not? I'm sure she'd love to spend some time with her grandson.'

'Want to bet? She's more interested in having a good time.'

'People change,' Billy said.

'Not her.' She'd been a selfish mother and she'd probably be an equally useless grandmother. 'I'll think of something. I don't need to get my family involved.'

'There's no shame in asking for help, you know.'

He dropped her off at home. 'What the hell is that outside your house?'

Roo looked, and blinked. Matt's wreck had been transformed with a paint job into a fluorescent orange monstrosity. It was now not only visible from her front window, but probably from outer space, too.

Ollie laughed. 'It's a clown car!'

'And I know just the clown who owns it.' Roo looked up. Matt was watching her from his bedroom window, gleefully awaiting her reaction.

'Do you want me to sort this out?' Billy asked.

It was a tempting offer, to hand over her problems to someone strong and capable. But that wasn't her style. 'I can handle him.'

'Like I said, there's nothing wrong with asking for help.'

As Billy drove off, Roo took one last look at the bright orange car, then took Ollie into the house. There was no point having another row. Actions spoke louder than words. It was time to get tough.

She looked up the number in the phone book. 'Hello, is that Normanford police? I'd like to report an abandoned car . . .'

'So I was wondering if you knew of any childminders in the area.' Roo looked out of the window at her son, who was playing in Nanna Moon's yard. The same yard she'd played in as a child. He was rooting around among the cracked flagstones, digging up the narrow strip of earth like an explorer who'd just found darkest Africa.

After another missed day at work desperately trying every other avenue, she'd finally taken Billy's advice and turned to her family. But it wasn't easy. Nanny was still frosty with her about missing Eric Pearson's funeral.

'Childminders?' Nanna bridled, as if she'd just suggested inviting the local paedophile round for tea. 'You don't want to send the kiddie to a stranger!'

Roo didn't like to tell her grandmother Ollie had been going to strangers since he was a month old. In fact, he knew some of the strangers better than he did his own mother. 'I don't think I've got any choice.'

'Your mother can look after him,' Nanna said.

Roo was disappointed. She'd hoped Nanna would offer to do it, the way she'd looked after Roo when she was small.

Irene Moon read her thoughts. 'I'm too old for looking after children,' she said. 'I can't run about after them like I used to. Sadie would enjoy it.'

'I doubt it. She's not interested in children.'

'But this is her grandson. You don't know how much she thinks of that little boy.' She nodded towards the photos crammed on to the mantelpiece. 'Always bragging about him, she is, and yet she hardly knows the lad.' She looked severely at Roo. 'You've got your mother all wrong, you know. She was hardly more than a bairn herself when you were born, and of course she made mistakes. But she deserves a second chance.'

'Who deserves a second chance?' Sadie appeared in the doorway, laden with shopping bags. She spotted Roo, and her smile dropped. 'Oh, it's you.'

'Our Ruby needs someone to look after her little lad for a few days,' Nanna said. 'I told her you'd do it.'

'Did you now? And what about my job?'

'You can take time off, can't you?'

She looked from one to the other. Then she said, 'No, I'm sorry, I can't.'

'Told you,' Ruby said, as Sadie left the room. Nanna was wrong to say her mother had changed. Sadie still looked out for number one.

Sadie dumped the carrier bags on the kitchen table, seething. Ruby had a nerve! After the way she'd ignored her over the years, she suddenly expected her to drop everything just because she'd decided she needed help.

She broke her nail and cursed. This was meant to be the best day of her life. Jan had phoned to say the agent would be at the

Ponderosa that night to hear her sing. She'd had her hair done and been planning all day what she'd sing. Now Ruby had ruined her happy mood.

Then she realised she wasn't alone. A small boy was watching her shyly from the back doorway. Fair-haired, with dark, serious eyes like his mother's. When Sadie said hello he ducked away and hid.

She turned her back on him, knowing he was still watching. She talked out loud, reciting the contents of the shopping bags as she unpacked them. When she reached the variety pack of biscuits, she unwrapped them, selected a chocolate one and left it carefully on the corner of the table, within Ollie's reach. Then she moved away to put the kettle on.

He edged forward. He reminded Sadie of the time she'd taken Ruby to the park when she was a toddler and they'd coaxed a squirrel across the grass with a trail of biscuit crumbs.

'Do you want a drink with that?' she said, still not turning round.

'Coke, please.' The hasty way he said it made her realise it was probably forbidden.

'Sorry, we don't have that in the house. How about a nice glass of milk?'

She poured it for him, then offered him another biscuit from the packet. Ollie went to take it, then drew back his hand. 'It might spoil my tea.'

'Another one won't kill you.' She sat down across the table from him. He spent a long time choosing, his hand hovering over the packet, as if it was the most important decision he would ever make. Finally he selected one with jam and cream in the middle.

'Your biscuits are nicer than ours,' he said. 'Ours are yukky. Daddy says they taste like doormats.'

'Aye, well, yukky things are generally good for you.'

'Who are you?' he asked.

'I'm your gran.' It felt odd, saying it out loud.

'No, you're not. My granny lives in the country.'

'That's your other granny. Your daddy's mum. I'm your mummy's mum.'

He eyed her suspiciously. 'You don't look like a granny.'

'I'll take that as a compliment.'

'So what shall I call you?'

'Most people just call me Sadie.' She brushed biscuit crumbs off her red pedal-pushers. 'So you're here for a holiday, are you?'

Ollie frowned. 'Sort of, but Mummy doesn't want me. She's too busy with her job to look after me. Can I have one of those pink biscuits?'

'Just one.' Sadie got up to pour boiling water into the teapot, so Ollie couldn't see her shocked expression. And Ruby had the cheek to call *her* a bad mother!

A moment later Ruby walked in. Ollie turned to her excitedly. 'Look Mummy, they have custard creams here. And pink biscuits. Why can't we have proper biscuits?'

Sadie glanced at her daughter. 'I've never known anyone get so excited over a chocolate digestive.'

'Be careful you don't get chocolate down your T-shirt.' Roo was instantly fussing, dabbing her son's chin with a tissue. Sadie wanted to tell her to stop, all kids got dirty, but she bit her tongue.

'Where's his dad?' she asked.

'On a course.'

'What happened to the nanny?'

'She's ill.'

Sadie arranged some biscuits on a plate and handed them to Ollie. 'Take these in to Nanna, will you love? Tell her I'll bring her a cup of tea in a minute.' As he trotted off, she said, 'He's a nice little lad.'

'Yes, he is.' There was a long silence.

'What made you ask me to look after him?'

'I know you haven't seen much of him over the years. I thought you might like a chance to get to know your grandson.'

'Nothing to do with the fact that you couldn't get anyone else to do it?'

Ruby looked flustered. 'Well—'

'Let's face it, the only reason you came here is because you're desperate. You wouldn't let me anywhere near him otherwise.

You'd rather pay a stranger to look after him than his own grandmother!' She shook her head. 'And you wonder why I said no.'

'Actually, I would have been amazed if you'd said yes. I stopped expecting you to help me a long time ago.'

'What's that supposed to mean?'

'Think about it. When was the last time you did anything for me? Even when I was a kid, it was always you first. You, you, you. Never mind that we couldn't afford to pay the gas bill because you'd spent the money on a new dress. Never mind that I had to go to bed in the cold and dark because you were out getting drunk with your latest boyfriend and we didn't have fifty pence for the electric meter. As long as you got what you wanted, that's all that mattered!'

Sadie felt the colour drain from her face. She'd never been that bad – had she? 'If you feel like that, I don't know why you bothered asking.'

'Like you said, I was desperate. But don't put yourself out, I'll sort out my own problems. I've had a lot of practice, living with you all those years!' She headed for the door.

Irene hobbled into the kitchen a moment after the front door banged closed, as Sadie knew she would. 'Made a right pig's ear of that, didn't you?'

'I don't know what you mean. Macaroni cheese all right for tea?' Without waiting for an answer, Sadie began pulling the ingredients out of the cupboard.

'You know perfectly well what I'm talking about. You had the chance to look after that little lad, and instead you cut off your nose to spite your face. You're too stubborn, that's your trouble.'

'Mum, I don't need this. It's my big night at the club tonight, remember?' Sadie tipped flour and butter into the pan, her hands shaking. 'Don't spoil it by talking about Ruby.'

'As if you haven't wasted enough years,' her mother went on, ignoring her. 'That little lad's not a baby any more, and you've barely seen him. You're like strangers.'

'And whose fault is that? She doesn't want me in his life, she made that clear. She only came round because she had nowhere else to go.'

'And you turned her down.' Irene shook her head. 'Where do you think we'd all be if we turned our backs on our kids every time they were desperate?'

They looked at each other for a long time. Then Sadie said, 'And what do you think would have happened after this week? That would have been it. She would have taken him back to London and that would have been the last I saw of him.'

'A week's better than nothing.'

'Not to me, it isn't.' Sadie brushed past her to reach the hob. 'Now do me a favour, Mum, and mind your own business. This is between Ruby and me.'

'If I'd minded my own business all this time, this family would have fallen apart years ago.'

She shuffled off to the sitting room. Sadie slammed the kitchen door shut. She didn't need this. Not tonight.

She was taking out her temper by attacking a lump of cheddar with a grater when she heard a thump followed by a cry from the hall.

'Mum?' She dropped the grater and rushed into the hall. 'Mum! Oh no!'

Roo drove home in a bad mood, hardly listening to Ollie's chatter. Every encounter with her mother left her feeling bruised.

There was something missing when she got back to Sykes Street. It wasn't until she'd backed easily into the space outside her house that she realised Matt's rusting eyesore had gone.

He threw open his front door as she was looking for her keys. 'I suppose you think that's funny?'

'I'm sorry?'

'So you should be! And don't bother trying to look innocent, I know it was you who called the police.'

It dawned on her. 'They've towed it away?'

'As if you didn't know. Thanks to you I've spent all afternoon on the phone, trying to get it back.'

'I'm sure if you show them your tax and insurance documents they'll let you have it. Or don't you have any?'

He reddened. 'I hadn't got round to it.'

'I thought not. So technically it was an abandoned vehicle, wasn't it? And as such I was well within my rights to get it removed.'

There wasn't much he could say to that. 'You just wait. You'll be sorry!'

'I'm already shaking,' Roo said, as her mobile rang. She reached into her bag to answer it.

'Ruby?' It was her Uncle Tom. 'Can you come to the hospital? It's Nanna.'

Chapter 14

'I don't know why you brought me here. Lot of fuss over nothing if you ask me.'

Underneath all the bluster, Sadie had never seen her mother looking so frightened. Her hand clutched Sadie's so hard she could feel the bones under her papery skin. She didn't look like the indomitable Irene Moon on the trolley in the curtained cubicle. She looked like a small, helpless old lady.

Sadie's heart hadn't stopped pounding since the moment she found her in a crumpled heap at the foot of the stairs.

'You've had a fall, Ma,' Tom explained, slowly and carefully. 'You've got to stay here until the doctor checks you over.'

'Doctors! What do they know? And you don't have to speak to me like that, I didn't fall on my head.' Irene looked around impatiently. 'How long have we been here? You do realise I'm missing *Emmerdale*?'

Thank God there didn't seem to be too much wrong with her. She'd been complaining from the moment they arrived in casualty.

'We wouldn't be here at all if you'd used your stairlift.'

'Stairlift! I wasn't even going upstairs. I told you, I tripped over my slippers.'

'Can I get you anything, Ma?' Tom asked.

'Yes, you can get my coat. I want to go home.' She tried to sound nonchalant but Sadie knew her mother was terrified of hospitals. She'd seen too many of her friends go in and never come out.

She looked at the clock. Seven fifteen. She should be at the Ponderosa now, getting ready for her big night. She was due on stage at eight. She should phone Jan and let her know what was happening.

At that moment Ruby arrived with Ollie in tow. 'What's happened? How is she?'

'We don't know yet,' Tom said. 'We're still waiting for the doctor to see her.'

'You don't have to talk about me as if I wasn't here,' Irene said.

'You mean you've been waiting all this time?' Ruby glanced at her watch. 'That's ridiculous. I'm going to sort this out.'

'Don't bother the doctors,' Irene said. 'They're busy enough without having to deal with an old fool like me.'

'That's not the point. I'll talk to the consultant, find out what's going on.'

As she left the cubicle, Sadie followed her. 'Don't go making a fuss.'

'But they can't just leave her like that. It's a disgrace.'

'I know, but your nanna's terrified. She'd sooner stay on that trolley all night than see a doctor.'

'We've got to do something.'

'The best thing you could do is just go in there and help take her mind off everything.' Sadie saw her daughter's troubled expression. 'I know you're only trying to do what's best, but getting her more agitated won't help anyone.'

Twenty minutes later, the consultant finally arrived. Without looking at Irene, he picked up her notes, flicked through them and said, 'Right, we'd better get you down to X-ray.'

As the porter moved to push the trolley out of the cubicle, Irene's bony fingers tightened around Sadie's. 'Don't leave me, will you?' she whispered.

'We're all here, Ma,' Tom said.

'Stay with me, won't you Sadie?'

Sadie squeezed her mother's hand. 'Of course I will.'

Roo and Tom watched them heading off towards the lifts. She

was surprised Nanna wanted Sadie with her and not Tom. She could hardly imagine her mother being good in a crisis.

'Maybe we should go down there with them,' she said.

'Ma wouldn't want anyone but Sadie with her.' Tom sat down in the waiting room and picked up a copy of *Country Life*. 'There's always been a bond between those two. They might fight like cat and dog, but you just try coming between them. I should know,' he said gruffly.

'I don't understand.' Sadie was a disaster area, she'd brought the family nothing but trouble ever since she was a teenager.

'Neither do I, believe me. I must admit it's got me down sometimes. But what can you do? It's a mother and daughter thing, I suppose. You know what it's like.'

No, I don't, Roo thought. She'd never had that mother and daughter bond with Sadie. She doubted if she ever would.

Half an hour later, Sadie emerged. 'There are no bones broken, but they're keeping her in overnight for observation,' she said.

'That's a relief.' Tom looked at his watch. 'Shouldn't you be getting to your club? You're supposed to be singing tonight, aren't you?'

'I already rang Jan and told her I couldn't make it. Mum wants me to stay with her.'

'But I thought it was your big night. Wasn't some agent bloke meant to be coming in to see you?'

Sadie darted a quick glance at Roo. 'It doesn't matter. There'll be other nights.'

'But I thought—'

'Leave it, Tom, please. Mum needs me, and that's all there is to it.' She looked drawn and tired. 'Now why don't you go up and say goodnight to her? She's on Ward Three.'

Roo followed her uncle to the lifts, feeling slightly confused. Had her mother really given up her big chance in order to stay and nurse her sick mother? It didn't tally with her memories of Sadie always putting herself first.

She glanced back at her, sitting in the reception area. Sadie had taken out her compact and was applying lipstick in the mirror.

She never faced a crisis without her lippy. Looking at her, Roo felt an unexpected twinge of affection.

It rained all the way down the motorway on Friday night, and Roo began to regret her impulsive decision to take Ollie back to London a day early instead of waiting for David to come and pick him up the following day.

'It'll be a lovely surprise for Daddy, won't it?' she told Ollie, full of excitement. She'd already planned how it would be. She'd get back on Friday night and spend all Saturday tidying up and cooking a meal for him.

She looked forward to immersing herself in some domestic bliss after such a stressful week. In desperation she'd taken Angie's offer of part-time childcare, which meant working late into the evenings to catch up. But at least she felt she was getting somewhere at Fairbanks. After the last round of job cuts she was well on the way to convincing the bank to lend them the extra money they needed. And with Billy and the sales team chasing all possible new avenues for orders, she hoped they could get the factory workers back to full-time soon.

And Nanna was getting better. At least she was home from hospital, although she complained bitterly at being made to use a walking stick. Roo was surprised by the fuss Sadie made of her, cooking her meals, fetching and carrying for her and gently bullying her into resting.

They got home just after six. As Roo bundled through the door with an excited Ollie and all their bags, she heard a noise upstairs. A moment later David appeared on the landing.

'Roo! What are you doing here?'

'It was meant to be a surprise. I thought your course didn't finish until tomorrow?'

'The last speaker didn't turn up, so . . . where are you going?' He swung round as Ollie cannoned past him up the stairs.

'To his room, probably. He's desperate for a reunion with his *Star Wars* DVDs.' Roo smiled. 'How was Bristol?'

'Great. Very . . . enlightening. Look, why don't you go and pour us a drink? You probably need one after that journey.'

'I've got a better idea. Why don't you get the drinks while I take these bags upstairs?' She moved to pick them up, but David had already bounded down to meet her.

'Let me take them.'

'But I need the loo.'

'Use the one downstairs.'

'You're very edgy, what's—' she was interrupted by Ollie on the landing above them, his face quizzical.

'Daddy, what's Shauna doing in your bed?'

A moment later Shauna emerged from the bedroom, wearing David's bathrobe and looking sheepish. 'Hello,' she said.

They all looked at each other, frozen. Then Roo said, 'Excuse me, I think I need that drink.' She dropped her bags and went into the kitchen.

Someone had spilt red wine on the table. She grabbed a cloth from beside the sink, sniffed it, rejected it, picked a new one and ran it under the tap before scrubbing away at the sticky patch, wondering all the while at her unnatural calm. She'd just discovered her husband *in flagrante* with the nanny and all she could think about was whether the wine would stain the wood.

She was still scrubbing when David came in. 'Where's Shauna?' she asked, not looking up.

'Upstairs, with Ollie.'

'Nice to see she still remembers what she's paid to do.'

He sighed. 'Don't be like that, please.'

'Like what?' She stopped cleaning. 'I'm sorry David, how should I be? What's the appropriate response for someone who comes home and finds their husband in bed with the hired help?' He stared at his shoes. 'So how long has it been going on?' she demanded.

'Does it matter?'

'Of course it bloody matters!'

'Not long. A few weeks.'

'Since I've been away?' He didn't answer. 'I see. So all the time

170

I've been working, you've been shagging the nanny. And you had the nerve to make *me* feel guilty!'

'I'm sorry.'

'Is that all you can say?' She threw the cloth in the sink, went to the fridge and poured herself a glass of wine. All the time she kept telling herself it wasn't happening. She couldn't allow it to be real, because then her whole world would collapse.

'So what is it? Some kind of midlife crisis? Thought you'd have one last fling before you're forty?' She shook her head pityingly. 'Shagging the nanny, for God's sake. That's such a cliché! Couldn't you think of anything more original?'

He flinched. 'It wasn't like that.'

'Then what was it like? Come on, David, there must be a reason why you'd go to bed with her?'

'Yes, there is!' Anger flared in his eyes. 'For a start, she isn't a control freak. She doesn't colour-code her underwear. She doesn't tell me what to eat, or where to live or what car to drive. And she doesn't make me feel like a pathetic loser just because I don't have a six-figure salary. You want to know why I slept with her, Roo? Because she isn't perfect.'

For a second she was shocked, then anger reasserted itself. 'Then you make a good couple, don't you? Because you're not perfect either!'

'I've been trying to tell you that for years,' he said.

She raged around the room, picking things up and putting them down again, fighting the urge to throw them at his head.

'Do you want me to go?' he asked.

She stared at the plate in her hand. It was discontinued Villeroy and Boch, too precious to smash. 'I don't know what I want.'

'That makes two of us.'

'David?' Shauna stood in the doorway, white-faced. She couldn't bring herself to look at Roo. 'Is everything all right?'

'What do you think?' Roo snapped.

'You'd better wait upstairs,' David said, but Shauna stood her ground.

'This affects me too. I want to stay.'

'Stay? You think I'd let you stay under my roof after this? I want you to pack your bags and leave now. I paid you to look after my son, not sleep with my husband!'

Shauna looked at David. 'Do you want me to go?'

'What are you asking him for? Just get out of my sight!' She dashed the plate to the ground, then stared at the shattered fragments. 'Fuck! Now look what you've made me do!'

'I think it might be best,' David said.

He went upstairs with Shauna. Roo gulped her wine and listened to the muted hum of their voices. Shauna sounded upset, and David was reassuring her. How dare he comfort that bitch, she thought. Shouldn't he be down here with her, trying to save their marriage?

She looked around the kitchen. Her dream kitchen, a perfect room for a perfect family. Or so she'd thought. She had no idea that while she'd been trying to live a dream, David had been seething with resentment.

What was wrong with wanting everything to be perfect? If she was a control freak, it was only because she wanted everything to be right for her family.

Finally she heard them thumping down the stairs with Shauna's bags. Roo went out to see them, feeling strangely calm. Shauna looked as if she'd been crying. She flinched as Roo held out her hand.

'Key,' she said flatly. 'I don't want you sneaking back in here any time you like.'

Shauna handed it over, tearful but defiant. 'You won't stop us seeing each other.'

'No? Have you ever heard the expression, "Out of sight, out of mind"?'

'Say what you like if it makes you feel better. But before you blame me, maybe you should ask yourself why David did it.'

'Because you were easy and available?'

Her face flooded with colour. 'Better than being a cold bitch!'

'That's enough!' David tried to step in between them. 'Your taxi's here. I'll call you,' he muttered to Shauna.

Roo went straight upstairs and ripped the sheets off their bed, still fighting not to lose control. It was all she had left.

David followed her. 'I've put Ollie to bed. I'll sleep in the spare room, shall I?'

'No, *I'll* sleep in the spare room. Do you honestly think I could sleep in the same bed when you and she—' She bundled the sheets up and threw them into the corner. She'd never feel the same about her beautiful Egyptian cotton again.

Neither of them slept much. As she lay awake, she could hear David prowling around downstairs. What was going through his mind? she wondered. Was it anything like hers, veering wildly from despair to disbelief and back again, encompassing every emotion in between?

She finally drifted to sleep just before dawn and awoke four hours later, confused and disorientated. For a split second she couldn't remember what had happened, then it all came flooding back in a sickening rush.

The house was silent. David was gone. Roo panicked until she found the note on the kitchen table saying he'd taken Ollie swimming. It seemed so normal, just like any other Saturday morning. All that family stuff she'd taken for granted. She longed for it back.

And she could get it back. Now some of the shock and pain of last night had worn off and she could think clearly, she realised her marriage was too important to throw away because of a fling.

That was all this was. A fling. How could it be anything else? Shauna was nineteen, rarely conversed with anyone over five years old, and her idea of foreign culture was Australian soap operas.

No, the only reason David had gone to bed with her was because he was lonely. Losing his job had affected his self-esteem. He needed someone to bolster his ego, make him feel like a man. It wasn't sex, it was a cry for help.

And she hadn't been there to hear it. She'd been so wrapped up in her career she hadn't thought about how bruised he must be feeling. The more she thought about it, the more she realised David's infidelity was as much her fault as his.

But it wasn't too late to put it right. Yes, she was hurt. But she wasn't about to let one silly mistake wreck ten years of marriage.

David came home just before lunch. 'I dropped Ollie off at Miriam's,' he said. 'I thought it would give us a chance to talk.'

'Good idea.' They sat on opposite sofas. For a long time neither of them could think of anything to say. Then they both started talking at once. 'You first,' David said.

Roo took a deep breath. 'I've been thinking about last night.'

'Me too.'

'I just want you to know I don't blame you for what happened. It was my fault as much as yours. I've been working too hard and neglecting you.'

'I haven't been very easy to live with, either.'

'You couldn't help it. I should have been more supportive. I should have realised your self-esteem was damaged when you lost your job.'

He frowned. 'Sorry?'

'But we can put things right. I've been thinking about it, and I reckon we should have counselling. And spend some time together as a couple.' She smiled. 'Which is why I've booked us a holiday.'

'You've done what?'

'A holiday. I called the travel agent this morning. After I finish in Normanford, we're jetting off to Tuscany for two weeks.'

David's brows drew together. 'I wish you'd asked me first.'

'I thought you'd be pleased.'

'I hate Italy.'

'But we always go there!'

'I know, and I've always hated it.'

'You've never said.'

'Oh, I have. Many times. But you never listen.'

'That's not true. You're just saying that because—'

'There, you see? You're not listening now. Why does it always have to be about you? Jesus, I can't even have an affair without it being something you've done! When are you going to stop telling me how I feel and actually listen to what I want?'

Roo sat back. 'Okay, I'm listening,' she said. 'What do you want, David?'

His eyes met hers, serious and direct. 'I want a divorce.'

Chapter 15

Roo felt as if she'd been punched in the solar plexus. 'You don't mean that.'

'There you go again, telling me what I'm feeling. I've been thinking about it for a while. Before all this business with Shauna happened.'

'But I thought we were happy!'

'We haven't been happy for a long time and you know it. When was the last time we talked? Laughed? Stayed in the same room for longer than five minutes without arguing?' She was silent. 'You see? There's nothing holding us together. Nothing really important, anyway.'

'We've got Ollie. Isn't he important?'

'You know he is.' A shadow passed across David's face. 'But he'd be better off if we weren't getting at each other all the time. God knows, he's virtually got two single parents as it is, the amount of time you're away.'

Roo seized on it eagerly. 'Is that what this is about? I could change that—'

'It wouldn't do any good. It's the time we spend together that's the problem, not the time we spend apart.'

This couldn't be happening. It shouldn't be happening. By now they should be holding hands and planning their second honeymoon. Instead her whole life was collapsing in front of her eyes and for once there wasn't a thing she could do about it.

'All couples go through bad patches,' she said.

'This isn't a bad patch, Roo. We want different things out of life. You want a successful career man, someone as driven and ambitious as you are. Someone who wants to go places.'

'And what do you want? A thick teenager who thinks Bartok is a brand of toilet cleaner?'

He winced. 'Leave Shauna out of this.'

'How can I? You brought her into it when you jumped into bed with her.' She stood up and paced the room. 'I can't believe this. She's half your age, David. You'll be a laughing stock.'

'It's better than being lonely,' he said.

His words struck her like a blow. 'Thanks a lot. I had no idea marriage to me was such torture.'

'It isn't. It wasn't.'

'So why do you want to throw it all away?'

'Because it isn't what I want any more.'

She stared out of the window at the common opposite. A woman walked by with a pair of laughing children and a black dog just like Harvey. For the first time in her life she didn't know what to say.

Finally she took refuge in bitterness. 'You're not having this house.'

'I don't want it. I never liked it much anyway.'

'But you chose it!'

'No, *you* chose it. Just like you chose everything else. I went along with it for a quiet life.'

Roo was shocked. She had no idea he'd been so resentful all these years. Her happy family life was built on a fantasy.

'All I want is Ollie,' David said. Roo swung round to face him.

'No way. You're not having my son!'

'He's my son, too.'

'But I'm his mother.'

'So what? You might have given birth to him but you haven't shown that much interest in him all these years.'

'That's not true!'

'Okay, where were you on his last birthday?'

She felt herself blush. 'I don't remember.'

'I do. And so does Ollie. You were in New York.'

'I couldn't help it. There was a flight delay—'

'You didn't even make it to his birthday party. How do you think he felt, listening to you singing "Happy Birthday" down the phone from three thousand miles away?'

'How do you think it felt for me? Anyway, I don't know why you're giving me a hard time. You missed more than your fair share of birthdays too!'

'At least I took an interest!' He twisted round in his seat to face her. 'Tell me, what football team does he support? Who's his best friend at school? You don't know, do you? You don't know the first thing about your own son. And you call yourself a mother!'

His words haunted her as she drove to pick up Ollie from Miriam's. Of course she was his mother! She loved him. And she did her best for him. He never wanted for anything, not like her when she'd been growing up. All right, so she didn't know which football team he supported, but what the hell did that prove? He was her baby, her flesh and blood, the most important person in her world.

And she couldn't lose him. She could already feel David slipping away from her; she couldn't let Ollie go too.

Miriam was madly curious when Roo arrived to collect Ollie. She greeted her with a baby at her breast as usual, her wild hair fastened up in a sock. 'Everything all right?' she asked. 'Why don't we crack open a bottle of Jeffrey's leek and potato wine and have a chat?'

Roo politely refused, which only brought an even more speculative gleam to Miriam's eye. Fortunately she was called away to deal with an emergency – Gustav had hung a noose from the branches of a tree and was trying to persuade his younger brother to try it out for size – so Roo managed to escape.

Maybe it would have been nice to pour her heart out to someone, she thought as she headed home. It shocked her that she couldn't think of anyone. Most of her friends were work colleagues, or mums from school, and not remotely close enough for her to confide in. Any real friends had gone by the wayside a long time ago when she'd stopped having time to return their calls and invitations.

She was half-tempted to drive straight back to Normanford with Ollie. But she knew David would only follow her, so in the end she went home.

David was waiting for her, in a far more subdued mood. 'I've been thinking,' he said. 'Perhaps it would be better if you took Ollie back with you, just for a couple of weeks. It's bound to be unsettling for him here, especially if I'm moving out. But that doesn't mean I'm handing him over to you permanently,' he added quickly. 'I'm still his father. And I won't have him used as some kind of emotional football.'

'Of course not!' Roo was shocked. 'I'd never do that.'

'I know. I shouldn't have said that. I'm sorry.'

'So what made you change your mind?'

He looked wary. 'I spoke to Shauna,' he admitted reluctantly. 'She convinced me it was for the best—'

'Shauna! What the hell's it got to do with her?'

'It might surprise you to know she understands our son a lot better than we do,' David said. 'Anyway, she's on your side. You should be thanking her.'

'For ruining my marriage?'

He smiled sadly. 'I think we managed that all by ourselves, don't you?'

She didn't see what was waiting for her in Sykes Street until she'd almost driven into it in the darkness. Ollie stirred and woke up. 'Mummy, what's that smell?'

'It's . . . um . . . compost, darling.' A great steaming mountain of it, right outside her house. 'For the garden.'

'What's it doing outside your house?'

Good question. She parked her car down the street and sat behind the wheel, staring straight ahead of her. She couldn't face this. Under her tough exterior she could feel all her strength sapping away.

Just let me get inside, just let me get through the night and in the morning I'll be strong enough to deal with it, she thought as she and Ollie marched bravely past the offending mountain of manure to their front doorstep. But as soon as she put her key in the door Matt appeared.

'What do you think?' he grinned. 'You said my car was a pile of shit, so I thought you'd like to know what the real thing is like!'

He was smiling all over his stupid face, so pleased with himself. Roo opened her mouth to retaliate and appalled herself by bursting into tears.

Matt's smile vanished. 'It was only a joke—' he stammered, as Roo fumbled with her key. She opened her door and fell through it, dragging Ollie and all her baggage behind her, then slammed it in Matt's bewildered face.

Once she'd started crying she couldn't stop. She sat on the sofa, hugging herself and rocking gently as the tears exploded out of her like the rush of a broken dam. Ollie pressed a scrap of toilet paper into her hand, wide-eyed at the sight of his fearless mummy dissolving in front of him.

She heard a man's voice. Matt stood over her, his face grave.

'How did you get in here?'

'The last tenant gave me a key so I could feed his goldfish while he was away.'

'You had no right to use it.' She covered her dripping nose with the shredded tissue. 'Can I have it back, please?'

'In a minute.' He crouched down so his face was level with hers. 'I just wanted to say I'm sorry. It was a joke. I didn't realise it would upset you so much.'

A hysterical laugh bubbled out through the tears. 'You think you've upset me? You really think that's why I'm in this state?'

'Isn't it?'

'I'll tell you what's upset me, shall I? I'm the most hated woman in town, I'm snowed under at work and I can't find anyone to look after my son because everyone detests me. Oh, and I've just caught my husband in bed with another woman. And he wants a divorce. I'd say next to all that a pile of horse shit is nothing, wouldn't you?'

'Bloody hell. I had no idea.'

'Well, now you know.' She stood up, mustering her dignity.

'Now I'm going to put my son to bed. See yourself out, would you? And leave the key.'

She went upstairs, washed her face and managed to pull herself together for Ollie's sake. He was still anxious as she tucked him into bed, but he was so tired he fell asleep straight away. Roo knelt beside his bed, stroking his fair hair off his angelic face. Poor baby. He didn't deserve to be caught up in this mess.

Matt was waiting for her downstairs with a large bottle of brandy and two glasses.

'I thought I told you to leave.'

He handed her a glass. 'Brandy. It's good for shock.'

'I don't drink spirits.'

'Now might be a good time to start.'

'If I start now I might not stop.'

'Does that worry you? Not being able to stop?'

She looked at him sharply. 'What do you mean?'

'You keep a lot of stuff bottled up, don't you? Why are you so frightened of losing control?'

'Because I'm a control freak.' That's what David called her. The thought of him made her down her brandy in one gulp.

'Blimey,' Matt said. 'For someone who doesn't drink you can really put it away.'

'Shut up and pour me another.'

'That's more like it.' He leaned across and refilled her glass. 'So what happened?'

She hadn't meant to tell him. The last thing she wanted was to drag the whole sorry mess up again. But the brandy loosened her tongue and somehow, bit by bit, he managed to coax the whole story out of her.

Why am I doing this? she kept thinking, as he filled up her glass again. Matt was the last person on earth she would ever dream of confiding in.

'I don't know how it happened,' she said. 'It was never meant to be like this.'

'No one ever means these things to happen. They just do.'

'Not to me they don't.'

'What makes you so sure?'

'That's why I chose David, because we were totally compatible and I knew he'd never cheat on me.'

Matt was amused. 'You make it sound like picking out a kettle in Argos!'

Roo couldn't see why he found it so funny. 'The principle's the same. Whatever you choose has to meet all your criteria, otherwise you end up with something totally unsuitable.'

Matt looked at her, caught between laughter and a frown, not sure whether to take her seriously. 'You're kidding, right? You're not telling me you went out with a shopping list for a man?'

'Well obviously love played a part in it.'

'I'm glad to hear it.'

'But I wouldn't have let myself fall in love with him if he hadn't been suitable.'

There had been boys at university she could have fallen for, if she'd been silly enough to let herself get carried away. Roo went out with some of them, but it always fizzled out after a few dates. Even if they didn't lose interest – which they nearly always did – Roo would have ended it. She didn't want to be like the other girls, getting drunk and suicidal because some man had dumped them. They reminded Roo too much of her mother, mascara running down her face as she worked her way through a bottle of gin after yet another broken romance.

If they'd listened to her, Roo could have told them their big mistake was in choosing the wrong man in the first place. They all went for the good-looking but feckless types. Roo couldn't understand the attraction – what good was a man who blew all his grant on dope and booze? – but the other girls were besotted. They slept with them, then got all hurt when they were dumped afterwards. But after two days of misery, they'd be back in the Student Union bar making exactly the same mistakes. Just like her mother always believed her latest charmer wasn't like all the others.

But Roo was different. She had no intention of having her heart broken so casually. Which was why she'd chosen David.

She didn't believe in love at first sight, but she'd known he was the right man for her within a few hours of meeting him at the bank where they both worked. And not just because he was tall, blond and good-looking. He owned his own home, he'd recently come out of a long-term relationship (although not too recently – she didn't want anyone on the rebound) and he was ambitious enough not to want a safe job in a bank for the rest of his life.

'Good husband material, in other words,' Matt said.

'Exactly.'

'I'm surprised you didn't run a credit check on him.'

'I did.' She was totally serious.

Matt spluttered with laughter. 'You're unbelievable, do you know that? Do you always let your head rule your heart?'

'It's the only way, unless you want to end up like—'

'Who?'

'My mother. And before you say anything, I don't want to talk about her,' she added warningly. 'Anyway, it worked for David and me. We were very compatible.'

'Maybe he decided he needed more than compatibility,' Matt said. 'Maybe he wanted chemistry.'

'I don't know what you mean.'

'You really don't, do you?' Matt shook his head in wonder. 'Haven't you ever seen someone across a crowded room and just thought even though they're the most unsuitable person in the world you had to have them there and then?'

Roo blinked at him. He seemed to be sitting a lot closer now, lounging on her sofa. He reminded her of an Australian surfer, all lean, tanned muscle and sun-bleached hair. Even his eyes were greeny blue like the ocean.

'Absolutely not,' she said tartly. 'Although you obviously have.'

'Meaning?'

'Meaning I've seen all those women you bring home. You're obviously some kind of serial shagger.'

He laughed. 'I think you'll find the term is "commitment phobic", so I'm reliably informed.'

'At least it's my head ruling my heart. With you it's a completely different part of your anatomy!' She twisted round on the sofa to face him. 'So why exactly do you find it so hard to commit, pizza boy? Did you have a difficult relationship with your mother? Are you secretly afraid you might be gay?'

Matt wasn't smiling any more. 'It's not complicated,' he said shortly, refilling her glass. 'I like women, that's all there is to it.'

'Maybe that's what I need,' Roo said.

'A woman?'

'A revenge shag.'

Their eyes met. It was a knowing look that spoke volumes. He was very attractive, she thought. And he had an awesome body. And he was only too willing and available. All she'd have to do was show the slightest bit of interest and—

'I don't think that would be a good idea,' he said. 'Two wrongs don't make a right and all that.'

'It might make me feel better.'

'It would make you feel better in the same way that brandy makes you feel better. The effect would wear off and in the morning you'd feel even more terrible.'

'You sound as if you're speaking from experience.'

'I am.' He finished his drink and stood up. 'I'd better go. It's getting late.'

'Don't you want another drink?' Roo was absurdly disappointed.

'No. And neither do you.' He picked up the bottle. 'Look, things will sort themselves out. Just try to relax. Life's too short.'

'That's an easy philosophy for someone who doesn't have the worries of the world on their shoulders.'

He sent her a long look. 'You'd be surprised,' he said.

She woke up on Saturday morning with a hangover and a deep sense of shame. Had she really made a pass at her next-door neighbour? Worse still, had he really turned her down? Matt

Collins, who was such a womaniser he practically had a revolving door fitted to his bedroom.

She would have preferred to avoid Matt, to spare her blushes. But he called round that afternoon while she was cleaning.

She threw herself behind the sofa, panicking. But as she lay sprawled out on the carpet, praying he wouldn't look through the window and see her, she heard voices at the back. Ollie had wandered into the yard and was talking to Matt over the fence.

There was no way she could avoid him. She had to brazen it out.

'Oh, hello.' Ollie was playing with Harvey, throwing a rubber ball which Harvey leapt up and caught.

'I knocked around the front but there was no answer.'

'Sorry. I was . . . um . . . on the phone.'

'Funny, your son said you were hiding behind the sofa.' He looked amused. 'I hope you weren't avoiding me.'

'Why should I?' Her blushing face gave her away. 'Look . . . um . . . thanks for last night. For listening, I mean.'

'Not at all. It was an interesting evening. We must do it again sometime.' Oh God, now he thought she was after him! She immediately saw herself through his eyes – newly separated and desperate. Easy pickings for a serial shagger.

'I just wanted to let you know I've got someone to get rid of the . . . er . . . you-know-what from the front of your house. And I came round to give you this.' He handed her a square box. Ollie recognised it before she did.

'A PlayStation!'

'It's not the newest model, but there are a couple of games on it. I thought it might help keep Ollie amused. Although it looks like he's already found a friend to keep him company.'

'Perhaps they'll keep each other out of trouble.' They both laughed as Harvey misjudged a catch and the hard rubber ball hit him squarely between the eyes. 'It's very kind of you to let us borrow this. Are you sure you don't need it?'

'Absolutely not. In fact you'd be doing me a favour taking it off my hands. I need to get on with some work and it's far too distracting.'

She frowned. 'Work?'

'My dissertation. Didn't I tell you, I'm doing a PhD in clinical psychology?' He grinned. 'Maybe you won't feel so bad now.'

She frowned. 'About what?'

'Propositioning me.' His brows lifted. 'Let's face it, it's got to be better than making a pass at a pizza boy.'

Chapter 16

Cat had made it to the front page of the *Normanford News* this time. She and her Fairbanks Action Group friends were clustered around the shiny black front door of 10 Downing Street clutching their petition.

Becky handed the paper to Roo with her morning mail. 'Honestly, you'd think Mum could have bought something decent to meet the Prime Minister. That suit's ages old,' she groaned. 'By the way, we've had a letter from them. They're organising a public meeting and they want to know if you'll come along and put Fairbanks' case.'

'Tell them I'll let them know.' Secretly she didn't relish the prospect. Public meetings had a habit of turning into public slanging matches. They were hardly a forum for reasoned argument and debate.

She tried to say as much to George Fairbanks later that morning. 'Nonsense, you've got to go,' he insisted.

'Even if I get lynched?'

'If you're so sure you're doing the right thing by Fairbanks and its workers you've got nothing to fear, have you?'

Roo glared at him. He didn't care if she was torn apart by an angry mob. Anything that might send her scuttling back to London with her tail between her legs. But she wasn't going anywhere.

'I'd be glad of the chance to put my case,' she said through gritted teeth.

'That's the spirit.' George Fairbanks chuckled. 'Oh, and by the way, I've organised a little staff outing for tonight. I hope you can come.'

She eyed him suspiciously. 'Why?'

'It'll give you a chance to get to know the staff a bit better. Break down a few barriers. I suppose you'd call it team-building.' He beamed at her. 'I think you'll enjoy it.'

She very much doubted it, but to show willing she told George she'd try and arrange a babysitter.

'You do that,' he said. 'We're meeting back here at seven thirty.'

'Tell me where to go and I'll make my own way there.'

'And spoil the surprise? No lass, you meet us back here at seven thirty.'

Billy caught up with her as she was walking back to her office. 'Penny for them?' he said.

She looked up, distracted. 'Sorry?'

'Your thoughts. Let me guess, it's only Monday morning and you're missing Ollie already?'

Roo suddenly realised that he thought Ollie had gone back to his father in London. 'There's been a change of plan. He's staying with me. David had to work,' she explained. She couldn't bring herself to talk about her marital problems, not yet. It was embarrassing enough that she'd confided in Matt.

'So have you got your childcare sorted out?'

'I managed to find someone in the end. A woman called Angie.' Although it had cost her dear. After bribing her with double rates Angie had finally agreed she could fit Ollie in full-time: 'Just for the next few weeks.'

'Angie Bennett?' Billy said. 'Lives on Stokehill Road?'

'Do you know her?'

'She looks after Megan and Liam after school.' He grinned. 'Small world, isn't it?'

'Isn't it?' That was all she needed, running into Cat every evening!

'I've got some good news for you,' Billy said. 'I've been talking to Roger Fleet, the MD of the Park Hotels group, about contract furniture. It turns out he's carrying out a major revamp of some of their older hotels and he's looking for a new supplier. It all looks pretty hopeful. I wondered if you'd like to come along to the meeting.'

'Yeah, sure,' she replied, her mind elsewhere. 'Get Becky to put it in the diary.'

'Of course, us winning this contract would depend on you sleeping with him.'

'No problem.'

Billy snapped his fingers in front of her face. 'Hello? Anyone there?'

'What? Oh, sorry. I've just got a lot on my mind, that's all. I take it you've seen this morning's paper?'

'Oh, that.' His face fell.

'Apparently they're organising a public meeting. George wants me to go along.'

'What for?'

'Sacrificial goat, I think.'

Billy sighed. 'I'm sorry.'

'It's not your fault.'

'It's my wife. Why did Cat have to start this? I told her not to get involved.'

'I think she's getting at me.'

He looked shocked. 'She wouldn't do that!'

'Maybe not. I just wonder if she'd be taking such an interest if it was someone else doing this job.'

'Do you want me to talk to her about it?'

She shook her head. 'This is something Cat and I have to sort out for ourselves.' As Billy walked away she called after him, 'I don't suppose you know anything about this trip George Fairbanks is organising tonight?'

Billy shook his head. 'He hasn't said anything to me. What's it all about?'

'I don't know,' Roo said. 'But I've got a nasty feeling I'm about to find out.'

Cat was surprised to see Elizabeth Montague back in the salon. There was a young woman with her, fair-haired and ethereally beautiful in designer jeans.

Maxine fell over herself to get to her. They spoke for a few minutes, then she called Cat over.

'Mrs Montague would like a word with you,' she said, her lips stretched in a fake smile.

'It's more of a favour, really.' Elizabeth turned to the young woman beside her. 'This is my daughter Charlotte – you know, the one I was telling you about? She's getting married in a month's time. I was telling her how terrific you are and she wondered if you'd be interested in doing her hair for the wedding.'

'It's just me and two bridesmaids – and Mum, if you have time,' Charlotte said. 'My usual hairdresser was going to come up from London but he's off to Cuba for a month. Mum reckons you'd be perfect.'

'Are you sure you wouldn't prefer Julie to do it?' Maxine interrupted, unable to contain herself. 'She is our senior stylist—'

'I wouldn't trust your senior stylist to trim my garden hedge.' Elizabeth smiled sweetly. 'I know it's short notice, but we'd be terribly grateful,' she said to Cat.

'I—'

'Of course she'll do it,' Maxine stepped in quickly. 'Why don't you come through to the office? We can talk about fees and so on.' As Maxine guided them past, she heard her say, 'So what's Sean Connery actually like close up? Is he a good kisser?'

Billy came home late that night, by which time Cat was bubbling over with excitement.

'Guess what?' she said.

He collapsed on the sofa. 'Don't tell me, you and your militant mates are going to throw yourselves under Frederick Fairbanks' Jag?'

Cat's smile faltered. 'You're in a funny mood. Have you had a bad day or something?'

'You could say that. Everyone's talking about that bloody photo in the paper. You've really done it now.'

'Good. It was supposed to stir things up.'

'You don't get it, do you? How do you think it makes me look? You do realise I could lose my job?'

'You'll all lose your jobs if she gets her way.'

He sighed. 'So this is about Roo, is it?'

'No!' She turned away so he wouldn't see her blushing face.

'Yes it is. What's she done to make you hate her so much?'

'I told you, it's got nothing to do with Ruby!'

'She's family, Cat. You should be on her side.'

'Why does she need me on her side? She's got you.'

He frowned. 'Don't tell me you're jealous.'

'Would you blame me if I was? The amount of time you two spend together—'

'We work together. What am I supposed to do, ignore her?'

'You don't have to be at her beck and call all the time. I bet if she called right now you'd be round to her place like a shot!'

'Maybe. But only because she's a friend and I know what a hard time she's having at the moment.'

'No more than she deserves,' Cat said in an undertone.

'Actually she doesn't deserve it. She's working bloody hard, trying to get Fairbanks back on its feet, and all she's getting is hassle. She doesn't need it, especially from you.'

'So tell me,' Cat said. 'Explain to me exactly how my cousin is doing such a fantastic job saving Fairbanks when all she's doing is putting half the town out of work.'

Billy regarded her coldly. 'You wouldn't understand.'

'Because I'm just a dumb hairdresser, you mean? Not like Ruby, with her brilliant business brain.'

'When are you going to stop comparing yourself to your cousin?'

When you do, Cat thought.

She'd been looking forward to telling him about her triumph at the salon. But now she realised he wouldn't be interested. Nothing she did could ever compare with Ruby's impressive achievements.

Including this campaign. If she was honest, the main reason she'd got involved was because she wanted to make her family proud of her. She wanted them to sit up and take notice, to realise she wasn't just a mum with a humdrum job. But it had all backfired on her.

★

191

'Is this your idea of team building?' Roo could hardly contain her dismay when the minibus pulled up outside the Ponderosa.

'It'll be a good night out. Your mum's doing a turn tonight.'

'So I noticed.' She'd already caught sight of the poster advertising 'Cabaret Singer Sadie Starr'.

As if this evening wasn't bad enough. She'd already had to endure being packed into a minibus with a gang of Fairbanks workers all giving her daggers looks. And now this. She wanted to turn tail and run, but she was trapped.

The club was surprisingly full, with most of the tables taken and people leaning on the bar. 'Looks like there's nowhere to sit,' Roo said hopefully.

'Don't fret, lass. I've had Jan keep us a table at the front. Don't want to miss anything, do we?'

Once they'd reached the table, all the others gathered at one end, leaving Roo at the other. When they ordered a round of drinks they left her out so she had to go to the bar and get her own.

'Doesn't look like this team-building lark is going to work, does it?' George said in her ear.

'You knew it wouldn't. That's why you brought me here, isn't it? To humiliate me.' Roo fought to stop her voice shaking with anger.

'You could always leave, if you don't like it.'

She stared at him. Wouldn't he love it if she walked out now? She put down her drink and stood up.

'You wish.' She headed to the bar and returned a few minutes later. 'I've put my credit card behind the bar,' she told the huddle of workers. 'All tonight's drinks are on me. Just to show there are no hard feelings.'

There was a murmur of approval from the other end of the table. Roo turned to George. 'Just so you know, I'm not going anywhere, Mr Fairbanks,' she hissed. 'And if you want a fight, you've got one.'

George was spared from answering by a blast of music from the stage. The man on the keyboard announced Sadie's name and suddenly there she was, in the spotlight. She wore a peacock-blue spangly dress split up the side, which showed far too much leg for Roo's liking, her blonde hair swept up on top of her head, sparkly earrings catching the light.

Jesus wept. Roo closed her eyes briefly to block out the shame as her mother went into a lively rendition of 'Copacabana'. She could hardly bear to look at anyone else, not wanting to see the pitying looks on their faces. Why did Sadie insist on embarrassing herself like this, night after night?

The song ended and suddenly there was rapturous applause. Roo steeled herself to glance around. They were enjoying it. Not just being polite, but really loving it. She looked back at the stage, wondering if she'd missed something. Surely she wasn't that good? Roo had been so embarrassed she'd hardly listened. But as Sadie slowed down the tempo and went into Patsy Cline's 'Crazy', she realised with a shock that her mother wasn't as bad as she'd thought. In fact, she was almost good. If she closed her eyes and forgot it was her mother up there in a dress ten years too young for her, she could imagine she was actually a decent singer.

Then, when the next song ended, Sadie did something that made Roo's blood run cold. She went over and had a word with the man on the keyboard, who started searching frantically through his music. Then she came to the front of the tiny platform stage and said, 'I'd like to dedicate this next song to my daughter, who's sitting in the front row.' Roo shrivelled in her seat as all eyes turned in her direction. 'It's a very special song and I hope you'll all like it.' She barely heard as Sadie began to sing 'Goodbye Ruby Tuesday', her heart was thumping so loudly in her ears. Oh God, why did she have to humiliate her like that?

She jumped as someone tapped her on the shoulder. 'Excuse me, are you Sadie's daughter?' Roo looked around cautiously at the middle-aged woman standing behind her. 'You won't re-member me, but I used to live next door to you. In Sykes Street.' she smiled. 'How's your nanna? I heard she wasn't too well.'

''She's . . . um . . . on the mend.'

'Give her my love, won't you? Tell her Elsie sends her best.'

'Thanks.'

As the woman moved away, another took her place. It turned out she'd gone to school with Sadie. 'She was always such a livewire. You never knew what she was going to do next.'

That sounded like Sadie, Roo thought.

Soon a small queue of people had formed, all wanting to say hello to Ruby Tuesday Moon. Even her fellow Fairbanks workers thawed slightly once they realised who she was. It seemed as if everyone knew her mother, or her grandmother. And she was surprised at the warm way they talked about Sadie, and asked about Nanna's health.

'You see? We're not such a bad lot once you get to know us,' George said.

Roo glanced at her mother, now belting out a Tina Turner number on stage. 'I suppose not,' she agreed.

'I'm sorry, Roo, I really am. But it's the bank's decision and there's nothing I can do about it.' Mike Garrett looked regretful. 'We can't approve any more funds.'

'But you've seen the cashflow forecasts. Now we've made all those savings to the overheads and tightened up our credit controls, our financial picture looks a lot healthier.'

'We're all delighted with what you've done. But we still don't consider Fairbanks a good financial risk.'

'What about the potential new markets I've outlined?'

'That's all they are. Potential. They mean nothing until they're translated into solid sales.'

Roo stared down at the rows of carefully prepared figures in front of her. She'd been up all night putting them together. Now it looked as if her hard work had been for nothing. 'So that's it. Fairbanks is finished.'

'Don't take it so personally,' Mike said. 'No one said you had to make this work. Your job was to find out if the company had a viable future, not to save it from ruin. You've already done more than enough.'

'But I could have done more.' It was maddening that she'd got so close and there was a big brick wall in front of her. She knew

194

she could make the factory work, if only she had more time and money.

Maybe Mike was right. Maybe she should just wind things up and leave. No one would blame her if she did.

But she couldn't. Somewhere along the line, it had become personal. She'd broken her own golden rule and got involved.

She felt like going straight home but she wanted to go and break the news to George Fairbanks. She wasn't looking forward to it, but knew she wouldn't sleep that night if she left it until the morning.

It was early evening and the sun was out for once as she drove through the factory gates. Most of the workers were leaving. They didn't greet Roo but at least they weren't hostile any more. In a way that made her feel worse.

George Fairbanks was still in his office. He gazed out of the window, leaning on his stick, watching the workers leave.

'There they go,' he said. 'I wonder how long it'll be before they're leaving permanently.' He turned to look at her, the shadows casting deep, troubled lines on his face. 'That's what you've come to tell me, isn't it?'

Roo chose her words carefully. 'The bank wasn't as helpful as I had hoped.'

'And you couldn't wait to come and tell me the good news.' He turned to look out of the window again. 'I daresay you're pleased. You can tick us off your list and go back to London.'

'That's not fair!' Roo protested. 'I've worked hard to keep this factory going. Okay, so maybe you didn't approve of some of the things I did, but at least they gave this place a fighting chance. Which is more than it had before.'

'I know.' To her surprise, George backed down. 'I'm sorry if I've given you a hard time. I suppose I was just blaming you for everything going wrong.' His eyes were sad. 'I do appreciate what you've done. I'm just sorry you didn't get here a year ago, then maybe you could have made a real difference.'

'So am I,' Roo said, and was surprised to realise she meant it.

He gazed at her with respect. 'You're a fighter, I'll give you

195

that. There aren't many that would put up with what you have over the past few weeks.'

'Thanks to you.'

'Aye, I know I haven't made it easy for you,' he chuckled. 'I'm a stubborn old fool, I know that. But this factory's been my life since I was a young lad, and it broke my heart to see it being torn apart by you and that son of mine.' There was a faraway look in his eye. 'I just wish I could have done something about it, before—' he broke off.

'Before what?' Roo asked.

He looked over his shoulder at her. 'Before I die,' he said.

Chapter 17

Roo laughed uneasily. 'You've got years yet!' But George shook his head, his face sombre.

'Cancer,' he said. 'The doctors found it last Christmas.'

'Can't they do anything?'

'It's too far gone. I've surprised them by lasting this long. They thought I'd be dead by Easter!' He smiled wistfully. 'I've hung on because I've been waiting for a miracle. Not for me, for this place. But it doesn't look like it's going to happen now, does it?'

Roo suddenly felt overwhelmingly sad. Against all the odds, she'd grown to like George Fairbanks. She'd begun to understand what the factory meant to him. It wasn't just a building, or numbers on a balance sheet. It was his whole life. And now he was going to die, and his factory was going to die with him.

'Do you know what hurts most?' he said. 'That I've let them all down. The workers, my father, my grandfather. They trusted me to keep this place going and I failed them all.'

'You can't say that.'

'Why not? It's true.' He turned away from her. 'I've been looking out at this same view for thirty years. It's changed a hell of a lot in that time. All that land over there used to belong to the pit. Now look what's happened to it.'

She followed George's gaze out of the window. Across the river, JCBs were churning up the ground to put in foundations for new houses. Some neat rows of homes had already been built. 'I expect they'll be building on this land when the factory closes,' he sighed. 'All these people living here, and not one of them with a job.'

'Would they be allowed to build on this site?'

'Try stopping them,' George said grimly. 'I've already had offers from property developers. As soon as they found out this place was in trouble they were sniffing around, asking me if I wanted to sell. Bloody vultures!'

'Is that right?' Roo gazed across the river. An idea was beginning to form in her mind. 'Mr Fairbanks,' she said. 'What if I told you I might be able to save this factory?'

George regarded her suspiciously. 'I'd say you were a flaming miracle worker,' he said.

'Sell the factory?' Frederick Fairbanks stared at her. 'Have you been drinking, Ms Hennessy?'

'It's the answer to all our problems. This site is prime development land. It's worth a small fortune. And the factory itself is a liability. It's too big and needs too many repairs. If we were to try and put everything right we'd be in the red for years.'

'I agree. Our heating bill alone is astronomical.'

'So why don't we sell it? We could use the money to lease a smaller, purpose-built unit out of town, which would be more efficient and cost less to run. And we'd have enough money left over to pay off our existing loan and buy the new machinery we need. We wouldn't have to take out another loan to get it, so we'd save money on repayments and interest.'

'I suppose it makes sense,' Frederick agreed.

'It makes perfect sense. I've already talked to a couple of management agents from the local business parks and I reckon we could negotiate very favourable rates on a new place. They're crying out for tenants.'

Frederick Fairbanks looked tempted. Then he shook his head. 'My father would never agree to it,' he said shortly. 'He's far too attached to this place.'

'I talked to him last night. He thinks we should do it.'

Frederick gazed at her in admiration. 'How the hell did you manage that? I've been trying to talk him into it for years.'

'I have my ways.' It had been a long, emotional conversation. But in the end George Fairbanks had reluctantly agreed that even his father would have approved of getting rid of the building if it meant keeping the family firm in business.

Cat was getting out of her car at the childminder's when Ruby's gleaming silver Audi glided into the parking space behind hers. Ruby got out, looking pleased with herself.

Cat greeted her coolly. 'Nanny's day off, is it?'

'Can't I spend some time with my son if I want to?'

'Of course.' In an undertone, she added, 'That'll be a novelty for him.'

Angie took a long time to answer the door. 'I'm afraid we've had a bit of an accident,' she said, just as Ollie appeared, looking tearful and wearing an unfamiliar pair of Manchester United football shorts.

'He wet himself,' Megan announced. 'All over Angie's sofa.'

Cat glanced at Ruby, who'd turned purple with mortification. She might feel sympathy for any other mum, but not her cousin.

'He's a baby.' Megan's nose wrinkled in disgust. 'Even Liam's more grown-up than *him*!'

'Shut up, Megan. Can't you see he's upset?' Cat hissed as she hustled her towards the car. She felt sorry for the poor little boy; he was obviously terrified of his overbearing mother. But she was also relieved, because it was usually Liam wearing those football shorts. And at least it wiped the smug look off Ruby's face!

Roo smoothed her Stella McCartney dress over her hips and twisted to catch her back view in the full-length mirror. It gave her a slight shock to see herself looking so sexy, especially with the Christian Louboutin heels. When she'd bought them, she'd never imagined she'd be wearing them to save her marriage.

She still had a chance, she thought. David had called every night this week. Admittedly it was to speak to Ollie, but they'd had a few words, and she sensed he was missing his family. His fling with Shauna was running its course.

Tonight he was coming up to Normanford to see Ollie, and she had a feeling she might be able to convince him to give their marriage another go.

She'd prepared carefully. She'd planned a special meal, medallions of beef in a red wine sauce. Laden with saturated fat but all in a good cause. They were marinating in the fridge now, along with some ready-prepared green beans and dauphinoise potatoes and a couple of Marks and Spencer crème brûlées.

She'd also shaved her legs, plucked her eyebrows, slathered herself in body lotion until her skin gleamed and now she set about putting her make-up on. It was an unfamiliar experience. Her usual make-up routine of mascara, pencil and lipgloss took about a minute and a half. All this extra stuff – foundation, blusher, several different shades of eyeshadow – was a new experience for her. It made her think of her mother, sitting at her dressing table, her make-up laid out before her. Her warpaint, she always called it. Roo understood why now. She felt as if she was going into battle.

She would have quite liked a mother's advice at the moment, to reassure her she was doing the right thing. But not her mother's. Sadie's judgement could hardly be relied on, especially when it came to men.

The crash from downstairs made her jab her mascara wand in her eye. She rushed downstairs to find pandemonium in the kitchen. Ollie stood by the open fridge amid a wreckage of broken crockery, scattered vegetables and red wine marinade. With him was Harvey, his muzzle dripping with what looked like crème brûlée.

At the same time Matt rushed out into his yard, yelling for Harvey. 'In here,' Roo called out.

He vaulted the fence and came in through the back door. 'What the – oh Christ!' He stopped dead. 'But I only let him out for a pee!'

They both looked at Ollie, who burst into tears. 'He was lonely!' he wailed.

'I take it that was meant for David?' Matt said.

'He's ruined everything.' She laughed to stop herself from crying.

'I'm really sorry. Is there anything I can do?'

'You could go to Pizza Paradise and get us a takeaway.'

Matt gazed around at the devastation. 'I've got a better idea. Why don't you take him out?'

'How am I supposed to find a babysitter?'

'I'll look after Ollie. It's the least I can do after Harvey ruined your evening. What do you say, Ollie? We could have a lads' night in. A few beers, a session on the PlayStation—'

'Yeah!' Ollie jumped up and down.

Roo smiled reluctantly. 'If you're sure . . .'

'Like I said, it's the least I can do.' He grabbed Harvey's collar. 'Come on, you. I'll be round about eight, if that's okay?'

'Fine.'

As he hauled Harvey to the door, he turned back and said, 'You look good, by the way.'

'Thanks.' Their eyes met, and she was astonished to see he was blushing.

Ten minutes later, when she'd cleared up the mess and Ollie was at the sitting room window watching out for his father's car, the phone rang.

'There's been a change of plan,' David said. 'I won't be able to make it.'

'No!' Roo looked at her son, his nose pressed to the glass. 'What am I going to tell Ollie? He's been looking forward to this.' And so have I, she thought.

'I know, I'm sorry.'

'You could have let us know sooner.' Disappointment lanced through her. 'Anyway, what's so bloody important you can't come up and see your own son?'

'It's a bit difficult. I just need to be at home at the moment, that's all.' Something in his voice sent warning signals up her spine. 'David, what is it? What's wrong?'

There was a long silence. 'Shauna's just found out she's pregnant. Roo? Are you still there?'

'Yes, I'm here.' She took a deep, steadying breath. 'I don't know what to say.'

'Neither did I, when she told me.'

There was a long pause. 'So what are you going to do?'

'I don't know yet. Shauna's in a bit of a state, which is why I have to stay with her.'

She glanced at Ollie and lowered her voice. 'Even if it means letting your own son down?'

'I'm sorry, okay? Believe me, I'd rather this wasn't happening! Tell Ollie I'll be up next weekend.'

'If Shauna lets you out of her sight.'

'And give him my love,' David said, ignoring her.

'He'll be heartbroken.'

'Now you know how I felt all those times I had to tell him you weren't coming home,' David said shortly, and hung up.

'Was that Daddy?' Ollie demanded as she put the phone down. 'When's he coming? Has he brought me a present?'

'Sorry, darling.' Roo steeled herself. 'Daddy can't come today. He's . . . um . . . had some bad news.'

She hugged him as sobs shook his little body. She tried to say all the right comforting things about how his daddy loved him and hated to let him down, but all the time she kept thinking what an utterly selfish bastard David was.

Ollie still hadn't calmed down when Matt turned up half an hour later, laden with popcorn and crisps. 'All ready for our boys' night in?' he said cheerily. 'I've brought a few provisions; I had a feeling your mum wouldn't be a junk food fan . . . what's wrong?' he stopped when he saw Ollie's tear-ravaged face, his head buried in Roo's lap.

'David's not coming,' Roo explained through tight lips. 'Something came up.'

'Ah.' Matt read the unspoken message in her eyes and immediately took charge of the situation. 'There's no reason why we shouldn't still have our fun. Why don't we take this lot next door and watch a video? We could even order a pizza, if you like. And Mummy can come too. She can be an honorary lad for the evening.'

'I don't know—' Roo began to say.

Ollie looked up tearfully. 'Have you got *Star Wars*?'

'Have I got *Star Wars*? I've got the lot. And *Lord of the Rings*.'

'*Star Wars* is better.'

'I don't know about that. I reckon Gandalf could beat Darth Vader any day.'

'But Darth's got a light sabre. Gandalf's only got a stupid old stick!'

'We'll see about that!' Matt winked at her. 'Everyone round to my place, then!'

Matt's house was messy and lined with books. More books and papers were strewn all over the table. 'Sorry, I didn't know I was going to be having guests.' He collected them up in an untidy pile.

Roo glanced at one of the closely typed sheets. 'Are you really doing a PhD?'

'No, I only say that to impress women. Of course I'm doing a PhD. My thesis is in non-verbal communication.' He swept last Sunday's newspapers off the sofa, clearing a space for her. 'Make yourself comfortable. Ollie and I will order the pizza.'

'Don't I get to choose too?'

He frowned, mock severe. 'Excuse me? Are you a man?'

'No, but—'

'Then stay out of it. Ordering pizza is men's work, isn't that right, Ollie?'

She smiled to herself, listening to them in the hall bickering over the takeaway menu. Matt was just what her son needed.

She examined the photos on his mantelpiece. Lots of studenty groups of lads in wacky poses. A couple of family shots. But only one girl. Surprising, considering the number of lady friends he seemed to have.

Roo studied it. She was red-haired, green-eyed, freckled and pretty. 'I haven't seen this one before,' she said when Matt came back from phoning his pizza order.

'No, you wouldn't.'

'Don't tell me, she was the one that got away?'

'You could say that. Ham and mushroom all right for you?' he changed the subject, his smile flashing into place. Roo put the photo back, wondering if she'd touched a nerve. Matt might know all about her private life, but she knew surprisingly little about his.

When the takeaway arrived they all huddled on the sofa and watched the film. Roo tried not to mind when Ollie absent-mindedly shared his pizza with Harvey. She was too tense to concentrate on the film, which she'd already seen a million times. She couldn't stop thinking about David and Shauna. Matt didn't seem to be paying much attention either. She hoped he wasn't too bored.

By the time the film finished Ollie had fallen asleep, propped up against Harvey. 'He missed the end,' Matt said.

'He knows it off by heart anyway.' Roo got up. 'Thanks for a lovely evening. It was just what he needed—'

'Don't go.'

'I need to get Ollie to bed.'

'He's okay there for a bit longer. We haven't had a chance to talk.'

'Are you sure I'm not keeping you from your work?' she asked as Matt fetched a couple of beers from the fridge.

'Believe me, you're a welcome break.' He snapped the top off one of the bottles and handed it to her. 'Sorry, did you want a glass?'

'This is fine.' She eyed the bottle warily, then sat with it on her lap.

'Why didn't your husband show?'

'His girlfriend's pregnant.'

'No way!'

'So it looks like there isn't going to be a reconciliation after all,' she said.

'I'm sorry.'

'To be honest, I didn't really think there would be. But I had to try, for this one's sake.' She pushed Ollie's fair hair back off his brow. 'It's him I feel sorry for. I feel like I've failed him.'

'How do you work that out?'

'If I hadn't screwed up he'd still have two parents. Now he's only got me.'

'He's still got his father.'

'It's not the same, is it? I was brought up with just my mother and I always wished I had two parents.'

'That depends on the parents. My mum brought me and my brother up after our dad died and she made a terrific job of it.'

'Lucky you. Mine was a nightmare. Half the time it felt as if I was looking after her, not the other way round.'

'What about your father?'

'I don't know anything about him.' Roo stroked Ollie's hair distractedly. She'd thought he might stay fair like David, but it was already turning from pale straw to the colour of golden syrup. Reminders of David were slowly slipping from her life.

'I should have tried harder,' she said. 'I could have held it together if I'd done things differently.'

'This is a marriage, not an exam. You don't get a better grade by putting in more effort. Not if the chemistry isn't there.'

'Chemistry! You mean your "eyes across a crowded room" thing?'

'That's what it's all about.' Their eyes met and held. Roo could instantly see why he was such an expert in non-verbal communication. His body language was sending her all kinds of messages.

And then the doorbell rang.

'Where the fuck have you been?' She heard the girl's voice, shrill with anger. 'Eleven, you said. Outside Ritzy's. I've been waiting hours!'

'I'm sorry.' Matt muttered something she couldn't make out. Seconds later the girl barged her way into the room. She was a tall, Scandinavian blonde with ice-blue eyes that raked over Roo like an arctic storm.

'This all looks very cosy,' she snapped. 'Who the hell are you?'

'This is Roo, my next-door neighbour.'

'I'm just leaving.' She gathered Ollie up in her arms.

'Let me.' Matt stepped forward to take him, but Roo held on.

'No, it's fine. Sorry if I ruined your evening,' she said in an undertone.

'You didn't,' Matt whispered.

As she left, she heard the girl say, 'Bit old for you, isn't she?'

She didn't hear Matt's reply. She didn't need to. Her face flamed as she let herself into her house, still with Ollie bundled in her arms.

Roo spent the rest of the weekend veering wildly in her emotions. Sometimes she felt utterly depressed, as if all the light had gone out of her life. And then sometimes she was filled with vengeful thoughts about how to make David as miserable as possible.

She spent a lot of time playing with Ollie, trying to make up for letting him down and losing his father so carelessly. Strangely, he didn't seem to mind too much.

'Are you and Daddy getting divorced?' he asked out of the blue, while they were watching a repeat of *You've Been Framed*.

Roo kept her eyes fixed on the screen, where yet another person was falling face first into their birthday cake. 'What makes you ask?'

'When Harry Patterson's mum and dad got divorced, he got a Gamecube.'

Roo slipped her arm around his shoulders and held him close. So much for being emotionally scarred!

Two days later it was a different story. Ollie trailed down the stairs, his pyjama trousers in his hand, looking distressed. 'I had an accident,' he mumbled.

'Oh dear, never mind.' She tried to be brisk and matter-of-fact about it as she stripped off the sheets and stuffed them in the washing machine, but deep down she was troubled. Ollie hadn't wet himself since he came out of nappies three years ago. Now he'd done it twice in a week. Perhaps all this business with David was getting to him more than he was letting on.

'Do I have to go to Angie's?' he pleaded, pushing his cereal around his bowl. 'I don't like it there.'

'Of course you do. You'll have a lovely time, playing with all the other boys and girls. Now hurry up. We don't want to be late, do we?'

Ollie grumbled all the way to the childminder's, but Roo

switched off, already mentally planning her day ahead. She had to call some local property developers, to find out what level of interest there might be in the Fairbanks site. She'd also arranged to visit a couple of business parks in the area with Frederick, to see if they might make suitable premises for the new factory.

And she would see Leonard about updating the machinery. She'd love to see his face when she broke the news to him about that!

It was a hugely busy and satisfying day, and she barely had time to think about all her other problems until her mobile rang around four o'clock that afternoon.

'Roo? It's Angie, the childminder.'

'Oh Lord, what is it now?' Roo scrolled through a file on her computer, her eyes fixed on the screen. Why did Angie have to call her about every little thing? 'Don't tell me he's wet himself again.'

'Nothing like that.' Angie sounded anxious. 'Look, I don't want you to panic, but . . . Ollie's gone missing!'

There was a police car outside Angie's house. Roo's heart sped up when she saw it. She'd raced straight there, crashing red lights and leaving blaring horns in her wake. It was a miracle she hadn't wrapped herself around a juggernaut.

Angie's door was open. Roo heard the clamour of voices coming from inside before she reached the gate. One of them stopped her in her tracks.

'What do you mean, you don't know how it happened? You're paid to keep an eye on these kids, not let them wander off! Christ, she could be anywhere!'

In the sitting room, Angie was on the sofa in tears while Cat raged at her. A young policewoman was trying to quieten her.

'Calm down, Mrs Kitchener. This isn't getting us anywhere.'

'Calm down? How do you expect me to calm down when my daughter is somewhere out on the streets? And what are you standing around here for? Why aren't you out there looking for her?'

'We're doing all we can.'

'She's been gone half an hour. Anything could have—' She spotted Roo in the doorway. 'What are you doing here?'

'Her little boy's missing too.' Angie fumbled with her tissue.

Their eyes met, and for a second they recognised the fear and panic in each other's faces. Then Cat lost her temper again. 'Great,' she said. 'So you let two kids just wander out of here? What kind of a place is this?'

'Is there anything we can do?' Roo asked the policewoman.

Cat turned on her. 'What the hell do you think we can do?'

'I don't know. But I know screaming the place down isn't going to help.' She turned back to the policewoman. 'Should we be out searching?'

'Good idea,' Cat said. 'I know Megan's favourite places. We could try there.'

The policewoman looked unsure. 'You don't want to hamper the search—'

'You don't seem to be getting very far, do you?' She hoisted her bag over her shoulder. 'That's it, I'm going.' She looked back at Roo. 'Are you coming?'

Out in the street their momentum deserted them. 'Where do we start?' Roo said.

'I don't know, do I? Megan likes going up to the common—'

'So let's go there.'

'Yes, but she likes to feed the ducks on the river, too.'

'Then we'll split up. You take the common and I'll go down by the river.'

'No!' Cat looked down at the ground. 'I don't want to be on my own,' she said quietly.

Roo knew what she meant. 'We'll start with the river,' she said.

The river bank seemed a wild, unfriendly place with its overgrown shaggy hedges and uneven, litter-strewn paths.

'I'm calling Billy.' Cat pressed the number into her mobile phone. She listened for a few moments, then gave up in frustration. 'Sod it, it's switched off.'

'He's gone to Wakefield for an account managers' meeting.'

'I do know where my own husband is, thanks very much!'

They searched in silence, both looking around. Roo shuddered, her mind filled with pictures she didn't want to see. Pictures of lurking figures, of their two innocent children being lured away. Ollie was so naïve, he'd go with anyone who seemed friendly . . .

'It's only been half an hour,' she said aloud. 'Nothing could have happened to them in that time.'

'You think so?' Cat's voice had a desperate edge.

'They've probably just gone off on an adventure and not realised the trouble they've caused. You know what children are like. They're in a world of their own most of the time. It never occurs to them their parents might be frantic.'

Cat's smile wobbled. 'Do you remember that time we decided to go to the pictures without telling anyone?'

Roo nodded. 'There we were, watching the film and stuffing our faces with popcorn, not realising how worried everyone was.'

'And then we came out and found ourselves in the middle of a police search!'

There was a long silence. 'At least they're together,' Cat said.

Roo's phone rang, disturbing the peace. They both looked at it, then at each other until Cat exclaimed, 'Oh, for God's sake!' and snatched it away from her.

She listened for a moment then hung up. Roo saw the colour drain out of her face and had just started to brace herself for the worst when Cat said, 'They're safe.'

That's when they realised they'd been holding hands, their nails scoring grooves into each other's flesh.

They were already back at Angie's, side by side on the sofa. Ollie's lip was trembling in terrified anticipation, but Megan looked composed and unrepentant.

'We picked them up on Masefield Road. They said they were on their way to the stables,' the policeman said.

'Ollie wanted to see the horses,' Megan said.

'I could have done that young lady for resisting arrest. She bit me when I tried to get her into the car.' He nursed his hand, which still bore tiny teeth marks.

'You told me never to go with strangers,' Megan said to Cat primly.

'I also told you never to wander off on your own, but you didn't take much notice of that, did you?'

'I wasn't on my own,' Megan pointed out. 'Ollie was with me.' Ollie hung his head in shame.

'Got an answer for everything, hasn't she?' the policeman said.

'Just like her mother,' Roo muttered.

Cat turned on her. 'What's that supposed to mean?'

'I might have known your child would be behind this. Ollie would never do anything like that on his own. He knows right from wrong.' She felt as if she'd been holding her breath for the past half-hour. Now emotion rushed through her, making her lash out.

'At least mine have got minds of their own. They don't have me breathing down their necks every five minutes, telling them what to do and what to think!'

'Ladies—' The policeman tried to step in but they both ignored him.

'Fat lot of good you'd be at that, since you never seem to think at all!'

Somewhere along the line Angie ushered the children out of the room, but neither of them noticed. They were too caught up in their argument.

'And you think you're so clever, don't you?' Cat thrust her face so close Roo could almost count the freckles sprinkling her snub nose. 'It didn't help get you the man you wanted, did it?'

'It didn't help you, either. You had to trap him instead. Do you really think Billy married you for your lightning wit? He married you because he had to. You were just a one-night stand that went wrong!'

'That's more than you ever were! It really bothers you, doesn't it? That he fancies me and not you, even with those brilliant brains of yours.'

'Who says he doesn't?' Roo hadn't meant to say it, but Cat had got her so riled she just wanted to wound her.

Cat took a step back as if Roo had struck her. 'Lying bitch,' she said. 'Billy didn't want you then and he doesn't want you now!'

'Then you've got nothing to worry about, have you?'

Roo went off, leaving Cat standing there, her mouth gaping.

By then it was almost five, and Cat took Megan and Liam straight home. She was still fuming as she bundled them in the car. Megan was silent, knowing better than to try to talk to her mother when she was so furious.

'It wasn't my fault,' she whimpered finally. 'Ollie wanted to run away. He doesn't like it at Angie's because all the other kids are mean to him. Their mums don't like his mum. Why don't you like her?'

'It's a long story. Oi!' she screeched at an oncoming four-wheel drive. 'What do you think you're driving, a bloody tank?'

For a moment, it had been her and Roo together, just like old times. Now she couldn't wait for the public meeting the following week, when she'd wipe that self-satisfied smirk off her face once and for all.

Chapter 18

'Mum, I don't feel well.' Ollie pushed his cereal around his bowl the following Wednesday.

Roo, in the middle of browsing the foreign markets in the *Financial Times*, putting another load of washing in and looking for his missing trainer, suppressed a sigh. 'Again? What is it this time?'

'My tummy hurts. And my head. Can't I stay at home?' he pleaded.

'You know Mummy has to go to work.'

'You could stay off too.'

'I can't, darling. I'm meeting Uncle Billy at a furniture show in—oh hell!'

She snatched Ollie's half-finished breakfast bowl away, found the missing shoe hidden behind a cushion in the sitting room and bundled him, still groaning, into the back of the car.

Angie greeted them at the door. She'd been incredibly contrite over letting the kids wander off, and Roo understood that it wasn't completely her fault that Megan had gone through her handbag and found the door-key. But even so she still felt a pang of anxiety at leaving him there. If she'd had any choice she might not have done it.

'I thought you'd stood me up,' Billy said as she roared into the car park of the exhibition centre half an hour later.

'Don't.' She reached into the back of the car, stuffing papers into her briefcase. Billy watched her with amusement.

'Surely this isn't Roo Hennessy, super-organised business-woman?'

'No, this is Roo Hennessy, working mother on the edge. So don't push it, okay?' She slammed the car door shut and straightened her shoulders. 'Right, let's go.'

'Not until I've done this.' He moved towards her and for one alarming second she thought he was going to kiss her. But he reached up and tucked a strand of hair behind her ear. 'There. Can't have you less than perfect, can we?'

'Heaven forbid.' He should have seen her an hour ago, still in her dressing gown and panicking because she'd lost a contact lens.

He was still standing very close to her, so close she could smell the lemony tang of his aftershave. Then Billy moved away hurriedly.

'We've, um, got quite a full day ahead of us,' he said, straightening his tie. 'There are lots of buyers I want you to meet. I'm hoping you can win them over.'

'With your looks and my brains how can we fail?' They walked towards the exhibition centre, as far apart as they could get, terrified of touching.

The hangar-like building was already packed. Buyers thronged between lavish room sets displaying sofas, chairs, tables, beds and wardrobes, each manufacturer vying to catch the eye of the milling retailers.

By contrast, the Fairbanks stand was subdued and uninspired. It stood out among their slick, modern competitors like a middle-aged maiden aunt at a disco.

'I know,' Billy said, seeing her look. 'But we were lucky to get this. Frederick reckons it's a waste of marketing budget.'

'What does George say about that?'

'Not much. He's been handing over the reins to Frederick a lot lately. I'm wondering if he's about to retire, actually.'

Roo was silent. She knew the truth, and it lay heavy with her.

They spent all morning luring potential customers over to the stand and giving them the big sales pitch. Roo had never talked so much or thought so fast in her life, trying to convince customers there was life in Fairbanks yet, and they should take a chance on them. Unfortunately, it didn't make people want to place any orders.

'It's not you, it's the furniture,' she kept hearing again and again. 'Fairbanks is a good company, but your range is too boring.'

Then Roger Fleet arrived. He was MD of the hotel chain Billy had been talking to about supplying contract furniture. Even he seemed less than impressed with what they were offering.

'Our hotels are exclusive and upmarket, and the styling should reflect that.' And your furniture doesn't, his look said.

'We are working on a new concept at the moment,' Roo said, ignoring the quizzical looks Billy gave her, and thinking off the top of her head. 'It's something totally new for Fairbanks. And frankly it's going to blow this lot out of the water.'

'Really? Can I see it?'

'I'm afraid not. We're keeping it under wraps at the moment. But let's just say Fairbanks is coming back with a bang.'

Roger Fleet was intrigued enough to invite her to look around the new flagship hotel they were building in Birmingham. 'And if this new concept of yours takes off, we could be in business,' he said.

'What new concept?' Billy asked, as soon as he'd gone.

'I've no idea,' Roo admitted. 'But I couldn't just let him walk away, could I?' She put down the sheaf of brochures she'd been trying unsuccessfully to offload. 'Let's have a coffee. I need to think.'

There was a long queue in the cafeteria. At the head of it, a foreign man was holding everyone up, trying to pay for his coffee with euros. 'What do you mean you can't take them?' he kept saying to the blank-looking woman at the cash desk. 'What kind of a country is this?'

In the end Roo lost patience and marched to the head of the queue. 'Here, let me.' She handed over cash for all their coffees to the unsmiling woman at the till. 'And next time go to the bank!'

She regretted being so sharp as soon as the man looked at her, his wicked smile lighting up his inky black eyes. 'I only flew in from Milan two hours ago.' He looked disreputable and sexy in a rumpled dark linen suit over a black T-shirt. His collar-length hair was dark and silky. Even his stubble was sexy, as if he'd just fallen out of his mistress's bed and on to a plane. 'I'm Sal.' His voice was as rich and smooth as espresso.

'Roo Hennessy.'

'Shall we sit down?' Billy hissed behind her. 'We're holding up the queue.'

To Billy's chagrin, Sal joined them at the only available table.

'So what do you do?' she asked. 'Are you a buyer, or a designer?'

'I make furniture. I have a stand over there.' He pointed vaguely towards the far end of the hall.

'Really? I must take a look.'

'Yes, you should. I'm very good.'

'So modest,' Billy muttered, toying moodily with a packet of sugar.

'You should come over and see us, too,' Roo said. 'Stand 207. Fairbanks Fine Furniture.'

He stifled a yawn. 'Your British furniture lacks – how you say? – imagination. Just like your food.' He put the cheese roll down with a grimace. 'And your men, maybe.'

Billy bristled beside her. 'And you think you can do better?' Roo asked quickly, before he could respond.

'Better than your furniture? Or better than your men?' He gave her a grin that could scorch a woman's underwear at fifty paces. 'I can show you my furniture. The rest you will have to find out for yourself.' He pushed a card across the table towards her. Roo glanced down at the name and recognised it instantly.

'Salvatore Bellini. You designed the interior of the Wharf Hotel in Leeds.'

'You've seen it?'

'I certainly have. And I was very impressed.'

'Of course.' He shrugged, unsurprised. 'My furniture is very beautiful.'

'And bloody expensive,' Billy said. Sal regarded him coolly.

'Money is not important. Beauty, that is what drives men to distraction.' He looked at Roo.

Billy pushed his cup away from him. 'We'd better get back to the stand.'

Roo stood up. 'It's been nice meeting you, Signor Bellini.'

'Ciao, bella.' He reached for her hand and planted a lingering kiss on it. 'And if you want to see how furniture should be made, come and see me.'

'He was a bit bloody full of himself,' Billy said as they left.

'He was Italian.' And very charming, she thought, glancing back over her shoulder at him.

'He was flirting with you.'

'So? I didn't mind. I quite enjoyed it, actually.'

Billy shook his head. 'Women! Just when we get to grips with feminism and equality in the workplace, you go all mushy over some smoothie Don Juan!'

'He was harmless.'

And intriguing. She couldn't stop thinking about him. Later that afternoon, when Billy was busy with a potential client, she slipped away to take a look at Salvatore's stand.

Roo spotted it straight away among the crowded room sets. A single chair, crafted in slices of cherry and walnut, sitting on a raised plinth. Moody low-voltage lighting picked out its exquisite lines. It was flanked by two gorgeous, snooty-looking Italian girls in cream designer suits that showed off their own exquisite lines.

'I knew you wouldn't be able to resist.' He lounged in the shadows at the edge of the stand, sleek as a panther. 'Is it the furniture you've come to see, or me?'

She nodded towards the chair. 'There isn't much to see.'

'I prefer quality to quantity. Every piece is flawless.'

'And stunningly expensive too, I'll bet.'

'Like I say to your friend, people will pay for something beautiful.'

Roo felt an idea stirring in her mind. Not just any idea. The big one.

'It's a shame more people can't enjoy your beautiful furniture,' she said.

'We can't always have what we want, can we?'

'We could if we combined our talents.'

His eyebrow rose. 'That sounds tempting.'

She ignored the suggestive look he gave her. 'You could design a capsule collection for Fairbanks. We'd make it in our factory and sell it under our joint names. And it wouldn't affect the exclusivity of your own range,' she went on, seeing him frown. 'As you said, there will always be people willing and able to pay premium prices for something exclusive.'

Sal pulled a face. 'I am not sure.'

'Our furniture is very well made.' Her mobile rang and she switched it off quickly. 'At least come and look around our factory, meet our production team. Then you can make your mind up.'

'Will you be there?'

Didn't he ever let up? 'If it would help,' she laughed.

'Okay, I will meet your factory people. But if I do not like what I see, that's it.'

'That's all I ask.' She could hardly conceal her delight and excitement.

He nodded past her shoulder. 'I think your boyfriend wants you.'

Roo glanced behind her. Billy was pushing his way through the crowd towards them. 'He isn't my boyfriend!'

'No? He's very jealous.' He smiled. 'We'll give him something to be jealous about, no?' Before she could stop him he'd pulled her towards him and kissed her lingeringly on both cheeks. His stubble grazed her skin. He smelt divine.

'You've got it wrong,' Roo said, shaken. 'Billy and I are just friends.'

Sal smiled enigmatically. 'If you say so, cara mia. But he still looks like he wants to kill me!'

Billy was surprisingly lukewarm about her idea. 'It would mean changing all our production methods.'

'That will be easy once we get our new machinery. I think it'll be just the shot in the arm we need. And it would be something different, something special. The stores would definitely go for it.'

'How do you know the Italian Stallion can deliver?'

'Oh, he can deliver. Ask your daughter. She's a big fan of his.'

'You too, by the look of it.'

As he stalked off to his car, Roo wondered if Sal was right. Billy certainly seemed to be acting like a jealous lover. But he couldn't really be jealous – could he?

She was still on a high about her idea when she rang Angie's doorbell. Angie greeted her with a bemused smile. 'Hello, what are you doing here?'

'I've come to pick up my son. You know, about this high? Fair hair? Thinks he's Luke Skywalker?'

'Hasn't your mum spoken to you? Ollie wasn't too well earlier on, so I rang her to take him home.'

'You rang my mother?'

'I tried calling you but I couldn't get through,' Angie said defensively. 'Sadie said she'd let you know.'

'She probably didn't think.' That was Sadie. She didn't think. God only knew what she was doing with her son now!

'Higher! Higher!' Ollie squealed with delight as Sadie pushed him on the swing, up and up until her arms ached. He'd made a miraculous recovery since she brought him home from the child-minder's.

She'd been surprised to get a call from Angie Bennett. She only knew her because her mum came into the salon.

'Sorry to call you like this, but we've got a bit of an emergency,' she'd explained. 'Your grandson's not very well. I can't reach Roo, she's not answering her mobile. I wondered if you could possibly come and pick him up.'

Sadie's first instinct was to drop everything, but she held back. 'Shouldn't you wait to hear from his mother?'

'I'd rather not. If he's got a bug I wouldn't want all the other kids to catch it. He's been looking peaky for a few days, actually. I'm surprised she sent him,' she sniffed.

'She has to earn her living, same as the rest of us,' Sadie said shortly, wondering why she was bothering to defend her daughter.

218

On the way home, she began to wonder if she'd done the right thing. Ruby wouldn't thank her for getting involved. And Ollie didn't seem half as sick as Angie made out. He was well enough to pester her for a detour to the park.

Sadie gave him one last push and massaged her stiff arms. 'Come on, we'd better head home. I've got to let your mum know where you are.'

'Can I have a lolly?'

'I thought you felt sick.'

He stared at his shoes. 'I'm better now.'

'That was quick.' She caught his blushing face. 'Maybe I should take you back to Angie's.'

'No! I don't want to go back there! I don't like it.'

She took him to the ice-cream kiosk, where he took a long time to choose, staring into the fridge as if his life depended on it. Finally he chose a Cornetto and Sadie had a Strawberry Split.

'You're too old for lollies,' Ollie reproved as they headed home through the avenue of beech trees.

'I'm too old for a lot of things but I still do them. So why don't you like Angie?'

'She's all right. It's the other children I don't like. They make fun of me because they say I talk posh, and . . . they say things.'

'What kind of things?'

'They say my mum's horrible and we don't belong here.'

'Have you told your mum about this?'

'She won't listen. Anyway, I don't want to make her sad.' He unwrapped his Cornetto carefully. 'She and Daddy are getting divorced.'

Sadie nearly dropped her lolly in shock. 'What?'

'I think it's a secret,' Ollie said, remembering suddenly. 'Mummy doesn't know I know. But I listen to them on the phone. He's got another woman.'

'I'm sure you've got that wrong, love.'

'I haven't! Her name's Shauna. She used to be my nanny but now she's Daddy's girlfriend. What's pregnant?' he asked suddenly.

'Ask your mum.' Sadie's mind reeled as she struggled to take it in. So Ruby was getting divorced. Why hadn't she said anything to her about it?

Because you're the last person in the world she'd confide in, a small voice inside her head reminded her.

As they turned the corner into Hope Street, Sadie saw Ruby's silver car parked outside her mother's house. They'd barely reached the gate before she ran down the path and gathered Ollie into her arms as if he'd spent the last six months held captive by white slave traders.

'Where the hell have you been?' She glared at Sadie over his head. 'I've been worried sick.'

Sadie's hackles rose. 'Let me see. We played a quick game of hopscotch in the middle of the M62, then I taught him how to juggle with hand grenades.'

Ollie looked at her, a frown creasing his angelic features. 'No, you didn't. We went to the park and had an ice-cream.'

'You could have let me know,' Ruby said.

'If you're that worried, try answering your phone next time.' Sadie stalked past her into the house, all her sympathy forgotten. That was absolutely the last time she ever tried to be helpful to her daughter!

She'd put the kettle on and was starting on supper when Ruby appeared in the kitchen doorway.

'Sorry,' she muttered. 'I didn't mean to snap. I was just worried, that's all. When I got here and you weren't back—'

'You assumed I'd done something daft? Thanks a lot,' she said bitterly.

She expected Ruby to go but she didn't. She stood at the window, staring out over the yard. 'Ollie really seems to like you.'

'Don't sound so surprised. Not everyone thinks the same as you.'

'Look, give me a chance, I'm trying to apologise!' Sadie glanced across at her daughter. She'd lost even more weight; in the early evening light, her face looked gaunt and tired. She fought the urge to put her arms around her.

'I wasn't interfering,' she said. 'I told Angie she should wait for you, but she insisted he wasn't well—'

'I know. You did the right thing,' Ruby said shortly.

'He's a lovely little boy. So bright. He's a credit to you.'

'Thanks.'

There was a long silence. Then Sadie said, 'He must miss his dad.'

Ruby looked up sharply. 'What makes you say that?'

'Being away from home for so long. It must be hard on him.'

'David's coming up this weekend.'

There was something about the way she said it that made Sadie realise Ollie was right. If Ruby's marriage hadn't broken up yet, it was heading that way. Kids knew more than their parents gave them credit for sometimes.

The kettle came to the boil and to Sadie's surprise Ruby offered to make the tea.

'I don't know,' Sadie said. 'You know how particular Nanna is.'

Ruby nodded. 'Always loose, never bags. Warm the pot first and let it stand for exactly seven minutes.' She smiled. 'You can't grow up in this house and not know how Nanna likes her tea!'

It was strange seeing her there in her chic cream jacket and black tailored trousers, sluicing Nanna's old brown teapot out over the sink. Strange but nice. Sadie wondered if she should risk ruining the mood by mentioning what Ollie had told her about being bullied at the childminder's. In the end she knew she had to say something; she couldn't let her grandson go on being miserable, even if her daughter did bite her head off.

Ruby was dismissive at first. 'What do you mean, not happy? How can he not be happy? Angie's lovely.'

'It's the other kids he doesn't get on with.'

'He'll be fine. He's just taking a bit of time to adjust.'

'I think it's more than that. He told me he tried to run away because he was so miserable.'

Her daughter's confident mask slipped a fraction. 'What else did he tell you?'

'That the other kids tease him and call him names.'

'He's never said anything to me.'

'I don't think he wants to worry you. He reckons you've got enough on your plate.'

She expected some smart reply. But Ruby sat down at the kitchen table, her head in her hands. 'Oh, God. Why didn't I notice it before? All those times he pretended to be ill, I had no idea—'

'You weren't to know.'

'But I'm his mother! I should know these things, shouldn't I?'

'You can't know everything.'

'That's just it, I don't know anything. I don't even know what his favourite football team is!' What the hell did that have to do with anything? Sadie wondered. 'I just wanted to do it right, and it's all going wrong!'

Sadie hesitated, then laid her hand tentatively on her daughter's shoulder. Under her jacket she was all bones and angles.

'What am I going to do?' Ruby said. 'I can't deal with another problem, not now. If he can't go to Angie's, where can he go?'

'You could let me look after him.' She felt Roo's muscles stiffen under her hand.

'You?'

'I managed to take care of him this afternoon without killing him, didn't I?'

'But I thought you didn't want to do it.'

'I've changed my mind. It'd be better than sending him somewhere he's unhappy.'

'It might not be for long,' Ruby said. Her mascara was smudged under her eyes, making her look less terrifyingly perfect, more vulnerable. 'Just a couple of weeks. And I'd pay you, of course.'

'There's no need for that.'

'I want to.'

Sadie saw her daughter's determined expression and realised that the only way Ruby could allow herself to accept her mother's help was by turning it into a business transaction. 'Suit yourself,' she said. 'We'll sort it out later.'

Ruby finished making the tea but politely refused Sadie's offer of supper. This far but no further, her cool look said. Sadie was disappointed, but at least they didn't part screaming at each other for once.

It was a start.

Chapter 19

The draughty church hall was packed for the public meeting the following day. Roo stood at the back, watching people shuffling down the rows looking for empty seats, knowing none of them were on her side. There was no sign of the Fairbanks family. They'd left her to face the ordeal alone.

'Ready?' She jumped as Billy touched her arm. 'No need to ask if you're nervous!' he smiled.

'I'm okay, honestly. You don't have to do this, you know.'

'You don't seriously think I'd let you face this lot on your own, do you?'

'What about Cat?'

His face clouded. 'Cat's got enough people on her side. She doesn't need me. You do.'

Roo was grateful to him, but uneasy too. She didn't want him to take sides. It would only make life difficult for him.

'Do I look all right?' After much thought she'd chosen an ass-kicking fitted Jasper Conran jacket in blood red, teamed with black trousers.

'You look great.'

'I just thought since everyone thinks I'm the devil in disguise I might as well dress the part.' She tweaked her jacket. 'And at least the rotten tomatoes won't show,' she added, only half-joking.

Up on the platform, Cat was suffering a similar crisis of nerves. She gazed over the rows and rows of faces and felt daunted. What the hell was she doing? She didn't belong up here. She was no public speaker.

Down in the packed audience, she caught her daughter Becky's disapproving scowl. Next to her, Dominic grinned and gave her the thumbs up. Cat tried to smile back, but her mouth wouldn't move. Beside her, Marjorie Prentice was white-faced as she shuffled her notes for the hundredth time.

Cat glanced through her prepared speech. The words, which she'd carefully worked on for the past week until her eyes ached, sounded clumsy as she read them through in her head. She could feel damp patches of perspiration under her arms, and prayed they weren't showing through her top.

There was a stir at the back of the hall as Ruby walked in. Her heels clicked on the tiled floor as she calmly walked the length of the hall to take her place on the platform. She looked cool and composed, and Cat was almost ready to throw in the towel there and then – until she saw Billy.

She had no idea he was going to be there. And she certainly didn't know he'd be with Ruby!

It couldn't have been a more public taunt. She felt everyone's eyes go from him to her, waiting for her reaction. Ruby caught her eye and nodded a greeting, but Billy stared straight ahead of him.

'Take no notice,' Marjorie whispered. 'That Fairbanks lot probably made him come to put you off.'

If they had, it hadn't worked. Anger sent a surge of adrenalin that chased her nerves away, and before she knew what she was doing she was standing at the microphone addressing the crowd.

'Ladies and gentlemen.' Her voice came out as a whisper. How did this stupid mike work? She leaned closer. 'If I can just have your attention.' Still nothing. She tapped the mike head, cursing under her breath.

Ruby leaned across. 'I think you have to turn it on,' she said, flicking the switch. Cat felt the heat rush into her face. 'Thanks,' she said, then flinched as her voice echoed around the hall.

She stumbled through her opening address, constantly looking down at her notes because her brain had gone blank and she couldn't remember a word. All the time she felt Ruby watching her, waiting for her to make a berk of herself. When she did look up briefly, she saw the reporter from the *Normanford News* stifling a yawn, his notebook unopened in his lap.

She quickly finished her opening speech and handed over to Ruby for her presentation. As she took her place at the microphone, the reporter woke up and reached for his pen.

Her voice was full of cool authority as she began her speech. 'Ladies and gentlemen, thank you for allowing me the opportunity to come here and explain what's really happening at Fairbanks—'

'We know what's happening!' someone shouted. 'You're closing the place down!'

'That's where you're wrong. It's true we've had to implement certain measures over the past few weeks, to ensure the company's survival—'

'To ensure bigger profits for you lot, you mean!'

Ruby turned on the heckler with an icy smile. 'You seem very well-informed. I take it you've read last year's company report?' Everyone looked at the man, who turned red and stared at his thumbs. 'No? Well if you cared to look at it you'd see that far from making a profit Fairbanks has been losing money for the past two years.'

Cat scanned the crowd. She recognised most of the people, but there were several in the back rows she didn't know.

'When I arrived at Fairbanks, the factory was facing insolvency,' Ruby continued. 'The situation was so bad, we were in danger of not being able to meet the following month's wage bill.'

'Management toadie!' someone out the back shouted half-heartedly. Everyone ignored him. They were all listening to Ruby now. Cat could feel them warming to her. She didn't know if what she said was true, but it was certainly convincing. She was a real pro, she thought. Until she saw the admiring way Billy was gazing at her; then the ice came back into her heart.

'Now we've made the necessary savings, hopefully we can start to rebuild the company,' Ruby was saying.

'Why should we believe you?' A voice came from the back of the hall. 'What do you care if Fairbanks goes down the drain?'

'I care because Fairbanks is part of my history too.' Now she was playing the local hero card. How sickening. 'I was born and brought up in Normanford—'

'Yeah, and you couldn't wait to get out of the place!' Everyone laughed. Cat looked round to see who'd shouted and realised to her horror that it was her. Billy stared at her coldly from the other side of the stage.

The people at the back took up her cue and began a Mexican wave of jeering.

'Capitalist pig!'

'Filthy scum!'

'Fairbanks fat cats!'

Ruby tried to stay composed, but as the shouting grew louder Cat could see she was beginning to crack. She stammered, lost her place in her notes. Cat stood up and seized the microphone from her.

'We're supposed to be here to find out what's going on, so why don't we shut up and listen to what she's got to say?' She pointed at the back rows. 'If you lot just want to make trouble, clear off and do it outside the kebab shop!'

She handed the microphone back and took her seat again. Ruby shot her a surprised, grateful look. But the heckling and cat calls went on, growing louder and more ferocious. Some members of the crowd were turning on the troublemakers. Scuffles broke out, and people were beginning to surge towards the stage. Ruby had given up trying to make herself heard. There was a sheen of perspiration on her brow.

Cat saw him before she did. A yob in an Adidas hoodie pushed his way to the front. Cat saw him raise his arm, caught the glint of something in his hand. 'Look out!' she screamed. Ruby turned towards her, just as the bottle flew through the air and struck her on the head. She fell. Cat dropped her notes and ran to her, but Billy was already there. He knelt beside her, cradling her in his arms, saying her name over and over again. Her blood was all over his shirt.

'I've got to get her to hospital,' he said.

'Shall I call an ambulance?'

'No, I'll take her.'

Cat looked down at her cousin. She was groggy but conscious, blood pouring down her face. 'Is there anything I can do?'

Billy glared at her. 'I think you've done enough for one night, don't you?'

'Honestly, Billy, I can make myself a cup of tea!' Roo reclined on the sofa, propped up with cushions, feeling slightly silly. 'You don't have to make such a fuss, it was only a tiny cut!'

'You still had to have stitches. And blows to the head can be dangerous. You heard what the doctor said; you have to rest in case of concussion.'

'He also said I was absolutely fine.' Roo sipped her tea and grimaced. 'Ugh! Did you put sugar in this?'

'It's good for shock.'

Roo put her cup down. His over-protectiveness was beginning to trouble her. 'Shouldn't you be going home? It's after ten. Cat will be wondering where you are.'

'I don't really care.' Billy's jaw was clenched. 'After tonight I don't think I want to be with her at the moment.'

'It wasn't her fault it turned into a riot!'

'She shouldn't have started this bloody protest in the first place.' He reached for the phone. 'Do you want me to ring David?'

'Why?'

'He'll want to know, won't he? I would, if—' he didn't finish the sentence.

'I don't think he'd be very interested.' She saw his quizzical expression and added, 'You might as well know. David and I have split up.'

'What?' He stared at her. 'When?'

'A couple of weeks ago. Although to be honest things haven't been right between us for a long time.' She looked down at her hands. Her wedding band still gleamed on her third finger. Maybe that was why she was coping with it. Deep down she'd known their break-up was inevitable. 'He's met someone else. And she's pregnant.'

'And you didn't think to mention it? I thought we were supposed to be friends.'

'It was my problem. I had to deal with it.'

'Christ, Roo, why do you have to be so bloody independent all the time?'

'Who else have I got to depend on?'

'You've got me.'

'Cat would love that, wouldn't she? She's bad enough about us working together. God knows what she'd do if I started crying on your shoulder.'

'You're probably right. I don't know what's got into her these days. She used to be so kind and loving but lately she's changed so much I hardly recognise her.'

He looked so confused, Roo wanted to shake Cat. She had a good man and a good marriage, and she risked throwing them away for the sake of some stupid feud.

'Perhaps you should be telling Cat, not me?'

'That's just it. I can't say anything to her at the moment without her getting jealous and flying off the handle.' He looked rueful. 'Listen to me going on. It's you we should be worrying about. I really wish you'd told me about you and David.'

'Like I said, it's my problem.'

She shifted against the cushions and Billy was instantly solicitous, reaching over to plump them up for her. 'Better?' He lifted his eyes to meet hers, dark and intense.

'Thank you.' He was very close to her. If she reached up, she could kiss him. And she realised with a sudden certainty that he was thinking the same thing.

She turned her face away, breaking the spell, just as the doorbell rang.

'I'll go.' Billy stood up. 'It might be a reporter.' They'd already called twice, begging for a quote about the evening's events. Roo listened to the voices on the front doorstep, trying to make out who would be calling at that time. Then Billy came back.

'It was some boy called Matt. He said he's a friend of yours.' He looked unconvinced. 'I told him to come back tomorrow.'

Roo felt a pang of disappointment. Suddenly the one person she wanted to see was Matt, if only to relieve the charged atmosphere between her and Billy.

Then he was there, shouldering past Billy into the sitting room.

'How the hell did you get in?' Billy demanded.

'I used my key.' He turned to Roo. 'I heard what happened. Are you okay?'

'I'm fine,' said Roo, although a dull ache was gathering behind her eyes.

'From the way they were talking at the pub, I expected to find you with at least one limb missing.'

'As you can see I'm all in one piece.'

'I'm glad to hear it.'

Billy loomed behind them, waiting for an introduction. 'Billy, this is my neighbour Matt. Billy's an old friend of mine,' she explained.

They nodded coolly, eyeing each other up. 'I can take over the patient now, if you need to go home,' Matt said.

'That won't be necessary.'

'Are you sure? Won't your wife be wondering where you are?' Matt looked pointedly at his wedding ring.

'I'm happy to stay.'

'I don't need anyone looking after me, thank you very much!' Roo said firmly. They collided with each other to get to her as she stood up. 'And Matt's right. You should go home, Billy.'

He looked as if he might argue, then gave up. 'If you're sure you're okay?'

'I'm here if she isn't,' Matt said.

'Really, I'm fine.' She saw him to the door. She felt guilty dismissing him after he'd been so kind. But she had a feeling he might never go home otherwise and she didn't need another reason for Cat to hate her.

'He didn't seem in any hurry to leave,' Matt said. He was in the armchair, his long legs stretched out in front of him. He was wearing black jeans and a Wallace and Gromit T-shirt.

'He and his wife are having problems at the moment.'

'Let me guess. You're the problem?'

She looked up sharply. 'What makes you say that?'

'I've spent three years studying non-verbal communication, remember? I get the feeling you two have a history.'

'You could say that.'

'Want to tell me about it?'

'Do I have a choice?' Matt had a way of getting her to open up. Perhaps it was all that psychology training.

She gave him a brief summary of her complicated relationship with Billy and Cat. 'But like you say, it's history,' she said.

'Are you sure? I reckon you could have him back any time you liked.'

'Don't be ridiculous!' But she couldn't help adding, 'What makes you say that?'

'Because he's vulnerable, and his marriage is in a mess. And now he's beginning to wonder if he made the right choice all those years ago. Is this anyone's tea?' He picked up her untouched cup.

'Help yourself.' Roo frowned. 'I don't want to break up his marriage.'

'No one would blame you if you did. After all, she pinched him from you.'

Roo was silent. Matt was right; something could have happened between her and Billy earlier on, if she had made the slightest move, given him a single word of encouragement. It was tempting. And it was hardly her fault that Cat had driven him away, was it?

But as soon as the thought crossed her mind she knew she couldn't do it. There was no way she could inflict that kind of pain on someone else.

And besides, she wasn't sure she felt that way about Billy now. He was still wildly fanciable, but the spark wasn't there any more.

'It would be a big mistake if you did.' Matt put the empty cup down.

'Why's that?'

'Because deep down he still loves his wife.'

231

'How can you say that? I don't know if he's ever loved her. She forced him to marry her, remember?'

'She couldn't force him to do anything he didn't want to,' Matt said. 'And even if he didn't love her when they married, that doesn't mean he hasn't grown to love her.'

'What about your instant chemistry thing?'

Matt shrugged. 'It doesn't always work like that. Sometimes it takes a while for people to realise how they feel about each other.'

He looked at her, and Roo felt alarming little prickles of electricity shoot up the back of her neck.

The phone rang, distracting them. It was Sadie, sounding frantic. 'Tom just called,' she said. 'Is it true? You've been attacked by a madman? Are you badly hurt? Why aren't you in hospital?'

It was weird, Roo thought as she reassured Sadie she hadn't been shot, or stabbed, or lynched by a hysterical mob. She sounded concerned. Almost like a real mother.

'Is there anything I can do? Shall I come round?'

'No, really. But it would help if you could keep Ollie with you tonight.'

'Of course. He's dropped off on the sofa with Nanna anyway. Although how he can sleep when she has that telly on full-blast I've no idea. Are you sure you don't want me to come round?'

Matt smiled when she put the phone down. 'I thought your mum was a selfish cow.'

'So did I.' Roo was thoughtful. 'She was different when she was younger.'

'Weren't we all?'

'Even you?' Roo curled up on the sofa, tucking her legs under her.

'Even me.'

'Are you seriously trying to tell me you weren't always the habitual womaniser you are today?' Roo teased.

He gazed into the empty fire grate. 'Actually I used to be a one-woman man.'

'That girl in the photo?'

He nodded. 'Emma.'

'Don't tell me, she broke your heart?'

'In a way.'

'So what did she do? Run off with your best friend? Grow a beard and become a lesbian?'

'She died.'

'Oh Lord, I'm sorry. When did it happen?'

'Three years ago. We were going to get married after we graduated, but then Emma found out she had leukaemia. I wanted to bring the wedding forward but she was determined she wasn't going down the aisle in a wheelchair. She really thought she was going to beat it, right up to the end.' His voice was flat. 'We buried her in the same church we were due to marry in. Now the only thing I've got left of her is Harvey.'

No wonder he'd been so angry when his dog was taken away. 'Is that why you don't want to commit to anyone now? Because you're still in love with Emma?'

'Possibly,' he agreed. 'Or maybe I just don't want to get hurt again.'

'What about all those girls you go out with? Don't you care about hurting them?'

'I don't set out to hurt anyone. They know the score. They know I'm not interested in anything long-term.'

'What if they are?'

'That's their problem.' His eyes were level with hers, warm turquoise fringed with thick, dark lashes. 'I don't make promises I can't keep.'

She suddenly felt very sad and tired. Matt caught her stifling a yawn. 'Are you okay? Can I get you anything?'

'I'm a bit tired. I think I might go to bed.'

'Let me help you.' Against her protests, he insisted on waiting on the landing while she took off her make-up, brushed her teeth and changed into her pyjamas. 'And before you argue, I'm spending the night here,' he said. 'You shouldn't be left alone for twenty-four hours after a blow to the head. Surely the doctor told you that?'

'He mentioned something about it. But I'm sure it's not necessary—'

'I'm staying, and that's all there is to it.' He noticed her wary face and laughed. 'Don't look so terrified; I'll sleep on the sofa. I'm not going to try anything while you're weak and defenceless.'

'The thought never crossed my mind.'

'Didn't it? It did mine!'

Chapter 20

'I want the whole lot off. And blonde. Like that girl on breakfast telly.' Laura Pardue smiled challengingly in the mirror. Cat stared back in disbelief. Laura had been coming into the salon for two years and in all that time she'd never known her have more than an inch trimmed off her long, straight, dark hair. And even then she practically had to be sedated.

'What's brought this on?'

'I just fancied something different,' Laura said, and promptly burst into tears.

Thank heavens the salon was empty, apart from Natalie, who was topping up the posh salon shampoo bottles with cheap stuff Maxine had bought at the cash and carry. Maxine and Julie were out having a 'senior management meeting', which meant a morning's shopping followed by a drunken lunch. Cat's next client wasn't due until eleven, so she had plenty of time to make Laura a fortifying cup of tea, calm her down and listen to her story.

It all sounded horribly familiar. Laura was convinced her husband was having an affair with a colleague at work and she wanted to win him back.

'You should see her,' she sniffed, dabbing her smudged mascara away with a tissue. 'She's young, blonde, and dead glamorous. I'm not surprised he fancies her. He spends more time with her than he does with me.' She smiled wanly at her reflection. She was roughly the same age as Cat, in her mid thirties, worn down by a full-time job and looking after three kids. 'She spends all her time in beauty salons, having her nails done and her tan topped up. I don't even own a lipstick since the kids pinched it to colour the walls!'

'How do you know he's having an affair?' Cat asked, as her dark locks fell to the floor.

'I've seen his credit card bill. All those charges for flowers I've never had, and restaurants I've never been to. And he stayed overnight in a hotel. He said the whole team was going, but it turned out to be just the two of them.' She blew her nose. 'But it's more than that. It's a feeling. You just know, don't you?'

You certainly do, Cat thought.

Billy hadn't come home until gone midnight the previous night, by which time she'd spent several nailbiting hours wondering if he was going to come home at all.

'Before you start, I left Roo's two hours ago,' he snapped before she could speak. 'I just couldn't face coming home.'

Cat bit her lip. 'I'm sorry.'

'It's not me you should be apologising to, is it?'

'Is she all right?'

'Just about. No thanks to you.'

'I didn't know those yobs were going to turn up, did I?'

'I'm too tired to argue,' he said. 'I'm going to bed.'

The following morning, as Billy got dressed, he said, 'And you might as well know now, I have to go to Birmingham to visit a hotel next week. It'll mean an overnight stay. And Roo's going.' He sent her a defiant look.

'Fine,' Cat said humbly, not daring to argue. As Billy left, she added, 'I can't help the way I feel, Billy. You two have always been so close.' Closer than us, she thought.

'But I married you,' Billy said. He didn't look happy about it.

She applied colour to Laura's newly shorn hair, made her another cup of tea and gave her a selection of magazines just as Sadie came into the salon with Ollie. Cat hadn't seen much of her since she'd taken time off to look after her grandson. She couldn't blame her for it, but sometimes it felt as if even her greatest ally had abandoned her and gone over to Roo's side.

236

'I suppose you've come to tell me how stupid I am?' Cat said. She'd already had Glenys on the phone, telling her off for not being more supportive of her husband's career. 'Do you think my Bernard would ever have been elected MP if I'd gone around organising riots?' she'd said.

'You weren't to know how it would turn out,' Sadie said. 'But you haven't done yourself any favours. It's hardly going to bring you and Billy closer, is it?'

'I know,' Cat sighed. She put the kettle on and they sat in the staffroom while Ollie played with the box of toys set aside for customers' children.

'He's a good man, Cat. But you're driving him away with all this silly jealousy and insecurity. Why can't you just accept that he's with you, not Ruby?'

'Because it's not me he wants! He's only with me because he felt he had to be.'

'For eighteen years?' Sadie said. 'If he'd wanted to go, he could have walked out on you years ago. He wouldn't have stuck around and had more kids.'

'Maybe he didn't have a reason to leave then.'

'You mean Ruby? You can't blame her for all this. Like I said, you're doing a grand job of driving him away all by your-self.'

'I might have known you'd take her side!' Cat felt a stab of betrayal. She'd always looked on Sadie as the mother she'd never had. But when it came down to it, she was Ruby's mum, not hers.

'I'm not taking anyone's side. I don't want to see you and Billy split up over nothing, that's all. And Ruby's not interested in taking him away from you. She's got enough problems of her own to deal with, what with work and her marriage—' she broke off.

Cat pounced. 'What about her marriage?'

Sadie hesitated, then said, 'You're probably going to find out sooner or later. She and David have split up.'

Cat felt as if someone had emptied a bucket of icy water over her. 'That's it, then.'

'What do you mean?'

'Work it out, Sadie. She's single again. No wonder she wants Billy back.'

Sadie shook her head. 'You haven't heard a word I've said, have you? Why can't you have a bit more confidence in yourself? You're a lovely girl, Cat. There's no reason why Billy would want to be with anyone else.'

Cat put down her cup and stood up. 'I'd better go and check if Laura's blonde enough.'

'Laura Pardue's going blonde?' Sadie looked amazed. 'Don't tell me she's heard they have more fun? Because if she has, tell her it's not true.' She twisted a strand of hair around her finger.

'Actually she's trying to get her husband back by making herself look like his mistress.'

Sadie looked at her shrewdly. 'She'd be better off being herself.'

Laura Pardue was pleased with her hair. She twisted her head this way and that, letting it swing around her face. 'I love it,' she said. But Cat couldn't help worrying that Sadie was right. Laura had turned herself into a clone of the other woman. Just like she was trying to turn herself into a pale imitation of Ruby, playing her at her own game. And it had all backfired on her.

Catching Cat's thoughtful expression Laura said, 'I suppose you think I'm a bit desperate.'

'Not at all. I admire you for trying. I just hope it works for you.' But she felt a pang of sadness at Laura's touching faith that something as simple as a new hairstyle could bring her husband back.

If only it was that straightforward.

Despite everyone telling her to take it easy, Roo insisted on going in to work the following day. But she was beginning to wish she hadn't, as all anyone wanted to talk about was the riot.

'I hear it was quite an evening!' Frederick Fairbanks grinned when they met for an update meeting.

'Oh, it was. It's a pity you weren't there,' Roo said with feeling.

'I heard all about it. It's made that action group lot look like a right rabble. I doubt if the papers will be so sympathetic now.'

'Great. So it was almost worth getting lynched?'

'That was regrettable,' Frederick agreed. 'I specifically said no one was to get hurt.'

It took a moment to realise what he'd said. 'You mean you were behind it?'

'I may have made a few phone calls to some anarchist friends of mine in Leeds.' Frederick looked pleased with himself.

Roo was disgusted. 'So much for free speech! I don't like playing dirty.'

'So what? It worked, didn't it? The Fairbanks Action Group are totally discredited. I don't suppose we'll be hearing much more from them!'

'Unless I go to the press and tell them what you've just told me.'

The colour drained from Frederick's face. 'You wouldn't,' he said. 'It would be disloyal to the company. Anyway, I'd deny it. And you've got no proof.' He leaned back in his seat, looking smug. 'We mustn't fall out, Ms Hennessy. Not when things are starting to go so well. Look, this will cheer you up.' He reached over and picked up a file. 'I've just signed the lease on our new business premises.'

'I thought we were going to discuss it before you made any decisions?'

Frederick looked irritable. 'I am the Finance Director. I don't have to discuss everything with you.'

She took the document from him and flicked through it, frowning. 'This isn't right. It says this lease is only for six months.'

'Ah. Yes.' Frederick toyed with his Mont Blanc pen. 'I know we talked about long-term leases, but this is more flexible. We can review the situation regularly, and move premises if a better deal comes up.'

'Surely the cost of moving all that heavy equipment every six months will cancel out any savings we might make?'

Frederick was condescending. 'You leave the finances to me, Ms Hennessy.'

Roo walked away before she was tempted to point out that it was leaving the finances to him that had landed the factory in so much trouble in the first place.

'What are you doing here?' Becky looked up from her computer when Roo walked back into the office. 'Aren't you supposed to be resting, or something?'

'I'm not an invalid! Life has to go on. Anyway, we've got an important meeting today. Salvatore Bellini's coming in.'

'You're kidding! You mean *the* Salvatore Bellini? What's he doing here?'

'He's meeting Leonard and our chief designer. If everything goes well he might be designing a capsule collection for us.'

'That's fantastic! How did you pull that one off?'

'I haven't yet. That's why I had to come in this morning.' She touched the dressing on her temple. 'I just hope he hasn't read the *Normanford News*.'

They'd already started the meeting by the time she got there. Roo was pleased to see they were all getting on famously. Salvatore and George made an unlikely pair, Sal with his flowing dark locks and leather jacket, George in his shabby, ancient suit and walking stick, but they impressed each other with their shared love of furniture-making. And even Billy was beginning to thaw towards the charismatic Italian as he realised the impact their new designer range could have on sales.

After the meeting, Sal invited them all to dinner that night at his hotel in Leeds. Roo called Sadie to check if it was okay for Ollie to stay the night.

'Again? You didn't see him last night either.'

'I could hardly help that, could I?' Roo bridled. 'Anyway, I'm not going out to enjoy myself. This is a business dinner.'

'I'm sorry, I have to go to work. It's my cabaret night at the Ponderosa.'

'Mustn't miss that, must we?'

'There's no need to talk like that. You're not the only one who has to work, you know. Look, if you tell me what time you'll be back I could ask Jan if I can start later.'

'Don't bother. I'll find someone else to look after him.'

But there was no one else. She'd already promised Becky she could go to the dinner and meet her idol, so she couldn't disappoint her. And Matt was working at the pizza place. So she was in a foul mood when she went to collect Ollie that night.

'What's the matter with you?' Sadie stood in the doorway of the spare bedroom downstairs, watching her throw Ollie's things into a bag.

'If you must know I had to cancel dinner. We could lose this deal.' Although she knew that wasn't true. Salvatore could see the advantages of going into partnership with Fairbanks, even without her being part of it. She was just pissed off at missing out.

'You should have checked with me first, shouldn't you? You're not the only one allowed to make plans. Anyway,' Sadie added, 'it will do you good to spend some time with Ollie. He's missed you.'

'I'm sorry?' Roo stared at her in disbelief. 'Are you trying to tell me I'm neglecting my own son? That's rich coming from you. How many times did you abandon me to go off and do your own thing?'

'And how many times did I stay with you when you needed me?' Sadie snapped back. 'But you forget about that, don't you? You're so wrapped up in yourself – poor, hard done-by Ruby having to put up with her nasty bitch of a mother.'

'At least I make sure my child's properly cared for. He doesn't have to put himself to bed in the dark because there's no money for the electric meter.'

'You're lucky, aren't you? Some of us didn't have a choice. You seem to think I was out having a grand old time, but I was working to keep a roof over our heads.'

'By singing in some poky nightclub for a couple of quid?'

'What else could I do? I didn't have a bunch of exams like you.'

'You could have got a proper job, like—' she broke off.

'Like everyone else's mother? Is that what you were going to say? Well, I'm sorry, but I wasn't like all those other mothers with their nice homes and their nice husbands. Believe me, I wish I had

241

been.' Sadie's voice shook. 'Do you really think I enjoyed bringing you up in those stinking dumps? Don't you think I used to lie
awake at night and wish I could give you what all the other kids
had? A proper home, a family?'

'It's a pity you didn't give me away when you had the chance
then, isn't it?'

She saw her mother's eyes fill with tears and immediately
wished she could take the words back.

'Isn't it?' Sadie said, and walked out.

She was still packing up Ollie's things when Nanna shuffled into
the room.

'You shouldn't be so hard on her, you know,' she said.

'She shouldn't try to tell me how to bring up my son. Have you
seen Ollie's pyjama bottoms?'

'Under the bed. She was a good mother. As good as she knew
how to be, anyway.'

'She wasn't interested in me.'

'If she wasn't interested, why did she fight so hard to keep you?
Why didn't she just leave you at that unmarried mothers' home,
instead of running away with you?'

Roo didn't know anything about Sadie running away, but she
wasn't in any mood to back down. 'I wish she'd left me there,' she
muttered truculently.

'How dare you talk like that!' Nanna rapped her walking stick
hard on the floor. 'Don't you let me hear you talk like that about
your mother. You don't know the half of what she went through
for you. Oh, she was young and stupid, I'm not denying that. But
do you think it was easy for her, bringing you up on her own? She
was sixteen years old! And it wasn't like it is these days, I can tell
you. Folk round here made her life a misery, gossiping about her
behind her back.'

Roo retrieved Ollie's pyjamas and stuffed them in her bag.
'That didn't stop her enjoying herself, did it?'

'And why shouldn't she have a bit of fun? God knows, she
didn't have much to laugh about. Sometimes she'd be up at dawn

cleaning offices, then off to work in a shop all day, then back to office-cleaning at teatime. Anything to put food on the table.'

Roo thought about her mother flitting out of the house, done up like a film star. 'She never kept a job for more than five minutes.'

'They all took liberties with her, just because she was young and desperate. And they usually ended up sacking her because she needed to take time off to look after you.' Nanna sent Roo a hard look. 'They made her choose between you and the job, and she chose you every time.'

'Except for her singing,' she said bitterly. She still needed something to cling on to, a reason to resent her mother. 'She never gave that up for me.'

'That was the only dream she had left,' Nanna said. 'She thought it would be the answer to her problems. She was going to become this big star, then she could give you everything you ever wanted. We all told her it wasn't going to happen, but no one ever said your mum was level-headed. She needed her dreams. She's not perfect, Ruby. But she's always cared, in her own way.' Nanna looked thoughtful, then beckoned to her. 'Come with me. I want to show you something.'

It took a long time to get up the stairs. At least Nanna used her lift, though she grumbled all the way up.

They ended up in Sadie's room. 'Should we be in here?' Roo said.

'It's my house. Anyway, she's got no secrets from me.'

The room was typical Sadie, a haphazard riot of bright colours. Clothes were heaped up on the bed, make-up scattered over the dressing table. A faint smell of cigarettes hung in the air.

'She thinks I don't know she smokes,' Nanna chuckled. 'As if I could do anything about it! What am I going to do, put her over my knee?'

There was a stereo in the corner with a pile of CDs beside it, most of them out of their cases. Roo fought the urge to tidy them up. Suddenly she saw her mother as she used to be, dancing around the room, her blonde hair in curlers, cigarette in one hand, G&T in the other. For once the memory didn't seem bitter. She could see Sadie for what she really was – a young girl, barely more than a child herself, trying to scrape some fun out of the miserable drudgery of her life.

Nanna gestured to a table in the corner. 'Under there,' she said. 'The box.'

Roo reached under the table and pulled it out. 'What's in it?'

'Have a look.'

It took her a moment to recognise the contents. 'My old schoolbooks!'

'Not just the books. There's every school report you ever had in there. And your GCSE certificates. She never threw anything away.'

Roo rifled through the papers. Deeper inside, there were old school photos, and a couple of clumsy, handmade Mother's Day cards she'd made for her at infant school.

'She was always there, you know,' Nanna said. 'All those school concerts and prizegivings.'

'I never saw her.' She'd always assumed she'd been too busy at the nightclub.

'You wouldn't. She used to sneak in late and stand at the back.'

'Why?'

'Because she didn't want to embarrass you.' Roo had a sudden flash of herself as a teenager, refusing to acknowledge her mother at a parents' evening. It only occurred to her now how much it must have hurt. 'She was so proud of you,' Nanna went on. ' "My Ruby," she used to say. "Always so clever. She'll never end up like her daft mum." And she was right, wasn't she?'

Roo felt hot tears sting the back of her eyes. She had started to put everything back when a photo fluttered out of her English book.

It was a tall, handsome boy with dark curly hair and laughing eyes. He looked like a young David Essex in faded jeans, T-shirt and leather jacket. He also looked like trouble.

On the back, scrawled in her mother's writing, were the words, 'Johnny Franks. November 1969.'

The year before she was born.

'What have you got there?'

'Nothing.' Roo stuffed the photo back in the book and put it with the rest.

But she did have something.

After all these years, she finally had a name.

Chapter 21

Bridge House, a rambling Victorian pile, sat comfortably amid spreading lawns, its grey stone walls softened by rampant ivy. Cat stood at the drawing-room window, clutching an armful of hair magazines. She'd never seen anything like this house, with its elegant, high-ceilinged rooms, polished mahogany furniture and antique rugs.

'Cat!' Elizabeth Montague came into the room, looking stylish in cream tailored trousers and a white T-shirt, a cream cotton sweater tied loosely around her shoulders. 'Thank you so much for coming. Charlotte won't be a moment. Shall we have some tea while we're waiting?'

The housekeeper served it. Cat perched on the sofa, not daring to take a biscuit in case she scattered crumbs on the pale lemon silk. In the distance she could hear the thwack of tennis balls and faint laughter.

'My other children,' Elizabeth explained. 'James and Victoria are just back from university for the summer.'

Soon Charlotte strolled in, her hair freshly washed from the shower, dressed in jeans and T-shirt.

'There you are!' Elizabeth said. 'You really shouldn't keep Cat waiting, you know. I'm sure she has better things to do than wait on you.'

'It's the bride's prerogative to be late,' Cat said. Charlotte beamed at her.

'Exactly!'

'Not three weeks before the wedding,' Elizabeth grumbled good-naturedly.

They talked about the wedding over tea and biscuits. It sounded very grand. A marquee in the garden, champagne, a string quartet, and a sit-down meal for five hundred guests. Cat's mind boggled. How could anyone have so many friends?

'I know!' Elizabeth rolled her eyes. 'I haven't broken the news to my husband yet. I should have put my foot down over the guest list a long time ago.'

'A lot of them are your friends,' Charlotte pointed out.

'Since we're paying for it I think we're entitled, don't you?'

Charlotte turned to Cat. 'Was your mother this bossy over your wedding arrangements?'

Cat lowered her eyes. 'She died before I got married.'

'Oh, you poor thing!' Elizabeth was instantly sympathetic. At least she didn't ask how she'd died. Cat always felt embarrassed telling strangers about her mother's suicide. As if it was somehow her fault.

Several cups of tea and a lot of chat later, they finally settled down to making some decisions. Charlotte flicked through the magazines Cat had brought, exclaiming over the styles. 'They're all lovely. It's so hard to know which would suit me,' she said.

'Maybe if I saw a picture of your dress it might help,' Cat suggested.

While she was gone, Elizabeth said, 'It's so kind of you to agree to do this.'

'I still don't understand why you asked me. I know Charlotte said her usual hairdresser was on holiday but surely she could have found someone else in London to do it?'

'Why should she go to all that trouble when you're on our doorstep?'

They were interrupted by Charlotte returning with sketches of her dress. Cat studied them and offered suggestions of some styles she thought would suit. She half-expected them to fall about laughing, but they seemed to take her opinions seriously, which only made her more nervous. What if she got it wrong? What if she made a mess of it and ruined Charlotte's big day?

Elizabeth seemed to read her thoughts. 'You should have more confidence in yourself. Look, I admit when I walked into your salon it was an emergency. I wasn't expecting a brilliant job,' she said. 'But I was really impressed by what you did.'

'Me too,' Charlotte chimed in. 'And it's so much easier having you close by. With everything to organise, it's a relief to know at least one thing's sorted out. Mummy's got great taste,' she confided. 'I knew you'd be perfect as soon as she told me about you. What do you think of this one with all the curls?'

Cat studied the magazine photo. 'It's pretty, but with your dress being so simple I think something more elegant might be better. Like this.' Cat pulled her brush and pins out of her bag. She swept Charlotte's long, silky curtain of hair up and twisted it, pinning it in seconds into a sleek pleat. 'Of course, the finished result would be a lot smoother than that,' she said. 'And I could weave some pearls into it to pick out the beading on the dress . . .' She caught the look that passed between Charlotte and her mother. Oh God, had she said something naff?

Then Elizabeth smiled. 'You see?' she said. 'I told you she was good, didn't I?'

But Cat still wasn't convinced as she left the house, her magazines tucked under her arm. She was sure Elizabeth would call and tell her it had all been a mistake and they were going to get Charles Worthington after all.

She looked around the grounds as she headed back down the drive, committing every detail to memory. She couldn't wait to tell Billy about this!

Then she remembered. She and Billy were barely speaking. She could have given the Queen a home perm and he wouldn't have been interested.

'Daddy's here!' Ollie bounced up and down at the window. 'And Shauna's with him.'

'What?' Roo looked up. Her neck and shoulders ached from where she'd been hunched over her laptop for several hours. She knew she would have to get used to seeing them together sometime, but she hadn't imagined it would be so soon.

Shauna looked pasty-faced and sullen. She hung on to David's arm so tightly he had to prise her off before he could hug his son. Roo, who'd been steeling herself for this moment, was amazed at how little it bothered her.

'Shauna, what a lovely surprise,' she greeted her, determined to be utterly charming. 'How are you?'

'Shauna's suffering from morning sickness,' David answered for her.

'All day bloody sickness,' Shauna mumbled.

Her hormones hadn't been kind to her. While they allowed some pregnant women to bloom, Shauna's appeared to have gone into reverse, giving her sallow, spotty skin and greasy hair.

David surprised Roo with a hug. 'You look . . . different,' he said.

'It's my new image.' The new, slim-fitting Earl jeans were a departure for her – she hadn't owned anything denim since she left university – as was the pink T-shirt with a sequinned heart on the front. 'You're not the only one who fancied something younger-looking!'

David's mouth fell open, then he laughed. Shauna looked grumpy. 'Can we sit down?' she whined. 'My ankles are swelling up.'

That's not all that's swelling up, Roo thought. She'd obviously been taking the eating for two bit very seriously.

It was a surreal situation. Ollie sat with David on the sofa, Shauna squashed in next to them, as if she couldn't bear to let him out of her reach. It amused Roo to watch how she bossed him around, telling him off for putting too much sugar in his tea and sulking when he showed his son more attention than her. And he thought *she* was controlling!

'What's with the computer?' David asked.

'I'm trying to do some research on the internet but I don't know where to start. If it's an information superhighway then I seem to be stuck up a one-way street.'

'Maybe I could help.'

She smiled. 'I was hoping you'd say that!'

'So what is it you're looking for?' he said, as he sat down at the keyboard.

'My father.'

'Really?' His brows lifted. 'You've found him?'

'That's what I want to find out.'

'Let's see what we can do, shall we?'

'What shall I do?' Shauna said.

David glanced over his shoulder. 'You and Ollie can amuse each other for a couple of minutes, can't you?'

It felt very strange, her and David busy while the nanny entertained their son. She kept having to remind herself that Shauna wasn't the nanny any more, but her husband's girlfriend. And she couldn't remember spending so much time with David without arguing.

And just when she thought the day couldn't get any more bizarre, Matt arrived.

Roo was shocked when he let himself in. When was he going to give back that wretched key? But she was completely thrown off guard when he took her in his arms and kissed her. 'Sorry I'm late, darling, I had some research to finish.' He glanced past her ear. 'Oh hi. You must be David.'

'Who are you?'

'This is Matt—'

'Her boyfriend,' he added, squeezing her shoulder.

She felt as if she'd entered the twilight zone. Matt stretched out in the armchair opposite David, who was surreptitiously sucking in his stomach. Shauna stared from one to the other, as if she couldn't quite believe how Roo had landed such a hunk.

Roo slipped away to get more drinks. Matt followed her. 'Alone at last,' he murmured suggestively.

'What are you playing at?'

'Trying to make your husband jealous, what do you think? I saw them pull up and I guessed you might be feeling outnumbered, so I came to lend you some moral support.' He grinned. 'If you ask me, your husband's beginning to realise he's made a big mistake. Why the hell did he trade you in for her?'

Before Roo could reply the kitchen door flew open and David stormed in.

'Sorry to break up the party, but Shauna says can she have mineral water?' he said.

Matt insisted on staying for a drink. Roo cringed as he chatted to David, all the while keeping his arm firmly around her shoulders.

'I didn't know you were so fond of toyboys,' David grunted after he'd gone.

'You can talk.' Roo stared at the door, absurdly disappointed that Matt hadn't kissed her goodbye. 'At least he's out of his teens.'

Shortly afterwards, Shauna nagged David into taking her back to their hotel in Leeds, saying she felt tired.

'Can I come?' Ollie asked. David and Roo looked at each other.

'Would you mind?' he asked.

'I don't see why not.'

As Roo followed Ollie upstairs to pack his overnight things, she heard Shauna grumble, 'You could have asked me if I minded!'

They were all smiles again by the time Roo and Ollie returned, although Shauna's appeared to have been nailed in place. 'I've called the hotel and it's all arranged,' David said. 'They're putting an extra bed in our room.'

'Can we go to McDonald's?' Ollie asked as they headed for the car.

'Definitely not,' Shauna said. 'The smell makes me heave.'

As they drove away, Roo could see Shauna's mouth moving in a constant litany of complaint. She almost felt sorry for David. Almost.

But she didn't want him back. She was surprised at how little she felt for him. She was sad that she hadn't been able to make it work, and wistful for what might have been. And she was still fond of him, but more as a friend than a husband. She hoped she hadn't driven him to make a terrible mistake with Shauna.

So Matt had been wasting his time, trying to make David jealous. But it was nice of him to try, she thought. On impulse, she grabbed a bottle of wine from the fridge and went round to thank him.

A girl answered the door. She was small, dark and curvaceous. Matt's Wallace and Gromit T-shirt skimmed her tanned thighs. 'Yes?' her voice was huskily foreign.

'Is Matt around?'

'He's in the shower. Can I help you?'

'I, er, just came to give him this.' She thrust the bottle into the girl's hands and fled, deeply embarrassed and cursing herself for being so stupid. It was Saturday night, for heaven's sake! How did she ever imagine Matt would be spending a quiet evening in front of the telly?

David brought Ollie back on his own the following afternoon. 'Shauna's back at the hotel. She isn't feeling too well.' He smiled wanly. 'I'd forgotten what all this pregnancy business is like,' he admitted.

'Luckily you're not the one with your head down the toilet. Coffee?' she offered.

'Please. Lots of sugar.' He grimaced. 'Shauna thinks it's bad for me.'

So did I, but it's not my problem any more, she thought, ladling in an extra spoonful. It occurred to her that David needed someone to boss him around, otherwise he felt totally lost.

As they drank their coffee he said, 'When is Ollie coming back to London?'

It was the question she'd been dreading. But she'd promised herself she would be utterly fair about it when the time came. 'When do you want him?'

'I'd like to take him home with me tonight.'

'No!' So much for being utterly fair. 'It's far too short notice.'

'It would mean you could get on with your work without worrying about childcare.'

'I can manage, thank you.' Funny how the thought of coping with childcare wasn't nearly so terrible as the thought of coping without her son these days. 'Sadie's looking after him.'

'Your mother?'

'What's wrong with that?'

'Nothing. I just thought she's the last person you'd ask for help.'

'I didn't ask. She offered. And I pay her, so it's a business arrangement.' She stirred her spoon around her mug, scraping the milky froth from the rim. 'Anyway, she's got quite close to Ollie. She'd be upset if I just sent him away without giving her a chance to say goodbye.'

'Why don't we ask Ollie what he wants?' David suggested.

'That's not fair. You can't expect him to choose!'

'What's wrong? Worried he might not choose you?'

As David called Ollie and put the question to him she prayed silently.

Ollie looked from one to the other. 'I want to stay with Mummy.'

Roo, who'd been steeling herself not to get upset, looked up sharply. So did David. 'What?' they said together.

'I'd miss Harvey,' Ollie said.

Roo smiled. That was honest. 'Matt's dog,' she explained to David.

'Ah.' She saw his disappointed face and felt sorry for him.

'Why don't you stay here for another week and then go and visit Daddy?' she said. 'That'll give you a chance to play with Harvey and see Sadie and then you can say goodbye to them properly before you go.'

'And will you come with me?' Ollie asked.

'I can't, sweetheart.' She was amazed at how sad she already felt at the prospect of him going. 'But I'll only be here for a couple of weeks longer and then I'll be coming back to London too.'

'And then you'll be going somewhere else,' Ollie said in a small, accusing voice. 'You're always going somewhere.'

'We'll see.' Now it was just her and Ollie she was going to have to cut back on travelling. And if Gerry Matthews didn't like it – tough.

As David left, she said, 'By the way, just in case you were wondering. Ollie's best friend is called George and he prefers cricket to football.'

David smiled. 'Very good. You'll make a mother yet.'

He was halfway to his car before he turned back. 'I almost forgot. I did a bit of digging on the internet when we got back to the hotel last night and found this for you.' He pulled a scrap of paper out of his pocket and gave it to her.

'What is it?'

'Your father's address and phone number.'

Roo stared down at the paper in her hand. 'Are you sure it's him?'

'No, but it's the only Johnny Franks I could find. And he's in Sheffield, so it's possible he's the same one.' He regarded her curiously. 'Do you know anything about this guy?'

'Nothing.'

A slow smile spread across David's face. 'Then I think you might be in for a bit of a shock,' he said.

'A lap-dancing club?' Matt said.

Roo was instantly defensive. 'We don't know that for sure. It says it's a "private gentlemen's establishment".'

'Roo, the place is called *Babes*. They're hardly going to be passing the port and swapping war stories, are they?' Matt was highly amused. 'Fancy that. Your long-lost dad is Peter String-fellow!'

'Don't.' Roo groaned. She was still trying to get used to the idea herself. It wasn't quite what she'd imagined. She'd sort of hoped Johnny Franks might turn out to be a doctor, or a bank manager. She never in her wildest nightmares thought he'd be a medallion-wearing nightclub owner.

'If you feel like that, maybe it would be better if you didn't find out any more,' Matt suggested.

'I can't leave it now.'

'It's better than being disappointed.'

'I've spent my whole life wondering who my father is. Now I finally get the chance to find out. Do you really think I'm going to give up just in case I'm disappointed?'

'I suppose not.' Matt looked at the scrap of paper in his hand. 'Are you going to tell your mother about this?'

'I don't see why I should.'

'She might not want her past dragged up. She might have a good reason for wanting it to stay buried. You ought to give her the chance to prepare herself, at least.'

'She's had over thirty years to prepare herself. Now I have a right to know.' Roo was beginning to wish she'd never shared her good news with Matt. She'd thought he might be pleased for her, but all he'd done was pour cold water over her excitement.

'What if she's trying to protect you?' Matt said.

'Look, I'm a big girl now. I make my own decisions and I certainly don't need protecting. I'm going to see this Johnny Franks.'

'Please yourself,' Matt shrugged. 'But don't say I didn't warn you.'

Chapter 22

Roo sat in the bar of the Park Solihull Hotel, feeling pleasantly drunk. It was rare that she allowed herself to indulge, but this was a special occasion. Earlier that day, she and Billy had secured a contract with Roger Fleet to supply the furniture for the refurbished Park Hotels.

Now they were celebrating, although neither of them could quite believe they'd pulled it off.

'I wonder what swung it in the end?' Billy mused as they started on their second bottle of Pinot Grigio.

'Salvatore,' Roo said. 'If that new range wasn't generating such a buzz Roger Fleet might not have been interested.' Everyone in the industry was talking about their partnership. People were beginning to look at Fairbanks with new respect.

Billy gazed into his glass. 'It was a good idea to get him on board.'

'I thought you didn't like him.'

'Only because I thought he was after you. I didn't want to see you getting hurt,' Billy went on.

'And there was me, thinking you were jealous.'

'Maybe I was. A bit.'

There was a second's charged silence and then suddenly they were both talking about something else.

'I can't wait to tell George the good news,' Roo said.

Billy regarded her thoughtfully. 'You've got quite close to the old man, haven't you? Do you always get this involved with your clients?'

'Never.' She'd broken all her own rules, letting it get personal and allowing her feelings to cloud her professional judgement. If Fairbanks had been any other company, she would probably have closed it down weeks ago.

But she'd done it for George's sake, because she felt he deserved better than to have his life's work die with him.

It was a pity his son didn't inspire the same loyalty. Roo couldn't imagine Frederick running the company after George was gone. He had some bright ideas, but he didn't strike her as very competent or committed to the company.

She said as much to Billy. 'I mean, when George retires,' she added, remembering just in time that Billy didn't have a clue that he was ill. No one did, apart from her and his family.

'I doubt if that will happen,' Billy said. 'They'll have to carry the old man out of that place in his box.'

Roo suppressed a shudder. He didn't know how close to the truth he was. 'I suppose it's inevitable Frederick will end up running the company,' she said.

'I'm certain of it. George wouldn't hear of anyone but a Fairbanks in charge. Not that there's much love lost between him and his son,' he went on. 'Between you and me, I'm not sure if George trusts Frederick to run the company in the time-honoured way.'

'Maybe he's got a point,' Roo said. 'Sticking to tradition hasn't done them a lot of good so far.'

'True, but that's the way George wants things done. Since Frederick's the last of the Fairbanks line, the company will have to go to him.' He sipped his drink. 'Let's hope it doesn't happen for a few more years.'

Roo was silent as he topped up her glass.

They finished the bottle and headed up to their rooms, drunk and happy. 'Fancy a nightcap?' Billy asked as they said goodnight outside his door. 'I could show you the new website we've set up.'

Roo hesitated. Every iota of common sense told her it was a bad idea. But lulled by alcohol and euphoria, she didn't want the evening to end. 'Why not?'

The message light was flashing on his bedside phone. 'Aren't you going to listen to that?' Roo asked.

'It'll only be Cat.' He peered inside the minibar. 'What can I get you? Whisky? Vodka? Gin?'

'Vodka and tonic would be nice.' She glanced back at the phone. 'Have you two had another row?'

'We can't seem to talk without it ending up in an argument these days.' He added tonic to her glass. 'Sorry, there's no ice.'

'It doesn't matter.' She took the glass from him. 'Is it because of this protest?'

'Not any more. It's gone beyond all that.' He took his laptop out of its case. 'Now, about this website. You've got to remember, it's just a work in progress . . .'

They lay side by side on the bed, their shoulders touching. Roo tried to concentrate on the screen. She looked down at his long fingers as they whispered over the keys, bringing up images on the screen.

'I wonder what Cat would say if she could see us now,' she said.

'She'd probably go mad, as usual.' Billy didn't smile as he tapped in his password.

'She's still jealous, then?'

'You could say that. I don't understand it. I've never given her any reason not to trust me. I've never even looked at another woman since we got married.'

'Lucky her,' Roo said. 'Mine did a lot more than look.'

Billy glanced at her. 'I'm sorry,' he said. 'I wasn't thinking. How are things between you two?'

'It's strange, we seem to get on better now we're apart than we ever did when we were together. I don't know why we ever got married,' she said wryly.

'Presumably you must have loved each other.'

'Like you loved Cat when you married her?'

'Touché.' His mouth twisted. 'So are you saying you didn't love him?'

Roo considered for a moment. 'I thought he was what I wanted. And so did he. But we were both wrong.'

258

'So what did you want?'

She looked at him. You, she wanted to say. Surely he knew that. 'Something I couldn't have,' she said.

Their eyes met and held. A second later he rolled away from her and stood up. 'I think I will get that ice after all,' he said. He grabbed the ice bucket and left.

Roo rolled over on to her back and covered her eyes. What the hell had she done? She didn't even fancy Billy any more. It must be the alcohol, she decided.

The phone rang on the bedside table. Without thinking, Roo reached across to answer it.

'Hello?' The line went dead.

Billy came back as she was hanging up. 'Who was that?'

'They hung up. Must be a wrong number.' She sat up, straightening down her clothes. 'Look, Billy, I don't think I can finish this drink. I'm tired, and I'm going to be wrecked in the morning.'

'To be honest I'm not really in the mood either.' He put the ice bucket down, not meeting her eye.

As she headed for the door he suddenly said, 'Roo?'

'Yes?'

He looked at her. 'I do love Cat, you know.'

Cat put the phone down, shaking. And to think she'd called Billy to try to apologise for their row! He hadn't wasted much time getting Ruby to console him, had he?

She'd been doing her best to keep her jealousy in check, telling herself she was being paranoid. Of course Billy couldn't ignore Ruby, he had to work with her. Just because they were friends it didn't mean he loved Cat less.

She'd even planned to leave the Fairbanks campaign so it wouldn't antagonise him. Of course, Marjorie had made some sarcastic remark about her bowing to her lord and master, but Cat didn't care. All she wanted was to save her marriage. Billy was far more important than anything else.

And he'd betrayed her. Not only that, he'd had the nerve to make her feel bad for suspecting them!

259

She didn't deserve that. Okay, so maybe he didn't love her as much as he loved Roo, but she'd tried so hard to be a good wife to him and make him happy. She couldn't help it if she wasn't her cousin.

She went to bed but couldn't sleep. The bed felt too big without Billy, and she kept hearing Ruby's voice on the other end of the phone. Every time she closed her eyes she saw them entwined in each other's arms.

All night she lay awake, wondering what to do. Should she confront Billy with it? Should she wait for him to confess? Or should she just pretend it hadn't happened and hope it would all go away?

The following morning she had a thumping headache from lack of sleep. Her neck muscles were like knotted ropes of tension. Megan and Liam, sensing her mood, ate their breakfast like lambs for once. They even went off to brush their teeth without her nagging them.

Maxine wasn't pleased when she called in sick, but for once Cat didn't care. It would do Julie good to cover for her clients for once; Cat was constantly covering for her while she took Dwayne to his many juvenile court appearances.

She was on her third cup of coffee and wondering whether it was too late to take up smoking when Dominic arrived to pick up Becky. 'She's still in the shower,' Cat told him.

'I'm in no hurry.' Dominic sat down and poured himself a bowl of Frosties. 'You all right, Mrs K? You look a bit peaky.'

'Just a headache.'

'I don't suppose we'll be meeting like this much longer,' Dominic said through a mouthful of cereal. 'Not after Becky moves to London.'

Oh Lord, she'd forgotten Becky was supposed to be going on that work placement to London soon. Another member of her family Ruby was stealing away. Soon she wouldn't have anyone left.

Would Becky still go when she found out her father was having an affair? She had a sudden, horrible picture of the three of them living together in Ruby's London house, one big happy family, leaving her with the shredded remnants of her old life.

'It's great news about her going, isn't it?' Dominic broke into her thoughts. 'I've always said she was wasted at Fairbanks.'

'Won't you miss her?'

'Of course I will. But I can't hold her back, can I? That would be selfish.'

Cat was stung. Why hadn't she been that generous all those years ago, when Billy wanted to leave Normanford, instead of clinging on so pathetically?

'I mean, I could tell her I didn't want her to go,' Dominic went on. 'But knowing Becky, she'd probably go anyway, and that'd be us finished. Or if she stayed she'd end up hating me for ruining her chance to make something of herself.'

Cat felt sick. He could have been talking about her and Billy.

'Anyway, you know what they say, don't you? "If you love someone, set them free." ' He screwed up his face. 'Shakespeare said that.'

'I think you'll find it was Sting, Dominic.'

Billy came home late that afternoon. Cat's heart lurched as she heard his key in the front door.

He must have seen her car in the drive because he came into the sitting room looking for her.

'Cat? What's wrong? Why aren't you at work?' As he swooped to kiss her, Cat turned her face so he caught her cheek instead.

'I wasn't feeling well.' She wasn't feeling well now. Her stomach was churning like a ferry in a force nine gale.

'Poor you. Why don't we go upstairs and I'll make you feel better?'

'As good as you made my cousin feel?' Cat shrugged him off. 'Don't touch me!'

His face fell. 'Not this again.'

'So what were the two of you doing in your room at eleven o'clock last night? Playing dominoes? Or was it another one of your "business meetings"?'

He couldn't hide the fleeting look of guilt. 'We were having a drink.'

'Very cosy, I'm sure. Do you think I'm stupid or something?'

'At this moment – yes.'

'Thank you. It's nice to know what you really think of me.'

'I didn't mean it like that. I'm just sick of your accusations.'

'And I'm sick of being treated like a fool. I might not be as clever as her, but I can see what's going on under my nose!'

'There's nothing going on. Roo and I aren't having an affair. Nothing could be further from the truth.'

'Why don't I believe you?'

'I don't know. Because you're fucked up and insecure?'

They glared at each other. Tears stung her eyes but she fought them back, determined not to cry. 'And do you wonder why? You sleep with my cousin and then try to make me feel bad about it!'

'I didn't sleep with her.' He sounded weary. 'All right, maybe I could have. But I wouldn't.'

'Why not?'

'Because I'm married to you! And believe it or not, I take those marriage vows seriously. If you don't trust me, I might as well not be here.'

So that was it. He was still trapped, tied to her. It wasn't that he loved her, he just couldn't bring himself to break a sacred promise.

Dominic's words came back to her. If you love someone, set them free.

She took a deep breath. 'Fine. You'd better go, hadn't you?'

He stared at her. 'You don't mean that.'

'Like you said, what's the point in staying if I can't trust you?'

'Fine. I'll go and pack my things.'

Cat listened to him overhead as he opened and closed cupboard doors, and felt a chill creep around her heart. It was all she could do not to beg him to stay. She kept thinking it was all an act, that he wouldn't really go through with it. However bad things were, he wouldn't leave her.

The next thing she knew he was standing in the hall with his bags. 'Tell the kids I'll call them later,' he said. 'Perhaps you can explain to them what's going on, because I don't have a bloody clue!'

Even then she didn't think he'd go. She held her breath, waiting for him to turn around and take her in his arms. All she needed was one word of reassurance.

'You know, you're right,' he said. 'Maybe it is better if we're apart. I don't know you any more. You're not the woman I married.'

'You mean I've stopped being a doormat?'

'No,' he said. 'You've started being a bitch.'

She flinched as the door slammed shut. He was gone. The nightmare she'd always dreaded had come true. She was alone.

Only then, alone in the house with no one to see her weakness, did she allow herself to cry.

From the outside, it was very discreet. So discreet Roo walked past the doorway three times before she noticed the tiny brass plaque bearing the words, 'BABES – Members Only'.

Down the narrow stairway that led from the street, it was a different story. Even in the middle of the afternoon the place was dark, hot and sleazy, with deep-plum-coloured walls and leopard-skin sofas. The room was dominated by a long catwalk surrounded by tables and chairs. A big-breasted blonde wearing a policeman's helmet, a G-string and a set of handcuffs was gyrating around a pole, watched by a group of bored-looking businessmen.

As Roo stared, a leggy black girl loomed out of the shadows towards her. 'Can I help you?'

'I'm here to see Johnny Franks.'

'Do you have an appointment?'

She was just about to reply when a big, shaven-headed man in a suit appeared and said, 'You're here for Mr Franks? He's in the VIP lounge.' He pointed to a door at the far end of the club.

The VIP lounge had fuschia pink walls, white leather sofas and heavily shaded lamps. Roo spotted Johnny Franks straight away. He was lounging on one of the sofas, flanked by a pair of heavies.

His curly hair had greyed to the colour of pewter, but it was definitely the man in the photo. He had an aura of menace and power, from his heavy-set body in his well-cut suit to the thick gold jewellery that adorned his deeply tanned wrists. Roo knew at once this was the kind of man who dropped people in the River Aire wearing concrete swimming trunks.

He looked up as she approached, his wolfish eyes sweeping over her.

'Mr Franks,' she stammered. 'Thanks for seeing me.'

One of the brawny men spoke for him. 'Get changed in the back,' he said brusquely.

She looked at him blankly. 'I'm sorry?'

'Into your gear. I take it you don't want to audition in that get-up?' He looked her sober navy suit up and down.

'Audition?' Suddenly it dawned on her. 'Oh no! I'm not a lap-dancer!'

'Thank Christ for that!' Johnny Franks muttered. They all laughed.

'So if you're not here for the audition what do you want?' the man asked.

'I . . . I'm . . .' Her brain deserted her. She hadn't expected to get this far, and had no idea what to say. So she just said the first thing that came into her head.

'I'm your daughter,' she told Johnny Franks.

At least it got his attention. Those silvery eyes fixed on her. Then the other man said, 'Are you some kind of nutter?'

He moved towards her but Roo stood her ground. 'My name is Ruby,' she said. 'Ruby Tuesday Moon. You might remember my mother – Sadie Moon?'

There was a long silence. The two henchmen glanced at each other then at their boss, like Rottweilers awaiting their master's command. Finally he said in a deep, gravelly voice, 'Get rid of her.'

Five minutes later she was back on the street. She headed back to her car, so furious she barely noticed the sleek black limo gliding to a halt alongside her, until the electric window slid down and a voice said, 'Get in.'

'Fuck off,' Roo said, not breaking her stride.

'I see you've got your mother's way with words.'

She stopped. 'So you admit you know her, then?'

'Oh aye, I know her all right. Now will you get in this car before I'm arrested for kerb-crawling?'

Inside the warm, musky-smelling interior of the car Johnny Franks seemed even more intimidating.

'So what makes you think I'm your father?' he said. 'Did Sadie tell you?'

'No, but I found a photo of you.'

'I've got a photo of the Queen, but that doesn't make her my bloody mother!'

'It was the only photo she had. I thought it might mean something.'

'Is that right?' He scratched his chin thoughtfully. 'And did your mother tell you where to find me?'

Roo shook her head. 'She doesn't know anything about this.'

Johnny gazed out of the smoky window as the car cruised steadily past rundown shops and houses. 'Sorry, I'm not your father,' he said finally.

'You would say that, wouldn't you?'

'I'm saying it because it's true!' He turned on her. 'Do you think I'd walk out on my own kid? If Sadie had been carrying my baby I would have married her.'

'But how do you know you're not my father?'

'Because she told me.' A muscle worked in his jaw. 'And because on the day you were conceived I was doing time in Armley jail. Satisfied now?'

'So do you know whose baby I was?'

'If I'd known that I would have killed him.' He signalled to the driver to stop the car. 'This is where we part company,' he said.

Roo didn't argue. As she got out of the car Johnny said, 'Your mother never got wed, then?'

She looked at him bleakly. 'Would I be here if she had?'

'I can't believe you did that,' Matt said.

'I know.' She was still shaking two hours later. 'I confronted a bunch of gangsters.'

'No, I can't believe you went to a lap-dancing club without me. You knew I was looking forward to it.'

Roo smiled in spite of herself. 'Be serious!'

'I am.' He grinned. 'Did they really mistake you for an exotic dancer?'

'Not for long. I think I'd flunked the audition without needing to take my clothes off.'

'I find that hard to believe.' Matt sent her the kind of look that might have turned her to a quivering heap if she didn't know he was joking.

'Anyway, I'm no nearer to finding out who my father is,' she said. 'Johnny Franks is certain it's not him.'

'And you believe him?'

'I don't know what to believe. I mean, he's the likeliest candidate. I don't have any other names. If it's not him, who else could it be?' Although secretly she didn't relish the thought of having a gangster for a father, it was better than nothing.

'Perhaps he is your father and he just needs some time to get used to it,' Matt suggested. 'After all, it's not every day someone turns up out of the blue claiming to be your daughter, is it?'

'Maybe. But how do you explain the bit about him being in jail?'

'There's only one person who can answer that. Your mum. You're going to have to ask her again.'

'I suppose so,' Roo agreed heavily. 'Although I doubt I'll get any further with her than I did with Johnny Franks.'

They sat in thoughtful silence for a while. Then Matt said, 'So tell me about this blonde in the G-string and the policeman's helmet.'

'And handcuffs,' Roo reminded him.

'Oh God, I forgot about the handcuffs. Tell me more about the handcuffs.'

'No.'

'If Johnny Franks does turn out to be your dad, do you think he'd let you borrow the handcuffs?'

'Matt!' She hit him as the doorbell rang.

Roo looked up. 'Who's that?'

'I suggest you open the door and find out. If it's a half-naked blonde in a police helmet, tell her she can take down my particulars!' he called after her.

But it wasn't. Billy stood on the doorstep looking doleful, his bags around his feet. 'Cat's kicked me out,' he said. 'Can I sleep on your sofa?'

Chapter 23

'She kicked you out?' Roo repeated. 'Why?'

'She said she couldn't trust me any more.' He spotted Matt in the hallway behind her. 'Sorry, I didn't know you had company. I'll go—'

'No. Stay.'

'Are you sure? I don't want to be in the way.'

'You're not.' She and Matt exchanged looks as she moved aside to let him in. Why was he frowning at her like that?

'I tried the B and B but it's full. And I couldn't face driving all the way to Leeds tonight.'

What he meant was he couldn't face being alone. Roo didn't blame him. 'Have you eaten? Can I get you a sandwich or something?'

'That would be good.' He smiled gratefully.

'Go and sit down and I'll bring it in to you.' Roo went into the kitchen. Matt followed, closing the door behind him.

'What's that all about?'

'What else can I do? He's got nowhere else to go. I can't just turn him away, can I?'

Matt pulled a leaf off a plant on her kitchen windowsill. 'It looks like you've finally got him to yourself. That's what you wanted, isn't it?'

'Don't be ridiculous.' Roo buttered bread furiously. 'You sound just like Cat.'

'You've got to admit, it's all worked out pretty well for you.'

'You think so, do you?' She swung round, brandishing the

knife. 'My marriage has broken up, my husband's run off with a pregnant teenager and that's your idea of things working out pretty well?'

Matt delicately turned the tip of the knife away from him. 'At least you're both free,' he said.

'But I'm not interested! Why can't anyone understand that? I DO NOT FANCY BILLY KITCHENER!' she shouted, as the door opened and Billy walked in.

'Am I interrupting something?'

'I'm going to work.' Matt pushed past him into the hall.

'I hope I haven't caused a row,' Billy said when the front door banged shut.

'No, it's fine.' Roo handed him the plate.

'I don't think your boyfriend likes me being here.'

'He's not my boyfriend. And it's nothing to do with him.'

'Where's Ollie?'

'In bed.' She paused, choosing her words carefully. 'I'm not saying this because I want you to go or anything, but do you really think it's a good idea for you to be here? If Cat thinks we're having an affair, it's hardly going to calm her down if she finds out you're with me, is it?'

'At the moment I couldn't care less,' Billy said. 'She wants to believe the worst of me anyway, so why should I worry about what she thinks?'

'Are you sure you're not just doing it to spite her?'

'No! Maybe. Oh God, I don't know. How did I ever get in this mess?'

'It sounds to me like it's Cat's fault. What brought this on, anyway?'

'She rang my room last night and you were there.'

'Oh Lord. Was that her?' No wonder she'd put the phone down. 'But nothing happened.' Although for a split second she'd wanted it to.

'That's not the point, is it? The point is we should never have been in that position. I knew Cat was as jealous as hell about you and what did I do? I invited you to my room. I knew she'd be hurt if she found out and I took no notice. I put myself first, just like I've always done.' He put down his plate, his food untouched. 'I've been a selfish bastard from the day we got married.'

'How can you say that, after everything you gave up for her?'

'I didn't give anything up. Nothing I didn't want to, anyway.'

'But what about all your hopes and dreams?'

'They weren't really mine. Even the whole idea of going to university was my mother's idea. She wanted me to make something of my life. She wanted to choose my future, just like she tried to choose everything else for me.' He looked bitter. 'That's partly why I was so determined to marry Cat. Because I knew how much it would piss my mother off. How pathetic is that?'

Roo could barely take it in. All this time she'd thought Cat had trapped him into marriage, but all she'd done was give him a way of escaping his mother's clutches. 'I need a drink,' she said, reaching into the fridge.

'So why didn't you leave?' she asked later, when she'd cracked open a bottle of wine.

'I thought about it. Especially after Becky was born. We were barely more than kids ourselves, and we were stuck with no money and a baby to look after. We argued all the time.'

'So why didn't you leave?' she repeated.

'I couldn't do it to Cat. I'd made a commitment and I meant to stick to it. I cared too much to let her down.' He swirled his drink around in his glass. 'And things started to get better after a while. Becky went to playschool, Cat got a part-time job and I went back to college. It really seemed as if we could see some light at the end of the tunnel. And then Cat got pregnant again.'

'That must have been pretty devastating.'

'It felt like the end of the world. And of course I blamed Cat. I just kept thinking, how stupid was she to accidentally get pregnant twice? It never occurred to me it might be my fault too. I was oh-so-perfect Billy Kitchener, the boy who never made mistakes.'

Roo gazed at his remorseful face, knowing she was as guilty as he was. She'd been so jealous and angry when Cat got pregnant, she hadn't stopped to think it might take two. 'So what happened then?'

'We stopped speaking to each other for months. I was so wrapped up in myself, I couldn't see what Cat was going through. And then she was rushed to hospital.' He stared up at the ceiling, controlling his emotions. 'Apparently her blood pressure had gone sky-high. The doctors had told her to rest but she insisted on going to work and looking after Becky. She said she didn't want to put any more pressure on me.' His voice shook. 'By the time they got her to hospital, it was too late. Michael was born dead, and they thought Cat was going to die too.' He looked at Roo. 'That was when I finally realised how much I'd grown to love her. Although God knows why she ever stuck with a self-pitying idiot like me.'

'Maybe she loves you.'

'Maybe she did. But I've thrown it all away, haven't I? Cat's right, I've never taken her seriously. Deep down I suppose I've always thought the same as everyone else: that I was doing her a favour being with her. When really she was the one doing me a favour.' He covered his eyes with his hand, his shoulders shaking. Roo fought the urge to put her arms around him. After last night she was terrified of getting too close. 'I need her,' he said. 'All this time I've acted like I was the strong one, and she needed me. I made her feel grateful just for being with me. But I'm nothing without her and the kids.'

'You'll sort it out,' Roo promised.

'Will we? I'm worried she might realise she's better off without me.'

Finally Billy was all talked out. He curled up on the sofa under the spare duvet while Roo went to bed. She felt sorry for Billy but she had problems of her own to deal with. Like the fact that she was going to have to tackle her mother the following day and find out the truth about Johnny Franks.

She waited until the following evening, when she picked Ollie up after work.

'I met an old friend of yours yesterday,' she said, as they stood in the back doorway waiting for Ollie to finish playing in the garden.

'Oh yes? Who was that?'

'Johnny Franks.'

Sadie was silent for a moment. Her face, fixed on Ollie, gave nothing away. Then in a carefully neutral voice she said, 'I can't say I remember the name.'

'So why do you keep his photo in that box of yours?'

Sadie turned on her. 'You've been going through my things? You had no right to do that!'

'Is he my father?'

'What? No!' Sadie's face was blanched with rage.

'So why do you keep his photo?'

'I don't know. I forgot I even had the bloody thing.'

'You're lying. Why can't you be honest with me?'

'I am. Johnny Franks isn't your father, all right? Oh God, why did you have to go and dig all this up?' She twisted her hands in agitation.

'Because I've got a right to know. If he isn't my father, who is?'

Sadie turned back to where Ollie was playing. The light flooding in from the back door caught the lines fanning out from her eyes. 'He wasn't worth knowing.'

'You must have thought so once, or you wouldn't have got pregnant.'

Sadie flashed her a look and for a second it seemed as if she was about to say something. Then she went into the yard and called Ollie in.

Frustrated, Roo had no choice but to end the conversation. In clipped voices they talked about arrangements for dropping Ollie off the next day. Then, as they were heading for the car, she said, 'You might as well tell me the truth, because I'm going to find out anyway.'

Not if I've got anything to do with it, Sadie thought as she watched them drive away. Why couldn't Ruby leave well alone? Why did she have to keep digging up the past?

And now she'd found Johnny. Hearing his name again after all this time had been a massive shock. She couldn't remember the last time she'd said it out loud. She'd closed the door on that part of her life over thirty years ago.

And yet she hadn't. There was still a part of her that was wretchedly in love with him. No man she'd met since had ever come close.

She made a start on her mother's supper, still thinking about Johnny and the time they'd first met. Everyone adored Johnny Franks. Especially the girls who hung around the fairground where he worked. They all wanted to tame the boy with the dark, gypsy good looks and wild reputation. But Sadie didn't. She was the only one who didn't want him to settle down and find a steady job. Which was probably why she was the only one he didn't want to love and leave. She took the trouble to see beyond his arrogance, to the frightened boy who kept moving to escape his troubled past. While everyone else thought of him as a tough street-fighter, she knew those scars on his face were the result of having his skull fractured by his drunken stepfather while trying to protect his mother from another beating. Later, when his mother died, he'd run away from home at the age of thirteen and taken his younger brother on the road. Sadie was the only one he'd ever confessed to about his past. He'd trusted her.

And she'd let him down.

Johnny was twenty-one when he was sent to jail. His kid brother Darren had fallen in with the wrong crowd and got involved with a burglary, and Johnny had taken the blame to keep him out of prison. He got six months. Sadie said she'd wait for him, of course. They'd already started to make plans about their future, and Johnny had promised to stop travelling and settle down once he got out.

But one night had changed all that.

The worst moment of her life was getting pregnant. The second worst was breaking the news to Johnny. Even now she could clearly remember the hurt and pain that flashed across his face when he found out.

And then came the anger. Sadie had braced herself, biting her lip to hold back the tears as he raged at her, calling her filthy names, making her feel dirty all over again. But she'd refused to tell him who the father was, no matter how much he screamed at her.

He left town the next day. She never saw him again. She let everyone think he'd left her alone and pregnant because it was easier that way. It meant there were no more awkward questions about who the real father was. But she felt guilty when Tom and her mother refused to have his name spoken in the house, because she knew she was the one at fault, not him. He would have done anything for her, and she'd let him down.

Irene was growing restless, wanting supper. She'd started to root around noisily in the cupboards, muttering about just needing 'a biscuit to keep me going'.

'I'm cooking sausages and mash,' Sadie told her. 'It'll be ready in five minutes.'

Irene glanced at the empty pan boiling away on the hob. 'It might help if you stuck a few potatoes in there.' She eyed her daughter narrowly. 'You're miles away, aren't you?'

Sadie sighed, reaching for the vegetable rack. 'I wish I was.'

Salvatore Bellini's drawings had been couriered overnight from Milan and were waiting for her when she got into the office the following day. Roo could hardly contain her excitement as she looked at them. Even to her untrained eye, they were something special. Simple but stunning designs, just as they'd asked for. Cherry wood dining table and chairs, sliced through with pale, contrasting slivers of ash. A long, low coffee table inlaid with two kinds of maple. Bookcases and storage units that could be mixed and matched to fit any room. For the first time she allowed herself to hope that their partnership might work.

She wished Becky was there to see them. But she'd taken some time off to deal with 'personal problems'.

No need to ask what they were. She wondered if Becky was listening to her mother endlessly going on about her break-up in the same way she had listened to Billy. After two sleepless nights on her sofa, he'd finally been persuaded it might be better for the sake of his marriage if he moved in to the B&B.

'I'm going up to show these drawings to George Fairbanks,' she told the girls in the main office. 'I should be back in half an hour if anyone wants me—'

They all stopped typing. 'You haven't heard, then?' one of them said.

'Heard what?'

'Mr Fairbanks was taken to hospital this morning.'

Frederick was talking on his mobile phone outside his father's room in the private hospital. He hung up abruptly when he spotted Roo approaching down the corridor.

'What are you doing here?' he demanded. 'This is a family matter.'

Roo ignored that. 'How is he?' she asked.

'Holding on. Mother's with him at the moment.'

Before Roo could say anything, the door opened and a tall, silver-haired woman emerged, dabbing her eyes. Frederick rushed to her side.

'How is he, Mother? Is there any news?'

She looked straight past him to Roo. 'Are you Ruby Moon?' she said in a voice full of quiet dignity.

'I . . . yes,' Roo nodded, not wanting to quibble over her name.

'He's asked to see you.'

Frederick looked petulant. 'How did he know she'd be here?'

'I don't know,' his mother said. 'He just said he knew she would be.' She touched Roo's arm as she passed. 'Be careful, my dear. He's very weak.'

It could have been a room in a luxury hotel, with billowing chintz curtain swags and reproductions of old masters on the eau de nil striped walls. Until you noticed all the tubes and bleeping machines surrounding the bed.

George Fairbanks was as white as the sheet he lay on. He seemed to have shrunk and shrivelled inside his skin.

He turned his head slightly to look at her, a smile lighting up his eyes. 'I told Agnes you'd be here,' he whispered.

'How are you?'

'I'll live to fight another day, lass.'

Roo could hardly speak herself. She kept thinking of the spirited old man she'd first met, who was so determined to save his company he'd staggered off his sick bed to confront her. They'd had some bitter arguments since then, but she'd never lost her respect for him.

'I've got something to show you,' she said, taking Salvatore's drawings out of her bag. She had to hold the papers up in front of his face because he was too weak to hold them for himself. But he studied them carefully, asking questions, not missing a single detail.

'You can tell he's Italian,' he said finally.

Roo laughed. 'Is that good or bad?'

'Bit flashy. But I reckon we can make a good job of it. And Billy says it'll sell, does he?'

'We've already had loads of interest and they haven't even seen the designs yet. We're planning a big marketing launch for a couple of months' time.'

'I'll have to put it in my diary,' George said.

'And we signed the Park Hotels deal two days ago,' she went on, feeling tears sting her eyes. 'I've talked to Leonard about it, and we should be in production again by the end of the month. We'll have all our staff back on full-time. We might even have to offer them overtime, to cope with retraining once our new machines arrive!' Suddenly all she wanted to do was please him, to bring a smile to that gaunt face.

'New machines, eh? That should make a big difference.' He lifted his head from the pillow, struggling to nod his approval. It took all his strength to do it. 'You did well, lass.'

Roo's heart swelled inside her chest. Those words meant more to her than any incentive bonus Warner and Hicks could come up with. 'I was just doing my job,' she said.

They talked a little more, until she could see George was getting tired. 'I'd better head back to the office,' she said.

'Aye. Thanks for coming in. I'll see you on Monday morning – if I can get them to unhook me from this bloody machine!' he growled.

Roo smiled. 'See you on Monday.'

But as she left the room she had the feeling that was the last time she was ever going to see George Fairbanks.

Jan was talking to a man in a suit when Sadie turned up for her stint at the Ponderosa that evening. Not wanting to disturb her, she nodded a greeting and went straight into the back room to get changed.

She was putting the finishing touches to her make-up when Jan knocked on the door. 'I've got something to tell you,' she said. 'Ray and I are getting married.'

'Jan, that's brilliant! Congratulations!' Sadie put down her lipstick and went to hug her friend. 'You don't waste much time, do you? Talk about a whirlwind romance!'

'Do you think it's too soon?' Jan looked anxious.

'I was kidding. Anyone can see you two are made for each other.' She'd never seen her as happy as she had been the last few weeks.

'That's what I thought.' Jan allowed herself to smile. 'But there's just one problem.'

'Don't tell me, he wants you to wear rhinestone cowboy boots for the wedding?'

'Funny! No, Ray's retiring in a few months. He wants us to go travelling.'

'Travelling where?'

'The States. He's always wanted to do some real line-dancing in Texas, apparently. I know,' she read Sadie's shocked face, 'I've never been further than Bridlington, but I think I'd like to give it a go. I reckon it's about time I had an adventure. What do you think?'

'Why not? But what about this place?'

Jan gazed down at her hands. 'I'm selling up. That man I was speaking to was an estate agent.' She looked imploringly at Sadie. 'I'm sorry, Sadie, I really am. I'm sure whoever buys this place will still want to keep you on.'

'Oh, don't worry about me. I'll be fine.' But they both knew that wasn't true. The new owners might keep her on as a barmaid, but they wouldn't want a fifty-something cabaret singer. Her performing days were numbered.

Perhaps it was just as well, she thought. It was about time she realised she was never going to make it as a singing star.

But she couldn't allow her fears about her own future to get in the way of Jan's happiness. She was delighted for her friend, finding someone to love again after the misery of her first marriage.

'And it just goes to show,' she said. 'If you can find your Prince Charming, there might still be some hope for the rest of us!'

But she was heavy-hearted as she took to the stage in her shimmering red dress. Her lucky dress, she always called it. It hadn't brought her much luck tonight, had it?

There was a good crowd in that night. The air was a fug of cigarette smoke and stale alcohol. It was hardly the London Palladium, but she still loved it. Beyond the dazzling footlights, she could make out dim shapes at the tables surrounding the stage. They were chatting, but as Dennis, the keyboard player, played the first bars of her opening number, everyone stopped to listen.

Sadie scanned the room, making eye contact with the crowd. She took a deep breath, opened her mouth to sing – and then she saw him. At a far corner table, flanked by a couple of other men, was Johnny Franks.

As his eyes met hers, direct and piercing as a laser beam, Sadie felt as if she'd been shot through the heart.

Behind her, Dennis was coasting into his third intro, still waiting for her to take her cue. Perspiration trickled from under his ginger toupée.

Somehow she managed to pick up the microphone and sing 'You Don't Have To Say You Love Me'. She'd been doing the old Dusty Springfield number for so many years, thank God, she didn't have to think about the words. She was in such a blind panic she would have been hard-pushed to remember her own name.

She managed to struggle through the set by pretending he wasn't there. Then, when she finally plucked up the nerve to look back at the corner table, she was horrified to find he wasn't.

She lurched from panic-stricken to poleaxed with disappointment. Bastard! He'd put her on edge and nearly wrecked her act, then he couldn't even be bothered to stay to the end!

Or maybe he'd seen enough? Maybe he'd turned up expecting to see the sexy Sadie he used to know, and instead he'd found some tired old bag trying to look twenty years younger.

She hardly noticed the appreciative applause as she fled back to her dressing room. She stripped off her dress, pulled on her old silky robe and was massaging cleansing cream into her face when there was a knock on the door.

Her heart stopped briefly, but it was only Jan. 'You've got an admirer,' she grinned, producing an enormous bouquet of red roses. 'Here's a note, look.'

Sadie opened it, her hands trembling, while Jan looked on excitedly. 'Well?' she said. 'What does it say? Don't keep me in suspense!'

'It just says he enjoyed the show.' Sadie screwed up the paper and threw it in the bin.

'Is that it?'

''Fraid so.'

'And there was me, thinking your Prince Charming had turned up after all.' She pulled a face. 'Coming round to the bar for a drink?'

'Not tonight. I'm a bit tired.'

Sadie waited until Jan had gone, then dived to rescue the note out of the bin. She smoothed it out on the dressing table.

'Meet me by the back door in ten minutes,' it said. No 'hello' or 'please' or 'what have you been doing for the past thirty-odd years?'. Not even a name.

Sadie went back to creaming off her make-up. Arrogant sod! she fumed. Did he really think he could just turn up out of the blue after all this time, snap his fingers and she'd come running? Who the hell did he think he was? 'Meet me in ten minutes' indeed!

She'd dressed, reapplied her make-up and was by the back door in five.

He was waiting for her in the back of a limo. 'Hello, Sadie Moon,' he said softly. 'It's been a long time.'

Sadie got in, determined not to be impressed. 'I can't stop,' she said. 'Mum will be expecting me home.'

'Some things never change.' His husky growl reminded her of old whisky and too many smoky bars. 'How is the lovely Irene? Still got my picture on her mantelpiece?'

'Only to throw darts at.' He looked every inch the successful businessman in his cashmere overcoat and polished shoes. Only his wicked smile reminded her of the Johnny she used to know.

'Thanks for the flowers,' she said. 'You didn't have to send so many.'

'There was a rose for every year since I last saw you.'

She blushed. 'A bunch from the petrol station would have done.'

'Not for you.' His eyes crinkled at the corners. 'How about a drink? Or better still, let me take you for a meal.'

'At this time? You won't find anywhere open.'

'I know somewhere.' Johnny gestured to the driver. In the front of the car, beyond the smoked glass screen, Sadie could see the dark shapes of his two henchmen.

She looked down at her denim skirt. 'I'm not dressed for going out!'

'You look fine.'

The limo was warm and smelled of leather and Johnny's musky aftershave. The sound system played a sexy, soulful Aretha Franklin number.

'Nice car,' Sadie commented, trying to break the seductive mood. 'Did you hire it for the night?'

He laughed. 'It's mine.'

'You've done well for yourself.'

'I have, haven't I?'

She peered out of the window at the passing streets. 'So where are we going?'

'You'll see. Somewhere very special.'

'Not too special, I hope?' She didn't want to go anywhere she might not be able to afford to pay her share. And she was still aware she had to get home to her mother.

'You call this special?' she said ten minutes later, as they stood in the queue at The Friendly Plaice fish and chip shop.

'Don't you remember? This is where I brought you on our first date.'

How could she forget? 'You really know how to show a girl a good time, don't you? Is this all I'm worth? A portion of haddock and chips?'

'I didn't want you to think I was being flash.'

'You? Flash?' she grinned as they got back into the limo with their fish and chips. 'Whyever would I think that?'

Johnny reached into the minibar and took out a bottle of champagne. The real thing. The best Sadie ever got was sparkling wine at Christmas.

'I suppose you keep a bottle handy just in case?'

'No, I put this one aside for you especially.'

'What made you so sure I'd come?'

'You never could resist me, Sadie.'

It wasn't fair that he'd got more attractive with age when all she'd got were crows' feet. 'So how come you can afford all this?'

'Like you said, I've done all right for myself.'

'And what is it you do?'

'Oh, you know. A bit of this, a bit of that.'

Sadie gazed at the thick Rolex watch on his tanned wrist. She didn't want to think about what he did to earn that kind of money.

Johnny noticed and smiled. 'All strictly legit. I run a club in Sheffield, and I've got a sideline in limo hire. Hence the flashy motors. You know, for hen nights and race days? Very popular these days.'

He gestured to the driver and they drove off again. Sadie licked grease and vinegar off her fingers. 'Where are we going now?'

'Another trip down Memory Lane.' They drove in silence, eating their chips. Then he said, 'I met your daughter.'

She took a deep breath. 'I'm sorry she came to see you. I had no idea.'

'She seemed to think I was her father.'

'She didn't get that from me.'

'So you've never told her who her father is? Just like you never told me.'

Sadie sighed. 'I've never told anyone.'

Five minutes later the car slowed down. Sadie wiped a patch of steam off the window and peered out. All she could see was darkness, with the faint sulphurous gleam of street lamps in the distance. 'Where are we?'

'Surely you remember?' The warm, still evening air hit her as the driver came around and opened the door.

Then, suddenly, she realised. 'The common?'

'Where we first met.' He reached for her hand to help her out of the car. 'Of course, it was a bit different that night, wasn't it?'

She nodded dreamily. 'The fair was in town.' She could still remember the excitement. The whirling, dizzying riot of coloured lights in the darkness. The loud music, the smell of candyfloss and frying onions. 'You were on the dodgems.'

'And you couldn't work your car so I jumped on the back to help you.'

'Actually, I could work it all right. I just wanted you to notice me.'

He laughed. 'How could I miss you?'

'Don't give me that. You had all the girls queuing up outside your caravan come closing time.'

'All except you. But you were the only one I wanted.'

'Only because I was the only one you couldn't have!'

'Maybe. Or maybe I just knew you were special.'

She walked on quickly, embarrassed, until they came to the wall marked 'Private'.

'As if that ever stopped us!' Johnny laughed. 'Do you remember how we used to sneak over there to be alone?' He looked at her, his eyes gleaming. 'Think you could still manage it?'

Sadie stared at the wall then back at him in horror. 'You're not serious?'

'Why not? Are you worried about getting arrested?'

'I'm more worried about getting a slipped disc! I'm not sixteen any more, and neither are you,' she reminded him.

'Come on, it's only four feet!' Johnny was already over. He

282

jumped to the ground and looked over at her. 'What's the matter? Don't tell me you've got boring in your old age.'

'Not so much of the old, if you don't mind.'

Rising to the challenge, she threw her shoes over first, the way she always used to. Giggling, she clambered over. She searched around in the dark for her shoes, but couldn't find them.

'Forget about them. It's better to go barefoot in the grass,' Johnny said.

'But they cost thirty quid!'

'I'll buy you a new pair.'

'You owe me a pair of tights, too. These have got a huge ladder.' She examined her legs in the dark, then stopped when she realised he was staring at them too. 'What are we doing here, anyway?'

'Don't you remember? This is where we had our first kiss. Over there, under that oak tree.'

'Fancy you remembering that.'

'How could I forget?' He turned to her, and even in the darkness she could see the sadness in his eyes. 'You broke my heart,' he said. 'I never got over it.'

'It didn't stop you getting married, did it?'

He looked shocked. 'How did you know?'

She nodded at his hand. 'You might have taken your ring off, but the mark's still there.'

He smiled admiringly. 'You don't miss a trick, do you?'

'Not when you've met as many cheating husbands as I have. So where is she? Back home in Sheffield, I suppose?'

'Actually, at this precise moment she and her toyboy are probably on their third bottle of sangria at our villa in Spain. We divorced last year,' he explained. 'After she'd taken me to the cleaners, of course.'

'You don't seem very upset about it.'

'To be honest, I shouldn't have married her. I knew she was only after my money. But she was younger than me, and I was flattered, so . . .' he shrugged.

'How long were you married?'

'Five years. She was my third.'

'Not a very good track record, is it?'

'I never found anyone to match up to you.'

They walked in the darkness. After Sadie had stumbled a few times, Johnny took her hand to guide her. His fingers felt warm and strong.

'You should have come back,' she said.

'I was tempted.'

'So why didn't you?'

'Because I was scared of what I might find. I thought you'd be married with loads of kids.'

'I never got married.'

'Why not?'

'Probably the same reason as you had three wives.'

His fingers tightened around hers. 'Why didn't you marry him? The baby's father.'

'I couldn't. It wasn't possible.'

'But you would have, if he'd asked you?'

'I don't want to talk about it.'

'Did you love him?' She didn't answer. Johnny gripped her arms and swung her round to face him. 'Is that why you kept the baby, hoping he'd marry you?'

'No!'

'So it was just a meaningless fling?' His face was bleak. 'You threw away everything we had for a one-night stand?'

'It wasn't like that.'

'Then what was it like?'

She stared at him. 'You wouldn't understand,' she said, and walked away, tripping and stumbling in the darkness.

They were silent in the car going home. But as Johnny dropped her at the end of Hope Street he suddenly said, 'Can I see you again?'

She was instantly wary. 'Not if you're going to keep talking about the past.'

'Fine,' he said. 'We'll talk about the future.'

Sadie went home, feeling a crazy sense of unreality. Had tonight really happened? She had a feeling she would wake up in the morning and find it had all been a dream.

But when the following morning a motorbike courier arrived with a pair of gift-wrapped Gucci shoes, she realised it hadn't been a dream after all.

Chapter 24

Bridge House was in chaos the following Saturday, the day Charlotte Montague was marrying Daniel Hetherington. Her mother's bedroom looked like an explosion in a taffeta factory, Cat thought, with billowing dresses hanging behind the door and draped over the bed, the chairs and every other available surface. Outside in the pink and white marquee, the caterers were setting out tables and chairs, chilling champagne and fluffing up flower arrangements.

Cat felt as if she was on a production line. Her fingers hurt from making pin curls and weaving tiny silk roses into intricate plaits. Her feet ached and she longed to sit down.

But the atmosphere made up for her weariness. Everyone was very high-spirited and giggly, thanks to a bottle of champagne one of the bridesmaids had smuggled upstairs.

'I wonder if the caterers have remembered the candles I asked for?' Elizabeth Montague gazed anxiously out of the window. She looked serene in her dove-grey couture coat dress, but Cat could tell she was fretting.

'Don't panic, Mummy. Have some champagne! It'll help you relax.' Charlotte handed her a glass. Unlike her mother, she seemed to have no worries about the day ahead.

Her mother eyed her severely. 'I hope you're not so relaxed you fall over!'

'Here, Cat. You can relax instead.' Charlotte offered her the glass. She was due at the church in less than half an hour, but she still wasn't dressed, much to her mother's dismay. Her towelling

286

dressing gown looked absurd with the tiara glittering on her beautifully upswept hair.

'Not while I'm working, thanks.'

'I'm glad Cat and I are keeping our heads,' Elizabeth said approvingly. 'When are you going to get dressed, Charlotte? I'm afraid Daddy will wear a groove in the hall floor if we leave him pacing for too long.'

'Calm down, Mummy. The wedding isn't for another half an hour.'

'It takes twenty minutes to get to the church.'

'So? I can't possibly be on time for my own wedding. It's a tradition, isn't it?'

'How do you know he'll wait?' one of the bridesmaids said. She was already dressed in a narrow sheath gown of gold raw silk.

'Of course he'll wait. I'm worth waiting for, aren't I?' Charlotte smiled complacently.

Cat felt a pang of envy. She couldn't remember feeling like that on her wedding day. All she'd felt was that she was lucky to be marrying Billy, and she'd better snatch him up quick before he came to his senses and realised he was throwing his life away.

But now when she thought about it she realised that perhaps she hadn't been such a bad bargain after all. Okay, so she might not be as brainy as her cousin, but she still had a lot going for her. She'd been a good wife and mother all these years. Billy could have done a lot worse, she thought.

'How do I look?' Cat looked up from threading roses into the last bridesmaid's hair. Charlotte stood in front of her, transformed into a radiant princess in an ivory silk gown that shimmered with thousands of iridescent beads.

'What do you think? Will I do?' Beneath her perfect make-up she looked young and anxious.

Cat nodded. 'Daniel's a lucky man.'

'I know!' Charlotte laughed delightedly. She looked back at herself and straightened the gold locket around her neck. Her grandmother's locket – something old, as Elizabeth had explained.

Cat finished the last bridesmaid's hair. 'There. All done.'

'And right on time, too. Thanks, Cat, we couldn't have managed without you.' Elizabeth smiled.

'It was my pleasure.' She meant it. It had taken her mind off her problems, and it had felt good to share in someone else's happiness for a while.

As she packed her brushes away, Charlotte said, 'You will come to the church, won't you?'

'Oh no, I couldn't—'

'Of course you must,' Elizabeth stepped in swiftly. 'We'd love you to be there.'

'But I'm not dressed for it.' She looked down at her T-shirt and linen trousers.

'You look fine. Anyway, it doesn't matter. Everyone will be looking at me!' Charlotte laughed.

In the end Cat allowed herself to be persuaded, although she felt out of place at the church among all the smart outfits, the big hats and the morning suits.

No one noticed her as she crept into the back pew. Daniel sat at the front, looking handsome but very nervous. He kept sneaking anxious glances towards the back of the church, waiting for his bride to arrive.

It hadn't been like that at her wedding, either. She'd been the first to arrive, and it was her who'd sat in the narrow hallway of the register office, staring at the frosted glass door, wondering if Billy would turn up. It made her laugh now to think how pathetically grateful she'd been when he did.

And she'd been grateful ever since.

There was a murmur of excitement as Elizabeth took her seat. The bridesmaids were already congregated outside. Then the organ struck up and everyone rose to their feet as Charlotte swept in on her father's arm. She looked so beautiful, Cat felt like crying.

Why wasn't her wedding day like this? She hadn't had a mother to tell her she looked beautiful, or any bridesmaids to fuss over her. And her father had never gazed at her with as much love and pride as Charlotte's father. Cat couldn't remember her father looking at her with anything but disappointment.

Come to think of it, apart from her aunt Sadie there hadn't been anyone on her side at all. No one to make her feel special, or that Billy was a lucky man for marrying her.

Billy was looking after Megan and Liam for the day, but Cat didn't mind the thought of going home to an empty house. She used to be afraid of being alone but now she found she quite enjoyed the peace and quiet. She was looking forward to a long hot soak in the bath, then half an hour with her feet up reading Jilly Cooper.

And then she spotted Billy's car in the drive.

Becky opened the door before Cat had a chance to get her key out. 'Dad's here,' she said.

He was waiting in the sitting room, perched on the edge of the sofa. He seemed ill at ease, like a visitor. 'I brought the kids back.' He sounded defensive. 'I know I said I'd keep them longer but Mum had a migraine so we had to come home.'

'You should have called me. I would have picked them up on my way back.' Cat headed for the kitchen. 'Would you like a coffee?'

'If you're making one.'

'It's only instant, I'm afraid. I can't be bothered to faff around with that other stuff.'

'Instant's fine.' Cat was surprised. Billy was usually a real coffee snob, forever messing about with grinding beans and steaming milk. Cat had stuffed the espresso machine away in the back of a cupboard the day he'd left.

He followed her into the kitchen and lingered in the doorway, watching her. The children, she noticed, had beat a tactful retreat upstairs, leaving them alone. 'Becky says you've been working today.'

'I had a wedding. At Bridge House.'

'Really? That big place? What's it like inside?'

'Incredibly glamorous.' She told him all about the wedding, and about Elizabeth Montague being a Bond girl. Billy seemed impressed. More than that, he seemed interested. It was odd to have a conversation that didn't involve the children.

Feeling bold, Cat decided to tell him about a plan that had been going through her mind for a few days. 'I'm thinking of branching out on my own,' she said.

'You mean open your own salon?'

'Nothing quite that ambitious. Not yet, anyway. I thought I'd start with mobile hairdressing. You know, going round to people's houses to do their hair? I was thinking about it this afternoon, while I was up at Bridge House. I think I could be quite successful. And it would mean I could work my own hours.' She was beginning to get sick of Maxine and her demands. Especially as there seemed to be no chance of her ever getting a promotion.

'Do you think you could handle it?' Billy asked.

'I don't see why not. I'm a pretty good hairdresser, and I know a lot of the customers would come to me.'

'There's more to it than that,' Billy warned. 'What about your accounts? And maybe VAT. And you'd have to think about pricing to cover your costs—'

'I've thought about all that. I'm not stupid, you know!' She wished she'd never said anything. Billy obviously didn't think she was capable of anything more mentally taxing than wielding a set of heated rollers.

'I'm sorry. I was only trying to help.'

He looked so crestfallen, Cat felt sorry for him. 'I know. Maybe I'm just over-sensitive.'

They finished their coffee and Billy got ready to leave. 'Are you sure you're okay?' he said. 'There's nothing you need?'

'I don't think so.' Except you, she thought. Although she didn't need him, not any more. She wanted him. There was a big difference. The past few days had taught her she could stand on her own two feet. But she still missed Billy. 'I'm coping fine on my own, thanks.'

'So I see.' Was it her imagination, or did he seem hurt?

On impulse, she said, 'Why don't you stay for supper? I'm sure the kids would like it,' she added quickly.

'I wish I could, but I've arranged to have dinner with one of our retailers.' He looked regretful. 'Why don't we have dinner sometime this week?'

'Okay,' she agreed with a shrug. 'But it'll have to be Pizza Paradise. Megan's gone off burgers since someone told her they put horses in them.'

He hesitated. 'I was thinking of just the two of us. Maybe we could go somewhere a bit more upmarket.'

Cat was puzzled. 'You mean, like a date?'

He smiled. 'Exactly like a date.'

Roo wasn't impressed when she went round to collect Ollie from Nanna's house on Hope Street the following Friday and found him getting out of Johnny Franks' limo.

'Mummy!' He launched himself into her arms. 'I've been for a ride in Uncle Johnny's car. It's got a telly in it and everything!'

'That's nice.' Roo glanced at Johnny Franks as he came towards them.

'Hello again,' he said. He still looked menacing, even in jeans and a polo shirt. Thick gold chains nestled around his tanned neck. How on earth could she have imagined he was her father?

'I didn't know you were back.'

'After you came to see me I decided to renew a few old acquaintances.'

At which point Sadie came out of the house, wiping her hands on a tea-towel. 'Hello you two, I didn't hear you—Oh!' she spotted Roo. 'You're early.'

'I'm taking Ollie back to London tonight, remember?'

'Of course.' She looked embarrassed. 'You've, um, met Johnny, haven't you?'

Johnny put his arm proprietorially around her mother's shoulders. Roo felt sick, remembering all the other men who'd mauled her like that over the years.

'Come and have a look, Mummy!' Ollie dragged her towards the big black car. 'It's huge inside. As big as a house! And I can go for a ride in it any time I like. Uncle Johnny says—'

'He's not your uncle!' Roo shouted. They all looked at her. Ollie's chin wobbled.

'There's no need to yell at the kid,' Johnny said quietly.

Roo whirled round to face him. 'Did I ask you to interfere?'

Johnny stared at her for a moment. Then he turned to Sadie and said, 'I think I'll leave you to it, love.'

She looked disappointed. 'Aren't you staying for your tea?'

'Not tonight.' He kissed her cheek. 'I'll call you.' He ruffled Ollie's hair affectionately and left without glancing in Roo's direction.

As soon as he'd gone Sadie turned on her. 'What did you do that for?'

'I don't like him.'

'That's obvious. What's he done to upset you?'

He's your boyfriend, Roo thought. Even now, at her age, she still couldn't look at her mother with a man and not feel ill. 'He's a thug,' she said, as Ollie wandered inside.

'No, he isn't. He's a legitimate businessman.'

'Oh come on, even you can't be that naïve. Do you think he got that car by putting money away in a post office savings account?'

'You know nothing about him,' Sadie said.

'Neither do you. He's just turned up out of the blue after thirty-odd years and suddenly you're all over him like a rash!'

'It's your fault he's here. You tracked him down.'

'I didn't know he'd turn up, did I? I didn't expect you two to start acting like love's young dream.'

'I thought you might be happy for me. Too much to hope for, I suppose.'

'Happy that you're making an idiot of yourself? Happy that he's going to end up making a fool of you, just like all the others?'

'Johnny's my friend,' she said quietly. 'It would be nice if you two could get along.'

'I'm not twelve years old. I don't have to be nice to your boyfriends.'

'I don't recall you ever being nice to anyone at that age!'

'And didn't you ever stop to wonder why?' Roo shot back. 'What do you think it was like for me, watching you parade all those men through the house? It's not easy, growing up knowing your mother's the town tart—'

The slap took them both by surprise. Roo stepped back, putting her hand to her stinging cheek.

'Don't you ever call me that again!' Sadie turned and stalked back into the house. A moment later Ollie came out. 'Why is Sadie crying?' he asked. 'And why are you crying too?'

'I'm not.' Roo blinked fiercely and opened the car door for him.

It felt odd being back in her own home, and yet it didn't feel like her home any more. When she went to unpack, she half-expected to find Shauna's clothes in her wardrobe instead of her own.

'She, um, hasn't moved in,' David said cagily, when Roo asked him about it. 'She didn't feel it was very sensitive, under the circumstances.'

Roo was about to point out that after getting pregnant by her husband it was a bit late to start considering her feelings, but David was in such an odd mood she didn't think he'd see the joke. He looked tired and rumpled. His face was stubbly, and she would have sworn he'd slept in that old creased blue shirt, except that he looked as if he hadn't slept for days.

He seemed awkward when Roo asked why Shauna wasn't there. 'She's spending some time with her parents,' he explained, as he unloaded the washing machine.

'Is she still on a twenty-four-hour vomiting marathon?'

'I don't think so.' He paused for a moment to sort out his socks, then added, 'Actually, she isn't pregnant. Not any more. She had an abortion last week.'

They didn't talk about it until Ollie had gone to bed. The story finally came out as they sat at the kitchen table, eating a picnic supper of leftover quiche and baked potatoes washed down with a bottle of Sancerre. Apparently Shauna had decided she couldn't face the idea of having a baby at her age, and booked herself in for a termination. But she hadn't told David about it until afterwards, when she called him to pick her up from the clinic.

'I don't understand it,' he kept saying, his face desolate. 'I mean, I know she was fed up about being pregnant, but not to tell me what she was going to do . . . It seems so unfair.'

'Maybe she thought you'd try to change her mind.'

'I would have liked the chance. It was my baby too.'

'So is she really with her parents?' Roo asked.

David shook his head. 'She's gone on holiday with her friends. To recuperate, she says.'

They both knew what that meant. Shauna had reclaimed her youth. Roo didn't blame her, but she felt desperately sorry for David, who seemed to have aged ten years in as many days. He'd lost everything.

She felt so sorry for him she ending up sleeping with him that night. She felt bad about it the next morning, especially when she realised she had absolutely no desire to get back together with him.

David sensed it too, although he made a feeble, half-joking remark about them making another go of it. Roo gently but firmly set him straight.

'I suppose it must be serious with the toyboy then?' David said.

'Sorry? Oh, you mean Matt?' She shook her head. 'That was over before it began,' she said truthfully.

As she left, David said, 'Sorry for screwing it all up.'

She shrugged. 'It takes two.'

She headed home, feeling shattered. The weekend with David had depressed her and sapped her energy. And after the exhausting row with her mother on Friday, she didn't think she could handle any more bad news.

When she got home she found a message on her answer machine. It was from Frederick Fairbanks, telling her his father was dead.

Chapter 25

It looked as if the whole of Normanford had turned out for the funeral the following Tuesday. The dull, grey day matched everyone's mood. People lined the streets to watch as the carriage, weighed down with flowers and drawn by a plumed black horse, travelled down the High Street towards the tiny modern church of St Pauline. Roo spotted Nanna and Sadie on the kerbside. Nanna nodded at her; Sadie looked away.

George's widow Agnes, tall and stately behind her veil, followed her husband's cortege, next to her son. Following behind, next to Billy and all the other Fairbanks senior staff, Roo desperately tried to hold herself together.

She kept telling herself she had no right to cry. She'd only known George Fairbanks for a matter of weeks, and for most of that time they'd been at loggerheads. So why should she feel so heartbroken now?

In the church, before a packed congregation, Frederick delivered a touching eulogy praising his father's contribution to the town's fortunes, and vowed to continue his life's work. His mother sat, stiff-spined and poker-faced, staring straight ahead of her, her eyes fixed on George's coffin.

Later they ended up at the Fairbanks family home for the ritual of the funeral tea. Roo had never understood why someone who had just lost a loved one should be forced to go through the ordeal of hosting a party straight afterwards, but everyone seemed to expect it. And Agnes played her part well, maintaining her dignity even when yet another person asked her how she was feeling.

Glenys, as the widow of another prominent Normanford resident, had naturally wangled herself an invitation. She spent a few minutes offering her condolences, and the rest surveying the Fairbanks home, satisfying herself it was nowhere near as lovely or well-appointed as her own.

'Garden's north-facing,' she said to Roo out of the corner of her mouth as she helped herself to a cucumber sandwich. 'And I certainly wouldn't have chosen those tiles in the downstairs cloakroom.'

Billy trailed after her, wearing a sombre dark suit, black tie and a 'somebody shoot me' expression. Roo was about to speak to him when she was accosted by a small man with thinning hair and round glasses, who introduced himself as Sidney Pennington, the Fairbanks family solicitor.

'I don't suppose you've seen Frederick, have you?' he said. 'I've been looking for him everywhere.'

Probably to tell him he now had control of the family business, Roo thought. 'I thought he was here a minute ago.'

She scanned the crowd, but he'd disappeared. It turned out no one had seen him since they'd arrived back from church.

She caught up with Glenys again as she was examining a Staffordshire figurine on the mantelpiece.

'Reproduction, of course,' she sniffed. 'But it's so easy to get caught out if you don't have a trained eye. I honed my antique-spotting skills watching *Bargain Hunt*.' Billy was on the far side of the room, having escaped his mother's clutches at last. Roo wished she could do the same.

'He looks tired, doesn't he?' Glenys followed her gaze. 'Poor boy, I keep telling him he should come home. He doesn't have to stay in that dreadful hotel.' Her mouth pursed. 'I notice she's kept the house, of course,' she said.

'It's the children's home too,' Roo pointed out.

'That's as may be. But my William pays for it. Still, at least he's got away from her now. They were never happy, you know.' Her bony fingers tightened on Roo's arm. 'You felt it too, didn't you?'

Behind her, Roo saw Billy wander over but stop short to listen. 'Well, I—'

'All she ever did was drag him down,' Glenys went on. 'I mean let's face it, she's nothing special—'

'That's where you're wrong, Mother.' Glenys swung round. Billy's face was dark with anger. 'Cat is special. She's kind, and beautiful, and no one in this whole bloody world makes me feel the way she does. But do you know what's really special about her? She loves me.'

Glenys glanced nervously around, aware they were being watched. 'We all love you, William.'

'No, you don't. You all wanted me to be something I wasn't. The top student, the captain of the rugger team, the head of some multinational company. You loved me as long as I was living up to your expectations. Cat was the only person who didn't care. She never wanted me to achieve anything, or be anything special. She was just happy to love me for what I am.'

Roo glanced at Glenys' pinched face but knew she was just as much to blame. She'd always assumed Billy was as ambitious as herself. But now she realised she was just the same as his ghastly, overreaching mother, wanting him to be something he wasn't. Cat hadn't held him back; the truth was, he didn't want to go anywhere.

'Y—your father and I only wanted the best for you,' Glenys stammered.

'But you never stopped to ask me what I wanted, did you? You were too concerned with me making you proud, not letting you down. You want to know the real reason I married Cat? To get away from you!'

'And a fat lot of good it's done you,' Glenys fought back. 'She doesn't want you now, does she?'

'No,' Billy admitted bleakly. 'And I think I'm beginning to understand why. Because all through our marriage people have been bringing her down, making her feel like she wasn't good enough for me. I'd even started to believe it myself. No wonder she's so bloody insecure!' His eyes blazed. 'But she is good enough. She's more than good enough. I'm only sorry I didn't see it until it was too late.' He put down his drink and stormed off, leaving Glenys with a sherry in her hand and a stunned expression on her face.

Roo caught up with him in the garden. He was sitting on a stone balustrade, his head in his hands. 'I've really done it now,' he groaned.

'It needed to be said. You were right.' She hesitated. 'I'm sorry, Billy.'

'Me too. I'm sorry I didn't show Cat how much I loved her when I had the chance.'

'Look, why don't we go out for a meal to cheer ourselves up?' she suggested. 'I don't know about you, but I don't fancy going home.'

Billy looked doleful. 'You're lucky to have a home to go to!'

Johnny listened in grim silence as Sadie told him about her row with Roo. She'd held off telling him for days, not wanting to burden him with her problems. But he'd noticed how depressed she was and had finally got it out of her.

'Do you want me to talk to her?' he asked.

'No!' The last thing they all needed was another confrontation. 'I don't know why I did it,' she said. 'I've never lifted a hand to Ruby before.' But her remarks had been so cruel, so cutting.

'She'll get over it,' Johnny said. 'She can't hold a grudge for ever, can she?'

'You don't know Ruby.' Whoever said time was a great healer had obviously never met her daughter.

Johnny gave her a lift to the Ponderosa. As usual, she felt like a film star stepping out of the limousine. It was amazing how quickly she'd got used to being driven around by a chauffeur. 'I feel like we should be going to The Talk of the Town, not the pub.'

'So you should,' Johnny said. 'You've got a terrific voice. You're wasted in this place.'

'I might not be here for much longer.' She told him about Jan's plans to sell up. 'It'll probably end up as some big fast-food

298

restaurant. And even if it doesn't, I don't suppose they'll want an old crock like me on stage.'

'Don't put yourself down.' He kissed her, sending the old familiar shivers down her spine. Then he got back into the limo.

Sadie was disappointed. 'Aren't you coming in for a drink?'

'Sorry, sweetheart, I can't. I've got some business to sort out in Sheffield. But I'll call you later. You've got your phone with you, haven't you?'

'That thing,' she grumbled, reaching into her bag for her brand new mobile. It was small, shiny and complicated. 'I'm still not sure how to switch it on. I don't know why you bought it.'

'I like to check up on you,' he said proprietorially. 'And it's useful if your mum needs to get in touch in an emergency.'

'Don't put that idea in her head or she'll be ringing every five minutes!' Sadie was pleased Johnny and her mother were getting on so well together. They'd had a frosty start but since Johnny let slip that he was a personal friend of Jimmy White and offered to get her front-row seats for the snooker final at the York Barbican, Irene had softened towards him.

'Keep your chin up.' He winked at her, and then he was gone. Sadie stood on the pavement, watching until the car disappeared down the road. Johnny Franks. She still couldn't believe he was back in her life again. She didn't care what Ruby thought. She deserved some happiness, after everything she'd been through.

And Johnny made her happy. She felt warm, secure and protected for the first time in years. She was too old and wise to call it love already, but she was beginning to wonder if perhaps it could be.

Her happiness stayed with her right up until the moment she stepped on stage and spotted her daughter holding hands with Billy Kitchener at a corner table.

'Your mum hasn't taken her eyes off us since she came on stage.' Billy glanced over his shoulder then looked away again.

'Ignore her.'

'It's a bit difficult. What have you done to upset her?'

'We're not exactly speaking at the moment.' Roo attacked her pasta. It was overcooked but she hardly noticed what she was eating.

'I thought you were getting on a lot better these days?'

'So did I.' She wished she hadn't flown off the handle, but she'd been so disappointed. Just when she'd let her guard down and allowed herself to admit her mother wasn't the selfish monster she'd always imagined her to be, Sadie had let her down again. Now the rift between them was wider than ever. 'Do we have to talk about my mother?'

'I certainly don't want to talk about mine.'

Inevitably, the conversation turned to Cat, who seemed to be the only thing on Billy's mind.

'She's so independent now,' he moaned. 'She doesn't need me any more.'

'Surely it's good for her to be less dependent, isn't it?'

'I liked being needed.' Billy speared his chicken. 'Pathetic, isn't it?'

'Sounds like you were the insecure one, not her,' Roo said.

'Maybe. Anyway, I've blown it. She's probably realised she's better off without me now.'

'What makes you say that?'

'All I ever did was hold her back. I never took her seriously, and I never encouraged her. I never let her believe she was any good at anything. I know I blamed my mother, but I was just as bad.'

'So what are you going to do about it?'

'I'm going to try to put things right, if she'll let me. I'm going to woo her back.'

'Woo her?' Roo laughed. 'How the hell are you going to do that?'

'I reckon a lot of our problems happened because we were thrown in at the deep end. We were married and then we had a baby without ever having any of that fun bit at the beginning. We never got to know each other. I'd like to try that. If Cat will give me a chance.'

Roo gazed at him. He was so handsome, and so touchingly

sincere, she couldn't imagine even her stubborn cousin passing him up. 'She will if she's got any sense,' she said.

The red message light was winking at her when she got home. It was Ollie, wishing her goodnight. Hearing him brought tears to her eyes. She missed his little arms wrapping fiercely around her neck as he hugged her goodnight. But much as she missed him, she knew David was in need of those hugs more than she was at the moment.

The doorbell rang as she was watching the ten o'clock news. Roo hit the mute button on the TV remote control and went to answer it.

She vaguely recognised the tall Scandinavian blonde on the doorstep. 'Have you seen Matt?' she demanded.

As soon as she heard her snappy tone Roo realised she was the girl who'd been so scathing about her age. 'No, I haven't,' she shot back, equally icy. I expect he's with his latest girlfriend, she felt like adding. But she was glad she hadn't when the girl broke down in tears.

'I don't know what to do,' she sobbed. 'He won't answer my calls, he's never there when I come round. I think he's got someone else!'

I'm bloody certain he has, Roo thought, knowing Matt. 'You'd better come in,' she sighed.

The girl, whose name was Monika, worked her way through a box of Kleenex while she told Roo how she'd met Matt at college, how she knew he had a reputation, but she thought she could be the one to change him. 'I played him at his own game,' she cried. 'I went out with other men, I didn't call or text him. I tried to play hard to get. Then I realised he wasn't trying to get me any more.' As she fumbled for another tissue, Roo realised this was the third person who'd cried on her shoulder in as many days. Since when had she become an agony aunt?

'I know I'm wasting my time, but I can't help it. I love him!' Monika said, mopping up her tears.

After half an hour, Roo finally managed to convince her that Matt was commitment-phobic, incapable of showing emotion and she was far too good for him. 'You're right,' Monika said, her confidence reasserting itself. 'Let's face it, if I can't hang on to him, who could?'

Roo closed the door gratefully, relieved to have some time to herself at last. Almost immediately, the doorbell rang. Thinking it was Monika again, she almost didn't open the door.

But it was Sadie. She must have come straight from work. Roo caught a glimpse of her pink spangly dress under her coat.

For a second she thought Sadie might be feeling as fed up as her and had come round to sort things out between them.

'Is he here?' She pushed past her and stepped into the hall, looking round.

'Excuse me? Is who here?'

'Don't play games with me!' Sadie swung around. 'You know who I mean. Billy Kitchener.'

'No, he isn't. Although I don't see what it's got to do with you—'

'You've got to stop seeing him.'

'I beg your pardon?'

'I mean it. Whatever you two have got going, you've got to finish it. Right now.' Her eyes looked unnatural, still caked with shiny gold stage make-up and ringed with black pencil.

Roo's surprise hardened into anger. 'You can't just barge in here and tell me what to do!'

'Okay, I'm asking you. I'm begging you. Don't see him any more.' She gripped Roo's arms, her fingers biting into her flesh. She looked so anguished for a moment Roo felt afraid.

'What's all this about?' she demanded.

Sadie faltered. 'I can't tell you. I'm just asking you, for once in your life trust me and do as I say. Please?'

'Not until you tell me why.' Roo pulled away. 'Why shouldn't I see him?' Her heart was pounding and she didn't know why.

'Because it isn't right.' Sadie couldn't meet her gaze. 'He's a married man—'

'That's got nothing to do with it, and you know it. So why don't you tell me the truth?'

Sadie put her head in her hands. 'I can't.'

'You're not leaving here until you do.' Roo moved against the front door, barring her way. 'Well? I'm waiting.' Her mother was silent. 'Maybe I should call Billy and ask him.'

'No! Don't say anything to him. He doesn't know—'

'Doesn't know what?' Roo grabbed Sadie's hands and dragged them away from her face. 'What doesn't he know? Tell me!'

Sadie looked up at her. Her mascara was smeared in thick black streaks under her eyes. The expression of utter defeat on her face frightened Roo so much that suddenly she didn't want her to speak.

'That he's your brother,' she said.

Chapter 26

Suddenly everything went so silent they could hear the steady drip of the tap down the hall in the kitchen.

'You were never meant to find out,' Sadie whispered.

Roo couldn't take it in. 'Bernard Kitchener is my *father*?' It didn't make sense.

'Look, it's not how you think—'

As if she could think anything! Her mind was a jumble of disconnected thoughts, as if someone had taken all the pieces of her life and thrown them into the air.

Bernard Kitchener. The whole time she was growing up, she'd looked at men – her mother's boyfriends, people they knew, strangers in the street – and wondered if they might be her father. But she'd never, ever suspected Bernard.

All kinds of questions scrambled over each other in her mind, wanting to be let out. 'Did you have an affair? How long did it go on for? Did Glenys know? Is that why she's always hated you?'

'No!' Sadie held up her hands, trying to ward off the barrage of words. 'It wasn't like that, it should never have happened. Please don't do this to me. I never wanted to tell you!'

'Did he know I was his daughter?' She thought of all the times he'd turned his professional politician's charm on her, asking her about her schoolwork. Was he just making polite conversation with his son's friend, or was he genuinely interested because he was her father?

And if he did know, why hadn't he done more to help them?

Why had he allowed her to be brought up dodging from one dump to the next?

'Ruby?' She'd almost forgotten her mother was there. Sadie's voice sounded as if it was coming from a long way away. 'I'm so sorry. I know you must hate me, but I never meant for you to find out. If you and Billy hadn't got so close—'

Her and Billy. Her brother. If things had been different, they might even have . . . oh God! Bile rose up in her throat again and she just made it to the bathroom before she threw up.

Afterwards she sat on the bathroom floor, hugging herself, the chill of the tiles creeping through her clothes.

'Ruby?' Sadie was outside the door, her voice anxious. 'Are you all right in there?'

'Go away.'

'I can't leave you like this.'

'I need to be on my own.'

There was a long silence. Then Sadie said, 'I'll go, then. If you're sure. I'll ring you later, okay?'

Roo said nothing. A moment later she heard her mother's footsteps on the stairs, and the door closing softly behind her. She relaxed slightly. She couldn't face anyone. After all this time of trying to find out the truth, suddenly she wanted to shut it all out, forget it.

But she couldn't. Disjointed thoughts kept coming into her mind, linking together and then coming apart again.

Billy was less than a year older than her. Which meant Glenys must have been pregnant when she was conceived. A horrible picture rose up in her mind. Surely Sadie couldn't have seduced Bernard while her friend was having a baby? She'd always been willing to think the worst of her mother, but even she couldn't believe her capable of that.

The insistent chirp of a mobile phone interrupted her thoughts. Roo got to her feet and went to look for it.

She tracked the sound down to the hall. Just inside the front door, under the hallstand, she found it. It must have fallen out of Sadie's bag.

She answered it without thinking.

'All right, love?' Johnny Franks' voice was deep, warm and rough around the edges.

'It's Roo,' she said wearily.

Johnny was instantly guarded. 'Where's Sadie? Is she all right? Has something happened?'

'Something's happened, all right. I've just found out who my father is.' She gripped the phone tighter. 'You'll be pleased to know it's not you.'

'And?' he said gruffly.

Roo hesitated, then disconnected. She couldn't be the one to tell him.

Matt didn't react when he found her in a sobbing heap on his doorstep. Without another word he put his arm round her and drew her inside. Then he poured her a large brandy and let her talk.

'I did try to warn you you might not like what you found,' he said when she'd finished.

'I never thought it would be like this! And don't try to tell me there are two sides to every story,' she glared at him over the rim of her glass. 'I don't feel like being reasonable, okay?'

'So what do you want me to say?' he asked.

She gazed at him. 'Nothing,' she said. 'Just hold me. I don't want to be on my own tonight.'

She woke up early the following morning with a thumping headache, staring at a poster of Sigmund Freud in a dress. It took her a moment to work out where she was, and when she did a wave of embarrassment washed over her.

Oh Lord, what had she done? She had a horrible feeling she'd just become Matt Collins' latest conquest. And the worst thing was that after so many glasses of brandy she couldn't even remember it.

The bed beside her was empty, the sheets cold. Matt must have been up for hours.

She found him in the kitchen, watching Harvey in the garden while he waited for the kettle to boil. His fair hair was rumpled, and his dressing gown hung open, revealing an Adonis-like body – broad, smooth, muscular chest, a rippling washboard stomach and endless legs.

Roo diverted her gaze sharply away from his boxer shorts as he turned to look at her. 'Coffee?' He turned away and reached into the cupboard for another mug.

'Not for me, thanks. I don't want to be late for work.' She glanced at her watch. It wasn't yet seven.

They looked at each other for a moment. Then she said, 'About last night . . .'

'What about it?'

'It probably wasn't the best idea, in the circumstances.'

'No.'

'Not that it wasn't really good,' she added hastily, not wanting to offend him. 'I just don't think we should repeat it, that's all. We've got a good friendship, and—'

'And you think sex could spoil it?'

'Exactly.' She sat down at the kitchen table. As usual, it was piled high with stalagmites of paperwork. 'Couldn't we just pretend it never happened?'

'That might be difficult. I'd have trouble forgetting a night like that.'

She gulped. 'Really?'

'But you're probably right,' he agreed.

Roo's shoulders sagged with relief. 'Good.'

'You're not really my type anyway.'

'Oh?'

'So it's not like we're going to be secretly lusting over each other, is it?'

'Of course not.' She fiddled with the neckline of her shirt. 'I'd, um, better go home.'

'You're sure you wouldn't like that coffee?'

'Some other time.'

He turned away to open the door for Harvey, who bounced in, tail wagging joyfully. 'Have you thought about what you're going to do yet? About your mother.'

'I've no idea.'

'You've got to sort it out with her sometime, you know.'

'I know.' She just wasn't sure if she could face it.

'Don't forget, my door's always open if you need to talk. Or anything else.'

'Er, thanks.'

As she fled, he called her back. 'Roo?'

'Hmm?'

His mouth twitched. 'Last night – it *was* pretty good, wasn't it?'

Roo found it hard to concentrate on work. She had a meeting scheduled with Frederick Fairbanks, but when she got to his office his secretary told her he'd decided to take some time off.

'Where is he?' Roo was keen to discuss the next phase of moving the factory to their new premises before they began production.

'I don't know, do I? I expect he's gone somewhere to grieve.'

On the way back to her office, she overheard Billy talking to Becky. Unable to face him, she darted into the ladies'. How could her mother make life so difficult for her? Now she couldn't even face her old friend.

Correction. Her new brother.

But deep down she knew it wasn't all Sadie's fault. She shouldn't have pushed her to find out the truth. Although, to be fair, she'd never imagined it would be such a nightmare.

But now she had half the story, she needed to know the rest. Matt was right; it was time she talked to her mother again.

And this time she was going to make sure Sadie told her everything.

Sadie was pleasantly surprised when Johnny turned up unexpectedly that evening. Tom had taken their mother to bingo, leaving her alone in the house.

'Thank heavens you didn't arrive ten minutes later, I would have been in the bath with a face pack on!' She saw his grim face and tensed. 'Is something wrong?'

'I spoke to your daughter last night.'

A knot of dread tightened in the pit of her stomach. 'You'd better come in.'

The house seemed strangely silent without her mother's TV blaring full blast. Sadie poured a whisky for Johnny and a large gin with a splash of tonic for herself. She had a feeling she'd be needing it.

'So you told her, then?' Johnny said. He looked menacing in his black leather jacket.

Sadie nodded. 'I had to.'

'And you couldn't tell me?'

'I was going to.' She dreaded dragging it all up again. But now Roo knew the truth she felt she owed it to Johnny. She'd been steeling herself to phone him but he'd beaten her to it.

He sat down on the sofa. 'I'm waiting,' he said.

Sadie perched on the armchair across the room from him, wondering where to begin. 'His name was Bernard,' she said quietly. 'Bernard Kitchener. He was a local councillor, a lot older than me. I didn't know him that well. Not until he married my friend Glenys—'

Johnny sat up. 'You slept with your friend's husband?'

'It wasn't like that,' she said in a rush. 'It only happened the once; it was a mistake.'

'Pity you didn't think about that beforehand, isn't it?'

Sadie couldn't bring herself to look at his face. It felt as painful as it did when she first broke the news to him that she was pregnant, more than thirty years ago.

Johnny stood up and paced the room. 'Do you know how much this has haunted me? All this time I've spent wondering what kind of man would make you break your word and turn your back on me.' His hand shook as he took a gulp from his glass. 'I kept telling myself it must be my fault. I couldn't blame you, could I? I was a jailbird with a criminal record. I had nothing to offer you. When you told me about the baby I was angry but deep down I thought maybe you'd found someone who could give you the kind of life I couldn't. But I was wrong, wasn't I?' His voice was bitter. 'It wasn't like that at all. You broke my heart for the sake of a one-night stand with a married man. I hope to God it was worth it.'

Sadie stared into the empty fire. 'You weren't the only one who got their heart broken.'

'What happened? Didn't he want to know you afterwards? Is that why you tried to come crawling back to me?'

'I never crawled to anyone!' She felt a flash of anger. 'I knew you'd never want me if I was carrying another man's child, but I needed to tell you myself. I owed you that much.'

Their eyes met. Johnny looked away in disgust. 'It's a pity you didn't tell me all this years ago. Then maybe I wouldn't have wasted so many years loving you.'

'I loved you too. I never stopped loving you.'

'Except when you slept with him?'

'Are you trying to tell me you've never made a mistake in your life?'

'Oh, I've made plenty. But I've never hurt anyone the way you hurt me.' He took a deep breath. 'The whole time I was in jail, the only thing that kept me going was the thought that you'd be there for me when I got out. I had all these dreams about what it would be like. I'd give up travelling, get a job . . .' he smiled, remembering. 'But then I got out and I found out you'd made plans of your own.' His face darkened. 'Do you know what the worst thing was? It wasn't just that you'd taken all my plans, all my hopes and dreams, and crushed them. The worst was that you just didn't care enough to wait for me!'

'Johnny, please.' She put out her hand but he turned away from her.

'I shouldn't have come back,' he said gruffly. 'I was wrong. There's no way we can turn back the clock. There's too much bitterness.'

He put down his glass and stood up. Panic shot through her. 'Johnny, don't go,' she pleaded. 'Don't let him ruin my life again.'

'No one made you sleep with him.'

Sadie looked at him, and realised the time had come to tell the truth.

'That's where you're wrong,' she said.

'Glenys had just had the baby. I went round with some flowers for him to take to her in hospital.' Sadie was aware of Johnny watching her intently, but she couldn't bring herself to look at him. If she did, she knew her courage would fail her.

'I knew straight away he'd been drinking. Wetting the baby's head, he called it. Oh, he was always very pompous, had a lot to say for himself. But this time he was different. He wanted me to have a drink with him. Most insistent, he was. Wouldn't take no for an answer—' She swallowed hard. 'I should have dumped the flowers and gone home, but he kept on and on at me to stay. So in the end I thought I'd have one, just to shut him up.'

'Go on,' Johnny said.

'He kept talking. He was saying all this stuff about how he'd always fancied me. And all the time he kept trying to touch me. Putting his arm around me, and all that. I said to him, "What about Glenys?" But he laughed and said she was frigid. He reckoned she hadn't let him touch her since she got pregnant. Then he said—'

'What? What did he say?'

'He said, "I bet you're missing it too, with your fella locked up."' Her voice was flat. The only way she could bring herself to say the words was to pretend she was talking about someone else. 'I tried to laugh it off. I told him not to be so stupid. I started to leave, but he wouldn't let me. That was when he turned really nasty.' She wrapped her arms around her body, shielding herself. 'I'd never seen him like that. It was like the drink had turned him into a monster. I tried to fight him off but it just seemed to make him worse. So in the end I just lay there.' She could still feel his wet mouth, reeking of alcohol, plundering hers, his pale, sweating body on top of her, pinning her down. The deranged look in his eyes. 'I should have fought him off. I should have done something. But I just wanted it to stop.'

'And then what happened?' Johnny's voice was gruff with emotion.

'Then it was all over. The next thing I knew, he was throwing my clothes back at me and telling me to go. He couldn't even bring himself to look at me.' She remembered the disgust in his voice. The same disgust she felt for herself. 'I got home, ran the bath as deep and as hot as I could, and scrubbed every inch of my skin with carbolic soap until it was red raw. But I could still smell him on me. I smelt him for months.'

'Why didn't you go to the police?'

'What was the point? He'd only deny it. And who do you think they'd believe? Anyway, I just wanted to block it out, pretend it never happened.'

'You should have told his wife.'

'I was going to. But when she came out of hospital, I couldn't bring myself to do it. She was so happy, you see. She had her baby son and her husband – the perfect family. She probably wouldn't have believed me, either. All she'd see was what she wanted to see: some tart making trouble for her beloved Bernard.'

Johnny reached into his pocket and lit up a cigarette. His hands were shaking.

'Did you ever speak to him again?'

She nodded. 'He came round when he found out I was pregnant. He was worried I'd try to make trouble, you see. He thought I might try to damage his political career. He denied the baby was his, but he gave me money to keep quiet. Five hundred pounds. More than I'd ever seen in my whole life. He said it was to help me out because I was Glenys' friend,' she said bitterly.

'And you took it?'

'Of course I took it. But I never spent a penny of it.' It was still upstairs, hidden away in the back of her wardrobe. A brown envelope full of yellowing old five-pound notes. 'There were times when we desperately needed that cash, I can tell you. But I didn't want his blood money. I thought if I spent it I'd be exactly what he thought I was – a cheap whore.'

'I'm surprised you could go on living here, go on facing him.'

'What choice did I have?'

Johnny took a long drag on his cigarette and watched the smoke curl towards the ceiling. 'You should have told me.'

'And what good would that have done?'

'I would have killed him,' he said flatly.

'And you would have ended up straight back in jail.'

'Maybe. But it would have saved me a lot of hurt.'

Their eyes met. 'So who else knows about this?'

'No one. And that's the way I want it to stay.'

He frowned. 'What about Ruby? Doesn't she have a right to know?'

'To know that she was born because of a cruel, brutal act? How do you think that would make her feel?' She shook her head. 'No, she must never know the truth.'

'Too late,' said a voice from the doorway. 'I already do.'

Chapter 27

Sadie stared at her. 'How long have you been there?'

'Long enough.' Thank God Nanna had given her a key to let herself in because she couldn't always hear the door when she had the TV turned up.

Roo looked at Johnny. 'Would you leave us alone, please?'

He turned to Sadie. 'Do you want me to stay?' She shook her head. 'Are you sure you'll be all right?'

'I'm fine. This is between Ruby and me.'

Outside, the sun was going down and the room was filling with shadows, but neither of them moved to light the lamps.

It was Sadie who spoke first. 'Whatever else has happened,' she said slowly, 'I just want you to know that I've always loved you.'

'How can you say that?' Roo felt sick. 'Every time you looked at me you must have remembered him.'

'I thought I would too,' Sadie said. 'When I first found out I was pregnant all I could think about was giving you away. I didn't want you anywhere near me. And then I saw you.'

'And it was love at first sight.' Roo's lip curled.

'That's exactly what it was. They put you in my arms at that hospital and from that moment I knew you were mine. My Ruby Tuesday. Nothing to do with him.' She looked at her daughter with tear-filled eyes. 'If anything good could have come out of something like that, it was you.'

Roo shook her head, unable to take it in. 'You can't just blank out something like that. It's too traumatic. Surely you would have needed counselling or something?'

'In those days? There was no counselling in that unmarried mothers' home, I can tell you. Just lots of prayers and back-breaking work and a reminder of what a sinner you were.'

'Is that why you ran away?'

'I ran away so they couldn't take you from me. I waited until they were all in the chapel then bunked out through the window with a suitcase full of nappies and the clothes I stood up in. I was terrified they were going to send the police after me.' She smiled wanly. 'Now does that sound like someone who didn't love you?'

Roo stared at the empty glasses on the coffee table. She'd never been more badly in need of a drink in her life. 'I didn't make it very easy to love me over the years,' she admitted.

'You and me both. You were right; I've not exactly been the perfect mother, have I?' She looked rueful. 'I was young and daft. But I was angry too. I'd been saddled with this reputation through no fault of my own, and instead of living it down I decided to live up to it. I thought if everyone reckoned I was a brazen hussy then that was what I'd be. I wanted to show everyone I didn't care.'

Roo looked at her mother, the picture of defiance in her bright yellow jumper, still done up to the nines even though her mascara was smudged and she'd chewed off most of her lipstick. For the first time she felt proud of Sadie, not embarrassed. She was filled with a sudden burst of outrage and anger. She wanted to put it all straight, right all the wrongs, make up for every bit of pain and humiliation Sadie had ever suffered.

'We can't let him get away with it,' she said. 'We must go to the police—'

'He's dead, Ruby. What are they going to do, dig him up and stick him in jail?'

'We'll go to the press, then. We'll tell them what he was really like.' It sickened her to think how Bernard Kitchener's reputation had remained spotless while her mother's had been so tarnished.

'And what good would that do?'

'They might stop naming hospital wards after him, for a start. And it would show Glenys what kind of a monster she was married to.'

'Glenys is a daft cow, but she doesn't deserve to be hurt,' Sadie said gently. 'And it wouldn't just be her everyone was gossiping about. It would be me, and you. And Billy.'

Oh God. Billy! She'd forgotten all about him. 'We should tell him, at least,' Roo said.

'Why? What good would it do?'

Roo opened and closed her mouth. 'He ought to know the truth,' she said finally.

'What, that his father was a rapist? Or that you're his illegitimate sister? Honesty isn't always the best policy, Ruby. And I don't want to rake up the past again. I've spent all these years trying to live it down; I don't want to go through all that again.'

Roo stared at a photo on the mantelpiece. Her, Sadie and Nanna on a picnic. She couldn't have been more than two years old. Sadie looked absurdly young, her arms wrapped around Roo, grinning into the camera.

'But he shouldn't get away with it,' she said.

'He didn't. He went to his grave knowing he'd done wrong. And I never let him forget it. Every time he turned round I was there, large as life, right under his nose. He lived in fear I was going to tell the papers and wreck his career. To be honest, that was probably what sent him to an early grave. That, and his guilty conscience.'

'Am I anything like him?' Roo caught a glimpse of her reflection in the polished brass fireplace and flinched.

'No! He was a weak, selfish man. You're brave and strong. You're a Moon.' She reached across and laid her hand on Roo's. 'I've got over this and so must you. You've got too much to be proud of.'

They heard a key in the door and sprang apart as Nanna shuffled into the room, followed by Uncle Tom. 'I don't know, three numbers short of the National jackpot . . . what's this? Why are you two sitting in the dark?' She flicked on the light switch, took one look at the pair's tear-stained faces and said, 'Put the kettle on, Tom.'

'What?' Tom looked at the scene and backed away. As he went, Roo heard him mutter, 'More bloody women's troubles, I suppose.'

Nanna looked sharply from one to the other. 'Have you two had a row or have you sorted things out finally?'

Roo and Sadie looked at each other. 'Sorted things out, I think,' Sadie said.

'About time too. I don't suppose there's anything you've got to tell me? No, I didn't think so,' she said when they were both silent. 'Oh well, I've been in the dark for this long, I don't suppose there's any point in knowing now.' She shuffled to the door. 'I hope Tom's not using teabags. They're never strong enough.'

After the traumatic events of that evening, it felt strange sipping tea and making conversation with Nanna and Uncle Tom. Nanna was especially interested in George Fairbanks' funeral. She wanted to know all the details of the service and who said what at the wake, even though she already seemed to know most of it.

'I hear young Frederick's gone abroad, is that right?' She shook her head. 'And his poor father barely cold. He's no respect, that lad.'

'I've no idea. I wish someone would tell me where he is. He's supposed to be running the company.' Or she assumed he was. The official will-reading wasn't until the following week. 'I need his permission before we can get moving on our new orders.'

'I expect your nanna could find out for you,' Uncle Tom joked.

'I daresay I could.' Nanna looked serious. 'I could ask at the Over 60s club. Or I expect you could find out something at the hairdressers', couldn't you Sadie?'

She nodded. 'Frederick's secretary Barbara often comes in for a blow-dry. I could ask her.'

'Good luck with that,' Roo said grimly. 'She won't tell me anything.'

Uncle Tom winked at her. 'Never underestimate the Moon mafia,' he said.

A man was hitching Matt's car to a tow truck when she arrived home.

'Don't tell me. Back to the garage?' she said.

'Off to the scrapyard, actually. It wasn't quite the vintage classic I thought it was.' He peered at her. 'Have you been crying?'

'Well spotted, Einstein.'

'Let me guess. You've been to see your mother. How did it go?'

If she was going to share Sadie's secret with someone, it would have been Matt. She knew he'd understand more than anyone. But she'd promised never to breathe a word and she had to respect that.

'We've reached an understanding,' she said.

'I'm pleased to hear it.'

She had a bath, changed into her pyjamas then searched through the freezer for something to eat. Was this what her life had become: getting excited over which microwave ready-meal to choose? She'd just selected a tuna and pasta bake when the doorbell rang. It was Matt, a bottle of wine in one hand and a couple of pizzas in the other.

'Can I come in?'

'Why?'

'I don't know. I just had this mad idea you might need some company.'

She was about to turn him down when she realised that was exactly what she needed.

They sat on the sofa together, sharing the pizza and watching an action thriller on TV.

'The only thing missing is Ollie,' Matt said. 'How is the little guy?'

'He's fine. Which is more than I can say for his father. David and Shauna have split up.'

'What about the baby?'

'There is no baby.' She explained about Shauna's decision to have an abortion.

'That's tough.' Matt chewed on his pizza thoughtfully. 'So there's nothing to stop the two of you getting back together?'

'I suppose not. Except I don't want to.'

'Really? Why's that?'

'I think we've both realised we're better off apart than to-gether.'

'Good.' He reached across and nabbed a piece of mushroom from her pizza. 'He wasn't right for you.'

'How come you're such a relationship expert, when you avoid them like the plague?'

'Talent, I suppose.'

They sat in silence, staring at the television. There was a car chase going on, but she was finding it so hard to concentrate on the film she couldn't work out whether the goodies were chasing the baddies or the other way round.

'I need to talk to you,' Matt said. 'About last night.'

Oh God. Roo twisted round to look at him. He was still staring at the screen. 'I thought that subject was closed.'

'I know, but I can't just leave it like this.'

'Why not? Look, I told you, you're sensational in bed but I don't want it to happen again.'

'Sensational, eh?' He looked pleased with himself. 'So what bit did you like best?'

'Sorry?'

'Oh come on, you must remember. If I was that good . . .'

Roo felt herself blushing. Then she saw his smile twitch. 'What's this about?'

'I'm afraid I have a confession to make. You know that sensational night you remember so well? It didn't happen.'

She stared at him. 'But I woke up in your bed.'

'And I woke up on the sofa. With Harvey. Come on, do you really think I'd be such a cad as to take advantage of an emotional wreck like you were?'

'You bastard! And you let me think—'

He shrugged. 'You seemed to think we'd had such a fabulous night, I didn't like to disappoint you.'

Roo stared at the TV screen. One of the cars was somersaulting through the air.

'I daresay I would have been disappointed,' she said tartly.

'Why don't you find out?'

Suddenly the air seemed charged with a million tiny crackling

319

particles of electricity. Roo felt her mouth tingle in anticipation, seconds before Matt leaned over and kissed her. He tasted of mouthwash and pizza. His teeth gently raked the softness of her lips, his tongue probing. Roo felt herself turning liquid with desire.

They went to bed, and this time she remembered every glorious moment. His gorgeous body with its lean, hard muscles. The way his warm, smooth, golden skin felt against hers, the tender way his lips explored every inch of her, making her arch with pleasure. Then the joyous concentration on his face as he slid into her, his body moving with hers until they both convulsed with ecstasy.

Afterwards he fell asleep straight away, his head against her shoulder, one arm flung protectively across her. Roo lay awake, her happiness giving way to unease. What had she done? She couldn't stop thinking about all those other girls, getting tense and tearful because he wouldn't commit, wouldn't answer their calls.

She had a horrible feeling she'd just become one of them.

The following morning she got a call from Sadie.

'I spoke to Barbara,' she said. 'You know, Frederick's secretary?'

'That was quick.'

'I know which bus she catches in the morning, so I made sure I just happened to be passing.'

Was there anything in Normanford that people didn't know about each other? Roo wondered. It was amazing that Sadie had managed to keep her secret for so long.

'Anyway, she was very talkative about old Freddie. She's expecting him back tomorrow. Apparently he's promised her a bottle of perfume from Duty Free.'

'Did she say where's he's been?'

'Now where was it? Somewhere I don't think I've heard of . . . ah, I remember. Croatia. Wasn't there a war there not long ago? Seems a strange place to go on holiday, don't you think?'

Roo gripped the phone tighter. 'I've got a feeling he wasn't on holiday.'

Agnes Fairbanks didn't seem too surprised to see her.

'I hoped you might call,' she said. 'I didn't get a chance to speak to you at the funeral. I wanted to thank you for all you've done for the company.'

'I was only doing my job.' Roo looked around the stately sitting room. She'd wondered if she was doing the right thing, coming here so soon after George's death. The last thing his widow probably needed was her talking shop. But after mulling over Frederick's absence all day, she'd decided she had to find out more. Fortunately Agnes seemed pleased to have the company.

'This place is so empty without him,' she said. 'I know he could be an old curmudgeon sometimes, but we were together a lot of years. I got used to his funny ways.'

'So did I.' She even missed him at the factory. She kept expecting him to creep up behind her and look over her shoulder.

Agnes regarded her thoughtfully. 'He had a lot of respect for you.'

'He didn't always show it.'

'That was just George. Always thought he knew best, especially when it came to that factory of his.' She turned her eyes to the ceiling. 'I wonder if he's looking down here now.'

'If he is, he's probably wondering why we haven't got that Park Hotels order started.'

Agnes didn't reply as she poured them both a cup of tea from a bone china pot.

'I suppose you're here about Frederick,' she said finally.

'Well, yes. I—'

'I just want you to know I don't approve. And neither would his father. Poor George would be turning in his grave if he knew what was going on.' She handed the cup to Roo. 'I've tried to talk to Frederick of course, but he insists it's for the best. Biscuit?' She held out the plate.

'No, thank you.' Roo shifted uneasily in her seat. 'Excuse me asking, but what are we talking about here?'

Agnes looked at her blankly. 'Frederick's plans to sell the factory, of course. What do you think I'm talking about?'

'What? He's selling Fairbanks?'

'Not selling. A merger. At least that's how he puts it. But I suppose it amounts to the same thing. All our production would move to eastern Europe. Apparently they can do things a lot cheaper over there.'

'And what would happen to the factory?'

'Oh, it would still be here.' Agnes stirred her tea. 'I don't know much about the details, but it would be more like a marketing and retail operation, Frederick says.'

A glorified warehouse, in other words. Roo closed her eyes. 'I didn't know any of this.'

'Frederick wanted to keep it all under his hat until he was sure of closing the deal. That's where he is at the moment. And of course he had to wait until he took control of the company. There was no way his father would agree to it.'

'And now the company's his he can do what he likes?'

'I'm afraid so.' Agnes nodded. 'Sidney Pennington is going through the will with us formally on Friday. But George always made it clear he wanted Frederick to take over. He insisted the factory should be kept in the family.'

How ironic, Roo thought. 'And what do you say about this?'

'I'm opposed to it, of course. George would have hated to see his factory run by foreigners. But what can I do? It's Frederick's factory, not mine.' She sighed. 'Perhaps he's right. Maybe the world has moved on. People don't want Fairbanks Fine Furniture any more. Frederick seems to think this is the only way to go. And at least this way the Fairbanks name stays around.'

Yes – stamped all over a load of cheap, mass-produced imports. It wasn't what George would have wanted.

And it wasn't what she wanted either.

Chapter 28

Frederick was surprised to see Roo waiting for him at the airport when he got off the plane, but he did his best to brazen it out.

There was a woman with him, dressed in white pedal-pushers and tanned to the colour of cheaply stained pine, weighed down by Duty Free bags.

'Ms Hennessy! This is a pleasant surprise. You didn't have to come all this way to meet me; I could have made my own way home.'

'I wasn't sure,' Roo smiled back just as falsely. 'You seem to be rather elusive these days.'

Frederick turned to the woman and pressed a few notes into her hand. 'Get a cab, Gloria,' he said. 'I'll see you back at the flat.'

Roo watched the woman stomping off towards the taxi rank, carrier bags swinging. 'I could have given your wife a lift, too.'

Frederick's teeth were white against his tan. 'That isn't my wife, Ms Hennessy.'

'I know, Mr Fairbanks. I spoke to her yesterday. She was as mystified as the rest of us about your little business trip.'

'Who said it was business?'

'Please don't insult my intelligence,' Roo snapped. 'I spoke to your mother. She told me all about your revised plans.'

He looked pleased with himself. 'So what do you think?'

'I can't believe you're doing it. I could understand it a few months ago when the factory was in serious trouble. But why sell now when the business is just starting to turn the corner?'

'Because it's still my father's business. It's still his name over the door.'

'It's your name, too.'

'And don't I bloody know it!' They reached her car and Frederick loaded his cases into the boot. 'Do you know what it's like to be born into the great Fairbanks family? No, of course you don't. Ever since I was a little boy I've had it drummed into me that the factory was my destiny. No question of whether I wanted it to be.' He slid into the passenger seat and slammed the door. 'And I don't like it. I fucking hated woodwork and I didn't much like my father, either!'

'Is that any reason to destroy a perfectly good business?'

'I didn't have to. My old man was doing a pretty good job of that all by himself. Until you came along.' He glanced sidelong at Roo. 'But you helped, in a way. The changes you've made will make this place an even more attractive proposition to our buyers.'

'I don't understand it,' Roo said, negotiating her way out of the car park. 'If you hated the business so much, why didn't you just tell your father you didn't want it?'

'And have him cut me off without a penny? Besides, he never listened. He might have seemed like a lovable old character to you, but he was a tyrant. He made me feel a failure just because I wasn't interested in making sideboards for the rest of my life.' He chuckled. 'I wish he was around to see what was happening to his precious factory. All those lovely MDF tables and chairs will soon be rolling off the production line with the blessed Fairbanks name and the words "Made in Croatia" stamped on them. He'd have a fit!'

Roo marvelled at the depths of his bitterness. How angry must Frederick be to want to hurt his father even after he was dead?

'So what are you planning to do with the money you make?' she asked.

'I don't know. But I want to do something on my own. Something that has nothing to do with furniture or my father. I can do it, you know,' he said. 'I've got what it takes to run a successful business.'

'I'm sure you have.' It was just a pity it wouldn't be Fairbanks. 'I take it this deal's signed and sealed?'

'It will be on Friday. That's when the buyers are coming over to take a look round. And that's when I take control of the company. Fairbanks will be all mine for a whole five minutes before I sign on the dotted line.' He looked at her. 'Cheer up, Ms Hennessy. I'm sure this will mean a big bonus for you. You've done a grand job.'

'It doesn't feel like it.'

'Why not? You did everything you had to do. You put the business back on track and thanks to you, I'll get an even better deal than I'd hoped for. Everyone's happy.'

'Except all those workers who'll be made redundant when it closes down.'

Frederick laughed. 'Oh dear. Don't tell me you've developed a social conscience? That could be very bad for your career!' He lowered his voice. 'Seriously, Roo, I'd advise you not to try to interfere with this deal. Not that there's anything you can do,' he added.

Maybe not, Roo thought. But I think I know a woman who can.

Cat put down the phone on another mother, eager to book her for her daughter's wedding. It was only Wednesday morning, but ever since the glossy colour spread of Charlotte Montague's wedding had appeared in *Hello Yorkshire* magazine the previous Saturday, they hadn't stopped ringing.

'I hope you don't mind,' Elizabeth had said when she called to tell her it was being featured.

How could she mind? *Hello Yorkshire* was her mother-in-law's bible, full of articles about wealthy, famous people in the area, and lots of glossy estate agents' ads, featuring grand country homes in acres of grounds that only a lottery winner could possibly afford.

And there, among the photos of rich people at York races and the Great Yorkshire Show, were Charlotte's wedding photos. And a photo of her, pinning Charlotte's hair up. Admittedly she didn't look too glamorous with her mouth full of hair grips, but underneath the caption read, 'Top local stylist Cat Kitchener puts the finishing touches to the beautiful bride.'

'I thought it would be good advertising for you,' Elizabeth said. And she was right. She'd already been booked for three more weddings. Even Glenys had been impressed and boasted to everyone about her 'clever daughter-in-law', much to Cat's surprise. The only one who wasn't delighted was Julie, who seethed every time one of Elizabeth's posh friends rang up for an appointment. And Maxine, who was furious the salon hadn't got a credit.

'Another wedding booking,' Cat said as Becky wandered in.

'You'll be as famous as Nicky Clarke soon,' Becky replied, and for once she wasn't being sarcastic. She'd stuck the wedding photos on the fridge door with a haphazard arrangement of magnets. She hadn't said anything, but Cat had the sneaking feeling she might be proud of her mother.

It was something else for her to tell Billy when she saw him that night. They'd been out a couple of times since they split up. It was a weird experience, going on a date with her own husband. But it gave her a good excuse to dress up. They talked, they laughed, and they had fun – something else that had been sadly missing from their marriage. He even bought her real presents, like flowers and perfume, rather than the Dyson he'd given her last Christmas.

The only thing she didn't like about it was saying goodbye at the end of the evening. Cat still fancied him like mad, and it was all she could do not to drag him off to bed. Unfortunately Billy seemed to be resisting the urge too. Cat was beginning to wonder if he was still interested in her.

But to her surprise, she found she quite enjoyed being on her own. She could slob around as much as she liked without worrying that she wasn't looking gorgeous enough for Billy.

Megan came in, slapping her riding crop against her thigh like an eight-year-old dominatrix. 'Liam's covered in spots,' she announced.

'Oh no, you haven't been using Becky's lipstick on him again?' Cat sighed. Then her son appeared and she realised at once they weren't the kind of spots she could scrub off with soap and a flannel.

'Jesus, what's wrong with him? He looks like he's got the plague.' Becky grabbed her cereal bowl and slouched off into the sitting room.

'More like chickenpox.' Cat counted Liam's spots. They seemed to be popping up before her eyes.

'If he dies, can I have his bedroom?' Megan asked, helping herself to a bowl of Frosties.

Julie answered when she called the salon to say she wouldn't be coming in. 'You can't keep being unreliable like this, you know,' she said. 'It's very unprofessional.'

'I'm sorry. I'm not leaving my son if he's ill.'

'I don't know why you bother coming in at all,' Julie grumbled. 'We could get a dozen stylists better and more reliable than you are.'

Cat had heard the same thing many times a day, and usually she ignored it. But today something inside her cracked. 'Fine,' she said. 'Why don't you?'

'What?'

'You heard. I quit.'

'You can't do that!' Julie spluttered. 'You're fired!'

'Whatever. Either way, I'm not coming in today. Or tomorrow,' she added, glancing at Liam's face, crammed with spots.

Five minutes later Maxine called back. 'I think there's been a misunderstanding,' she said in a wheedling voice.

'I don't. Julie's sacked me.'

'She had no authority to do that.'

'You made her senior stylist, remember? Anyway, I've resigned.'

'But you can't do that. We need you,' she pleaded. 'You're the best hairdresser we've got. Look, why don't I sack Julie and make you senior stylist?' In the background Cat could hear enraged squawking. 'I'll give you a pay rise. Ten per cent, how about that?'

'Twenty,' Cat said.

'If that's what you want,' Maxine said. There were more

squawks in the background. It sounded as if Julie was having another body-piercing, this time without anaesthetic.

'And I want to leave at three thirty every day. Even when there's no one else to cover the salon.'

'Whatever.'

'And you'll have to say please.'

'Please. PLEASE!'

'I'll think about it.' Cat paused. 'There, I've thought about it and the answer's thanks, but no thanks.'

'But you can't do this to me!'

'Why not? You're always telling me I can be replaced, so why don't you do it? If you can find someone to work for the slave wages you pay!' she added, and slammed the phone down.

'Way to go, Mum,' Becky grinned from the doorway.

Cat smiled back, feeling heady with her own power. She must be a good hairdresser after all, if Maxine was so desperate to have her back.

Her euphoria evaporated when she realised she didn't actually have a job any more, but she forced herself to stay positive. When Becky had taken Megan to the childminder's on her way to work, and Cat had settled Liam on the sofa wrapped in his duvet in front of *The Tweenies*, she sat at the kitchen table with a notebook and started working on the ideas she'd had about starting up on her own. She'd been thinking about it for weeks but had never got round to doing anything practical. Perhaps this might give her the boost she needed. Especially with the *Hello Yorkshire* article generating so much interest, and Elizabeth Montague telling all her friends how great she was. And she already had loads of regular clients she knew would follow her if she started her own business.

She was sketching out some ideas for ads and wondering if she could ask Billy to help her with marketing, when the doorbell rang.

The person she least expected to see was Ruby. Cat was instantly on her guard. 'What do you want?'

'Can I come in?'

Reluctantly she stood aside to let her in. The hall was littered with the kids' bikes, Liam's skateboard and Megan's riding paraphernalia, but Cat refused to apologise for the mess. So what if it was cluttered? It was her home and she liked it that way.

She led the way into the kitchen. 'I rang the salon and they said you were off today,' Ruby said.

'As a matter of fact I've resigned. I'm going into business on my own.'

'Really?' Ruby picked up the notes she'd been scribbling. 'You've spelt "professional" wrong,' she said.

'Oh, fuck off!' Cat snatched the notebook away from her. She should have known better than to expect anything nice from her cousin. 'What do you want, anyway?'

'I need your help.'

'Yeah, right.' Cat filled the kettle. 'Since when have you ever needed my help?'

'I need it now.' Ruby laced and unlaced her fingers. 'Is that action group of yours still going?'

'We wound it up a few days ago. There didn't seem to be any reason to carry on now the factory's out of danger.'

'That's just it. It isn't out of danger. It's going to be closed down if we don't do something.'

Cat made coffee while Ruby explained how Frederick Fairbanks planned to sell the factory off to the highest bidder.

'Sly bastard,' Cat muttered. 'I've never liked him since he tried to grope my bum at the last office Christmas party Billy took me to.'

'The buyers are all lined up,' Ruby said. 'They're due to come in and sign on Friday. Frederick's getting the company then, so he wants to sign the contracts straight away.'

'But what about all your hard work?' Cat asked. Much as she hated to admit it, Ruby had done a fantastic job getting Fairbanks back on its feet.

'All for nothing,' she shrugged. 'But that's not what bothers me. It's the thought of all those workers being put out of jobs for no reason.'

'So why can't you do something about it?'

'There's nothing I can do. The bank's happy about it; they don't

329

care who owns the place. Besides, you've got all the contacts. People will listen to you. They'd never listen to me,' she admitted.

They drank their coffee in silence. Cat wondered how much desperation it had taken for Ruby to come and ask for her help. Suddenly she didn't seem so confident or all-powerful after all. For all her designer suit and power heels, she was just an ordinary woman like her.

Finally Cat said, 'It's only two days away. That doesn't give us a lot of time to organise anything.'

'I know.' Ruby put down her cup. 'I've already made a few notes. I thought perhaps if you got all your old action group friends together, you could—'

Cat held up her hand. 'Hang on a minute. Who's organising this, you or me?'

'You are, but—'

'Then we do it my way, okay?'

They stared at each other for a moment. Then, to Cat's amazement, Ruby backed down. 'Sorry.' She smiled weakly. 'It's just my natural bossiness taking over.'

'Tell me about it,' Cat muttered.

Just then Liam wandered in, still wrapped in the duvet. He was sucking his thumb, his dark hair sticking up on end. Ruby took one look at his face and said, 'No need to ask what's wrong with him!'

'It's better when they get it young.' Cat pulled him into her arms, smoothing down his hair. 'Luckily the other kids have already had it or it would go through this family like wildfire.'

'Ollie got it when he was eighteen months old.'

'Was it very bad?'

'I don't know.' She gazed down at her hands. 'I was in Madrid at a conference on Integrated Performance Management.'

'Sounds very important.'

'Not as important as being there to look after your little boy.' Her face was bleak. 'I envy you.'

Cat laughed. 'Me? Why?'

'Because you've got your priorities right. Maybe if I'd done things differently I'd still have a family.'

She looked sad, almost vulnerable. How could Cat have been so in awe of her for all those years? She was just Ruby, the cousin who'd shared a bedroom with her, listened to all her secrets, laughed and cried with her. Cat suddenly felt sorry for all the years they'd wasted hating each other.

'You're not the only one who's made mistakes, you know,' she said. 'Look at me and Billy.'

She steeled herself, waiting for a smart comment about them never being suited in the first place. But Ruby just said, 'Yes, but you're different. Billy still loves you. And if you stopped being so bloody insecure you'd realise that.'

Cat was shocked. 'Don't speak to me like that!'

'Why not? Someone has to talk some sense into you.' She was back to her old bossy self again, laying down the law, always thinking she knew best. 'Billy loves you. And it's breaking his heart, you not being together. So it's about time you stopped being so pig-headed and took him back.'

Cat's hackles rose. 'What gives you the right to tell me what to do?'

Ruby glared at her. 'Because I love you too, you silly cow!'

Chapter 29

Roo still wasn't convinced Cat was going to help. She wasn't even sure how much use she could be in just two days. What they really needed was a miracle.

She spent the next two days waiting and worrying. It wasn't in her nature to be passive. She was used to taking control, driving the decisions.

Matt did his best to help her relax. 'You really should try to chill out,' he said, as he massaged her tense shoulders.

'How can I chill out when Fairbanks could be sold down the river tomorrow?' And there wasn't a damn thing she could do about it. 'This is no good,' she said, shaking him off. 'I should be doing something constructive.'

'I can think of something constructive.' He kissed the back of her neck, his breath warm against her skin.

She moved away from him. 'I meant *really* constructive. Do some research on the internet. Write a report.'

'I'll tell you what.' Matt pulled her towards him. 'You can give me a performance review, how about that?'

Roo relented, knowing she couldn't resist him for long. She was becoming seriously addicted to him, she thought later as they lay in bed. And like most addictive things, he was incredibly bad for her.

Their relationship, if she could call it that, had lasted a whole week. Not too long for most people, but a lifetime for Matt Collins. He hadn't shown any signs of wanting to move on. Just the opposite, in fact – he'd even taken the drastic step of leaving his spare toothbrush in her bathroom. But that didn't stop her feeling wary, waiting for him to tell her it was over.

And the worst thing was, as each day passed she was growing closer and more dependent on him. Falling in love with him, in other words. It was scary. Especially as it was exactly the kind of behaviour guaranteed to drive him away.

She'd made up her mind not to push him. But the following morning, as she watched him munching toast, she said very casually, 'I suppose I'll be going back to London when this is all over.'

He looked up. 'How soon?'

'I don't know. It depends how this protest works out. If Frederick sells the factory there won't be much more for me to do.'

'I expect Ollie will be pleased to have you back.'

'I'm looking forward to seeing him.' She waited. No reaction. 'David's found a flat, so I'll have the house to myself when I get back.' Still no reaction. 'You could come and visit me?'

'I could.' He fed a toast crust to Harvey. 'Or I could come with you.'

She almost dropped her mug. 'What?'

'I could come to London with you. My research is almost finished. All I have to do is write it all up, and I could do that anywhere.' He frowned. 'Unless you don't want me to come.'

'No! I mean, yes. I'd love you to come. It's just a shock, that's all. Isn't that a bit too much like commitment for you?'

'All I know is that I want to be with you.' Matt stood up and cleared his plate into the sink. Then he dropped a kiss on her forehead. 'I'll see you later, okay? Good luck with the protest.'

'Aren't you coming?'

'I'll try, if I can get away from college early.'

'I'd like you to be there.'

'Like I said, I'll try. But I can't promise anything.'

Typical Matt, she thought as the front door banged shut. He couldn't even commit to something two hours away, so how could she seriously expect anything long term?

He might think coming to London was a good idea now, but

she wondered if he was just saying it to make her happy. Who could say they'd even still be together by then?

She wasn't sure what to expect as she drove to work that Friday morning. But she certainly didn't expect the crowd that greeted her as she turned the corner. It was a fine, sunny day and it seemed like the whole of Normanford had turned out to enjoy the sunshine. She couldn't see the factory gates for the people gathered there, all waving their placards and chanting. Not just the factory workers themselves, but hordes of local shopkeepers, mums from the school gates and office workers.

And in the middle of it all was Cat. Roo caught her eye as she drove past. Neither of them smiled, but the slightest nod of acknowledgement passed between them.

There was huge excitement in the office. Becky and the other girls had their noses pressed to the glass, trying to see out. 'I don't understand,' Becky was saying. 'Why is Mum doing it? Why would she want to cause trouble now?'

'I'm not sure,' Roo replied coolly, sifting through the morning's post. 'But I think it's got something to do with Frederick Fairbanks selling the factory to a company in eastern Europe.'

They all exchanged horrified looks. 'Will we lose our jobs?' one of the girls asked.

'Probably. Unless you're fluent in Croatian.'

Next she went to see Billy. He was standing at the window too, staring down at the protesters. Or at one in particular, Roo guessed.

'I wonder how they knew those buyers were coming today.'

'I've no idea.'

'Are you sure about that?' He gave her a quizzical look. 'You didn't tip them off, did you?'

'Me? And risk losing my job? Where's Frederick, by the way?'

'Holed up in his office, fuming. Serves him right, the scheming little shit.' He turned back to the window. 'I should be down there with them, showing Cat some support.'

'So why don't you?'

'You're not the only one who could lose their job.'

334

'You'll lose it anyway once this new bunch takes over.' She looked at him. A pair of brown eyes startlingly similar to her own stared back at her. How could she have failed to realise he was her brother? 'Billy, there comes a time in every man's life when he has to stand up for what he believes in. The question is, do you want to save your marriage, or your job?'

Once Billy had gone, Roo went back to her office. It was deserted, apart from Becky, who insisted on giving Roo a running commentary on what was going on down in the yard.

'There must be hundreds of them now. The Normanford Gorillas have just turned up. Ooh, and a brass band. And what are those people doing in cowboy hats?'

In the end Roo could stand it no more. 'Becky, please go down there and join that protest right this minute!'

'I can't leave you here by yourself. What if the mob smashes its way in and lynches you?'

Roo glanced out of the window, where the Normanford and District Darby and Joan club were mustering by the gates, forming an impenetrable barrier with their Zimmer frames. 'I don't think I'm in much danger, do you?'

Then something else caught her eye. A flash of black as Johnny Franks' sleek and sinister gangster limo, driven by one of his shaven-headed henchmen, glided slowly into the fray like a prowling shark. Hanging out of the sunroof were Sadie and Nanna, the latter waving her walking stick with gay abandon.

All the Moon women were there. Except her.

'Where are you going?' Becky said, as she grabbed her bag.

'You don't think I'm going to miss out on the fun, do you? For heaven's sake, Becky! Are you coming, or not?'

There was a carnival atmosphere by the factory gates. The town's rugby league team, the Normanford Gorillas, were there as Becky had said, showing off a disturbing amount of solid muscle. The local brass band were leading everyone in a rousing chorus of 'Roll Out the Barrel'.

Cat shouldered her way through the crowd to Roo. 'What are you doing here? You'll lose your job if Frederick catches you.'

'Like I said to your husband, there are more important things in life than work.' Could that really be her saying that? 'Who *are* those people in the cowboy hats, by the way?'

'That's the local line-dancing club. Jan and her fiancé Ray brought them along. They're friends of Sadie's.'

'Now why doesn't that surprise me?' Roo said.

Suddenly the crowd parted like the Red Sea as Frederick Fairbanks bore down on them across the yard, looking furious. The brass band burst into a spontaneous chorus of *Colonel Bogey*.

'You have no right to create a disturbance,' he shouted. 'I'll have you all arrested for causing a breach of the peace!'

'Try it,' someone called back. The policeman who'd been sent to keep an eye on the situation looked up guiltily from having his palm read by one of the Darby and Joan ladies.

'You have no right to sell this factory from under us!' someone else yelled.

'If you think this is going to put off our new buyers, you're sadly mistaken. I've already telephoned them to put off their visit.'

'So we'll just come back on Monday,' Cat shouted. 'And the next day, and the next, until your buyers finally get the message!'

A roar of support went up from the crowd. Roo tried to lose herself behind a wall of rugby players but Frederick spotted her. 'Can't you do something to get rid of this lot?' he demanded.

'Why should I? They're exercising their democratic right to protest. Besides, I fully support them.'

Frederick was apoplectic with rage. 'We'll see what your boss has to say about *that*. I'm dispensing with your services.'

A jeer went up from the crowd. Roo stood her ground.

'It's not up to you. I was brought in by the bank, remember? Besides, you don't own this company yet.'

'I wouldn't be so sure about that.' Frederick pointed to a silver grey car pulling up at the gates. 'If I'm not mistaken, this is our lawyer with my father's last will and testament.'

Sidney Pennington looked around apprehensively as he got out of his car, clutching his briefcase. 'Have I come at a bad time?' he said.

'It couldn't be better,' Frederick said. 'Perhaps you'll tell these good people exactly who is in charge of this factory?'

Sidney looked nervous. 'Shall we go inside and discuss it?'

'I'd rather do it out here, if you don't mind.' Frederick scanned the crowd in triumph. 'I want everyone to hear who my father trusted to run this place after his death.'

'Judas!' someone called out.

Sidney Pennington took off his spectacles and polished them. 'I have to say this is most irregular—'

'Just do it, man!'

A hush fell as Sidney broke the seal on the thick white envelope containing George Fairbanks' last will and testament.

'This is better than the telly!' Nanna hissed.

He glanced through it for a moment, then intoned gravely, 'I, George Arthur Fairbanks, being of sound mind—'

The first section was all about his estate and how it was to be left to his widow Agnes. Frederick stood at his shoulder, twitching with anticipation.

'The company, man! What does it say about the company?'

Sidney sent him a severe look. He wasn't used to being hurried. 'You are aware your father had me draw up a new will shortly before he died?'

'Of course I know. He showed it to me, remember?'

'Not that one. He ordered another to be written after that.'

Frederick frowned. 'Why would he do that?'

Sidney Pennington didn't answer. His gaze swept the crowd. 'Is there a Ruby Moon here?'

Roo lifted her hand. 'That's me.'

Sidney smiled benignly over the top of his spectacles. 'Congratulations, my dear,' he said. 'It seems you've just inherited a factory!'

Roo packed her bags, marvelling at how much she'd managed to accumulate over the past months. But at least she was leaving behind a lot of other baggage.

'I've never seen you wear this.' Cat held up a strappy top.

'I haven't. It's never been warm enough.'

'Southern softy.'

'Take it, if you like it.'

'Are you sure? It's Dolce and Whatsit.'

'I'm sure. Unless you're too posh for my cast-offs these days?'

'Are you kidding?' Cat stuffed it in her bag before Roo had a chance to change her mind.

'I suppose you'll be buying your own designer labels once you're a rich and successful businesswoman?' she teased.

'Don't,' Cat blushed. 'I'm strictly a chainstore girl. Anyway, I've only got a bag full of brushes and scissors to my name so far. That hardly makes me millionaire material, does it?'

'It's a start. You wait, this time next year you'll have your own thriving business.'

'Yeah, right.' Cat sat on the bed, hugging her knees. 'It feels so weird, going it alone. Even Glenys hasn't stopped bragging about her daughter-in-law, the businesswoman!'

She tried to sound self-deprecating, but Roo could see she was chuffed that someone was proud of her.

'You might not be the only one starting out on your own,' Roo told her. 'I'm thinking about it myself.'

'You mean leave that posh job of yours? Never.'

'That posh job takes me away from home and makes me live out of a suitcase,' Roo said. She'd done some hard thinking and had begun to wonder if her future was at Warner and Hicks. The lifestyle wasn't for her. She wanted to spend more time with Ollie while he was still young enough to need her.

'You could have had a job here,' Cat said. 'You had a factory to run, remember?'

'I know, but it wasn't really my factory. Anyway, I've got to get back to London. Your daughter will kill me if I don't. She's due to start her work placement on Monday.'

Cat's smile faded. 'You will look after her, won't you?'

'Of course I will! I've told you a hundred times, what harm can she come to when she's living in our attic flat?'

'I know, but I can't help worrying. And London's so far away—'

'Cat, it's a couple of hours down the motorway, not Siberia! And you can come and see us as often as you like.'

She carefully refolded the tops Cat had slung into her suitcase. Old habits died hard.

'Billy will be sorry to have missed you,' Cat said. 'He had to fly to Milan to see Salvatore this morning about the final details for the capsule collection.' She picked up a pair of Roo's shoes. 'I never thanked you properly for making him Managing Director and giving him those shares.'

'I gave them to both of you. In joint names,' Roo reminded her. 'And I expect you to get in there and make some decisions too!'

'I couldn't do that. I don't know much about business—'

'Then you'd better learn, hadn't you?' Roo smiled. 'Don't do yourself down so much, Cat Kitchener. If it wasn't for you organising that brilliant protest, there might not even be a Fairbanks now.'

'It was more to do with George leaving you the factory. It still makes me laugh when I think of Frederick's face. I thought he was going to explode!'

'He nearly did.' He'd also threatened to contest the will on the grounds of his father not being of sound mind. At least they'd managed to reach a compromise. She'd agreed to buy Frederick out, allowing him to go off and start his own business.

After two weeks of thinking about it, Roo had handed a large number of her shares over to Billy and Cat. He deserved a chance to show what he could do, and she could trust him to do his best for the company. And it was yet another thing for Glenys to brag to her friends at the bridge club about.

'Anyway, thanks again for giving them to us,' Cat said.

Roo shrugged it off. 'Call it the wedding present I never gave you.'

They looked at each other. 'Billy really is lucky to have you, you know,' Roo said.

Cat twisted her wedding band on her finger. 'I don't know about that.'

'He is! And I think he's just beginning to realise it.'

'We're getting there. Slowly.'

Roo smiled. They hadn't seemed that slow off the mark when

she'd spotted them kissing passionately after the protest. And when she'd looked for Billy later, and his secretary had told her that he'd gone home, she didn't need to imagine what they were doing.

She was pleased for them. She couldn't have chosen a more loving wife for her brother.

She just wished she could be as happy as they were.

'Are you ready?' Cat asked half an hour later as she struggled to close the suitcase.

'In a minute.' Roo pulled the curtain aside and gazed out into the street. It was deserted, apart from a couple of kids playing football with an empty beer can.

Cat watched her shrewdly. 'What are you waiting for? Or should that be who?'

'What do you mean?'

'Oh come on. You've been rushing over to that window every five minutes, looking out for someone. Who are you expecting, Brad Pitt? Or your dishy next-door neighbour?'

Roo smiled. 'I think Brad's more likely.'

Matt wasn't coming. Right up until two days ago he'd insisted he was. But since then she hadn't seen him. There was no answer from his house, not even Harvey barking. He'd taken off and now she guessed he was lying low, too scared to face her and tell her he'd changed his mind.

She let the curtain drop and picked up her case from the bed. 'Come on, then,' she said. 'I want to miss the traffic.'

She'd allowed for a quick fifteen-minute visit to Hope Street to say goodbye. But she'd reckoned without her family. Johnny Franks was already there, his limo taking up most of the street. Nanna liked to go out and polish it occasionally with her sleeve, just so all the neighbours knew it was her visitor.

Nanna had also insisted that Sadie make Roo up a flask of coffee and a carrier bag full of food. 'For the journey,' she explained.

'They do have food on motorways, you know,' Roo pointed out.

'That rubbish! You might as well eat your own tyres.'

'How would you know? You've never been on a motorway in your life,' Sadie teased.

'I read, don't I? And I watch *Watchdog*.' Nanna briskly wiped a tear from her eye. 'Now I hope you're not going to make a fool of yourself saying goodbye, Sadie. Our Ruby doesn't need you having hysterics.'

'She's my daughter, and I'll make a bloody fool of myself if I want to. Don't leave me with her,' she begged Roo. 'She'll drive me mad.'

'You can always change your mind and come with me.'

Four months ago she could never have imagined asking Sadie to move down to London to live with her. And she was actually disappointed when her mother refused, saying her life was up in Normanford.

'I'm too old to uproot myself now,' she said. 'Nanna needs looking after and all my friends are up here.'

And she had her own business to run now. Johnny had bought the Ponderosa from Jan, so Sadie could sing to her heart's content, every night if she wanted to. He even planned to rename it The Talk of the Town, after the famous London nightspot where Sadie had always dreamed of topping the bill.

Sadie's expression softened. 'Thanks for the offer; you don't know what it means to me. But somehow I don't think the big city's ready for Sadie Moon yet!'

Roo looked at her mother's leather trousers and bright yellow sleeveless vest. Maybe she was right. She'd certainly raise a few eyebrows among her well-to-do neighbours.

'Besides, I wouldn't want to be without her, now I've found her again.' Johnny put his arm around Sadie.

'But you will come and visit, won't you? Both of you,' Roo added, looking at Johnny. They'd made their peace since she realised how much he adored her mother. If only they'd managed to stay together thirty-odd years ago, it could have saved them all a lot of heartache.

'Try and stop me. I have to see that grandson of mine, don't I?'

There was a screech of brakes as Uncle Tom's taxi came to

a halt outside. Johnny rushed to the window. 'Your bloody brother!' he cursed. 'If he scratches my paintwork—'

But Roo wasn't looking at the limo. She was looking at the black Labrador bounding out of the back of the taxi.

She rushed to the door, fighting her racing heart, and tried to stay calm when she saw Matt standing there, holding Harvey's collar.

'I thought we'd missed you,' he said.

'Come to say goodbye?'

'No way. We're coming with you. Harvey's looking forward to London. I can't disappoint him, can I?'

'But your house was empty. I thought—'

'You thought I'd changed my mind?' He shook his head. 'I've been working all hours to get the last of my research done. You didn't think I'd let you down, did you?'

Roo stared past him as Uncle Tom began pulling luggage out of the boot of his taxi. 'I wasn't sure.'

He held her at arms' length, his warm turquoise eyes meeting hers. 'I told you, I want to be with you.'

'For how long?'

'For as long as it takes to convince you I love you.'

Their kiss was interrupted by her family, spilling out into the street to say goodbye. Uncle Tom tutted. 'Just like your mother,' he grumbled.

'Ignore him. Miserable old goat.' Sadie hugged her. She still smelt of Charlie perfume. 'Goodbye, Ruby Tuesday,' she whispered. 'Take care of yourself.'

'And you, Mum.' They stared at each other in shock, both realising at the same moment that Roo hadn't called her that since she left junior school.

As they got into the car, Matt said, 'Ruby Tuesday, eh? No wonder you kept it quiet. What kind of a name is that?'

Roo glanced in the rearview mirror at her mother, who was waving frantically on the doorstep.

'A bloody good one,' she said.